Chol (Mayan) Folktales

Chol (Mayan) Folktales

A COLLECTION OF STORIES FROM THE MODERN MAYA OF SOUTHERN MEXICO

Nicholas A. Hopkins and J. Kathryn Josserand
with Ausencio Cruz Guzmán

UNIVERSITY PRESS OF COLORADO

Boulder

Published by University Press of Colorado
5589 Arapahoe Avenue, Suite 206C
Boulder, Colorado 80303

The University Press of Colorado is a proud member of
The Association of University Presses.

The University Press of Colorado is a cooperative publishing enterprise supported, in part, by Adams State University, Colorado State University, Fort Lewis College, Metropolitan State University of Denver, Regis University, University of Colorado, University of Northern Colorado, Utah State University, and Western State Colorado University.

ISBN: 978-1-60732-487-4 (paper)
ISBN: 978-1-60732-488-1 (e-book)

Library of Congress Cataloging-in-Publication Data

Names: Hopkins, Nicholas A., author. | Josserand, J. Kathryn, author.
Title: Chol (Mayan) folktales : a collection of stories from the modern Maya of southern Mexico / Nicholas A. Hopkins and J. Kathryn Josserand.
Other titles: Collection of stories from the modern Maya of southern Mexico
Description: Boulder, CO : University of Colorado Press, [2016] | Includes bibliographical references.
Identifiers: LCCN 2015039583 | ISBN 9781607324874 (pbk.) | ISBN 9781607324881 (ebook)
Subjects: LCSH: Chol Indians—Folklore. | Tales—Mexico. | Chol language—Texts.
Classification: LCC F1221.C57 H67 | DDC 398.20897/428—dc23
LC record available at http://lccn.loc.gov/2015039583

Cover photograph by Nicholas A. Hopkins

The audio files are housed at http://www.upcolorado.com/university-press-of-colorado/item/2929-chol-mayan-folktales.

With heartfelt thanks to Ausencio Cruz Guzmán,
without whom none of this could ever have happened.

*Ausencio (Chencho) Cruz Guzmán, Zoh-Laguna, Campeche, 2002
(photo by J. Kathryn Josserand)*

Contents

Preface

On Collecting Chol Folklore

Nicholas A. Hopkins

Kathryn Josserand and I began to collect folktales in our first fieldwork on the Chol language. We had worked independently on other Mayan languages when we were graduate students. After graduating from Texas A&M, I had gone to the University of Texas to study linguistics. While completing my coursework for a master's degree, I took a summer course on modern Yucatec Maya (taught by Moisés Romero) at Mexico City College in 1959 and then was hired on to the University of Chicago's Chiapas Study Projects the following year. I spent two years in Chiapas collecting data on the northern varieties of Tzotzil (McQuown and Pitt-Rivers 1970:9–20; Hopkins 1967b, 1970, 1974) and then went to graduate school at Chicago. There I worked as a language lab assistant in the production of the tapes for the courses Spoken Yucatec (Maya) and Spoken Quiché. I also produced a master's thesis on Tzotzil phonology (Hopkins 1964) and a PhD dissertation on Chuj grammar (Hopkins 1967a).

Kathryn earned a bachelor's degree in geography and anthropology from Louisiana State University, and her major professor, Robert C. West, had introduced her to Mexico on vacation field trips. She went to Tulane University intending to become a Maya archaeologist but was encouraged to go into linguistics instead. She studied Maya at Tulane through the *Spoken Yucatec* tapes and spent a year in Yucatán doing research on Maya in preparation for a doctoral project (1967–68). The two of us accompanied Terry Kaufman to the field in 1969 and did a small amount of work with his Huastec informants. We were married in 1970. In 1972, at the University of Texas, we team-taught a course on Maya Civilization, during which Kathryn worked out her correlation between the history of the Mayan-language family and the archaeological record (Josserand 1975). However, after 1973, when we took positions in Mexico at CIS-INAH (Centro de Investigaciones Superiores del Instituto Nacional de Antropología e Historia), our research was focused on Otomanguean languages, and we did not work on Mayan for several years.

While we were graduate students, we had both learned what was known about Maya hieroglyphic writing, mainly from the work of J. Eric S. Thompson (1960). I had taken a course under César Lizardi Ramos, a student of Thompson's, in 1959, and Kathryn had worked at the Middle American Research Institute at Tulane on the materials left by Herman Beyer. We had both attended the First Seminar for the Study of Maya Writing in Mexico City in 1966 (Hopkins 1967b, 1968a, 1968b). In 1976, three years into establishing residency in Mexico, we were in Austin, Texas, to check on our house there when we saw an announcement for a workshop on Maya hieroglyphics to be led by Linda Schele (among the first of her many workshops). We attended and were swept away by the progress that had been made since we last looked at Classic Maya. At the same time, Linda recognized that we had knowledge of the languages that she needed to acquire, and a long period of cooperative work began. We evaluated the state of knowledge on Mayan languages vis-à-vis Maya hieroglyphics and realized that much more needed to be known about Chol, since its Colonial distribution had covered much of the Classic Maya territory (Aulie and Aulie 1978; Thompson 1938). From our positions in Mexico City (Kathryn at CIS-INAH and I at the UAM, the Universidad Autónoma Metropolitana, Iztapalapa), we planned fieldwork in the region of Palenque, incorporating students and research assistants from our respective institutions.

Our first fieldwork on Chol, in 1978, was scheduled to allow us to attend the Palenque Round Table, the Tercera Mesa Redonda de Palenque (Robertson 1980). Through Linda we had met Merle Greene Robertson, who maintained a research center in Palenque, and we housed ourselves and our students in close proximity. From there we went out to try to find good informants. There ensued a frustrating week, as we could not find anyone who spoke both Chol and Spanish well enough for our purposes. We spent a couple of days working with a group of near-monolingual Chol speakers from a nearby *ejido* (small agricultural community), only to realize that none of us understood what was going on in the interactions. We spent another couple of days working with a local guide who was said to speak fluent Chol. Unfortunately, his Chol ended just when we were getting interested. Finally, one day, when we were voicing our frustration to Merle, she suggested we try to work with her assistant, Ausencio Cruz Guzmán.

Chencho, as he is universally known, had been working with Merle for several years as a carpenter and master of all trades, helping her carry out her photographic project at Palenque (Robertson 1983, 1985a, 1985b, 1991, 2006:118). He grew up in the small Chol community of San Pedro Sabana, on the banks of the Río Tulijá. His father was a Spanish speaker who had learned Chol in the course of becoming a canoe master, ferrying goods up and down the Tulijá between the communities and plantations and the railhead at Salto de Agua. Chencho's mother died early in his life, and he was raised by a Tzeltal-speaking nanny. However, the primary language of the community was Chol, and Chencho learned Chol at an early age from the children he went to school with. He perfected his knowledge of the language working with his father and other Chol speakers making canoes (Hopkins, Josserand, and Cruz Guzmán 1985).

After having several children and losing his first wife, he remarried and moved his family to Palenque, where he met Merle and began to serve as her chief assistant. Even though he identifies himself as a Ladino, not an ethnic Chol, for our purposes he was the perfect informant. He spoke both Spanish and Chol as a native speaker, he had lots of experience in many parts of the Chol-speaking world, he had Chol-speaking relatives scattered across the area, he had acquired an extensive repertory of folktales and stories, and, best of all, he not only had an excellent feel for the language, but he was easygoing, tolerant of our ignorance, and very pleasant to work with.

We began as linguists commonly begin, by eliciting a series of wordlists. A set of isolated words is the primary data for working out the sound system of a language. We began with the standard Swadesh list, a 100-word vocabulary that can be expected to occur in any language (the so-called basic vocabulary used for glottochronological reckoning). Since we had both worked on Mayan languages before, we could design a working orthography fairly quickly (although it would be years before we would achieve a more or less definitive orthography that is also culturally appropriate). We immediately elicited a much longer list, Terry Kaufman's Mayan Vocabulary Survey list of 1,400 words that are typical of Mayan and Mesoamerican languages in general (i.e., with many Mesoamerican cultural items included and not concerned with universality). The tapes of this elicitation have been delivered to the Archive of the Indigenous Languages of Latin America (AILLA), where they were digitized and made available to the general public through AILLA's website (www.ailla.utexas.org), along with the field recordings of many of the texts published here (some of which were edited for publication after the initial recording). The audio recordings of texts included in this volume are also housed at www.upcolorado.com.

Using these lexical data for information on the phonology and morphology of Chol, we then recorded a series of texts, the normal next step in a preliminary linguistic investigation. This was the point at which we confirmed Chencho as the perfect informant. He could tell a story, and he could tell it in an engaging fashion, like the best of the other Maya informants we had worked with over the years. The first long story we recorded with him turned out to have relevance to the Palenque Round Table publication, since it concerned the cave lord, Don Juan, and the volume resulting from the Round Table was to be dedicated to Dennis Puleston, an archaeologist who had done basic work on Maya cave use and been fatally struck by lightning while standing at the top of the Castillo of Chichén Itzá the week after the Mesa Redonda. We rushed through a translation of the text and sent it in for publication in a crude initial orthography that was more linguistic than practical (Cruz Guzmán, Josserand, and Hopkins 1980). A revised version of that text is included here (The Cave of Don Juan).

We have been working with Chencho ever since. For several years we alternated between going to Palenque to work with him and bringing him to Mexico City to work with us. After he had problems with the altitude in Mexico City, we limited ourselves to work in Chiapas. As Merle's presence in Palenque dwindled and she moved her operations to the United States, CIS-INAH (and after 1981 its successor, CIESAS, the Centro de Investigaciones y Estudios Superiores en Antropología Social) became his principal employer. During these years we began a dialect survey of Chol, visiting as many of the ejidos as possible to get a firm idea of the range of variation in the language and the distribution of variants (Hopkins 1983; Josserand 1996; de la Torre Yarza 1994). I directed a field school for anthropology students at the UAM in 1981, and three students spent significant time in separate Chol ejidos doing basic ethnography. We directed thesis research on the language as well (Koob 1979). We continued to research the history of the language (Hopkins 1985, 1995), learn about local ethnography (Hopkins, Josserand, and Cruz Guzmán 1985), and use our knowledge to shed light on precolumbian affairs (Folan, Josserand, and Hopkins 1983; Hopkins 1984, 1988, 1991).

By 1983 a combination of health problems and institutional reorganization led to our departure from Mexico City. Now free to turn away from the interests and concerns of our students, we concentrated more on Maya hieroglyphics. Since the late 1970s we had been working with Linda Schele to run the Texas workshops, which had evolved from a small meeting of specialists to a huge get-together of a wide range of Maya scholars and fans and had gone from a weekend lecture by Linda to add a week-long hands-on workshop that required a dozen people to coordinate activities and supervise learners. Seeing that there was a market for workshops, we began to offer ourselves as the "roadies" of Maya hieroglyphics, and for the next few years we supported ourselves with a combination of research grants, workshops, and then tours of archaeological sites and Maya villages (doing business as Jaguar Tours). All these activities fed into our research on Chol and its antecedents, and most of our writing and presentations were related to Maya hieroglyphs (Josserand, Schele, and Hopkins 1985; Josserand 1986, 1987a, 1992, 1994; Hopkins 1997; Hopkins and Josserand 1995, 1998; Josserand and Hopkins 2002b [1998]).

Grant-supported research kept us in the field for significant periods. Our first grant, "Chol Texts, Vocabulary and Grammar," 1983–84 (Hopkins and Josserand 1986b), gave us the opportunity to organize our Chol texts, compile vocabulary lists, and sketch out the basic grammar (Josserand and Martin 1986; Hopkins and Josserand 1994). A second grant, "Chol (Mayan) Dictionary Database," 1986–88, got us into computer processing of texts and vocabulary lists, and the related field-work involved going over every Chol vocabulary list published from 1789 to the twentieth century, checking each and every entry with Chencho for modern intelligibility, correcting typos, and confirming forms (Josserand and Hopkins 1988). The results of this effort are beginning to be published (Hopkins, Cruz Guzmán, and Josserand 2008), and all the derived databases have been merged into a historical dictionary of Chol that is online as one of the extensive resources of the Foundation for the Advancement of Mesoamerican Studies, Inc. (FAMSI) (www.famsi.org/mayawriting/dictionary/hopkins/dictionary/Chol.html; Hopkins, Josserand, and Cruz Guzmán 2011). A third federal grant, "A Handbook of Classic Maya Inscriptions (Western Lowlands)," 1989–90, allowed us to explore the Classic inscriptions in detail and work out the patterns we have proposed as the canons of Classic Maya literature (Josserand and Hopkins 1991; Josserand 1998, 1999). After several years of support from granting agencies and family funds, Kathryn was hired by Florida State University in a tenure-track job, and I began to teach there as an adjunct professor.

In these years we learned a lot about Classic texts by teaching them. Our weekend workshops, sponsored by museums, study groups, and occasionally universities, were focused on particular sites or particular topics. For each, a workbook would be prepared that had sample hieroglyphic texts, laid out on pages in convenient format with spaces for notes to be taken, along with front matter that explained the basics of Maya writing as we understood them (a revised version of our basic workbook is online [www.famsi.org/mayawriting/hopkins/index.html; Josserand and Hopkins 2011]). For two days, then, we would work on the inscriptions with the attendees, pointing out the features we had observed and answering questions. An analogy with this experience would be an itinerant English literature teacher who went from place to place, picking for each venue selected works of a particular author and then going over them line by line with an educated, interested audience. In all, from 1987 to 2005 we carried out more than seventy such workshops, including several in Mexico and Guatemala for native Maya scholars (as I continue to do).

The notebooks prepared for these workshops were complemented by those prepared for our tours. For each tour a notebook was compiled that included maps of the region and the sites to be visited, along with brief introductions to each site and its history and a set of inscriptions we would be seeing. The experience of taking interested parties around these sites, discussing their history and their inscriptions, gave us a much more profound appreciation for the relationship of the public monuments to local architecture and site planning. From 1988 to 2006, we led more than thirty such tours (and I continue to do so).

As we became more familiar with the storytelling styles of Chol speakers—and at the same time were studying ancient hieroglyphic inscriptions—we came to the realization that there were significant parallels between the two (Josserand, Schele, and Hopkins 1979). The breakthrough occurred when Kathryn and I took a break from caring for my father after his ultimately fatal stroke in 1984 and left Gloucester to spend a long weekend in the mountains of western Virginia. Linda had told Kathryn that to solidify her understanding of inscriptions, she needed to work her way though a set of texts by herself rather than just following one of Linda's presentations. She took on the set of inscriptions from the Cross Group at Palenque, and during that bucolic weekend she saw the connections. In November 1984 Kathryn and Linda drafted a paper on the discourse structure of Maya hieroglyphic texts (Josserand and Schele 1984). Linda read the paper at the American Anthropological Association meetings in Denver, as we had to return to Gloucester on news that my father had died the night before. Linda came to stay with us for several days in December, and she and Kathryn drafted a second paper, "Discourse Analysis of Narrative Hieroglyphic Texts," in 1985. Because of differences in opinion that now seem trivial (where to break episodes), the paper was never published, although copies were circulated at the annual Maya Meetings in Texas. Kathryn presented her version of the paper at the 1986 Palenque Round Table (Josserand 1991a). Meanwhile, Kathryn and I laid out the rhetorical structures we had discovered in Chol texts (Hopkins and Josserand 1990) and went on to discuss such phenomena in Classic period texts (Josserand 1991b, 1995a, 1995b, 1995c, 1997b; Josserand and Hopkins 1994) and the implications about Classic Maya society that could be drawn from an examination of its literature (Josserand and Hopkins 2002a, 2002b; Josserand 2002, 2004, 2007a).

In 1995, with a grant from FAMSI, we took two students from Florida State University (FSU) to the field in Tila, Chiapas, an active ceremonial center where many daily activities and ritual events are carried out in Chol. Our goal was to investigate the ritual vocabulary of this traditional pilgrimage center, since we suspected that some words and phrases might survive there that had been lost in less traditional communities like the ejidos on which we had been concentrating. The results of that investigation have been published online (Josserand and Hopkins 1996) and in an anthropological journal (Josserand and Hopkins 2005). The students wrote theses on evidentiality statements in Chol texts (Altman 1996) and the taxonomy of Chol birds (Folmar 1996). Our observations on the Black Christ of Tila were published much later (Josserand and Hopkins 2007).

In 2001, supported by an FSU faculty research grant, we went to do fieldwork in southern Campeche, where during a tour we had discovered two dozen relatively new Chol ejido settlements south of Xpujil. Our focus in this fieldwork was to interview the pioneer generation, the men and women who had moved their families out of the highlands of Chiapas and into the jungles of Campeche. We recorded and videotaped narrative histories of this migration. Noting how much traditional knowledge had been lost in these progressive communities, we decided to try to collect as much material as we could as soon as possible. In 2002, with another grant from FAMSI and with Chencho and two new students, we spent the summer in Chiapas and Campeche trying to get as many folktales as we could, recording and videotaping the narrators. We compiled from our work and other sources an inventory of Chol stories and their protagonists (Josserand et al. 2003). One of the students documented the use of Spanish loan words in these interviews and other texts and investigated the theoretical distinction between loan words and code-switching, both phenomena in which words of one language are employed while speaking the other (Kistler 2003).

In the summer of 2006 we returned to the field to introduce three female graduate students from FSU to the region and its people and to work with Chencho on the Chol materials. We visited many of the people we had worked with in the past but spent most of our time orienting the students and getting them ready to do their thesis research (see Litka 2011). Toward the end of the field season, the students departed from our research headquarters in Palenque to go to their respective field sites and begin independent work. I went back to work keyboarding the questionnaires from the Archivo de Lenguas Indígenas we had recorded with Chencho (who speaks the Tumbalá variety of Chol) and his brother-in-law Bernardo Pérez Martínez (who speaks the Tila variety). The tapes of these elicitation sessions have been delivered to AILLA for digitization and posting online, and they will sooner or later be published in Mexico in the Archivo de Lenguas Indígenas monograph series. Kathryn went back to work on an outline of Chol grammar she hoped to include in a volume of our texts. On July 18, 2006, she worked all day with Chencho trying to puzzle out the rather irregular patterns of derivation of Chol positional verbs. We took a break to go visit another old friend, Moisés Morales, and spent a pleasant couple of hours talking over old times and bemoaning new ones. Back at the house before supper, Kathryn went upstairs to take a shower. While showering, she was struck down by a cerebral hemorrhage, and she died later that night in the hospital in Palenque.

Since her death, I have been trying to finish up all the papers we had in progress and to make some dent in the huge backlog of research materials we have gathered over all these years. At the end of the summer of 2006, we had a number of papers in press; they had been accepted for publication but were lacking final corrections and adjustments. One of these papers reported our analysis of the history of the Black Christ of Tila and the cult that surrounds him (Josserand and Hopkins 2007). A second paper presented and commented on the 1789 word list recorded in Tila, the first known data on the Chol language (Hopkins, Cruz Guzmán, and Josserand 2008). The third paper, a revision of one of Kathryn's papers that had long languished awaiting final corrections, presented her argument for the presence of a "missing heir" at Yaxchilan and is based on her structural analysis of an obscure inscription at that Classic site (Josserand 2007b). Kathryn's final paper returned to her interest in archaeology and presented a discussion of the linguistic situation along the Pacific Coast of Guatemala and Chiapas in the Preclassic period (Josserand 2011). I worked from her notes to produce a summary statement on the structure of Chol folktales (Hopkins and Josserand 2012, a revised version of which is included below) and an analysis of the Palace Tablet of Palenque (Bassie-Sweet, Hopkins, and Josserand 2012). The volumes in which these chapters were published were dedicated to her memory, as was a volume on related work in the Chortí area (Metz, McNeil, and Hull 2009) that included a chapter expressing our position on the relation of Chol to Classic period texts (Mora-Marín, Hopkins, and Josserand 2009).

The present collection of Chol texts is a revision and extension of a set of texts we had originally planned to publish in Mexico with the title *T'an ti wajali*, "Stories from Long Ago." Some presentations and analyses had been circulated in our research reports, but there was no definitive publication of most of our text collection. Since many of the earlier texts were collected while we were employed at CIS-INAH/CIESAS, we first submitted the manuscript of *T'an ti wajali* to CIESAS in 1986. The Spanish introductions and text translations had been corrected by the institutional editor, Victoria Miret, and we hoped for prompt publication in the institution's *Cuaderno* series, where the results of several of our projects had been published. After more than a year and numerous inquiries as to the progress of the manuscript, we were informed that it had not been accepted for publication, apparently because of political maneuvering within our old program, which was undergoing reorganization under a new director.

A second publishing possibility in Mexico was offered by the Centro de Estudios Indígenas, a branch of the Universidad Autónoma de Chiapas located in San Cristóbal de Las Casas, Chiapas. This effort floundered. The manuscript was accepted for publication, pending preparation of camera-ready copy. At this point we experienced equipment failure; our aging daisy-wheel printer (Diablo 630 ECS) was suffering daisy-wheel decline, and we could not produce printable copy. In that early age of personal computers, our text files were produced on an Osborne Executive and a Kaypro 10, both CP/M platform computers, using WordStar as the word processor and storing files on large diskettes (the original "floppies"); it was next to impossible to move data from one proprietary system to another. We were by now engaged in another research project, and the publication effort was put aside.

In 1994 we finally submitted our Final Performance Report for our 1983–86 NSF project, "Chol Texts, Vocabulary and Grammar" (Hopkins and Josserand 1994), and we included in that report the entire volume of six *T'an ti wajali* texts with their introductory material, all in Spanish and Chol. That version as submitted demonstrates the low-quality printouts we were able to produce at that time; the manuscript as it appears in the report still bears Miret's editorial marks.

The Chol texts are presented here for the first time in a modern orthography. All the texts have had to be re-keyboarded in modern electronic media (in WordPerfect, on Macintosh computers), and the Chol text has been rewritten in accordance with the orthographic norms established by the Academia de las Lenguas Mayas de Guatemala. This is the first time these texts have appeared with an English translation; the translations were all done by me in 2007, directly from the Chol but referring to the previous Spanish translations for occasional guidance.

CHOL TEXTS ON THE SUPERNATURAL

This is not the first extensive set of Chol folktales to appear with English translation. An important early contribution to the literature was a publication of the Summer Institute of Linguistics, *Chol Texts on the Supernatural* (Whittaker and Warkentin 1965). Forty brief narrations, occupying nearly 150 pages, present the (Tumbalá) Chol texts in numbered sentences, with words and phrases marked with subscript numbers corresponding to footnoted English translations. A phonological key and orthographic notes precede the texts, and a glossary follows. The texts were collected between 1948 and 1962, some dictated and some written but all from the same informant (personal communication, Viola Warkentin, SIL Dallas, 1985). Topically, they are divided into Creation Stories, Religious Ceremonies, and the Spirit World and Witchcraft.

Now out of print, this volume was an essential reference for anyone interested in the language. A basic grammar could be gleaned from the entries (superceded by the publication of Warkentin and Scott's *Gramática ch'ol* in 1980), and the stories and commentaries were intriguing. The ethnographic information was clearly colored by the conversion of the informant to Protestant Christianity, but unlike foreign anthropologists and linguists, a considerable segment of the Chol-speaking population would have no problem with that. From the point of view of the present collection of texts, the problem is that these texts were heavily edited, and significant features of traditional storytelling are missing. There are no evidentiality statements, although the language of the texts implies a relation to traditional lore (use of *mi yälob'* "they say" and *'ab'i* "it is said"). Background information is limited, and tales begin abruptly; they also end abruptly, with no formal closing. Consequently, while the content of the stories is adequately presented, the collection as a whole does not satisfactorily portray the nature of Chol storytelling. It is our fervent hope that the present volume goes beyond this pioneer work in conveying a more nuanced sense of the oral tradition.

Chol (Mayan) Folktales

I

The Chol Maya and Their Folktales

Nicholas A. Hopkins and J. Kathryn Josserand

Since its discovery by explorers in the nineteenth century, Maya civilization has held a fascination for Europeans and Americans. As archaeological investigations and ethnohistorical research proceeded, it became clear that this was one of the world's most advanced civilizations for its time, with sophisticated knowledge of mathematics and astronomy and magnificent works of art and architecture. As the mysteries of Maya writing began to be untangled, the details of Maya history were revealed. All in all, this new world civilization rivaled those of the old world in complexity and achievement.

What has gone little noticed, as Classic period hieroglyphic inscriptions have been dissected for their historical data, is the fact that the Classic Maya also had great literature. The history of Maya kings and queens, their exploits in warfare and their attention to ceremonial affairs, is not simply stated as a sequence of events. The story is narrated in a highly structured literary style, the details of which are only now becoming clear.

With the conquest of the Maya by the intrusive Spanish culture, much of the culture of the Maya elite disappeared. The contexts in which elite culture thrived ceased to exist. There were no longer schools to prepare the rulers and their families for lives devoted to governance, to science, art, and religion. The books that recorded knowledge and preserved the models for ritual activity were collected and destroyed. The ruling classes were eliminated or absorbed into the emerging Colonial society. Without royal courts, there was no context in which courtly living

DOI: 10.5876/9781607324881.c001

could survive. Introduced diseases decimated the population. New rulers subjugated the remaining peoples and converted them to servants of the Christian crown and its administrators.

But the Maya survived. And in many places, key elements of Maya culture survived with them. Adaptations were made that allowed native customs to be integrated into the new reality. Native gods took on new guises and joined the Christian pantheon. Native practices were reinterpreted and understood to be popular Christianity. Now cloaked in Christian doctrine, Maya folk religion persisted, and it lives on today.

Studying the modern Maya of Yucatán, the anthropologist Robert Redfield (1941) developed the idea of the Great and Little Traditions. The Great Tradition is practiced by the elite—elaborate ceremonies supported by complex, esoteric explanations of the world, a proliferation of deities corresponding to a complex of interests, a culture that requires writing, formal study, specialization of roles, extensive investment of resources—the culture of the Classic Maya and their descendants up until the sixteenth century.

The Little Tradition is a pale reflection of the culture of the elite, carried on by the common folk. Ceremonial activity may be performed at the level of households rather than in huge public performances. Community celebrations are far less elaborate that those directed by the elite. The rationale behind ceremonial activity may be a simple appeal to tradition or a sense of community identity and not be motivated by philosophical or ideological principles. In place of writing, formal study, and specialized roles, folk culture is passed on informally through the oral tradition, from generation to generation within the family, within the community, and without major investment of scarce resources. However, since both the Great and the Little Traditions have a common origin and a symbiotic relationship, the Little Tradition may encode in its behaviors—often unrecognized by its practitioners—the same underlying principles as its elite counterpart.

In this collection of modern Maya folklore, tales told by the Chol Maya of southern Mexico, we see elements of the elite Classic culture we know from archaeological excavations and scholarly research. Such elements have taken on new meanings, and they exist in a distinct context. But they have been preserved, and a greater understanding of them may well shed light on Classic society. In interpreting these elements, we must keep in mind that they are derived from the Little Tradition and have survived as folk culture; they are not directly descended from the related elements as expressed in the elite culture of the Classic Great Tradition but are collateral descendants, derived from the Little Tradition of Classic times.

One such element is the modern Earth Owner, or Earth Lord, a figure known across Mesoamerica under various names but with similar characteristics. At present, he is surely the most prominent deity in Maya folk culture and religious practice, and he appears in many ethnographic studies. In Zinacantan, a Tzotzil community in Chiapas, for example, he appears as Yahval Balumil, the Owner/Lord of the World/Earth. For the Chuj of northwestern Guatemala he is Witz-ak'lik, Mountain-Plain, a metonym for "Earth." Elsewhere in Guatemala he is known simply as Mundo "Earth/World." In Guatemala he also appears under the guise of Maximón, "Saint Simon." In Yucatán his rain-bringer aspect is emphasized, and he is known as Chaak, and Chajk is one of his various avatars in the Chol area.

This earth deity lives underground, inside mountains and in caves, and he is the owner of all material resources, as some of his names imply. He owns the earth, the water, the land, the trees, the animals, the minerals, and all other material things. To make use of his properties—an absolute necessity for survival—people must ask his permission, treat his possessions with respect, make proper gifts in return for their use, and in general keep up an equitable relationship with him. He is not only the source of wealth and health, he is also dangerous and potentially deadly. Since he has so many properties to manage—great herds of animals, plantations, deposits of minerals, and the like—he needs laborers, and he takes the souls of transgressors as eternal slaves. Or, if the violation of contract is a lesser offense, he may simply withdraw his support and deny benefits by withholding rain, sending destructive winds, and so on.

In the Chol area, he appears in several guises. Chajk is the distant rain god and has little direct interaction with people. He brings the rain. He also rumbles in the distance when rain is coming; now an old man, he does not throw lightning as much as do his sons, who precede him, throwing flashing bolts of lightning and generally acting up. Physical evidence of his existence is seen in the polished stone axes found in the fields, called *'acha Lak Mam*, "Our Grandfather's axes," thought to be the results of his lightning bolts, and in the slivers of obsidian blades, *yejch'ak Lak Mam*, "Our Grandfather's fingernails," that he breaks off while digging caterpillars out of rotten trees. Under the rubric of "Our Grandfather," Lak Mam, he is known to take human form and interact with people, as in one of the tales that follows. He is also widely known as Don Juan, a title derived from the identification of John the Baptist as the rain-bringer (he sprinkles water to bring blessings on humans; by his festival day, June 24, rains should be coming regularly). Tales of encounters with Don Juan are especially prominent along the Río Tulijá valley, separated from Palenque by the mountain range known as the Sierra de Don Juan, where we have been told he maintains many "branch offices" in the caves scattered throughout the limestone massif (see A Visit to Don Juan). Pilgrims have visited these caves for hundreds of years (Bassie 2001). We have also argued that the Earth Lord has been incorporated into the persona of the Black Christ of Tila (Señor de Tila), who may be prayed to in caves as well as in churches (Josserand and Hopkins 2007).

Since this underworld deity is more important to farmers and hunters than to the urban elite, his presence in Classic art is somewhat subdued. However, Maya stelae often represent the three levels of the universe—the sky above (with ancestors and supernaturals), the earth (with the stela's human protagonist), and the underworld (on which the protagonist stands). At the base of many stelae the underworld is represented by the Earth Lord. These images are known in art history literature as the Earth Monster, the Cauac Monster (from the stone/cave markings that also appear in the glyph for the day name Cauac) or, more recently, as Witz "Mountain." The representation may be a generalized Mountain, or it may be a reference to a specific nearby location, but this motif is a ubiquitous icon that appears on architecture as well as stelae. The evidence does not tell us much about what the Classic Maya thought about the Earth Lord, but it surely suggests that he was present in the pantheon, and we are probably safe if we project backward from the widespread modern beliefs to attribute many of the same characteristics to him in the Classic period.

A second element that appears fleetingly in modern folktales but is more prominent in Classic iconography is the Celestial Bird, sometimes called the Principal Bird Deity. This elaborate avian frequently appears atop trees, as on the Palenque Sacophagus Lid, where he sits at the apex of the "world tree" that dominates the scene. Celestial birds appear in Maya art as early as the San Bartolo murals (Taube et al. 2010:96–102), where one (in this case, a Laughing Falcon) sits in a tree, tearing the head off a sacrificial snake while humans make offerings representing the other three major classes of animals. Maya ethnozoology recognizes four classes of vertebrates, based on locomotion (Hopkins 1980): mammals (walkers), reptiles and amphibians (crawlers), birds (flyers), and fish (swimmers). These four classes are present in excavated Classic offering caches as well as in offerings depicted in the Dresden Codex. Birds sometimes appear at the top of stelae as the representation of the celestial level of the world, as on Stela 11 at Piedras Negras (Schele and Miller 1986:112). The role of the Celestial Bird appears to be one of harbinger, a messenger of the gods, descending to the earth from the heavens.

In the Chol folktales, we see this messenger transformed to a more humble creature in the brief tale of the Celestial Bird, the *tyaty muty* "father-bird" that tells earthly roosters when to crow in the morning. But he also appears in the most sacred of narratives, the story of the Moon and her sons (Our Holy Mother), where he is described as *ixi lekoj bä 'ajtzo'*, literally, "that exotic turkey/peacock." Here he plays his role of celestial messenger, as he descends from heaven in the night to tell the plants to stand up again (after they were felled by the Sun's older brother).

Finally, these tales are populated by a number of strange and frightful creatures not seen in Classic period public art but very much present on ceramics (see the

Kerr archive of Maya ceramics, www.mayavase.com, or www.famsi.org/research/ kerr/). These are the creatures of the underworld, although they are not necessarily restricted to appearances down under. Death gods, skeletal creatures, severed heads, supernatural animals, and enough monsters to populate a dozen horror movies are seen on Classic ceramics and find counterparts in the Chol folktales. They are especially prominent in the "ghost stories" told while men are camped out in the fields on extended work periods, like the tales we tell our children at summer camp.

Beyond the inferences that may be gleaned from the cast of characters, there are valuable insights into Maya morality and worldview that emerge from these stories and that can be hypothesized to represent the values of common folk in earlier times. Certainly, they are not introduced from Europe, although many of the principles of Chol belief are compatible with Christian ideals (if not Christian practice). The emphasis in religious practice of making offerings to the gods is certainly common in the Classic period as well as modern times. Perhaps an understanding of what underlies modern practice—keeping up a harmonious relationship with the universe and its natural forces, paying for what we receive—could inform our ideas about the Classic, so thoroughly contaminated by the demonization of native cultures during the Colonial period and, for that matter, during modern campaigns to missionize and change the culture of modern Mayas. It is instructive to compare two descriptions of the "cave god," that is, the Earth Lord, one from a dictionary compiled by Christian missionaries, one from a reworking of that dictionary by secular Chols (translations from the Spanish and the Chol by the authors):

> *ajaw* 1. Evil spirit of the earth (called "our father"). It is believed that a person can make a pact with him. This person can make petitions to this spirit in favor [of] or against another person. The man who has relations with the *ajaw* is called the *sacristán*. If a man or a woman offends the sacristan, he goes to this spirit to curse the person, and within a short time that person dies . . . The spirit of water . . . If we enter the water, the spirit of water will eat us . . . A companion of the devil: The evil of the *ajaw* is the same as that of the devil. (Aulie and Aulie 1978:27–28)
>
> *ajaw* The lord of the mountains and caves who is the owner of all there is on earth; our lord, to whom we pray; welfare, health, and good comes with the end of offense . . . he is prayed to for good weather at the mouth of the cave. (López et al. 2000:42)

MODERN CHOL COMMUNITIES AND CULTURE

In historic times, the Chol Maya have occupied a continuous area in southern Mexico, in the state of Chiapas and adjacent parts of the state of Tabasco, with concentrations in the Chiapas *municipios* (county-like political subdivisions of the state) of Tila, Tumbalá, Salto de Agua, Yajalón, Palenque, and Sabanilla (Hopkins 1995). Chols have expanded in modern times into jungle areas to the southeast (in Ocosingo) and into a small area in the southern part of the state of Campeche, to the east (in the new municipio of Calakmul). The great majority live in small rural settlements with only a few hundred residents, but several urban centers are dominated by Chols, notably Tila, Tumbalá, and Salto de Agua.

Census figures for 1980, representing the period when these folktales were gathered, registered 26,000 Chol speakers among 35,000 residents in Tila; 16,000 residents, almost all Chol speakers, in Salto de Agua; 12,000 Chols of 16,000 residents in Tumbalá; 13,000 Chols among 35,000 residents in Palenque; 8,000 Chols, 12,000 residents in Sabanilla; and 5,000 Chols, 10,000 residents in Yajalón. Approximately 5,000 Chols resided in the new municipio of Calakmul, in the state of Campeche. These figures total only 85,000 speakers. Now, thirty-plus years later, the Chol population has increased significantly. The Instituto Nacional de las Lenguas Indígenas (2000) reported 145,000 Chol speakers in 2000 and a few years later (Instituto Nacional de las Lenguas Indígenas 2008) credited Chol with 185,299 speakers in a catalog of indigenous languages. Allowing for more recent growth and some undercounting in the census, the Chol-speaking population may now number close to 200,000. These figures are not unreasonable given the tremendous increase in the territory occupied by Chol speakers, brought about by the continual creation of new settlements (de la Torre Yarza 1994).

At the end of the sixteenth century, Chol settlements, including some large towns, were located along the Usumacinta River and its lowland tributaries as well as in the areas mentioned above. These lowland settlements resisted the Spanish, including Christian missionary activity, and carried out raids on highland areas pacified and controlled by the Spanish crown. As a consequence, they were subjected to a 100-year military effort (1590–1690) that conquered and resettled Chols area by area, beginning with the lower Usumacinta and Río Tulijá areas and proceeding upriver in successive campaigns, concluding with the conquest of the Mopán and Itzá Maya to the east (de Vos 1980, 1988, 1990).

Chols who survived pacification were resettled among highland Maya Indians along the border of the conquered lowlands, including the new town of Palenque as well as Tila, Tumbalá, and Bachajón in Chiapas and Retalhuleu in Guatemala. The only Chol populations to survive into the twentieth century were those that had been resettled in the highlands surrounding Tila and Tumbalá. Other Chols either assimilated or disappeared in all other areas. Distinct dialects of Chol developed in Tila, Tumbalá, and nearby Sabanilla (Aulie and Aulie 1978). In the late Colonial period, Salto de Agua was founded with Chols who had colonized the Río Tulijá valley from the highland towns.

John Lloyd Stephens, an American explorer who passed through the Chol area in 1840 (Stephens 1841), remarked that the Indians there lived in essentially aboriginal conditions, with little sign of Spanish influence. He encountered men in loincloths carrying crude clubs. However, after mid-century, German and North American interests founded coffee plantations and incorporated Chols in a system of debt peonage (Alejos García 1994; Alejos García and Ortega Peña 1991). This system gradually disappeared after the Mexican Revolution in the early twentieth century, and Chols eventually gained control of many coffee plantations through land reform in the 1930s, under the administration of President Lázaro Cárdenas. These lands became the first dozen or so Chol *ejidos* (federally sanctioned collective farms).

About 1960, a major new development took place when the federal government authorized the expansion of highland populations into lowland jungle areas left essentially unpopulated since the seventeenth century. Hundreds of new settlements have resulted as groups organize and petition for lands under the ejido system, and the population expansion has taken Chols back to virtually all of the Mexican territory their ancestors occupied at the time of the Conquest (de la Torre Yarza 1994).

Ejido settlements tend to be small, as the laws governing land reform specify how many heads of family will have land rights and restrict inheritance to one child, usually a son. Land-poor younger sons are a major factor in the formation of newer ejidos. As a consequence, ejidos tend to be peculiar demographically, as they are founded by young generation-mates and initially have few elders. By the same token, they are innovative socially, and little traditional life survives in the ejidos. A great majority are dominated by Protestant sects, in contrast to the well-entrenched Catholicism of the older highland settlements and evidenced by biblical place names like Jerusalén and Babilonia rather than saints' names like Santa Maria and San Miguel or Chol place names like Tiemopa and Joloniel.

The economy of Chol settlements is diverse, although there is a strong component of subsistence agriculture based on the Mesoamerican triad of maize, beans, and squash, with the addition of manioc, chile peppers, tomatoes, and other vegetables, as well as tropical fruits. Cacao was prominent in early Colonial times but was replaced by coffee. Nineteenth- and early-twentieth-century plantations also produced cattle, mahogany and other tropical hardwoods, rubber, and vanilla. In Colonial times there was a lucrative business exporting *zarzaparrilla* (*Smilax* spp.) to Spain as a medicinal (West, Psuty, and Thom 1985). (Ultimately, in the United States this vine yielded a refreshing drink: sasparrilla.) Commercial agriculture is now centered on coffee production, but low market values have recently resulted in the destruction of established coffee plantations and their replacement by maize and other crops.

Weaving and embroidery, once essential crafts for women, have disappeared almost entirely, replaced by sewing. Western-style dresses of brightly decorated satin-like cloth, worn with rows of beads and numerous hair clips, are a hallmark of ejido Chol women. Males do most agricultural work, women do domestic work—that is, men produce food, women process it, as in other Mayan communities. Family units are important and positively valued. Relations between brothers are said to be strained and competitive (as in mythology, see Our Holy Mother), while relations with cousins are friendly. People with the same surname are assumed to be related and can be called on for aid if necessary, a reflection of the now-defunct system of patrilineal clans (Hopkins 1988, 1991; Josserand and Hopkins 2002a). Uncles are counselors and helpers, grandparents are treated with respect and are sought out for advice.

Ejidos are governed by prescribed structures (a commissioner and councils) but often function more democratically, with men meeting daily for public discussions and more formal weekly public assemblies, with decisions made by consensus. Religious authorities exercise considerable authority over community members. Highland and urban settlements have legally prescribed systems of governance under federal law, balanced against a traditional "cargo" system, which now has mainly religious functions but nonetheless constitutes a political power base capable of opposing civil authority (Josserand and Hopkins 2007).

The cargo system survives best in Tila, where more than fifty citizens at a time hold ritual offices for one-year terms, with responsibilities for organizing festivals, caring for sacred images, and receiving and interceding on petitions from supplicants, including pilgrims from outside the community. Marriage is a prerequisite for these offices, and wives share the privileges and responsibilities of office with their husbands. Apart from legal institutions introduced from outside, social control is largely accomplished through socialization and internal social control. Individuals believe they are responsible for their acts not only to others but to the supernatural world and that bad actions will result in illness and other forms of supernatural discipline.

Traditional syncretic Maya-Catholic beliefs, as manifested in the Chol area, have merged the Sun with Christ and the Moon with the Virgin Mary, in accordance with precolumbian mythology, where the Moon is the mother of the Sun (see Our Holy Mother). Tila is the center of a syncretic tradition featuring a Black Christ, the Señor de Tila, and Tila is a major pilgrimage site for southern Mexico, similar to Santiago Esquipulas, the pilgrimage site of the Señor de Esquipulas, at the other extreme of precolumbian Cholan territory in eastern Guatemala. Both of these Christian icons have incorporated elements of the precolumbian Earth Lord (ibid.).

Caves figure prominently in religious practice as the domain of the principal earth deity, the owner of earthly goods who must be petitioned for reasonable use of his plants and animals. An overriding philosophy reigns that gifts must be repaid, and evil will turn back against its agent. Offerings in caves for success in hunting and other pursuits continue to be made (see A Visit to Don Juan). Apart from priests and pastors serving mainstream Christian churches, shamanistic curers are the principal religious practitioners. Summoned to their responsibility in dreams, curers visit caves to solidify their powers (Pérez Chacón 1988).

Curing practices involve invoking supernatural powers, both good and evil (the latter must be controlled by the shaman and made to act positively). Petitions to supernaturals are made through intermediaries and are accompanied by offerings of candles, incense, and liquor. An essential element is the pledge (*promesa*) made by the interlocutor, in effect a contract exchanging offerings and good behavior for divine assistance. Most shamans are male, but a similar position is held by female midwives, who likewise draw their powers from the supernatural and are destined to serve from birth. Men who have held a series of ceremonial offices and become respected elders, *tatuches*, also serve as intercessors for petitioners to the saints (Josserand and Hopkins 1996).

Major illness results from souls being imprisoned by earth powers (such as caves, rivers). Shamans cure with a combination of spiritual and herbal treatments; curers bargain for release of the soul with prayers, offerings, and threats and treat with herbs. Some illness may result from witchcraft, accomplished by pacts with earth powers. Principal illnesses are caused by fright, envy, and wrong thoughts, all involving disharmony with the spirit world. Curing techniques include ritual bathing, spraying (from the mouth) or sprinkling with herbal preparations, herbal remedies and diets, prayers and offerings. All utilize the shaman's special relation with good or harnessed evil powers. Midwives care for pregnant women and assist in deliveries.

Death is considered a natural process; people must die to make room for others, and this is part of God's plan. Burial is within twenty-four hours, in wooden coffins, in cemeteries, with Christian rites. (This was not always the case; a Colonial official reported in 1737 that the priest in Tila had not heard a confession in nine years of service and deaths were not reported to the church to avoid Christian burial [Breton 1988].) A wake features prayers and offerings on behalf of the soul of the departed. Gifts of food and candles are received by a designated family member of the same sex as the departed, and money, candles, and incense are ritually presented to the cadaver. The dead are recalled on All Saints' Day, when house altars are supplied with food for the dead and religious services are held in the graveyards.

THE PRACTICE OF STORYTELLING

Storytelling takes place in various contexts—at least where traditional ways have not been altered by new circumstances. A key element is not locational but temporal.

Stories are not told during the workday, which starts well before dawn and begins to wind down in the afternoon. Men—the principal storytellers but by no means the only ones—go out to work as soon as (and sometimes before) they can see the trails, to take advantage of the cool early morning hours. They will have broken their fast with a few tortillas and perhaps some coffee, and they carry with them a ration of *pozol* (Chol *sa'*, essentially the same as the ground maize dough tortillas are made of) and some additives or flavoring, varying from sugar to chiles, as well as a gourd bowl in which to mix the dough and other ingredients with water. This refreshing drink they will consume about the time the heat begins to rise, after several hours of labor, around 9:00 or 10:00. They return to work for another few hours, and when the heat becomes intense or the rains begin, they will rest, perhaps work a little more, and then return home to clean up.

By late afternoon the men are back in the settlement, rested and bathed, and they begin to gather in a central location, perhaps a town square or a grassy central clearing that serves the same purpose. They might hang around an ejido headquarters building if such exists. This is a time devoted to the discussion of civil affairs and the exchange of news, but important decisions await the weekly Sunday afternoon assembly ideally attended by all men (and no women). When the light fades it is time to head home for an evening meal and family time, the family gathered inside the single-room home around the cooking fire. Now, before the children are put to bed, is a good time for storytelling.

We learned early on that it was useless to ask informants to tell us stories in the morning. If they even tried, the results were disappointing. After trying repeatedly all day to elicit stories, we would give up and in the late afternoon decide to have a beer and forget it. As soon as the day's work was over and we were all relaxed and comfortable, the stories would come out. It just didn't feel right to spend work time in entertainment. The context was not right. It was like asking someone to tell bawdy jokes in a church. You might try to do it, but you wouldn't do it well. Of course, after we had been working with specific individuals for a few years and they treated storytelling as part of their employment, we might have better results. But still, the best time to get stories was in prime time, as part of the evening's activities. Several of the stories presented here were recorded after a long day's work thatching Merle Greene Robertson's house in Palenque, when the workers (including us) were kicking back and having a little refreshment.

During parts of the agricultural calendar, men may go out to distant fields and stay for several days, sleeping in makeshift huts in the fields they are working. At night they gather around the fire and tell stories. A similar context was provided by the canoe-making expeditions Ausencio Cruz Guzmán participated in with his father and brothers. They would camp for several days at the site of the tree they had felled while they carved the trunk into a canoe. Other men present would tell tales they hadn't heard. Mayas in general are wary of being out in the woods alone, especially at night, and the anxiety inspired by being away from the protection of the village may encourage the recitation of tales of things that come out of the woods. These stories are frightening, but all are resolved in the same way. The savage creatures that are likely to appear at your campfire are dangerous, but they can be outwitted, and these tales revolve around the ways that might be done. They are at once frightening and reassuring, a surefire formula for a good story.

Other contexts may be appropriate to storytelling. Cruz reports hearing about the Lightning God's encounter with fishermen while out fishing with a pair of adult men when he was just a young boy. There are probably other circumstances that would elicit certain kinds of stories, since one motivation for telling a story is to instruct, and the context might be appropriate for instruction.

The majority of the stories we have recorded were told by men, in part because men deal more with the outside world than do their female counterparts. However, when we have had the confidence of the family, we have recorded tales told by females, and they are every bit as well told as those we elicited from men. That is, women know how to tell a story as well as men do, they just don't get out as much. While we have had little opportunity to observe it, women probably tell each other stories as much as men do.

Storytelling does require an audience; it is an interactive activity. On several occasions we have recorded in the absence of other people, but only with informants who are used to such activities and can imagine an appropriate audience is present. Bernardo Pérez, for instance, a schoolteacher, was used to working out and rehearsing his classroom presentations (at least to himself). He was completely comfortable sitting down and dictating to a tape recorder (see The Blackman).

Imagine, then, as you are reading these stories, that it is evening and you are in a dimly lit thatch-roofed hut in the American tropics, the sounds of insects rising in the dusk. A small fire is smoldering in the three-stone hearth on the dirt floor in the center of the room to keep the mosquitoes away. It gives just enough light to get around in but not enough to illuminate all the nooks and crannies. The light flickers against the rafters and the ears of corn hanging there, waiting to be planted next season. The males of the family are resting in hammocks or sitting around the fire on small chairs, the women still working on domestic tasks, and it's not quite time to go to sleep. The children are about to be put down, the little ones already asleep. Conversation has lagged, and then from one side of the fire an elderly man begins to speak:

A long time ago, they say, our ancestors used to tell this story. I heard it from my mother and father. They say there once was a man . . .

2

The Narrative Structure of Chol Folktales

J. KATHRYN JOSSERAND

I first heard Maya storytellers during my 1967–68 fieldwork in Pustunich, Yucatán, where I had gone to study the Maya language with the goal of contributing to work on Maya hieroglyphic writing. At that time it was assumed that Maya was the appropriate language to associate with the Classic inscriptions. My major professor at Tulane, Marshall Durbin, assigned me an impossible dissertation project: go to Yucatán and write a grammar of Maya, then write a grammar of the language of the inscriptions and compare the two. I made some progress on the first task (Josserand 1968) but not on the rest. In the 1960s, before Xerox copies, it was virtually impossible to assemble a corpus of Classic inscriptions, and in any case no scholar could yet extract linguistic information from the graphics of Maya writing.

In 1976 my husband, Nick Hopkins, and I learned from Linda Schele that much progress had been made in deciphering the script, and it was time to work on Mayan languages again. We chose Chol as the language most indicated and began fieldwork from our headquarters in Mexico City, where we were employed in a program of training Mexican students to work on indigenous languages (Centro de Investigaciones Superiores del Instituto Nacional de Antropología e Historia, CIS-INAH, later renamed Centro de Investigaciones y Estudios en Antropología Social, CIESAS). By 1978 we had begun to record and analyze modern Chol texts (Cruz Guzmán, Josserand, and Hopkins 1980), and by 1980 we had begun to appreciate the relationship of Chol grammar to that of the language of the inscriptions (Josserand, Schele, and Hopkins 1985). It was the combination of studying Classic

DOI: 10.5876/9781607324881.c002

Maya inscriptions on the one hand and contemporary Chol narratives on the other that led to the insights discussed below.

We learned about modern Maya epigraphy from Linda Schele first by attending her workshops and then by teaching beginners' workshops and lecturing to workshop participants about Mayan languages and their history. By the spring workshop in 1984 we had produced a virtual workbook, a collection of source material on Mayan languages that we used as a didactic tool in the workshops (Josserand and Hopkins 1984). This package was made available to workshop participants through the Kinko's Files (papers on file at a Kinko's Copy store, to be copied on request). This collection included several maps and charts of Mayan-language distribution and genealogical relationships, cognate sets and phonological correspondences, and a model of diversification drawn from an earlier paper of mine (Josserand 1975). There was a sketch of Chol grammar and, finally, a set of excerpts of Chol texts, formatted to show their structure and translated to English.

At the 1984 Texas Maya Meeting, Linda had suggested that to advance my understanding of Classic texts, I should work my way through inscriptions on my own rather than take her presentations as given. That summer I took on the inscriptions of the Cross Group at Palenque. As I sketched out their discourse structures, I came to the realization that there were clear parallels between the Classic and modern narrative styles. I met with Linda at the Dumbarton Oaks meeting that October, and we drafted a paper on narrative discourse for a November symposium at the Annual Meeting of the American Anthropological Association (AAA) in Denver, held in honor of my major professor, Marshall Durbin, recently deceased (Josserand and Schele 1984). The night before that symposium was held, my father-in-law, Sewell H. Hopkins, died, and Nick and I left Denver immediately for Gloucester; Linda read the paper to the symposium. That December Linda came to Virginia to spend a few days with us, and we drafted a paper on the narrative style of Classic texts, for publication. While we agreed on almost all points, we disagreed about where to break episodes (Linda wanted to break after the Distance Numbers, I wanted to break before them), and this issue was never resolved. The paper (Josserand and Schele 1985) was never published, although it did find its way into the Kinko's Files. Schele's 1985 Texas Notebook incorporated aspects of what we had discussed.

I presented my analysis of Classic discourse to the Sixth Mesa Redonda de Palenque in 1986 (Josserand 1991b, 1997a). That same year, Nick and I presented a parallel paper on Chol narrative discourse at the Annual Meeting of the AAA (Hopkins and Josserand 1986a), and a version of that paper was later published in a Festschrift for Jorge Suárez (Hopkins and Josserand 1990). It included an analysis of Palenque's Tablet of the Slaves to illustrate the parallels between modern and

Classic discourse. I continued to apply what I had learned to Classic and modern texts in papers presented in 1987 (Josserand 1987a, 1987b, 1987c), and based on discourse principles I developed a new reading order for Palenque's Sarcophagus Rim inscription (Josserand 1989), followed by a commentary on the literary structure of the inscription on the Tablet of the 96 Glyphs, Palenque (Josserand 1995b). Over the next few years we continued to investigate aspects of the Chol language as well as the Classic inscriptions (see the references).

Throughout this period, inspired by our discoveries of literary structures in Classic texts, we expanded and worked on our collection of modern narratives in Chol (Hopkins and Josserand 1986a; Josserand et al. 2003), ultimately resulting in the present volume. It became clear that modern Chol storytellers shared a style of narration. We noted many of the same rhetorical devices in stories told by different narrators, and the responses to narration by listeners suggested that the norms of storytelling were shared by speakers and listeners alike. That is, there is an established tradition of narration whose norms are followed by those considered to be the best storytellers and disregarded by those who are not.

The devices employed by good storytellers create a dramatic narrative by anticipating the reactions of the audience. Old information is recalled as background, new information is introduced in the right way at the right time. Some details are suppressed, others are emphasized. Transitions from one episode to another are clearly marked. Peak events are clearly distinguished from the ordinary event line. Throughout a narration, back-channeling from the audience encourages the speaker, and if the story is not being told in a satisfactory way, the audience may intervene and set things right. In fact, there is a regular place in the presentation of a narrative that calls for audience participation and a retelling of major events in the story, perhaps even the introduction of untold events. Clearly, there is a common sense of how a story should be told and an appreciation for storytellers who tell stories well. We have only begun to appreciate all the aspects of this tradition, but from our observations of narrators and their audiences, we can offer the following generalizations.

THE EVIDENTIALITY STATEMENT

The telling of a story typically begins with what linguists call an evidentiality statement (Altman 1996). This is a statement of where and from whom the narrator first heard the story, that is, on what evidence does the storyteller draw. In the case of a personal experience, this may involve only relating the place and time when the events took place. For instance, the text A Visit to Don Juan, which relates the personal experiences of the storyteller, begins with the recorder (Ausencio Cruz

Guzmán) saying "This story we're going to tell, now, it took place about fifteen years ago. Mariano was a young boy still." Mariano, the storyteller, continues, "A long time ago, when I was still . . . when I was still where my brothers are, in Paso Naranjo . . ." A telling of the experiences of someone else may begin with a statement of how the teller knows it. The text of The Messengers begins with Cruz saying "This story I'm going to tell you all, a man told it to me when we went to carve out a canoe there at Arroyo Palenque."

A statement attributing the story to another source may be brief and without detail. The text The Celestial Bird begins with the simple statement: "Like this, they told me that it's like this. When the roosters crow . . ." We don't know who told the narrator the story or where or when it was learned, but it is clearly stated not to be something that comes from his personal knowledge. The narration of a traditional tale will have a statement, often quite elaborate, assigning authority to the ancestors. The story of the Older Brother Sun and Younger Brother Sun begins simply with "It was a long time ago, our ancestors [used to] say . . ."

Since these evidentiality statements are made prior to the actual telling of the tale, they are often edited out in published versions. A reader of much of the published literature would have no idea such things were common, even required, in a proper telling. We ourselves did not recognize this fact at first and inadvertently began our transcriptions of texts with the actual event line, disregarding the necessary introductory material. For a review of published literature on Chol, some more severely edited than others, see Josserand et al. (2003:appendix I). Translations to Spanish often adopt a Western storytelling style that differs starkly from the original texts. A tale that comes out of the ancient tradition of mythological and sacred stories should have an evidentiality statement that attributes the story to the ancestors, near or remote. For example, Our Holy Mother, one of the most sacred stories, begins:

Wajali 'ab'i,	A long time ago, it is said,
mi yälob' laj tyatyña'älob'	—our ancestors used to say;
mi yälob', mi kub'iñ	they speak, I listen—
jtyaty, jña', tzi sub'eñoñ,	my father, my mother, told me,
wajali.	long ago.

This opening contains several of the discourse elements that indicate a story is part of the ancient tradition. It starts with the word *wajali*, "a long time ago." The use of this temporal adverb indicates that the events to be related happened well before the life of any contemporary person. (It is occasionally employed to refer to recent historical time, but this seems to be an innovation, a usage that is coming into vogue as the tradition of oral literature is declining and traditional markers no longer hold their old meanings.)

The second word, *'ab'i*, glossed 'they say', is the reportative marker that accompanies the telling of events known as traditional knowledge, stories passed down from generation to generation. It appears to be a reduced form of the past participle of the verb *'al* 'to say', that is, *'al-b'il* '(it is) said', although we have frequently glossed it 'they say'. Typically, this marker is used heavily at the beginning of a story to establish its time frame and genre, and it will then reappear in the text only at peak events (to remind the listener that the story bears the authority of the ancestors).

The next phrase, *mi yälob' laj tyatyña'älob'*, 'say our father-mother-s', has two parts. The subject of the clause is a compound noun composed of *tyaty* 'father' and *ña'* 'mother', the generalizing suffix *-äl*, and the plural suffix *-ob'*. The compound is possessed by *laj-* 'our'. A compound of this sort in a Mayan language represents a metonym. The terms for two members of a class are juxtaposed in this fashion to index the class that includes them, not them themselves. Thus, "father-mother-plural" indexes 'ancestors', just as *'al-p'eñel-ob'* (child of woman–child of man–plural) indexes 'descendents'. The verb in this expression, *mi yälob'*, is in incompletive aspect (with preclitic *mi*), indicating that this is (or was) an ongoing behavior, not a single incident in time. We sometimes gloss this 'they used to say'.

In the next-to-last line, there is a couplet that constitutes another kind of metonymic expression: *jtyaty, jña'* 'my father, my mother'. Again, what is indexed is the class that includes them both, that is, 'my parents'. Note that the verb in this clause is in completive aspect (with preclitic *tzi*), that is, it refers to a specific act, not an ongoing behavior: *tzi sub'eñoñ* 'they told me'. So the narrator's ancestors used to tell this story, and his parents told it to him.

The phrase *mi yälob'*, 'they say', may be used alone without identifying the sayers. Here the tellers are identified as 'ancestors', but the phrase can occur by itself. In *Chol Texts on the Supernatural* (Whittaker and Warkentin 1965), the story of the Moon and her sons (Our Holy Father, the Sun, Is Born, 13–17) begins abruptly: *Jiñäch ñaxañ jiñi i yäskuñ tza' tyili tyi pañimil*, 'he it was, first his older brother came to earth' (ibid.:13; original orthography replaced). We believe the opening phrases were edited out of this story (and have been told by colleagues of the authors that this is the case). Later segments of traditional lore are introduced by phrases like *'añ yamb'ä mi yälob'* 'there is another one they tell' (ibid.:49), *'añ mi yälob' ja'el* 'there is something they say also' (ibid.:51), and *'añ ja'el mi yälob'* 'there is also something they say' (ibid.:58), or just *mi yälob'* 'they say', as in *'añ yamb'ä mi ña'tyañob' cha'añ mi' käñätyañ jiñi dios, mi yälob'*, 'there is another thing they believe in order to care for the god, they say' (ibid.:74). All such attributions to anonymous tellers are veiled references to the ancestors and the oral tradition. That is, these stories are common knowledge, passed down from generation to generation.

In the introductory statement quoted above, the same phrase appears again in a structural opposition, another kind of metonymic phrase. *Mi yälob', mi kub'iñ*, 'they say, I listen', refers to the transmission of tales from one generation to the next, in the oral tradition. The opening paragraph of Our Holy Mother, then, contains at least six markers that indicate that this is a traditional tale, passed down through the generations, and it carries the authority of the ancestors, delegated to the storyteller.

THE ESTABLISHMENT OF BACKGROUND

Following the statement of evidentiality and sometimes incorporated into it we find background information that is necessary to situate the story in time and place, to give us necessary context. We have used the term *background* in two senses. At the beginning of a story, "background" statements introduce such elements as the time, place, and protagonists. These statements might more properly be called "scene setting." This is new information, and it is stated in sentences that have non-punctual aspect, that is, they are not expressed in the completive aspect but in incompletive aspect, or they may use the timeless existential verb (*'añ*) or non-verbal predicates. Completive aspect is reserved for the event line, and the first use of the completive marks the transition from scene-setting background information to the action of the story.

The second sense of "background" involves back references made in the text to incidents reported earlier or information the hearer is assumed to know, what is called "old information" in the linguistic literature. These are statements like "He went to the cave … *When he had arrived at the cave*, he entered it." Such back references are usually distinguished by their grammar; they may be marked with *-ix* 'already' or some other morphology that distinguishes them from the event-line events (for a discussion of *-ix* as an aspectual clitic, see Vázquez Álvarez 2011:208–9). In oral performance the distinction is sometimes one of inflection (non-falling intonation on the final syllables), and this is difficult to convey in a written text.

Evidentiality statements may be incorporated into the scene-setting background statements. As an alternative to the elaborate phrases referring to the ancestors, a text can be marked as traditional lore by simply using the reportative clitic *ab'i* 'it is said'. Thus in the Tila Chol story The Blackman, where the form has been reduced to *b'i*, the text begins: *'Añ b'i wajali juñ tyikil lak pi'äl*, 'there was, it is said, a long time ago, a man'. The use of *b'i* and *wajali* clearly marks this as a story from the traditional repertory; they are the equivalent of "Once upon a time." However, some of these texts may have been edited to remove the preceding evidentiality statements, leaving the background to be the initial part of the narration.

Another text that mixes evidentiality with the background statements is Our Grandfather, told by Ausencio Cruz Guzmán. It begins:

Wajali 'añ mi yälob'	A long time ago, they say,
ke jiñ lak mam	that Our Grandfather
mu 'ab'i 'i jub'eltyak 'ila tyi lum.	used to come down here to earth.
'Añäch 'ab'i 'i ch'ujlel.	They say he had a soul [took human form].
Mu 'ab'i 'i jub'eltyak tyi mäk' b'itz'	He used to come down to eat *bitz'*
che 'i yorajlel b'itz'.	when it was the tme for *bitz'* [*Inga* spp.].

With the genre of the text having been established as traditional lore, the evidentiality marker *'ab'i* can now disappear, although it will come back into the text at critical points during the story. In fact, the recurrence of *'ab'i* later in a story is a sign that a peak event is about to be related.

We have noticed a broadening of *'ab'i* to general past among younger speakers and those divorced from the oral tradition, especially residents of Protestant ejidos distant from the homeland, for example, the Chol communities in Campeche. In a text recorded in Zoh Laguna by Kristin Cahn von Seelen (2004:312; orthography changed from the original, translation by the authors), a younger speaker begins a family history by saying:

Bueno. 'Añ kmama, tzax jili.	Okay. My mother, she died.
Ksajtyoñ lojoñ, 'añ 'uxp'e jab' wäle.	We lost her, about three years ago.
Pe[ro], 'añ 'ab'i	But she had, it is said,
kab'älob' 'i yijtz'iñob',	a lot of younger siblings,
ch'oktyakob' b'ä.	they were all girls.

This is not traditional lore, it is family history. For a conservative speaker, there is no proper place for *'ab'i* in this text. Among younger speakers, *'ab'i* seems to be used even when reporting relatively recent events, things told by people the speaker knows, not ancient traditional knowledge. We have even heard it used as a substitute for the quotative *che'eñ* 'he/she said' in a personal narrative.

The necessity of using markers of evidentiality at the beginning of a text is illustrated by "the exception that proves the rule," the text Jaguar-Man, narrated by Nicolás Arcos. Nicolás began this narration abruptly: *Jiñäch 'i tyejchib'ali* 'This is its beginning'. He then related a series of events without using a single genre or evidentiality marker. Events were simply stated as things that happened. He was promptly called down by his listeners, who intervened with questions about context and suggestions that he start over and tell it right. When he did so he was obviously annoyed, and he laid it on unusually thick (lines 45–48):

> *’Añ ’ab’i jun tyikil wiñik wajali;*
> *weñ yujil ’ab’i lemb’al.*
> *Mu ’ab’i ’i majlel tyi tyejklum;*
> *mu ’ab’i ’i cha’leñ lemb’al ya’i.*

> *They say* there was a man, *long ago*;
> he really knew, *they say,* how to drink liquor.
> *They say* he would go to town;
> *they say* he would drink liquor there.

Scene-setting background information ends when the event line begins, and this is marked by the first use of the completive aspect. After the evidentiality statements of The Messengers, the text continues (lines 16–22):

> *’Añ ’ab’i juñ tyikil korreyo’*
> *mu ’ab’i ’i majlel tyi ’ak’juñ.*
> *Pero komo wajali*
> *maxtyo ’ab’i ’añik xchumtyil;*
> *maxtyo ’añik xchumtyil.*
> *’I tza majli;*
> *tzi tyaja jochob’ b’ä ’otyoty.*

> There was, it is said, a messenger
> who was, it is said, going to deliver a letter.
> But since long ago
> there still, it is said, were no settlements;
> there still were no settlements.
> And *he left;*
> *he found* an abandoned house.

The background statements are all expressed in timeless existential verbs (*’añ*) or with non-completive aspect (*mu*). The transition to the event line is signaled by the use of the completive aspect: *tza majli* 'he went', *tzi tyaja* 'he found'. These report events that took place in a punctual fashion. This is no longer background; this is now the event line.

Background information may include phrases in the completive aspect, but these must be buried in subordinate clauses. In The Turtle and the Deer, the opening statement is:

Añ ’ab’i ’ajk tza k’otyiyob’ tyi juñ p’e preba yik’oty me’

There was, it is said, a turtle who came to a race with a deer.
(Literally, There was . . . a turtle, they came to a race, [he] with a deer.)

The subordinated clause *tza k’otyiyob’* '[they] came' is in completive aspect, but this is not the main clause of the sentence, which is expressed with the timeless existential verb *’añ*. It would not be correct to say that the turtle regularly engaged in a race with the deer (*mu ’i k’otyelob’* 'they [used to] come'), since this is presumably a onetime event, so the completive is proper here, but it could not have been used in the main verb of a background statement.

Scene-setting background statements may be extensive. In the text Our Holy Mother, the scene setting goes on for more than fifty lines before there is an event expressed with the completive aspect: *Tzi choko tyilel jiñ lekoj b’u muty* 'He (God) sent down that fabulous bird' (to tell the trees to stand up). But then the scene setting continues, describing the altered situation, and it is much later that the true event line begins.

In The Blackman, the narrator Bernardo Pérez first introduces the protagonist and the setting ("There was, it is said, a man. He had, it is said, a maize granary"). But he then goes on for two paragraphs to describe the custom of keeping a granary in the fields to guard the corn from wild animals and to introduce the Blackman and his characteristics. Only then does the event line begin (in Tila Chol the completive preclitic has become *ta*, corresponding to Tumbalá *tza*):

Jiñi lak pi'äl, ta b'i majli tyi käñtyañ i yixim,

That man came, it is said, to take care of his corn.

We have examined narrative texts from more than a dozen Mayan languages, a sample representing all branches of the language family (Josserand and Hopkins 2000). In all the narratives we looked at, the same pattern emerged: non-completive predicates are used in presenting scene-setting background information, and the completive aspect is not employed until the event line begins. Since we can also identify this pattern as a characteristic of Classic Maya hieroglyphic narratives (Josserand 1991a, 1991b), it is safe to state that this is part of the Maya canon, if indeed it is not a universal characteristic of narrative texts (for an opposing view, see Houston 1997).

THE EVENT LINE

My treatment of narrative texts is based on the model proposed by Robert Longacre (1985, 1986; Jones 1979); this model has proved useful not only for Chol but for Classic Maya hieroglyphic inscriptions as well (Josserand 1991a). It is also applicable to many other narrative traditions (e.g., Diarassouba 2007, where this model is applied to folktales in Nafara, a Gur language of Ivory Coast, a study done under my supervision). The basics of this model are as follows:

A narrative text has an "event line," or storyline, that relates the series of occurrences that constitute the story. In the narration, other events are presented as background; these events are "off the event line," not part of the storyline but essential to its narration. There are at least two kinds of backgrounding: scene-setting information given early in the narrative, introducing time, place, and participants; and, later in the text, back reference to events already narrated or understood to have occurred.

A series of connected events that normally share topic, syntax, and chronology form an "episode" within the narration; this is the rough equivalent of a paragraph in English composition: a series of related statements that share a common theme. Texts may consist of a single episode or multiple episodes, and these may be further organized into "sections"; these are the rough equivalent of chapters, large divisions of long texts, each containing a number of paragraphs. Within each episode there is a "peak event," which may be the only event. Within the set of episodes there may be a peak episode as well. Peaks are marked by special devices, such as coupleting, focus markers, and marked syntax (in Mesoamerican texts, Longacre [1979:ix] referred to this as "the zone of turbulence surrounding the peak").

A narrative text is normally framed by an "opening" and a "closing," and the transition between episodes may be marked by the use of special devices (lexical items, phrases, and temporal statements).

A Note on Chol Verbs

Mayan verbs in general mark "aspect" rather than "tense." The latter places an event in linear time, before, during, or after some reference point, usually the speech act itself. The former refers more to the state of the action than to its time of occurrence: is/was/will be the action only anticipated, just beginning, in progress, or completed? Spanish speakers will recognize the distinction in past-tense verbs in the "imperfective" (actions not yet completed) versus those in the "preterite" (actions completed): *iba* 'he was going' versus *fue* 'he went'. Still, in Spanish, past tense is implied in both imperfective and preterite aspects. In Chol, it is not necessarily implied. Verbs in the "completive aspect" usually refer to past actions, since the actions have been completed. But verbs in the "incompletive aspect" may describe actions taking place in the past, the present, or the future. Placement in time is clear only from the context.

In Chol, verbs that are to be expressed in distinct aspects take distinct "status markers," suffixes that are necessary to complete the verb stem (described below). In addition to the status markers, they take further suffixes that correspond to the different aspects. Additional marking for aspect takes the form of preclitics; "clitics" are verbal elements that are loosely tied to the verb, more like independent words, as opposed to prefixes, which are tightly attached to the following verb. Preclitics (*tza'* 'completive', *mu* 'incompletive', among others) precede the verb and mark the upcoming construction as either "completive" or "incompletive" aspect.

Applying this model to Chol narratives, we may note that events on the event line are stated in the completive aspect, with the appropriate status markers for each of the three main classes of verbs: transitive, intransitive, and positional. All verb classes share the same aspect preclitics.

The Marking of Event-Line Verbs

In the completive aspect, transitive verbs are suffixed with a vowel of the same quality as the root vowel and an epenthetic "(y)" that is present only if a vowel-initial suffix follows: *-V(y)*. Intransitive verbs take the suffix *-i(y)*, positional verbs take *-le(y)*. For example, *tzi yälä* 'he said (it)' is composed of the completive preclitic *tza'*, combined with third-person subject *'i(y)-* and transitive verb *'al~'äl*, followed by the transitive completive status marker *-ä(y)* and the unseen third-person object suffix *-ø*, that is, *tza' ('i)y-äl-ä-ø*. *Tza k'otyi* 'he arrived' is composed of the completive preclitic *tza'*, the intransitive verb *k'oty*, the completive intransitive status marker *-i(y)*, and the unseen third-person subject suffix *-ø*, that is, *tza' k'oty-i-ø*. *Tza b'uchle* 'he sat down' is composed of the completive preclitic *tza'*, the positional verb *b'uch*, the completive positional status marker *-le(y)*, and the unseen third-person subject suffix *-ø*, that is, *tza' b'uch-le-ø*. Epenthetic "(y)" appears only when the stem is further suffixed with a vowel-initial suffix, for example, *tza' k'oty-iy-oñ* 'I arrived', *tza' b'uch-ley-oñ* 'I sat down', with first-person subject suffix *-oñ*.

The Marking of Background Events

Background events are stated in non-completive aspects, for example, incompletive aspect, with the appropriate status markers. Transitive verbs take the inaudible *-ø* or less frequently the near-obsolete suffix *-e'*. Intransitive verbs take *-el*, and positional verbs take *-tyäl*. For example, *mi yäl* 'he says (it)' is composed of the incompletive preclitic *mu* combined with the third-person subject prefix *'i(y)-*, the transitive verb *'äl*, the transitive incompletive status marker *-ø*, and the unseen third-person object *-ø*, that is, *m(u)-'i y-äl-ø-ø*. *Mi k'otyel* 'he arrives' is composed of the incompletive preclitic *mu* combined with the third-person subject prefix *'i(y)-*, the intransitive verb *k'oty*, and the intransitive incompletive status marker *-el*, that is, *m(u)-'i-k'oty-el*. *Mi b'uchtyäl* 'he sits down' is composed of the incompletive preclitic *mu* combined with the third-person subject prefix *'i(y)-*, the positional verb *buch*, and the positional incompletive status marker *-tyäl*, that is, *m(u)-'i-b'uch-tyäl*.

As an alternative to using the incompletive aspect, background information may be presented with other non-completive predicates. They may employ the existential verb *'añ* 'to be', which has no marking for aspect: *añ ab'i juñ tyikil wiñik* 'there was, it is said, a man', with the existential verb suffixed with the unseen third-person subject *'añ-ø*. Other possible non-completive constructions, unmarked for aspect, are the non-verbal predicates (predicate nominatives or predicate adjectives), and participles commonly serve as predicate nominatives. The participles are formed using *-b'il* or *-Vl* for transitive verbs, the former indicating a result, the latter a state; *-em* for intransitive verbs and *-Vl* for positional verbs. For example, *'alb'il '*(that which is) said' is composed of the transitive verb *'al* and the participle suffix *-b'il*. *Kalal* '(that which is) open' is composed of the transitive verb *kal* and the participle suffix *-Vl*. *K'otyem* '(one who has) arrived' is composed of the intransitive verb *k'oty* and the participle suffix *-em*. *B'uchul* '(that which is) seated' is composed of the positional verb *b'uch* and the participle suffix *-Vl*. These participles commonly occur as inflected predicates, for example, *b'uchuloñ, b'uch-ul-oñ*, 'I am seated'.

Other examples of non-verbal predicates, unmarked for aspect, are the predicate nominative (i.e., a noun substituting for the verb), for example, *wiñik-oñ* 'I am a man', composed of the noun *wiñik* and the first-person subject suffix *-oñ*, and the predicate adjective *chañ-oñ* 'I am tall', similarly composed.

Back reference within the text sometimes employs the aspectual clitic *-ix* 'already', attached to completive stems, for example, *k'otyemoñix, k'oty-em-oñ-ix*, 'I having arrived already'. In oral texts, stress, intonation, and other prosodics may accomplish the same function.

The Marking of Episode Boundaries

Short, paragraph-like divisions of a narrative text are called "episodes." Within an episode there is a common setting, common protagonists, and a common theme. Narrative events are directly related to each other. There may be a "topic," a personage who is the featured actor, and within an episode this person may be the unstated subject of action verbs. (The "protagonist" is not necessarily a person; see Bassie-Sweet, Hopkins, and Josserand 2012.) In the text about The Messengers and the demons, the first topic is established in the opening line of the event line (line 16): *'añ ab'i juñ tyikil korreyo*, 'there was, it is said, a messenger'. The messenger is then the unstated subject of several sentences that follow. When the subject is not this person, the subject is stated overtly. The recognition of episode topics is critical for the identification of the antecedents of third-person pronouns, as I have shown for hieroglyphic inscriptions (Josserand 1995c).

The beginning of a new series of events, a new episode, is often marked by special expressions, some of which are fossilized and no longer have clear etymologies. The most common such marker in these Chol stories is the phrase *'añ che' jiñi* 'it was like that', which we have often translated 'so it was'. The phrase may be shortened to simply *che jiñ,* and we find some phonologically altered variants such as *che jeñ*, with assimilation of the vowels, and even *cheñ*.

An alternative marker is *('añ) mañik*, literally '(it is) not'. Paradoxically, this phrase seems to have the same function as *'añ che jiñi*, although the literal meanings of the two phrases are the opposite of each other. There may be subtle shades of difference we have not yet understood. Curiously, we have heard the equivalent phrase in local Spanish narrations, as in "*Ah, no, pero al otro día . . .*" ("Ah, no, but the next day . . ."). Some storytellers will use the loan word *'entonse* (from Spanish *entonces*, 'then') rather than the native *'añ che' jiñi*.

One device for breaking the text to begin a new episode is a back-step in time. This is the equivalent of "Meanwhile, back at the ranch" in that it marks the beginning of a new scene and new protagonists. We first recognized this device while editing the story Our Grandfather. The Lightning god sends a man off to bring him his hat and shirt, and the man returns. Lak Mam, "our grandfather," prepares to throw a bolt of lightning. But then the narrator says *Pero ñaxañ che' tza majli, tza ki sub'eñ . . .* 'But before he [the man] went, he [Lightning] told him . . . [not to shake his clothing]'. We discussed with the narrator (Ausencio Cruz Guzmán) the fact that this act was out of sequence and proposed moving this incident back to its proper place in chronological order. None of the three of us was satisfied with the change, and we kept it in its original place. It was only later that we realized this was a deliberate device that served to mark an episode boundary and reinforced the upcoming peak event. (In Classic hieroglyphic inscriptions, where series of historical events are being related and considerable attention is paid to putting precise dates on events, such back-steps are overtly marked and easily recognized [Josserand 1991b:14, Hopkins and Josserand 2012:31–39].)

THE PEAK EVENT

Toward the end of a narrative text there is a peak event, the climax of the story and its most dramatic moment. There may be lesser peaks within earlier episodes as well. In oral performance, peaks may be marked by special voice qualities and body movements or gestures, but there are also verbal devices that do not depend on the presence of the speaker but which can be seen in a written text. Unusual things go on; sentence syntax may be odd, information may be suppressed, and the like. Robert Longacre (1979:ix, 1985) has characterized Mesoamerican narratives as having a "zone of turbulence surrounding the peak." That turbulence can take many forms. (Before this principle was recognized, epigraphers described the turbulence around peaks as "scrambled syntax" and were unable to account for it.)

Perhaps the most common verbal device to be found at peak events is the couplet, a pair of lines that are sometimes identical and sometimes only structurally or semantically parallel. The couplet is the hallmark of formal speech in Mayan languages and is one of the distinctive features that distinguishes one genre of speech from another (see Gossen 1974). The most formal of speech genres, prayers, typically consist of nothing but couplets, as in this excerpt from a Tzotzil prayer (Vogt 1969:649–50):

Ta hhok'an hutuk 'un,	I shall visit your shrines,
Ta htsoyan hutuk 'un,	I shall entrust my soul to you,
Ta sba yol 'avok,	To your feet,
Ta sba yol 'ak'ob,	To your hands,
Tavalabike,	For your sons,
Tanich'nabike,	For your children,
Tanichike,	For your flowers,
Tak'elomike,	For your sprouts,
Ha' ta hk'an 'o ch'ul pertonal,	For these I beseech divine pardon,
Ha' ta hk'an 'o ch'ul lesensia.	For these I beg divine forgiveness.

The less formal Maya genres, for example, sacred and secular narratives, tend to have couplets only at peak events (Hopkins and Josserand 1990). Even conversation, the least formal genre, has a form of coupleting, as Jill Brody (1986) has pointed out. Speakers couplet each other by repeating part of the last phrase spoken by the other speaker (e.g., see the conversation in A Visit to Don Juan). Couplets may be extended to triplets, and other alterations are possible. A typical example is from the denouement of The Messengers, the final episode (lines 405–11):

'Añ che jiñ.	So it was.
Tzax b'äk'ñi wälej.	He was frightened now.
Tzax kaj tyi tzäñal.	He began to have chills.
Tzax kaj tyi k'ajk.	He began to have fever.
Max tzi ñusa jum p'ejl semanaj,	Not even a week went by,
tza chämi.	and he died.
Chämi.	He died.

A pattern we have observed in many texts (including hieroglyphic texts; see Josserand 1995b) is what we have called "nested couplets," a structure that places one couplet inside another to form a chiasmic structure, for example, two couplets AA BB rearranged as ABBA. An example of this device is found at the peak event of the story Our Grandfather, where Lak Mam throws a lightning bolt to free himself from the grip of the animal that has him by the foot (lines 155–67):

Tza tyojmi jiñ chajki.	Lightning exploded
b'a tzi' ñijka 'i b'ä.	when he shook himself.
Tza jach 'i ñijka 'i b'ä,	He just shook himself,
tza tyojmi jiñ chajki.	(and) Lightning exploded.

Another indication that an event is important is the reappearance of evidentiality markers such as *'ab'i* or *mi yälob'*. In the story about The Messengers and the demons, *'ab'i* marks the first storyline event that introduces the messenger(s): *'Añ*

'ab'i juñ tyikil korreyo, 'There was, it is said, a messenger'. The next appearance of
'ab'i in the text is when the messengers come to the abandoned house, then again, as
they begin to hear noises around midnight and the demons arrive. The peak events,
the flight from the demons and the fight at the corn granary, are related without
the reportative *'ab'i* but with other repetitive devices appropriate to a peak. The last
occurrence of *ab'i* in the text is in the discussion of the fate of the man who ate the
flesh of the dead woman, the moral of the story (lines 386–98, just before the passage of The Messengers cited above):

'A pero koñ 'añ tyo juñ tyikil jiñ wiñik	Ah, but there was still one of those men
tza b'u 'i mero mitz'añ 'ub'i we'eli;	who had really tasted that food;
mach 'ab'i 'utz, tza yub'i.	that wasn't good, it seemed, they say.
Jiñäch 'a mi ki k'extyañ,	He himself would have to replace it,
'o jiñ mi ki majlel tyi wentajil	or go in place of it,
'añ tza b'u 'i k'uxu 'i waji.	the one who ate that food.
'I k'exol 'ab'i,	Its replacement, they say,
'añ waj tzi k'uxu.	for the food he ate.
Machiki,	If not him,
jiñ 'ab'i 'i kuktyal,	his own flesh, they say,
'o 'i pi'äl,	or his wife,
'o 'i ña',	or his mother,
mi cha' k'extyiyel 'i cha'añ.	would be exchanged for it.

Thus it appears that when the most important events are being related, the narrator
tends to remind the listener that this is traditional lore; he isn't just making this stuff
up, and he invokes the authority of the oral tradition.

THE DENOUEMENT AND THE REPETITION OF THE MAJOR EVENTS

In the oral tradition, it is common for the narrator to introduce some incident that
allows him to retell the story, or at least to review its high points, after the peak
event and before the closing of the text. This often involves a discussion of the moral
of the story, the lesson to be learned. At this point one or more listeners may join in
and review the storyline.

In the story about The Messengers and the demons, after the big fight at the maize
granary (the peak event), the owner of the corn shows up and asks "What did y'all
do to make it like this?" (lines 298–303). The messengers then proceed to tell him
the whole story, from start to finish (lines 325–54). Then they deliver the letter, and
the recipient gives them advice: when you travel, leave early enough to avoid being
caught by nightfall on the road (the first moral, lines 373–82). They return home,

and the final episode, the death of one of the messengers (lines 405–11, cited above), illustrates the second moral of this story: don't take anything that doesn't belong to you; you will have to pay it back (lines 386–98 anticipate the death, stating the second moral).

The same thing happens in the story The Comadre. After relating the pursuit of a woman and her child by a jaguar masquerading as her comadre and her defeat of the jaguar, the narrator, Rafael López Vásquez, ends the event line with the return of the woman to her house (line 236). But then she goes to her real comadre and reviews the series of events (242–80), ending: *Che chi, komare, 'añ chäch wäläyi* 'So it is, comadre, that's the way it is here'. Her comadre adds a word of advice (the moral): *Yamb'ä 'ora, komare, mach 'a jak' majlel. Ame 'i k'uxety.* 'Next time, comadre, don't get called out. So he doesn't eat you.'

In the story about the Jaguar-Man, told after a rocky start by Nicolás Arcos, when the mother has successfully beaten off the attack by the jaguar (the peak event), the listeners Mateo and Chencho intervene with questions. Nicolás replies and then tries to end the story (line 199): *Che tzi' mele 'añ b'ajche jiñ* 'Thus she did it like that'. Chencho asks a question that leads to Mateo adding a denouement to the tale (lines 203–41), which includes the woman retelling the incidents. Mateo then tries to end the story: *Che tza 'ujtyi b'ajche jiñi* 'That's the way that ended' (243). Another question by Chencho leads Mateo to go back and review the entire story again, with back-channeling from Nicolás and Chencho (lines 245–89). All having agreed on the details, Mateo finally brings things to a close: *Che tza 'ujtyi b'ajche jiñi.* The last retelling brings up the brief moral: if the little girl hadn't been alert, we would never have known what happened.

THE CLOSING

Just as a narrative text has an opening, it has a closing, where the narrator announces the end of the story. A common ending is just to say (as above, in Jaguar-Man) *Che tza 'ujtyi b'ajche jiñi,* 'thus it ended like that'. Alternatively, the closing can be stated like a final episode, as in the story Our Grandfather:

'Añ che jiñi,	So it was,
che jach tza 'ujtyi b'ajche jiñi.	just like that it ended so.

The story of The Turtle and the Deer who race each other ends with a couplet:

Che tza yälä b'ajche jiñi.	That's what he [the turtle] said.
Che tza 'ujtyi b'ajche jiñi.	That's the way it ended.

The story of The Messengers and the demons ends with a similar expression:

Che jax b'ajche jiñi	Thus just like that
tza 'ujtyi jsub'eñety laj.	ended what I am telling you all.

One of the stories about the Moon and her sons (Older Brother Sun and Younger Brother Sun) ends with

Che' mi yälob' wajali.	Thus they tell of long ago.
Ya' tza' 'ujtyi.	There it ended.

The narrator may be overruled by his audience if they feel his ending is too abrupt. In the story of the Jaguar-Man, discussed above, Nicolás, the principal narrator, closes the story abruptly after the peak event, when the woman has killed the jaguar: *Che tzi' mele 'añ b'ajche jiñ*, 'thus she did it like that'. But Chencho and Mateo pick up the story and go over it again, and Mateo ends the retelling with *Che' tza 'ujtyi b'ajche jiñi*. But Chencho is still not satisfied and asks a question that requires another episode, the denouement, in which the villagers come out to see what is going on, and the whole story gets repeated again. Finally, after that review and some discussion of principal events, the story now having been told properly, Mateo is able to end the story with one last *Che tza 'ujtyi b'ajche jiñi*.

BACK-CHANNELING AND AUDIENCE INTERACTION

In an oral performance, the telling of a story to an audience, listeners do not just listen, they participate by back-channeling and even offering additions and corrections. Back-channeling consists of supportive utterances that have the effect of informing the storyteller that the listener is engaged in the story: a simple "uh-huh" or "hmm" or a repeat of some of the last words spoken, a normal part of Chol and other Mayan conversations (Brody 1986). Because we were preparing texts for native speakers, we edited out these interventions in some of the present stories, as they are edited out in virtually all of the published literature. This is proper when the goal is to establish prescriptive norms in the process of promoting a literary tradition, but it distorts the reality of the storytelling tradition and should be avoided when the goal is documentation, not promotion. Editors tend to look on back-channeling as unnecessary audience interruption, when in fact it is an essential part of the native tradition of storytelling. Even when we remain silent during a recording session, we back-channel visually with head nods and eye contact, since storytellers expect feedback from their audiences. The nature of these interventions can be seen in the texts of The Turtle and the Deer, The Jaguar-Man, A Visit to Don Juan, and The Comadre, where the transcriptions faithfully record audience participation. For other texts, the audio recordings archived by AILLA are unedited tapes.

3

Introduction to the Texts

NICHOLAS A. HOPKINS AND J. KATHRYN JOSSERAND

This collection includes texts from the Chol (Mayan) language that have mythological, folkloric, and traditional content and, in one case, personal experience. The protagonists of many stories are supernaturals. There is the Lightning god, the Moon and the Sun, the Lord of the Underworld, and other demons. More toward the range of reality, there is a celestial rooster, a turtle that races against a deer, and jaguars that convert themselves into men. The first set overlaps with figures known from ancient Maya literature, including precolumbian hieroglyphic inscriptions. Chajk, the god who throws lightning bolts and brings the rain, is a principal deity in Maya folk religion and is prominent in Maya art and iconography. Many pages of the Maya Codices, a small set of hieroglyphic books that survived the Inquisition's suppression of native religion, are devoted to Chajk. The children of the Moon goddess, "twin" brothers (but one older than the other), often called the Hero Twins, are not only seen in Classic period Maya art but also in the postconquest Popol Vuj, a sixteenth-century manuscript that relates the traditions of the Quiché (K'iche') Maya. The lords of the underworld that are defeated by the Hero Twins in a famous ballgame are the same figures that chase the messengers in one of our stories. One of the demons is called Gourd Head because he is skeletal, like many underworld figures recorded on Classic Maya ceramics. It is difficult to escape the conclusion that there is a long and continuous tradition of stories about these protagonists that stretches back to at least the first century and that is miraculously alive and well 2,000 years later.

DOI: 10.5876/9781607324881.c003

"""

The story about the slow turtle that beats the swift deer in a footrace can be recognized as one of the Greek fables collected by Aesop, albeit adapted to a new environment, with a deer instead of a hare as the swift but inconsistent contestant. (We have heard a variant of this story that features toads in place of the turtle; the toads line up and leap one by one, simulating a single toad and winning the race.) In another story, the principal actor, a rooster, represents an animal imported into the new world in historic times, but his actions reflect those of a fabulous native bird that is the messenger of the gods. Finally, the theme of transformation between human and animal shape is common in Mesoamerican folklore, although our transformers are not witches but wild animals, and they transform from animal to human, not the other way around. The Jaguar-Man is but one of the many characters in the Chol oral tradition that represent the dangerous side of nature. Others are the Blackman (see below), Bouncing Head, Sombrerón (Big Hat), Feet-on-Backward, the Savage, Spiny Man, and Flesh Dropper. The latter are described in the tales reported in another of our publications, an inventory of published Chol folktales and narrations (Josserand et al. 2003:appendix I). Here, we add our own contributions to this literature.

The style of narration varies with the content. The most traditional tales, concerning gods and demons, are presented in a more poetic form than stories that are more secular. In these sacred stories there is greater use of rhetorical devices, alterations of normal syntax, and patterned repetition. The texts are presented here in a format that represents the rhythm of speech and the structure of the language, so that, for instance, couplets are displayed on successive lines rather than in run-on text. Lines are numbered for convenience of reference. The English translation that accompanies each text is also formatted to correspond line for line with the original, wherever possible.

Several of these stories were edited for publication as *T'an ti Wajali* by the three of us (Josserand, Hopkins, and Cruz Guzmán), and some elements, like mistakes and back-channeling, were deleted (Our Holy Mother, The Celestial Bird, Our Grandfather, The Cave of Don Juan, The Messengers); Older Brother Sun and Younger Brother Sun received the same kind of editorial tampering. The Blackman was self-edited by the narrator, a schoolteacher. Other texts (The Turtle and the Deer, A Visit to Don Juan, Jaguar-Man, The Comadre) were recorded in conversational settings and are minimally edited. Repetitions and apparent errors have not been "corrected"; that is, we have made no attempt to out-guess the narrators and present what we suppose they might have wanted to say instead of what they actually did say. Back-channeling is preserved. Presented in this fashion, the poetic quality of many of the texts becomes obvious. A tale told by an experienced storyteller is the fine-tuned product of many years of telling and retelling, as the narrator seeks to find the language that best expresses the spirit of the story and keeps his audience's attention. Some of the texts are virtual lessons in storytelling, as listeners join in to suggest different strategies of presentation and performance or to clear up points that have not been well expressed (e.g., Jaguar-Man).

All these texts were transcribed from tape recordings of unrehearsed oral performances, some done in the privacy of home offices, others in more traditional contexts, among a group of friends relaxing at the end of a workday. The tape recordings were then transcribed by a native speaker of Chol (usually Cruz Guzmán), and a rough Spanish translation was appended. In the process of keyboarding the texts (usually by Hopkins or Josserand) the transcriptions were checked for orthographic consistency, and discussion between the authors and others cleared up the meanings of expressions and previously unknown words. At some point a more refined Spanish translation was prepared and checked, the first priority being to make the texts available to speakers of the language and scholars who could be expected to read and understand Spanish. The English translations presented here were done last (mostly by Hopkins in 2007), consulting both the original Chol text and the Spanish translations.

A Note on Orthography

There is no single standard orthography for Chol. Each presenter of Chol material has tended to use his or her own particular choice of alternatives, and the criteria for making such choices have evolved over the ages. Earlier transcriptions of Chol tended to follow Spanish orthographic norms, such as the use of the letters <c> and <qu> to represent the phoneme /k/ (before the vowels /a, o, u/ and /i, e/, respectively). Modern transcriptions are more likely to be modeled after the norms established for Guatemalan Mayan languages by the Academia de las Lenguas Mayas de Guatemala and use <k> for /k/.

A particularly difficult problem has been the representation of the "sixth vowel," a mid- to high-central vowel that is in the range of the vowels in the English words "but" and "would" (with variants conditioned by the surrounding sounds). Having no traditional standard representation (as opposed to the other five vowels, <a e i o u>), the sixth vowel has been represented by symbols as diverse as an upside-down wedge or inverted v <Λ>, a "barred i" (an <i> with a line through it, <i>), a plus sign <+>, an <o> or a <u> with umlaut, <ö ü>, and probably others. In this presentation we have followed the Guatemalan norms and used an <a> with umlaut, <ä>. Besides being easy to type or key, this choice has the advantage of stressing the historical relationship between the vowels /a/ and /ä/, which often vary within the same root. Careful readers will note that in the presence of bilabials, /ä/ often assimilates to /u/, for example, the relativizer *b'ä* becomes *b'u*.

Glottalized consonants are represented with the standard postposed apostrophe, for example, <k'>, and we have chosen to write the alveolar affricate (the consonants of English "tze-tze fly") as <tz>, a more traditional representation than the sometimes employed <ts>. Modern Chol has the peculiarity of palatalizing its alveolars, so that what appears in other languages as /t/ is transcribed here as /ty/ (and likewise for the glottalized consonant /ty'/). The alveolar nasal is represented consistently as <ñ>, even though it does have some non-palatalized allophones. In Spanish loan words, where speakers may vary in the palatalization of /t/ and /n/, we have tried to follow the speaker's preferences. As is traditional in Mesoamerican linguistics, the alveopalatal fricative [ʃ] (English "sh") is transcribed <x>. We use <j> rather than <h> for the so-called glottal fricative, but this represents non-syllabic voiceless vocoids (like English "h") rather than the velar fricative represented by <j> in Spanish orthography. In general the transcriptions are descriptive rather than prescriptive; they record the language as spoken rather than as it "should" be. Consequently, there are many instances of "missing" final glottal stops (and occasionally laterals and semi-vowels), the consonants most likely to be dropped in casual speech.

ACKNOWLEDGMENTS

Many of these texts were collected while the authors were employed by the Centro de Investigaciones Superiores del Instituto Nacional de Antropología e Historia (CIS-INAH) in Mexico City or by its successor, the Centro de Investigaciones y Estudios Superiores en Antropología Social (CIESAS). Some material was gathered during a field school led by Hopkins under the auspices of the Universidad Autónoma Metropolitana, Iztapalapa. Further fieldwork was carried out under grants from the National Science Foundation (BNS-8308506, BNS-8520749) and the National Endowment for the Humanities (RT-20643-86, RT-21090-89), as well as the Foundation for the Advancement of Mesoamerican Studies, Inc., Crystal River, Florida (Projects 1994.018 and 01085), and the Council on Research and Creativity, Florida State University. We gratefully acknowledge the support of these institutions, but the opinions and conclusions expressed are those of the authors and do not necessarily reflect the views of the sponsors.

Many of the original recordings of these narrations are now posted on AILLA, the Archive of the Indigenous Languages of Latin America (www.ailla.utexas.org). The archive is a work in progress and undergoes periodic changes as language codes are renegotiated, materials are reassessed, and similar factors. The record names below were assigned by graduate assistants whose translations of our tape labels were not always accurate (Our Grandfather was initially named The Story of the Ray, from Spanish *Rayo*), and in any case we have changed the names of the stories ourselves. In addition to the tales included here, many more Chol narratives are available in the archive, from us and from others. There is other material as well, including many field interviews. Among our contributions are several discussions of the stories themselves and discussions of local history and customs, as well as interviews with the pioneers who established the Chol ejidos in Campeche (Interviews: Migration). There is an interesting discussion by Bernardo Pérez Martínez about how he teaches mathematics in Chol to his students in Tila. Pertinent to this collection, there are two interviews with Ausencio Cruz Guzmán—actually long monologues—in which he discusses his life and his work with us: CTU010R013 and CTU010R014. At present, the structure of file names is CTU (the ISO code for Chol), followed by a three-digit number representing the deposit (e.g., CTU001); there follow record numbers (R and three digits) and Item numbers (I and three digits); some items are more complex and include numbered parts, for example, #3. These recordings are available for downloading without cost to the public, requiring only registration and agreement to abide by the terms of use. We hope you enjoy these stories as much as we have.

Title in This Collection	Title on AILLA	AILLA Reference Number (.mp3)
Our Holy Mother	The Tale of the Moon (partial Chol text; Spanish retelling later added to Chol)	CTU002R002I001
Older Brother Sun and Younger Brother Sun	The Major Sun and the Minor Sun	CTU006R012I001, #3
The Celestial Bird	Story of the Rooster (Spanish and Chol)	CTU006R006I001, #2
The Turtle and the Deer	[Not archived]	
Our Grandfather	The Tale of the Lightning (Spanish retelling)	CTU002R003I001 CTU002R017I001
The Cave of Don Juan	Story of the Cave of Don Juan (Chol and Spanish)	CTU006R006I001, #3
A Visit to Don Juan	Visit to Don Juan	CTU002R005I001
The Messengers	Story of the Witches (Chol and Spanish)	CTU006R006I001, #1
Jaguar-Man	[Not archived]	
The Blackman	The Xnek's Tale	CTU002R019I001
The Comadre	Interview 2002-2	CTU010R002I003

Part 1
Myths and Fables

4

Our Holy Mother

Ausencio Cruz Guzmán

The story of Our Holy Mother the Moon and her two sons is an ancient tale, with versions recorded from many parts of the Maya world (another telling of this story in Chol is found in Whittaker and Warkentin 1965:13–49). The Chol version is quite different from the related story of twin brothers told in the Popol Vuj, where two successive generations of "twins" are involved and the mother is not explicitly said to be the Moon. The identification of the moon with the Holy Mother carries over into Chol Christianity, where the Virgin Mary is also known as Lak Ch'ujul Ña', Our Holy Mother. From a Mesoamerican perspective, it is no accident that the Virgin of Guadalupe, the most significant appearance of Mary in the new world, is borne aloft by an angel standing on a crescent moon.

The story presented here was recorded in Mexico City in 1979 by Josserand and Hopkins; the narrator is Ausencio Cruz Guzmán. He first heard this tale from his father, in Spanish, and then from a sister-in-law, in Tzeltal. Later he heard versions told in Chol. Each of these versions of the story contained elements lacking in others, but all are agreed on the essential details. The Moon had two male children, and the younger child became the Sun. But not only did he become the Sun, he also brought knowledge to the world, that is, he is a culture bearer. He taught his mother to plant crops and care for domestic animals, and he introduced the milpa system of slash-and-burn horticulture. Still today it is the women who plant the chayote squash and the men who follow his example as agriculturalists. He who is to become the Sun also made the first gophers and is indirectly responsible for the

DOI: 10.5876/9781607324881.c004

other animals, the result of the death of the older brother. The fact that gophers were made of beeswax, with teeth and claws made of hard tropical wood, explains why they are the only animal whose bones are so soft the entire body can be eaten (except for the very hard teeth and claws). The story also explains why some animals don't have tails and why others have long ears.

OUR HOLY MOTHER

Ty'añ Lak Ch'ujul Ña'
Ausencio Cruz Guzmán (1978c)

Wajali 'ab'i,	1	A long time ago, they say,
mi yälob' laj tyatyña'älob';		our ancestors used to say
mi yälob', mi kub'iñ,		they speak, I listen—
jtyaty, jña', tzi sub'eñoñ,		my father, my mother, told me,
wajali.	5	long ago.
Jiñ Laj Ch'ujul Ña',		Our Holy Mother,
mi sub'eñoñ,		they tell us,
wäle, 'uj b'u,		now, she is the moon,
mi sub'eñob'.		they tell us.
Jiñi wajali	10	In that age long ago
max tyo 'ab'i 'añik majch' añ 'ila tyi pañämil;		there still wasn't anything here on earth;
max tyo 'ab'i 'añik 'i b'äl pañämil;		there still weren't any things of the earth;
max tyo 'añik muty;		there still weren't any birds;
max tyo 'añik chu'añ;		there still wasn't anything;
b'ä tye'eltyak max tyo 'añik.	15	wild animals there still were none.
Jiñ jach 'ab'i Laj Ch'ujul Ña'		Just Our Holy Mother, they say,
wol 'ab'i 'añ tyi lum.		was here on earth, they say.
'Añ 'ab'i		It happened, they say,
tza 'ajñi cha' tyikil 'i yalob'il.		there came to be two children of hers.
Juñ tyikil,	20	One of them
weñ joñtyoljax;		was really bad;
yamb'ä,		the other one
mero weñ 'i pusik'al.		had a really good heart.
'Añ che jiñi,		So it was,
mu 'ab'i 'i meltyak 'i chol	25	he would make his milpas, they say,
ñaxañ b'ä yalob'il;		the one who was the first child;
mi meltyak 'ab'i 'i chob'altyak.		he made many clearings, they say.
Pero max tyo 'ab'i chek wokol		But it still wasn't such a problem, they say,
mi lak mel lak chob'al,		as when we make our clearings,
b'ajche 'ilili wäleyi.	30	like here and now.
Max tyo mi laj k'äñ machity;		The machete was still unknown;

max tyo 'añik
chu' mi laj k'äñ tyi sek',
chu'tyak.
Jiñ jach mi käch 'i yab'
ya' tyi tye'eli;
mi kaj tyi jäjmel.
Che' woli 'i jäjmesañ 'i b'äj,
woli 'ab'i yajleltyak majlel jiñ tye'.
'A ko mañik,
'añ 'ab'i 'ixi lekoj b'u 'ajtzo',
mi sub'eñob';
'ixi pavo real.
Jiñ 'ab'i mi yajñeltyak tyi 'uk'el,
tyi 'uk'el tyi 'ak'älel.
'A koñ kab'älix
chu' woli 'i mel jiñ wiñik,
mi k'el jiñ Laj Ch'ujul Tyaty.
'I komo mañik 'i wokol
b'ajche' mi yäsañtyak jiñ tye'el,
'i wolix 'i jisañtyak jiñ tye'el.
Che jiñi,
tzi k'ele
jiñ Lak Ch'ujul Tyaty,
jiñ lak Dios:
Mach 'ab'i weñik
b'ajche woli 'i mel,
mi loñ k'el.
Tzi choko tyilel jiñ lekoj b'u muty.
Mu 'ab'i 'i tyilel
che' tyi yolil 'ak'älel.
Mi kaj tyi 'uk'el;
mi kaj tyi ty'añ;
mi sub'eñtyak tyejchel jiñ tye'el.
Che jiñi,
mi tyejcheltyak.
Mi k'otyel
che' mi säk'añ jiñ wiñik.
Mi cha' k'oty 'i k'el 'i chob'al;
laj cha' tyejchemix jiñi choleltyak;
mi laj cha' tyejchel jiñ tye'el.
Mach chäñ cholob'ilix, yilal.

there wasn't anything
to use to cut down trees
or whatever.
35 So he would just hang his hammock
there in the forest;
he would start to swing.
When he was swinging himself,
they say the trees would come falling down.
40 Ah, but no,
there was, they say, that exotic turkey
they tell about;
that peacock.
He would come down to cry out, they say,
45 to cry out in the night.
Ah, since so much
that that man was doing
Our Holy Father saw.
And since it wasn't difficult for him
50 the way he made the trees fall,
and the forest was being destroyed.
So it was,
he saw
Our Holy Father,
55 our God:
It wasn't good
how he was doing it,
he saw it was wrong.
He sent down the exotic bird.
60 He would come down, they say,
when it was midnight.
He would start to cry out;
he would start to speak;
he would tell all the trees to stand up.
65 So it was,
they would all stand up.
The man would arrive
when it was dawn.
He would come and see his clearing;
70 all of the brush was standing up again;
all of the trees were standing up again.
There was no clearing anymore, it seemed.

Mi loñ cha'mel	He would do it again
b'ajche' mi meltyak;	the way he did it;
mi jäjmesañ 'i b'äj tyi yab',	75 he would swing himself in his hammock,
pero mañix mi chän yajleltyak.	but nothing at all would fall down.
'I che jiñi,	And so it was,
pero jiñi ñaxañ b'ä 'i yalob'il Laj Ch'ujul Ña'	but that first child of Our Holy Mother
mach mi ña'tyañ	didn't know
mi 'añ yamb'ä	80 that there was another,
'i yijtz'iñ.	his younger brother.
Mi yäl ke jiñ jach	They say that that one
'añ tyi pañumil	was on earth.
Porke jiñ Laj Ch'ujul Ña'	Because Our Holy Mother
mak mi yäk'eñ 'i k'el.	85 didn't let him see.
Porke koñ joñtyoljax jiñi yalob'il,	Because since her son was so bad,
repente mi mi tzäñsañ.	he might just kill him.
Jiñ cha'añ, mi muktyak	For that reason, she hid him repeatedly
chañ mach mi k'el,	so that he didn't see him,
porke koñ k'ajk'atyax,	90 because he was so hot blooded,
'i repente 'añ chu' mi tyumb'eñ.	and he just might do something to him.
Mi yälob' ke che' ya 'añ	They say that since there he was,
'añ yäskuñ,	the older brother,
mukb'il, 'ab'i.	he was hidden, they say.
Jiñ jach,	95 That one,
che' mi majlel tyi xämb'al	when he would go out walking
'o tyi 'e'tyel,	or to work,
mu 'ab'i 'i lok'sañ tyi 'alas yik'oty.	she would take him out to play with her.
Che' weñ wäyäl 'añ yäskuñ,	When the older brother was well asleep
mi we'sañ, o mi chu'sañ.	100 she would feed him, or nurse him.
Pero woli 'i b'ejb'e kolel.	But he got bigger and bigger.
Pero 'añtyak mi lok'el tyi 'alas,	But many times he would come out to play
'i mu tyo 'i mejlel	and it was still possible
'i mukb'eñtyak 'i yälas.	for her to hide away all of his toys.
Pero 'añ juñ yajl,	105 But there was one time
max tzi laj lotyo,	she didn't gather them all up,
'i tzi käyä tyi juñ paty	and they were left there at one side
mu b'u 'i yäsiñ 'añ 'alob'.	where the child would play.
Pero jiñi 'i yäskuñ	But that older brother
tzax kaji 'i ña'tyañ	110 began to realize
ke repente 'añäch yamb'ä 'alob,	that all of a sudden there was another child,
'o yamb'ä 'i yijtz'iñ,	or another younger brother,
'i mach mi sub' 'i ña'.	and his mother wasn't telling him.

Pero 'añ ch'ityoñ　　　　　　　　　But the young man
tzax kaji 'ña'tyañ　　　115　　　started to think
b'ajche mi kaj 'i mel.　　　　　　how he would act.
Lix tyo b'ej 'ajñik.　　　　　　　He let some time go by.
Pero juñ yajl tza seb' sujtyi,　　　But one day he suddenly turned around,
'i tza k'otyi tyaj 'añ 'alob'　　　　and he came home to find the boy
ke woli tyi 'alas.　　　120　　　who was playing with his toys.
Pero 'i ña', tyoj b'äk'ñijel;　　　　But his mother was really frightened;
max tzi tyaja chuki mi yäl　　　　she couldn't find words to say
tyi 'i b'äk'eñ.　　　　　　　　　she was so afraid.
'Ix ku yerañ　　　　　　　　　As for the brother
weñ 'utz tzi päsä 'i b'äj.　　　125　　he made himself be good.
Pero chañ k'uñtye' mi ña'tyañ　　　But little by little he thought about
b'ajche mi kaj 'i tzäñsañ 'añ yijtz'iñ.　how he would kill his younger brother.
Koñ tz'a'atyax mi k'el,　　　　　Since he looked on him with hatred,
koñ 'añ 'ab'i 'i ch'ujlel.　　　　　since he had a soul, they say.
Koñ jiñ 'ab'i laj k'iñ, 'ab'i,　　　130　　Since he, they say, was our sun, they say,
mi yajñel.　　　　　　　　　who would come down.
Mi kaj 'i yajñel tyi pañämil,　　　He would come down to earth,
tzi yälä.　　　　　　　　　　they said.
Jiñ cha'añ,　　　　　　　　　For that reason,
mero tz'a mi k'el.　　　135　　　with hatred he looked on him.
Mach yomik 'i k'el　　　　　　He didn't want to see him
'ila tyi pañämil;　　　　　　　here on earth;
'i b'ajñel jach yom 'ajñel.　　　　and he wanted to be the only one.
'A mañik,　　　　　　　　　Ah, no, but
'i ña',　　　140　　　　　　his mother,
k'uxäch mi yub'iñ.　　　　　　she felt love for him.
'Añ che jiñi,　　　　　　　　So it was,
'añ yijtz'iñ ñukix.　　　　　　　the younger brother grew up.
'Añ mi lok'el tyi 'alas　　　　　He would go out to play
tyi mal tye'el yik'oty yulej.　　145　　in the forest with his slingshot.
'I 'añ tzi tyaja juñ tyejk tye'　　　And it happened that he found a tree
b'a 'añ chab'.　　　　　　　　where there was honey.
'I tza k'otyi 'i sub'eñ 'añ yäskuñ:　　And he went and told his older brother:
"Wäle käskuñ,　　　　　　　　"Now, my brother,
koñla sek' chab';　　　150　　　let's go cut out honey;
ya 'añix tyi tye';　　　　　　　it's there in the tree.
Koñla mäk',　　　　　　　　Let's go eat,"
che'eñ.　　　　　　　　　　he said.
"Koñla,"　　　　　　　　　"Let's go,"

che'eñ 'añ yäskuñ ja'el.
Che jiñi,
tza majliyob' tyi mäk' chab'
ya' tyi b'ij.
'Añ juñ p'ejl b'ij
b'a' 'añ juñ tyejk tye';
ya' tza majliyob' tyi mäk' chab'.
Che jiñi,
tza loñ majliyob' tyi mäk' chab'.
Tza loñ letzi 'ub'i 'askuñil b'ä.
Tza letzi tyi tye',
ya' woli 'i lom 'añ chab', 'ab'i.
Tza kaj 'i mäk'.
'Añ yijtz'iñi,
tza ki k'ajtyib'eñ.
'A mañik,
jiñ 'i yäskuñi,
mach mi loñ 'ak'eñ ja'el chab'i.
Jiñ jach 'i tya'chäb'lel,
mi loñ chokb'eñ jub'el.
K'oslaw,
mi jub'el ya' tyi jol.
'A che jiñi,
we'ekña tyi 'uk'el ja'el 'alob'i,
ko mach woli 'i yäk'eñ 'i mäk'.

Jiñ jach 'i tya'chäb'lel
woli 'i yäk'eñ.
'A tza ki mel 'ub'i ch'ityoñ,
tza ki mel 'i yaläl b'aj
tyi tya'chäb'lel.
Tza ki pajliñ b'äk ch'ib';
tzi tzäp'b'eñtyak cha' tzijty tyi cha'añ,
'i cha' tzijty tyi yeb'al tyi yej 'añ b'aji.

Tza' ki yotzañtyak tyi lum.
Che jiñi,
tza kaji loñ paxoñ sek' jiñ tye';

tzi loñ mele jiñ 'alob'.
Mañik,

155	said the older brother, too.
	So it was,
	they went to eat honey
	there on the road.
	There was a road
160	where there was a tree;
	they went there to eat honey.
	So it was,
	they just went to eat honey.
	The older brother just climbed up.
165	He climbed up in the tree,
	there he chopped at the beehive, they say.
	He started to eat.
	The younger brother
	started to ask him for some.
170	Ah, no,
	that older brother
	just wouldn't give him any honey.
	Just the beeswax,
	he just threw it down at him.
175	Bam!
	it came down on his head.
	So it was,
	the child was crying and shouting,
	because he wouldn't give him anything to eat.
180	Only the beeswax
	was he giving him.
	So the boy began to make things,
	he started to make little gophers
	out of the wax.
185	He carved some hard palm wood;
	he inserted into two pieces above,
	and two below, in the mouths of the gophers.
	He started to put them into the ground.
	So it was,
190	he just started to pretend to chop on the tree;
	that's all the boy did.
	No,

tza kaj tyi ty'añ 'i yäskuñ:
"Ma me ku kajik 'a sek'oñ,
porke k'ele me ku 'a bä
mi tza' yajliyoñ;"
che' mi loñ sub'eñ 'i yäskuñ.
'A mañik,
"Kom b'ajche' mi kaj sek'ety,
kom ma tza 'añ b'ajche' ya' k'amel
'iliya Lukum Ch'ejl,"
che' mi sub'eñ.
'I Lukum Ch'ejl,
'i yaläl machity;
mak ñoj 'añix 'i yej.
Jiñ' ab'i woli 'i käñ tyi sek'.
'A mi loñ 'al:
"Pero max mi low ja' tye'."
'A mañik,
koñ jiñ 'añ b'aj,
koñ kab'älix 'añ b'aj,
tzi loñ 'otza tyi yeb'al tye',
tyi wi'tye'tyak.
'A che jiñi,
tza kaji 'i yotzañtyak wäle 'añ b'aji.
Tza kaji tyi we'el ja'el b'aji,
ki sety'b'eñ 'i wi' 'añ tye'i.
'A mañik,
ya'ix 'añ
cha' p'ejl, 'ux p'ejl 'ora;
wäle 'añ
woli tyi 'e'tyel 'añ b'aji.
Tza ki yub'iñ 'i yäskuñi
ke tza ty'iño juñ yajl jiñi tye'
Che jiñi,
tzi yälä:
"Ma ma sek'oñ!"
Jiñ jax tza yub'i
ke wolix 'i jub'el majlel ya' tyi tye'i,
kiñlaw, ñup'law jub'el.
Ya' tyi ñi' tye',
ya b'a' woli tyi mäk' chab',
tza yajli.

his older brother started to say:
"Don't you go cutting me down,
because you'll see what happens   195
if I fall,"
that's all the older brother told him.
Ah, no,
"But how am I going to cut you down,
since it really isn't very big   200
this Angry Snake,"
so he told him.
His Angry Snake
was his little machete,
it wasn't very sharp.   205
This is what he was using to chop with.
So he just said:
"But it doesn't hurt the tree."
Ah, no,
since those gophers,   210
since there were already a lot of them,
he just put them under the tree,
in all the roots.
So it was,
he started to put all the gophers there.   215
The gophers started to chew,
to cut away the roots of the tree.
Ah, no,
there they were
two, three hours,   220
there they were
working away, those gophers.
The older brother started to sense
that the tree cracked all at once.
So it was,   225
he said:
"Don't cut me down!"
He just felt
that he was falling out of the tree,
crashing, smashing, falling.   230
There from the tip of the tree,
there where he was eating honey,
he fell.

'Añ che tza yajli,
tzax meku sujtyi majlel
'añ ch'ityoñ, 'alob'.
Tza k'otyi
b'a 'añ Lak Ña',
b'a 'añ Lak Ch'ujul Ña';
Lak Ña' b'ä
mi lak sub'eñ 'ili 'uji.
Tza k'otyi;
tza' ki k'ajtyib'eñ 'i ña':
"B'aki tza' majli 'a wäskuñ?"
loñ che' tzi sub'e.
'A mañik,
tza ki jak' 'añ ch'ityoñ,
"Majki? Käskuñi?
Sajmäx tza' tyili.
Ñaxañ tyo tza tyili.
Ya' tzi käyäyoñ tyi tye'el
max tzi sub'u 'i b'ä
tza tyili."
'Añ che jiñi,
"Ma'añik,
jatyety tza' tzäñsa.
'Añ chuki tza tyumb'e,"
che' tzi sub'e 'i ña'.
'A mañik,
"Mañik,
si ñaxañ tyo tza tyili.
Wi'patyoñix
tza tyiliyoñ 'añ joñoñ."
'Añ che jiñi,
tza majli 'i sajkañ 'i ña'.
Tza ki sub'eñ 'ub'i Laj Ña', uji,
tzi sub'e:
"Wäle, koñla k'el
b'aki tza' käyä;
b'aki 'añ tza' käyä
jiñ 'a wäskuñi,"
che mi loñ sub'eñ.
'A che jiñ,
tza majli 'i k'elob'.

And when he fell,
235   running back home went
the boy, the child.
He arrived
where Our Mother was,
where Our Holy Mother was,
240   the one who was Our Mother,
that we say is the moon.
He arrived;
his mother began to ask him:
"Where did your older brother go?"
245   she just asked him.
Ah, no,
the boy began to answer,
"Who? My older brother?
He came in earlier.
250   He came in first.
He left me there in the woods,
he didn't say he himself
was coming."
So it was,
255   "No,
you killed him!
You did something to him."
his mother told him.
Ah, no.
260   "No,
because he came in first.
Way behind
came I."
So it was,
265   'his mother went out to look for him.
Our Mother, the moon, started to speak,
she told him:
"Now, let's go see
where he remained;
270   where it is he remained,
that older brother of yours,"
she just said to him.
So it was,
they went out to look.

Tza ki k'el 'ub'i Lak Ña',
Laj Chuchu'i.
Ya' 'añ b'a tzi yäsañtyak
tyi ñi' tye';
ya' 'añ b'a tzi yäsa.
'I che tza yajli
tza laj b'ik'tyiyi.
'I jiñx, b'aki tza lok'i jiñ muty,

b'ä tye'el,
tyi kuktyal 'i yäskuñ.
Pero 'i ña, mak woli 'i ña'tyañ
mi chämeñix 'i yalob'il.
Jiñ tyo tzi sub'e yambä 'i yalob'il
che tza k'otyiyob' tyi 'otyoty.
Pero tyi ñaxañ,
tzi jak'ä 'alob':
"Wäle, mama',
'ixma 'añix 'a wixim,
chañ ma mäk'lañ 'a wälak'.
Kab'älix 'añ 'a wälak';
kab'älix 'a muty;
kab'älix 'a chityam.
K'ele chu' ma chäm.
Pero mach me ku kajik 'a chuk
ya' tyi ñej,
porke mach me weñik
mu mi b'ojkel 'i ñej."
'A mak tzi jak'ä ja' Laj Ch'ujul Ña'
che' tza cha' sujtyi 'i mäk'lañ.
Tza kaji loñ chuktyak 'añ xkulukab'
ya' tyi ñej.
Chityam, me', tye'lal,
yik'oty pejtyel jiñtyak b'ä
mach b'ä 'añik 'i ñej,
puro 'ab'i tzi chuku jiñ Laj Ña'.
Por eso,
jiñtyak b'ä tye'el,
mach b'ä 'añik 'i ñej,
b'oroltyak 'i ñej,
porke koñ jiñ 'añ Laj Ch'ujul Ña',

275 Our Mother started to look,
That Grandmother of ours.
There he was where he was felled
from the tip of the tree;
there he was where he fell.
280 And when he fell
he broke up into little pieces.
And it was from there that the birds came
   out,
the animals,
from the body of his older brother.
285 But his mother, she didn't know
if her child was dead already.
Not until her other child told her
when they arrived at the house.
But first,
290 the boy told her:
"Now, Momma,
shuck your corn,
so you can feed your animals.
You have a lot of animals now;
295 a lot of birds,
a lot of pigs.
Watch what you grab.
But don't start catching them
there by their tails,
300 because it's not good
if you pull out their tails."
Ah, Our Holy Mother didn't pay attention
when she went back again to feed them.
She just grabbed all the tinamous
305 there by the tail.
Pigs, deer, pacas,
and all those that
don't have a tail,
it's because Mother grabbed them, they say.
310 For this reason,
any animal
that doesn't have a tail,
that has a stub for a tail,
it's because Our Holy Mother

tzi laj chuku ya' tyi ñej,
tzi laj b'okb'e 'i ñej.
'Añ che jiñi,
tza ki k'ajtyiñ
che' tza k'otyiyob' tyi 'otyoty:
"Peru 'a wäskuñ?
B'aki tza käle?
chuki tza tyumb'e?"
che'eñ 'añ Lak Ña'.
"Käskuñi?
B'i jiñ tza
woli b'u 'a mäk'lañ."
"Chuki tza tyumb'e?"
che'eñ.
"Bä 'i b'äji;
mak tzi yäk'oñ jmäk' chab'.
Jiñ cha'añ,
tzak meletyak ya 'alä b'ajtyak
tyi tya'chäb'lel
tza bä 'i mäk'b'e 'i chäb'il.
Jiñ b'aj
tzi sety'b'e 'i wi' 'añ tye'.
Jiñ cha'añ
tza yajli,
'i che' tza chämi.
'I tyi kuktyal,
tza lok'ityak jiñ 'a b'ätye'eltyak,
yik'oty 'a muty."
'A che jiñi,
wajali 'añ tyo 'ab'i
mi melob' 'i chol.
'Añ tyo 'ab'i
mi pulob' 'ab'i 'i pulem lum.
Mu 'ab'i sub' 'i ña':
"Wäle, Mama,
ma maj tyi päk',
päk' ñi'uk'
päk' ch'ixch'ujm,
chu' ma' päk'.
Jiñ jach ma sajkañ
b'a weñ pulemtyak;

315 grabbed them all there by the tail,
she pulled out all their tails.
So it was,
she started to ask him
when they arrived at the house:
320 "But your older brother?
Where did he stay?
What did you do to him?"
said Our Mother.
"My older brother?
325 That was him
that you went to feed."
"What did you do to him?"
she said.
"It's his own fault;
330 he didn't give me honey to eat.
For that reason,
I made a bunch of little gophers
out of beeswax
that he ate the honey from.
335 Those gophers
chewed away the roots of the tree.
For that reason,
he fell,
and thus he died.
340 And from his body
came all your animals
and your birds."
So it was,
it was still a long time ago, they say,
345 they made their milpa.
Still, they say
they burned their fields for planting.
They say he told his mother:
"Now, Momma,
350 you are going to plant,
plant smooth chayote,
plant spiny chayote,
whatever you plant.
Just look for
355 where it is well burned;

ya' ma päk'		there you plant
chu' ma' päk,"		whatever you plant,"
che' mi sub'eñ.		so he told her.
"A koy,"		"Okay,"
che jach 'i ña.	360	so said his mother.
Tza loñ majli.		They just went.
Loñ päk'		They just planted
chu mi päk'.		whatever they planted.
'Añ jiñi 'ab'i ñi'uk'i;		They say that that smooth chayote,
jiñ 'ab'i b'a mi koleltyak jiñ ñi'uk'i,	365	where that chayote grows really big,
jiñ ab'i b'a mi yajñeltyak tyi pich		that's all the places she urinated, they say,
jiñ Lak Ña'i.		that Mother of Ours.
Ya' ab'i tza koli jiñ ñi'uk'i,		There, they say, that chayote grew big,
xch'ixch'ujm.		and the spiny chayote.
'Añ che jiñi,	370	So it was,
tzax me ku kaji tyi 'e'tyel 'ub'i 'alob'i.		the child began to work.
Tza kaji tyi lok'eltyak 'ab'i		He started to go out, they say,
tyi juñ p'ejl tyi 'otyoty.		by one door of the house.
Mu 'ab'i letzel		He would climb up, they say,
ya' tyi jol 'otyoty;	375	there to the peak of the house;
mi cha' 'ochel		he would come in again
che' tyi mal.		to the inside.
Jiñ 'ab'i k'iñ 'añ,		That one, they say, is the sun,
mi yälob'.		they say.
Jiñäch 'ab'i 'añ k'iñ,	380	That very one, they say, is the sun
'añ 'ili wäleyi.		that is here today.
Tza kaji tyi kolel majlel.		He started to grow big.
Tza kaji tyi kolel majlel.		He started to grow big.
Mi lok'eltyak tyi säk'añ;		He would go out at dawn;
mi ñumel ya' tyi jol 'otyoty;	385	he would pass by the peak of the house,
mi cha' 'ochel		he would enter again
che' tyi juñ p'ejl tyi otyotyi.		where there was a door to the house.
Jiñ 'ab'i		He, they say,
che' wolix 'i yik'añtyak majlel,		when it was getting to be dusk,
jiñ che' mux 'i yochel tyi mal,	390	then he would come inside again,
'ik'ix 'ab'i 'añ che jiñi.		and it would get dark, they say.
'A che jiñi		So it was,
tza kaj tyi kolel.		he started to grow.
Tza kaj tyi kolel majlel.		He started to grow bigger.
Pero 'añ Laj Ch'ujul Ña'	395	But Our Holy Mother

mu tyo 'i pi'leñtyak tyi xämb'al.	still went out to accompany him on his walks.
Pero koñ wowoli 'i kolel,	But as he got bigger and bigger,
chäch woli 'i ñajty'añ ja'el.	she was falling further behind.
'I che jiñi,	And so it was,
wowoli 'i ñajty'añ,	she was falling further behind,
tza b'ejb'e käle majlel Laj Ña',	Our Mother was left behind,
'uj b'ä.	the one who is the moon.
'I che jach tzi käyäyob' 'i b'äj	And that's the way they remained
tyi xämb'al.	on their walks.

400

5

Older Brother Sun and Younger Brother Sun

Marcos Arcos Mendoza

This version of the story of the Moon and her sons was narrated by Marcos Arcos Mendoza during a storytelling contest we organized one evening in 1985 in Palenque, resting after a hard day of thatching Merle Greene Robertson's house. It complements the version narrated by Ausencio Cruz Guzmán; it is shorter and limited to the peak event—the death of the older brother and its aftermath—but it contains some details not found in the other version. Of particular interest is the reference to the two suns as "the white sun" and "the green sun." Color terms often occur in Classic period hieroglyphic texts in association with ceremonial titles, and their usage has been difficult to understand. There are "white" titles and "red" titles, "black" titles and "yellow" titles, as well as "green" titles; that is, all five basic color terms are used as some sort of modifier. Here we may note that the older brother is the "white" sun and the younger one is the "green" sun. This may indicate an association of age and higher status with the color white, as we know that in the directional terms, white is associated with the north, or the zenith of the sun's path, where the sun is at its brightest, producing the most intense heat. Green, in contrast, is often associated with new, fresh, emergent things and here is associated with the younger brother.

It is also of interest that both narrators give specific identifications to the plants used to make the gophers' teeth (and in this version, their hearts). The teeth are made of *xb'äk ch'ib'*, a variety of the edible palm *ch'ib'*. The wood of this palm is known to be extremely hard (*b'äk* is related to 'bone'). The gopher hearts were

DOI: 10.5876/9781607324881.c005

made of another edible palm, *chapäy*, the Spanish *pacaya*, or *Chamaedorea* palm. The inclusion of such details adds to this traditional story information the listeners may find useful later on. One of the most effective means of transmitting cultural knowledge is to encapsulate it in folktales, so it is passed down from generation to generation along with the story. We can now all remember that gophers can be eaten in their entirety, bones and all, except for those teeth and claws.

OLDER BROTHER SUN AND YOUNGER BROTHER SUN

K'iñ 'Askuñälbä y K'iñ 'Ijtz'iñälbä (Arcos Mendoza 1986)
Marcos Arcos Mendoza

'Añ wajali	1	It was a long time ago,
mi yäl lak tyaty, lak ña'ob',		our ancestors say,
tza' bä 'i k'eleyob' wajali		those who saw it long ago,
b'ajche' tza' 'ujtyi tyilel.		how it came to pass.
Jiñi mu bä 'i yälob':	5	This is what they say:
'añ 'ab'i jiñi k'iñ;		they say there was a sun;
pero cha' tyikil, 'ab'i.		but there were two, they say.
Jun tyikil 'askuñäl 'ab'i;		One was the older brother, they say,
yambä 'añ 'ab'i 'ijtz'iñäl b'äy.		the other was, they say, that younger brother.
'Ixku jiñi 'askuñäl b'ä	10	As for the older brother,
pero jiñi säsäkbä k'iñ.		well, he was the white sun.
'Ixku jiñi 'ijtz'iñäl b'ä		As for the younger brother,
jiñi yäjyäx b'ä k'iñ.		he was the green sun.
Tyi jimbä 'i yorajlel		At this same time
tza' majliyob' tyi matye'el	15	they went into the forest
'i säklañob' chab'.		looking for honey.
Che' jiñi,		So it was,
tyi cha' tyiklel tza' majliyob',		as a pair they went,
yik'oty jiñi 'askuñäl b'ä,		with the one who was the older brother,
yik'oty 'ijtz'iñäl b'ä.	20	with the one who was the younger brother.
Che' tza' k'otyiyob' tyi yojlil matye'el,		When they came to the middle of the forest,
tza' ki säklañob' ñumel jiñi chab'.		they began to look around for honey.
Che' jiñi,		So it was,
tza' kaji k'elb'eñ		they began to see
b'a wo tyi lok'el jiñi 'i chäñi chab'	25	where the honey bees were coming out,
ya' tyi ñi' tye'.		there in the tip of a tree.
Tza' kaji 'i yäl jiñi 'askuñäl bä:		The older brother began to say:
"'Ix 'an chab'i,"		"There is the honey,"
che' tzi sub'e jiñi 'i yijtz'iñ.		thus he told his younger brother.
'Ixku che' jiñi.	30	As for that, so it was.

Tza' letzi jiñi 'askuñäl b'ä
ya' tyi ñi' tye'.
Tzi' kuchu letzel
jiñi 'i jachaj.
Tza' letzi
ya' tyi ñi' tye',
tza' kaji 'i lom jiñi chab'
b'a 'añ 'i tyi'.
Che' jiñi,
tza kaji 'i tyaj jiñi chab'.
Mi sub'eñob' chäk'ox.
Tyi 'orajach,
tza' kaji 'i bäk' mäk'e'
jiñi 'askuñäl b'ä.
Che' jiñi,
tza' kaji 'i k'ajtyib'eñ chab' ja'el
'i yijtz'iñ
ya' tyi lum:
"'Ak'eñoñ jiñi chab';
kom jmäk' ja'el," che'eñ.
Che' jiñi,
tza' kaji 'i chokb'eñ jub'e jiñi chab'
ya' tyi ñi' tye'.
Che' tza' kaji 'i mäk' chab'
jiñi 'i yijtz'iñ
ya' tyi yeb'al lum,
tza' kaji 'i mel jiñi kabäl b'aj.
Tza' b'i kaji 'i woxiñ
jiñi tya'chäb'lel jiñi chab'.
Tza' kaji 'i sutyk'iñ tyi baj.
Che' jiñi,
'ixku 'i yej 'ab'i jiñi b'aj,
jiñ 'ab'i tzi' yotzb'e jiñi xb'äk ch'ib',

yik'oty 'ab'i tzi' yotzb'e jiñi 'i tyulmal
jiñi 'i tye'el, jiñi chapäy.
Tza' b'i kaj tyi tyejchel;
tza' b'i kaj 'i yotzañ jiñi b'aj
ya' tyi wi' tye'.
Tza' b'i kaji 'i yub'iñ jiñi 'askuñäl b'ä
ya' tyi ñi' tye',

	The older brother climbed up
	there to the tip of the tree.
	He carried up
	that ax of his.
35	He climbed up
	there to the tip of the tree,
	he began to cut out the honey
	where its entrance was.
	So it was,
40	he began to find the honey.
	They call them red bees (mosca real).
	Then,
	he began right away to eat it,
	the one who was the older brother.
45	So it was,
	he started to ask him for some honey, too,
	his younger brother
	there on the ground:
	"Give me some honey;
50	I want to eat, too," he said.
	So it was,
	he started to throw him down the honey
	there from the tip of the tree.
	When his younger brother
55	began to eat the honey
	there below on the ground,
	he started to make a lot of gophers.
	They say he started to make balls
	of the beeswax of the honey.
60	They started to turn into gophers.
	So it was,
	as for the teeth of the gophers, they say,
	they say he inserted in them hard palm wood,
	and he put in them hearts of palm fruit
65	from that palm tree, the chapay.
	They began to get up, they say,
	he began to put them in, they say,
	there in the roots of the tree.
	They say the older brother began to hear,
70	there at the tip of the tree,

wo 'ab'i tyi ty'añ,
jäch'la 'ab'i jiñi kolem tye'.
Che' jiñi,
tza' kaji 'i yäl jiñ 'askuñal b'ä:
"Chuki wol 'a mel   75
ya' tyi yeb'al tye'?," che'eñ.
Tzi' jak'ä jiñ yijtz'iñ:
"Mañik chuki woli jmel;
woli jkatz' 'ili wi' tye," che' 'ab'i.
Tyi jumuk' jach che' jiñi.   80
'Ora, 'ora, tza kaji 'i bäk' mel jiñi b'aj.

Tza' tyij p'ojli jiñi b'aj.
Tza' kaji 'i sety' jiñi tye'
ya' tyi yeb'al.
Che' jiñi,   85
tza' b'i 'i cha' sub'e jiñi yäskuñi:
"Chuki wol 'a mel
ya' tyi yeb'al jiñi tye'?," che' 'ab'i.

"Mañik,
joñoñ woli jkatz' 'ili wi' tye,"   90
che' 'ab'i jiñ 'i yijtz'iñ.
Che' jiñi,
che' jale 'ora,
tza' b'i kaj tyi ty'añ jiñi kolem tye'.
Jäch'law 'ab'i tza' kaji.   95
'Ixku che' jiñi,
mux 'ab'i kaj 'i chok jub'el 'i bäj.
Tza' 'i yälä jiñi 'askuñälbä,
we'ekña 'ab'i tyi 'oñel:
"Chuki wa' mel?   100
Chukoch wa' sek' jiñi tye'?,"
che' 'ab'i.
"Mañik woli jsek',
woli jach jkatz'b'eñ 'i wi' jiñi tye',
che' 'ab'i.   105
Tyi jiñ jach b'ä yorajlel,
tza' b'i kaj tyi yajle jub'el jiñi kolem tye'
b'a k'ächäl jiñi 'askuñäl b'ä.

---

it was starting to speak, they say,
creaking, they say, was that big tree.
So it was,
the older brother began to say:
"What are you doing
there at the foot of the tree?" he said.
The younger brother answered:
"I'm not doing anything;
I'm hitting this tree root," they say he said.
For a minute it was just like that.
Then, then, the gophers went quickly to
  work.
The gophers happily multiplied.
They began to gnaw the tree
there below.
So it was,
they say the older brother said again:
"What are you doing
there at the foot of the tree?" they say he
  said.
"Nothing,
I'm hitting this tree root,"
they say the younger brother said.
So it was,
all of a sudden,
they say the big tree began to make noise.
Creaking, they say, it began.
As for that, so it was,
they say it began to throw itself down.
The older brother said,
crying, they say, yelling,
"What are you doing?
Why are you cutting down the tree?"
they say he said.
"I'm not cutting it down,
I'm just hitting the roots of the tree,"
they say he said.
At that very moment,
the big tree started to fall, they say,
where the older brother was straddling a
  limb.

Che' jiñi,
k'äläl tyi lum 'ab'i tza' jub'i.
Tyeme 'ab'i tza' jub'i
yik'oty jiñi kolem tye'.
Tyi jiñ jach bä yorajlel,
tza' b'i laj b'ek'i 'i ch'ich'el jiñi 'i yäskuñ,
pejtye 'i bäk'tyal wisi p'i'iltyak 'ab'i
b'a tza' majli.
Che' jiñi,
'ixku jiñi 'i ch'ich'lel,
yik'oty jiñi 'i bäk'tyal jiñi yäskuñ,
tza' laj sujtyi tyi b'ätye'el.
Yamb'ä tza' sujtyi tyi chityam,
yamb'ä tyi wakax,
yamb'ä tyi chijmay.
Yamb'ä tza' sujtyi tyi tye'lal,
yamb'ä tyi wech,
yamb'ä tyi muty.
'Ixaku jiñi 'i yijtz'iñ,
tza' b'i ki 'i päy jiñi chityam,
tza' b'i ki tyuxb'añ jiñi chityam,
'i chityam, we'ekña 'ab'i.
Tza' ki 'i wetz' majlel jiñi 'aläk'äl
ya' tyi yotyoty,
käläl tyi yotyoty.
Che' jiñi,
'i ña', 'i mamaj mi yälob'i,
jiñ 'ab'i jiñi lak ña' 'uj.

Che' jiñi,
tza' b'i ki 'i k'ajtyib'eñ jiñi 'i mamaj:
"B'ak 'añ 'a werañ?
B'ak 'añ 'a wäskuñ?," che' 'ab'i.
Tzi sub'e jiñi 'i yijtz'iñ:
"Mañik woli jk'el käskuñ,
che' 'ab'i.
"Chukoch mach,
jatyety tza' majli 'a wik'oty 'a wäskuñ,
tyi la' cha' tyiklel," che' 'ab'i.
Che' jiñi,
tza' b'i ki 'i mel 'i pusik'al jiñi 'i mamaj.

So it was,
110   all the way to the ground, they say, he fell.
Together, they say, they fell,
he and the big tree.
At that very moment,
they say his blood all spilled out,
115   all his body broke into little pieces, they say,
where he fell.
So it was,
as for his blood,
and the body of the older brother,
120   it all turned into animals.
One part turned to pigs,
another to cattle,
another to deer.
Another part turned to pacas,
125   another to armadillos,
another to birds.
As for the younger brother,
they say he started to call the pigs,
they say he started to whistle up the pigs,
130   his pigs were squealing, they say.
He started to herd along the animals
there to his house,
all the way to his house.
So it was,
135   his mother, his "momma," they call her,
that one, they say, was our mother the
    moon.
So it was,
They say his momma began to ask him:
"Where is your brother?
140   Where is your older brother?" she said.
The younger brother told her:
"I don't see my older brother,"
they say he said.
"Why not?
145   You went out with your older brother,
as a pair," they say she said.
So it was,
his momma began to worry, they say.

Tza' b'i kaj tyi 'uk'el.
Che' jiñi,
tza' kaji 'i yäl jiñi 'i ña',
wo'wo'ña tza' b'i kaj tyi 'uk'el.
Komo tza' b'i kaj tyi 'uk'el jiñi 'i mamaj,
tza' b'i laj pujki pejtyel jiñi 'aläk'äl.
Yambä tza' majli tyi paty,
tza' laj sujtyi,
tza' 'ochi tyi matye'el.
Jiñ 'ab'i cha'añ,
pejtye matye' chityam
yik'oty jiñi tye'lal,
yik'oty jiñi chijmay,
yik'oty jiñi wech,
lak cha'añ 'ab'i 'añ wajali.
Pero komo 'i mamaj jiñi k'iñ
tza' b'i kaj tyi 'uk'el,
tzi laj bäk'tyesa jiñi bätye'el.
Lamtya tza putz'i,
lamtya tza käle.
Tzäch bä käle,
jiñ b'ajche lak muty,
yik'oty 'ab'i lak chityam.
'Ixaku jiñi chijmay,
lak cha'añ 'ab'i wajali.
'Ixaku jiñi wech
yik'oty tye'lal,
lak cha'añ 'ab'i wajali.
Pero tyi kaj, 'ab'i,
tza' kaj tyi 'uk'el 'i mamaj,
tza' b'i 'ochi tyi matye'el
pejtye 'ab'i jiñi 'aläk'äl.
Che' mi yälob' wajali.
Ya' tza' 'ujtyi.

She began to cry, they say.
150   So it was,
his mother began to speak,
sobbing, they say, she began to cry.
Because his momma started crying, they say,
all of the animals began to scatter, they say.
155   Some of them went back,
they went all the way back,
they went into the forest.
For that reason, they say,
all of the wild pigs
160   and the pacas,
and the deer,
and the armadillos,
all were ours, they say, long ago.
But since the momma of the sun
165   started to cry, they say,
all of the animals were frightened.
Half of them fled,
half of them stayed behind.
The ones that stayed,
170   those are like our chickens,
and our pigs, they say.
As for the deer,
they were ours, they say, long ago.
As for the armadillos
175   and the pacas,
they were ours, they say, long ago.
But because, they say,
his momma began to cry,
they say they went into the woods,
180   all the animals, they say.
Thus they tell of long ago.
There it ended.

6

The Celestial Bird

Ausencio Cruz Guzmán

This story was recorded in 1979, narrated by Cruz Guzmán and recorded by Josserand and Hopkins. It is one of the stories Cruz learned when he went with his brother to make a dugout canoe in Arroyo Palenque, an ejido community on the Río Bascán. Domingo López, the owner of the canoe, told the story of the celestial rooster in Chol. He also told the story of the messengers pursued by the lord of the underworld (The Messengers). This story is a simple one; it explains how roosters know when to crow in the morning. The great rooster in heaven gives the order, and earthly roosters wake up the people on earth. This "rooster" is surely related to the Classic Maya "Principal Bird Deity," prominent in Classic iconography, and to the celestial messenger bird that came down to tell the plants to rise up in the tale of Our Holy Mother.

Discussing this story, Cruz Guzmán remarked that it reminded him of festival day in San Pedro Sabana, the village on the Río Tulijá where he grew up. When music is heard coming from the heavens, people know it is time to celebrate the festival of San Pedro (the patron saint of the town, Saint Peter). On this day San Pedro is put to sleep, as he is extremely tired. It is he who holds the world in his hands, like an atlantean figure. At the end of a year, he is exhausted and ready to let the weight of the world fall from his hands. So his disciples put him down to sleep, to rest. They make a festival for him and sing to him. When he is awakened the next day, he is rested and ready to take up his work again. A new year begins. If people didn't hear the celestial music, perhaps they would forget his day. And if they didn't put him to

DOI: 10.5876/9781607324881.c006

rest, he could let the world fall, and everyone would die. So people must respond like the roosters. Hearing the message from heaven, one must obey.

The Celestial Bird

Ty'añ Jiñi Tyaty Muty
Ausencio Cruz Guzmán (Josserand, Hopkins, and Cruz Guzmán 1978b)

Che jach,	1	Just like this,
tzi sub'eñoñ ke che'i,		they told me that it's like this.
che mu tyi 'uk'el muty,		When the roosters crow
'ila tyi lum,		here on earth,
'ila tyi b'a 'añoñlaj,	5	here where we are,
ñaxañ 'añ mi yub'iñ		first they hear
'ub'i tyaty muty.		that father rooster.
Mu 'ab'i tyi 'uk'el		They say it crows,
ñoj bä lak muty		our great rooster
ya' tyi pañchañ.	10	there in heaven.
'I jiñ chañ,		And for that reason,
che' yomix tyilel säk'ajel,		when dawn is about to come,
mero yom säk'ajel,		just before dawn,
mu 'ab'i 'i ñich'tyañ.		they say they hear him.
Ñaxañ mi cha'leñ 'uk'el	15	First crows
'ub'i tyaty muty tyi pañchañ.		that father rooster in heaven.
'Entonses mux 'ab'i jak'ob'		Then, they say, answer
wu bu 'añ tyi lum ja'el;		those that are on earth as well;
mux 'i laj pam jak'ob'.		from all over they answer.
Komo 'añ tza'	20	Because it is that
mach mi yub'iñob' ja' li säk'ajel,		they don't sense the dawn,
mach ke jiñtyo mi ñaxañ cha'leñ 'uk'el		not unless first crows
'añ tyi pañchañ.		the one that is in heaven.
Mañik 'añ mach mi tyejchel.		There is no one who would get up,
porke jiñach 'añ mi ñaxañ 'ak' 'orden	25	because he is the one who gives the order
che mi laj tyejchel,		that we arise,
ya' bä 'añ tyi pañchañ.		the one that is in heaven.
Che mi sub'eñob',		That's why they call him
"tyaty muty."		"father rooster."

7

The Turtle and the Deer

Mateo Alvaro López, Nicolás Arcos Alvaro,
and Ausencio Cruz Guzmán

The story of the race between the turtle and the deer is widely known, and not just among Chols. It is easily recognized as a variant of one of Aesop's fables, although the Greek version features a tortoise and a hare. This telling of the story was recorded by Josserand, Hopkins, and Cruz Guzmán in Palenque in April 1985, during the rethatching of Merle Greene Robertson's house. The narrators were Nicolás Arcos Alvaro (25) and his uncle, Mateo Alvaro López (30), both natives of the ejido León Brindis. The same narrators told the story of the Jaguar-Man (also in this collection). Since this is not a tale from the Mayan tradition, it is not marked with evidentiality statements referring the story to the ancestors, although the opening statement, "They say there was a turtle . . ." is marked as traditional lore by use of the reportative particle *'ab'i.*

The incorporation of European folklore in the repertory of Mayan folktales is not uncommon. During his dissertation research in northwestern Guatemala in the 1960s, Hopkins recorded (from a virtually monolingual Chuj speaker) a version of Oedipus Rex, complete to the riddle that had to be solved to win the hand of the widowed queen. Likewise, many of the West African rabbit trickster tales (Diarassouba 2007) have been incorporated into the Coyote-Rabbit stories of the Chuj and others (see Hopkins's contributions to AILLA).

The ejido León Brindis is currently located on the Río Axupá, a tributary of the Río Chacamax, a few meters north of the highway that runs from Palenque to Chancalá. In earlier years the ejido was located nearer Palenque, on the

Palenque-Ocosingo highway just before the road to Chancalá, near the bridge over the Río Axupá. The ejidatarios were of diverse origins, including Salto de Agua (Potiojá, Trinidad, Zapote, Tortuguero), Tumbalá (El Triunfo), and Yajalón, the latter speakers of Tzeltal and Spanish who have now learned Chol. The original lands were ceded to the ejido Belisario Domínguez, and León Brindis moved to where it has now been for more than forty years.

THE TURTLE AND THE DEER

Ty'añ 'Ajk Yik'oty Me'
Mateo Alvaro López
Nicolás Arcos Alvaro
Ausencio (Chencho) Cruz Guzmán

[MATEO:]		[MATEO:]
'Añ 'ab'i 'ajk	1	They say there was a turtle
tza kajiyob' tyi juñ p'e preba		that started a contest
yik'oty me',		with a deer,
kome jiñi 'ajk		but that turtle
che ya lalak tyi yok.	5	had short legs, like this.
Tzi ña'tya		He knew
'añ cha' tz'ijty b'ij;		there were two roads;
'añ 'i xäk' jiñi b'ij.		the road had a fork.
Tza k'otyiyob' ya tyi xäk' jiñi b'ij.		They went there to the fork in the road.
Tzi ña'tya chañ yom 'i lajob' 'i b'ij,	10	He knew that the roads should be equal,
majki mi mäl jiñi 'ajñel.		to see who won the race.
Che' b'a 'ora tza k'otyi jiñi me',		When the deer arrived,
lajal woli tyi tyilelob'		at the same time arrived
yik'oty jiñi 'ajk		the turtle
tyi jiñi b'ij.	15	at that road.
Che jeñ,		So it was,
tza kaj tyi ty'añ jiñi me'.		the deer started to speak.
Tzi yälä che b'ajche jiñi:		He spoke like this:
"Wäle, koñ laj, lak laj lak b'ij,"		"Now, let's go, let's race,"
che'eñ.	20	he said.
"Chañ mi laj k'el,		"So that we will see,
ya mi ka majlel ya'i;		you go that way;
joñoñ mi kaj majlel 'ilayi.		I'll go this way.
Mi ka laj k'el		We will see
majki ñaxañ mi ki lok'el ya',	25	who gets there first,
b'aki lok'em 'ili xäk' b'ij."		where the split in the road ends."
Che tzi ña'tya tyi pusik'al jiñ me',		So thought the deer in his heart,

chañ jiñ mi ñumen mäl,
ko me chañ 'i yok
'i ñajty mi tyijp'el,
jiñi 'ajk ya' k'ax k'uñtyejax.
Jiñ cha'añ yom 'i yäk' tyi kisiñ,
tzi ña'tya 'añ jiñi me'.
Che' mi yub'iñ 'i tyijikñel,
tzi ña'tya jiñ me'.
"Weno, 'utz'aty;
koñ laj,"
che'eñ.
"La laj cha'leñ 'ajñel,
che jiñi,"
che'eñ jiñi 'ajk.
Jiñi me', tzi chuku 'i yajñel;
'ajñel tza majli.
Pero mach laj kujilik
b'ajche ñajtyel jiñi xäk' b'ij,
b'a lok'em.
[NICOLÁS:]
Pero tyi' ja' b'a tza k'otyiyob'.

[MATEO:]
Tyi' ja'.
[NICOLÁS:]
Tyi' ja'.
[MATEO:]
Mach laj kujilik b'ajche ñajtyel.
'I che jiñi,
jiñi me'
tzi cha'le weñ 'ajñel.
Kome jiñi me'
mux tyi kab'äl tyijp'el,
tyijp' 'i majlel.
Jiñ cha'añ
tza lujb'a;
tza lujb'a.
[NICOLÁS:]
Tza päkle.
[MATEO:]
Che jiñ.

that he would win,
since his legs were long
30   and he jumped a long way,
and the turtle was really slow.
For that reason he would surely shame him,
so thought the deer.
So he would be happy,
35   thought the deer.
"Okay, that's good;
let's go,"
he said.
"Let's run,
40   so be it,"
said the turtle.
The deer, he took off running;
running he went.
But we don't know
45   how far it was from that fork,
where it left the road.
[NICOLÁS:]
But the riverbank is where they would
   arrive.
[MATEO:]
The bank of the river.
[NICOLÁS:]
The bank of the river.
[MATEO:]
50   We don't know how far it was.
And so it was,
the deer
ran really fast.
Since the deer
55   took a lot of leaps,
jumping he went.
For that reason
he got tired;
he got tired.
[NICOLÁS:]
60   He laid down.
[MATEO:]
So it was.

Tza ʼi kʼele ʼi paty;		He looked over his shoulder;
mañik majki tzikil.		no one was visible.
"Mañik ñumeñ,"		"No one has passed,"
tzi ñaʼtya.	65	he thought.
"Wäle tyo tyal;		"Now he's still coming;
tzax jmälä.		I've already won.
Jiñ chaʼañ,		For that reason,
wäle chañ mi jkʼotye		now that I'm arriving
ya tyi tyiʼ jaʼ,	70	there to the riverbank,
laʼtyo jkʼaj koj,		it's okay for me to rest,
kome lujbʼoñix,"		because I'm tired already,"
cheʼeñ.		he said.
Tza päkle jiñ jiñiʼ.		He laid down.
[CHENCHO:]		[CHENCHO:]
¿Che ʼañ meʼ?	75	That's what the deer said?
[MATEO:]		[MATEO:]
Jäjäʼ.		Uh-huh.
Tza päkle ʼañ meʼ.		The deer laid down.
Pero jiñi ʼajk		But the turtle
ya wo tyi kʼuñtyeʼ tyilel,		he was slowly coming,
ya wo tyi tyilel;	80	there he was coming,
pero cheʼ.		but like this.
[NICOLÁS:]		[NICOLÁS:]
Tza ʼochi ʼi wäyel jiñi meʼ		The deer went to sleep
bʼa tzi kʼaja ʼi yoj.		where he was resting.
[MATEO:]		[MATEO:]
Tza wäyi ʼañ meʼ.		The deer went to sleep.
Tza bäläkʼ wäyi tyi ʼora.	85	He went right to sleep.
Che jiñi,		So it was,
ya päkäl tyi bʼij,		there he was lying down
tza kʼotyi jiñ ʼajk.		when the turtle arrived.
Kome tzi kʼele chañ ya ʼañi,		So he saw that he was there,
wäyälix,	90	already asleep,
weñ wäyälix ʼan jiñ meʼ.		sound asleep was the deer.
[NICOLÁS:]		[NICOLÁS:]
Koñ kʼuñtyeʼ wo tyi xämbʼal,		Since he was walking really slowly,
tza ñumi.		he passed him.
[MATEO:]		[MATEO:]
Che jiñ.		So it was.
Tza kʼuñtyeʼ ñumi ʼañ ʼajki.	95	The turtle slowly passed him.
Tza ñumi;		He passed him;

tza ñumi;
tza majli.
Tza majli
k'äläl tyi tyi' ja'.
Che jiñ,
tza kajñi 'i wuty jiñi me'i.
"Maxtyo 'añik ñumen,"
tzi ña'tya.
Tzi cha' kañ k'ele 'i paty.
Tza tyejchi majlel.
Pero jiñ 'ajk,
yax 'añ tyi tyi' ja'
che' tza k'otyi.
Jiñ cha'añ,
tzi weñ cha'le kisin me',
komo tzi ña'tya chañ jiñ
ñaxañ mi k'otyel.
Koñ mach 'i ty'ojolik
mi ñumel jiñ 'ajk,
kon che ya lalaktyäl 'i yok.
Che jach
tzi meleyob' b'ajche jiñi.
[CHENCHO:]
¿A b'ajchje tza 'ujtyi 'añ me'?
¿B'ajche yälä?
[MATEO:]
"Jiñi,
koñ tza k'otyi che jiñi?"
Ma wo 'i ña'tyañ
mi yax 'añ jiñ 'ajk
ya tyi tyi' ja'.
Tza tyo k'otyi k'el
cheñ tyoj kisñijel.
'I kisiñtyik tzi yub'i,
kome tzax käle tyi wi' paty,
'i weñ kolem che' b'ajche jiñ.
[CHENCHO:]
Tza putz'i.
Tzax majli.
[NICOLÁS:]
Tzax majli.

he passed him;
he went by.
He went on
100 all the way to the riverbank.
So it was,
the deer opened his eyes.
"Still nobody has passed,"
he thought.
105 He looked back over his shoulder again.
He got up and left.
But the turtle
was already there at the riverbank
when he arrived.
110 So it was,
the deer was really ashamed,
since he thought that he
would come in first.
Since it wasn't right
115 that the turtle passed him,
since his legs were only so long.
So it was,
they did it like that.
[CHENCHO:]
And how did the deer end up?
120 What did he say?
[MATEO:]
"That one,
how did he get here like that?"
He didn't think
the turtle would be first
125 there at the riverbank.
When he arrived and saw,
he was really ashamed.
And he felt ashamed,
since he had been left behind,
130 and by a long way.
[CHENCHO:]
He fled.
He went away.
[NICOLÁS:]
He left.

[MATEO:]		[MATEO:]
Tza majli.		He left.
[NICOLÁS:]		[NICOLÁS:]
Tzi yälä jiñi me':	135	The deer said:
"Weno, 'utz'aty;		"Okay, that's all right;
mak chu' mi cha'leñ		it doesn't matter
mi mak tza kmälä."		if I didn't win."
[CHENCHO:]		[CHENCHO:]
Che'eñ.		He said.
[NICOLÁS:]		[NICOLÁS:]
Che'eñ, "Wäle,	140	He said, "Now,
wä mi laj käy laj b'äj."		here we leave each other."
Tyijikña 'ajk,		Happy was the turtle,
tza majli tyi yeb'al ja'.		and he went under the water.
[CHENCHO:]		[CHENCHO:]
'Aja.		Aha.
[NICOLÁS:]		[NICOLÁS:]
Pero jiñi me', tza majli ja'el.	145	But that deer, he left also.
Pero weñ kontento 'ajk tza majli,		But the turtle left really happy,
koñ tzi mälä;		since he won;
koñ tzi yälä jiñ		since the other one had said
mach kajik 'i mäl tzi ña'tya.		he wasn't going to win, he thought.
Che tzi yälä b'ajche jiñi.	150	That's what he said.
Che tza 'ujtyi b'ajche jiñi.		That's the way that ended.

PART 2
Tales of the Earth Lord

8

Our Grandfather

Ausencio Cruz Guzmán

This story is one of many that concern Lak Mam, Our Grandfather, an old god also known as Chajk (or in Yucatec Maya, Chaak). He throws lightning, and he brings the rain. The narrator of this version of his adventures is Ausencio Cruz Guzmán, and this telling was recorded in Mexico City in 1979 by Josserand and Hopkins. It is a story Cruz learned as a child, and he has not heard it told since. It was told to him by two elderly men of San Pedro Sabana, where he grew up: Felipe ("el Jueche") Arcos and Miguel ("Seco") López. At the time, Cruz was learning to fish, and the men had taken him out in a dugout canoe. It was the custom for men to fish in small groups, including young boys. One man took the stern position and paddled the canoe with a long steering oar. Another man would take the bow and fish with a long pole, baiting the hook with the seeds of *b'itz'* (Spanish *guatope*), *Inga spuria,* a pod-bearing tree that grows along the edges of rivers. In this instance, the boy seated in the middle of the canoe baited the hooks. While they were fishing, the two men told Cruz the story.

The rainy season is the season for the *bitz'* and laurel to be flowering and producing seeds. The *bitz'* has small white flowers that produce seed pods more than a foot long. The fleshy insides of the pods are edible. The fruit ripens from September to December, and in these same months one fishes for turtles and *macabil* fish, since these two species come out to eat the seeds that have fallen into the water. Macabil is a fish that has lots of small bones and teeth that are so sharp they are used as knives. Dark greenish in tint with a yellow belly, sixty centimeters long and thirty centimeters wide, it is a tasty fish.

DOI: 10.5876/9781607324881.c008

Lak Mam also eats other foods. He throws lightning (his ax) to split open trees so he can get at the juicy caterpillars, a hand-span in length, that grow in rotten branches. Sometimes people find these axes; they are the polished stone axes known from archaeological collections. Lak Mam also breaks off his fingernails when he is clawing out these delicacies; they are found in the form of obsidian flakes.

Lak Mam has sons who are more powerful than he is, since he is now very old. When a storm blows up, it is they who throw the lightning. The old man just rumbles with thunder and doesn't do any damage himself. It is he who is heard in the distance, but it is his sons who light up the sky with their bolts.

Lak Mam needs his hat and his shirt to throw lightning. They have powers of their own and are activated when shaken. In the story, the man who brings them to Lak Mam is told to be careful as to how he handles them. In the Maya Codices and on Classic ceramics we find representations of a character like Lak Mam, God L, who is pictured wearing his special hat and shirt (on the door panels of the Temple of the Cross at Palenque, for example). Lak Mam's wife, who figures in this story, is seen as a huge toad that lives in a cave along the banks of the river.

In 1987, at the Taller Maya IX in Antigua, Guatemala, Josserand presented a pair of papers, one on the various forms in which a text could be presented (with parallel lines of analysis, in poetic structures, as a cartoon, and similar forms; Josserand 1987c) and one on Classic inscriptions (Josserand 1987b). Since our friends from the Tzotzil Writers' Co-op (Sna Jtz'ibajom) in San Cristóbal de Las Casas, Chiapas, were attending with their road manager, Bob Laughlin, she asked them if they could put on a play, using the text as a script. They were experienced in puppet theater but had yet to begin their successful run at live theater. Laughlin (Laughlin 1999:496; Laughlin and Sna Jtz'ibajom 2008:7–8) has published the insider's view of how this performance launched Sna on its fabulous international stage career.

The other paper alerted the Mayas studying linguistics at the Programa Lingüístico Francisco Marroquín (PLFM) that scholars were now reading Classic texts. They asked us for a workshop, which we presented on the last day of the Taller. As we went over the ruler list from Palenque's Tablet of the Cross, one of the participants declared, "This is our history! This is what they have kept from us!" That weekend the participants of the Taller went on a field trip to Copán, and we introduced two of the PLFM leaders, Martín Chacach and Narciso Cojtí, to Linda Schele, in Honduras on a Fulbright scholarship. With organizational help from Nora England, this encounter led to a hieroglyph workshop back in Antigua, the first of many that have introduced Classic Maya writing back to the modern Maya (see, for instance, the activities sponsored by MAM, Maya Antiguo para los Mayas, on its website at discovermam.org). In 2012 the Primer Congreso de Epigrafistas Mayas took place in Valladolid, Yucatán, with the participation of dozens of Mayas from

Mexico, Guatemala, and Belize (on the Maya-speaking campus of the Universidad de Oriente). A Second Congress took place in Ocosingo, Chiapas, in 2014.

OUR GRANDFATHER

Ty'añ Lak Mam
Ausencio Cruz Guzmán (1978a, 1978b)

Wajali 'añ mi yälob'	1	A long time ago, they say,
ke jiñ lak mam		that Our Grandfather
mu 'ab'i 'i jub'eltyak 'ila tyi lum.		used to come down here to earth.
'Añäch 'ab'i 'i ch'ujlel.		They say he had a soul [took human form].
Mu 'ab'i 'i jub'eltyak tyi mäk' b'itz'	5	He used to come down to eat bitz'.
che 'i yorajlel b'itz'		when it was the time for bitz',
che 'i yorajlel b'uty' ja'lel		when it was the time for floods.
Porke jiñ jach		Because then it is
'añtyak 'i wuty jiñ b'itz'		that the bitz' has lots of fruit—
ambä tyi tyi' ja'	10	the kind on the banks of the rivers—
che 'i yorajlel ja'lel,		when it's the time for rains,
b'uty' ja'lel.		flood rains.
'A mañik,		Ah, no,
'añ 'ab'i tzi' tyajb'e 'i yora.		it was, they say, that the time came.
'Añob' 'ab'i xlukb'äl.	15	There were fishermen, they say,
'Ux tyikilob' xlukb'äl.		three fishermen.
Woliyob' 'ab'i tyi luk ch'akäl		They were fishing for macabil, they say,
komo jiñ 'i yorajlel luk ch'akäl		since the time to fish for macabil
che' woli tyi yajlel 'i b'äk jiñ b'itz'i.		is when the seeds of the bitz' are falling.
Woli 'i jub'elob' tyi luk ch'akäli.	20	They came down to fish for macabil.
Mañik,		Ah, no,
tza ki 'i k'elob'		then they saw that
k'ächäkña 'ab'i tyi ñi' b'itz'		straddled on a limb of bitz', they say,
jiñ lak mam.		was Our Grandfather.
'A mañik,	25	Ah, no,
tza' k'otyiyob'		they arrived
ya' b'a k'achäli.		there where he was astraddle.
Tza ki' k'ajtyib'eñ:		They started to ask him:
"Chu' wol 'a cha'leñ, mam?"		"What are you doing, Grandfather?"
"Mañik.	30	"Nothing.
Woliyoñ tyi mäk' b'itz'," che'eñ.		I'm eating bitz'," he said.
'A che jiñi,		So it was,
"Kom mi la' koltyañoñ		"I want you all to help me out
porke 'añoñ tyi wokol 'ili."		because I'm in trouble here."

'A che jiñi.
"Pero chuk wol 'a cha'leñ, mam?
Chuk wol 'a cha'leñ?
Chuk 'añ 'a chañ?" che'eñ.
'A che jiñi.
"Mañik.
Tzi' chukuyoñ chäñil ja',
chuxka,
mi 'ajiñ,
mi chäñil ja'
wäle, chuxka,
koñ ma tza 'añ tzikil,
koñ b'uty'ul tza ja'.
Tyity, mak laj tyaj laj k'el.
Wäle, mi la' koltyañoñ,
poj koltyañoñlaj jumuk'.
Jiñ jach la' majlel;
la' poj ch'ämb'eñoñ tyilel jpixol, jb'ujk,
ya' tyi kotyoty."
"Weno, koñ,"
che'ob' ja'el 'ili wiñikob',
kom 'utzäch mi k'el,
mi k'elob'.
'A che jiñ.
Tza lok'iyob' ya' tyi tyi' ja',
'i kächäyob' 'i jukub'.
Tza lok'iyob' majlel.
"Wäle, ma majlel
ya' tyi kotyoty,
ya' poj 'añ kotyoty 'ixixi.
Jumuk' jach ma majlel."
'Añ tza loñ majli 'añ juñtyikili.
Tza' käleyob' 'añ yambä cha' tyikilob'
ya' tyi tyi' ja',
tyi jukub'.
'Añ tza majli 'ab'i 'añ juñtyikili;
tza' k'otyi
ya' tyi yotyoty.
"Pero mak majch 'añ," che'eñ.
Tza' cha' sujtyi tyilel.
"Chukoch mach majch 'añ,

35   So it was.
"But what are you doing, Grandfather?
What are you doing?
What is your affair?" they said.
So it was.
40   "Nothing.
A water animal grabbed me,
whatever,
maybe an alligator,
maybe a water animal,
45   now, whatever,
since it can't be seen well,
because the river is in big flood.
It's turbid, I can't manage to see it.
Now, you all help me out,
50   please help us out a little.
You all just go;
please go bring me my hat and my shirt,
there from my house."
"Okay, let's go,"
55   the men said, too,
since they saw that he was good,
they saw it.
So it was.
They went to the edge of the water;
60   they tied up their canoe.
They arrived there.
"Now, you all go
there to my house,
there should be my house over there.
65   Just for a minute, you go there."
One man went, but in vain.
The other two men stayed
there at the edge of the water,
in the canoe.
70   So that one man went, they say,
he arrived
there at his house.
"But there isn't anyone here," he said.
He returned.
75   "Why is there no one there,

si ya''añ
tza'k'otyiyety,
b'a tza'k'otyiyety
tyi kaj wa'tyili.
Jiñ kijñam,
jiñ kaj wa'al tyi tyi''otyoty.
Chañ jach mach ma käñ," che'eñ.
"Cha' kuku," che' tzi sub'e.
'A che jiñ,
tza'cha'majli 'ub'i 'ili wiñiki.
Tza'k'otyi 'i k'el ya'
tyi tyi' ch'eñ,
tyi tyokolbä lum;
k'otyi 'i tyaj
weñ koleñ ña'pokok,
koleñ x'oñkoñak,
chuxka.
Jiñ yijñam lak mam 'añ jiñi.
Che jiñ,
tza'ki sub'e:
"Wäle, mu 'ab'i 'a wäk'eñoñ majlel
jiñ 'i pixol,
yik'oty 'i b'ujk jiñ kmam
porke 'añ 'ab'i tyi wokol."
"Chuk woli 'i cha'leñ?"
"Chuxka!
Tyik'äl mi chukul
tyi 'ajiñ,
tyi chäñil ja',
chuxka.
Jiñ tzi chokoyoñ tyilel.
Ya'k'ächäl tyi 'i k'äb' b'itz'.
Woli 'i mäk' b'itz'.
'A mañik,
koñ 'ochem 'i yok
ya' tyi mal ja',
ya' tzi' chuku."
"Weno," che jach 'i yijñami.
Tzi' yäk'e majlel.
Tza majli.
Che jiñ,

if it's there
that you went;
when you arrived
she was standing there.
80 My wife,
she was standing at the door of the house.
You just didn't recognize her," he said.
"Go again," he told him.
So it was,
85 the man went a second time.
He arrived and saw there
at the entrance to a cave,
at a crack in the earth;
he arrived to find
90 a big female toad,
a big toad,
whatever.
That was the wife of Our Grandfather.
So it was,
95 he said to her:
"Now, they say you are to give me
that hat of his,
and the shirt of my Grandfather,
because they say he is in trouble."
100 "What is he doing?"
"Whatever!
Perhaps he is caught
by an alligator,
by a water animal,
105 whatever.
He sent me to come here.
There he is straddled on a branch of bitz'.
He is eating bitz'.
Ah, no,
110 since his foot had gone in
there into the water,
there it caught him."
"Okay," said his wife.
She gave it to him.
115 He left.
So it was,

tza k'otyi ya' b'a lak mami.	he arrived there where Our Grandfather was.
Tza' ki yäk'eñ 'i pixol.	He gave him his hat.
Pero ñaxañ che' tza majli, tza' ki sub'eñ:	But before he went, Grandfather told him:
"Che ma kaj 'a ch'äm tyilel jiñ jpixoli,	120 "When you bring that hat of mine,
yik'oty jb'ujki,	and that shirt of mine,
ma meku kajk 'a käläx ñijkañ!	don't let it shake at all!
Ma me tzi' tz'ijiyety;	Don't let it strike you;
ma me 'i tzäñsañety."	don't let it kill you."
Loñ che jiñi;	125 In vain it was;
che jach woli 'i ña'tyañ majlel ja'el wiñiki,	just so the man was thinking as well,
porke koñ meleläch 'añ mi yäl,	since what he said was possible,
koñ lak mam tza'.	since he really was Our Grandfather.
'A che jiñi,	So it was,
tza' k'otyi yik'oty 'i pixol,	130 he arrived with his hat,
yik'oty 'i b'ujk.	with his shirt.
Tza' ki' sub'eñ:	He told him:
"'Uxeku b'a 'añ, kmam."	"Here it is, My Grandfather."
"Yoñku," che'eñ.	"Okay," he said.
Tza' ki' läp 'i b'ujk.	135 He put on his shirt.
Tza' ki' läp 'i pixol.	He put on his hat.
Tzi' k'äkä 'i pixol.	He lifted up his hat.
Che jiñ,	So it was,
tza' ki' sub'eñ:	he said to them:
"Wäle, kukula ya' tyi pañlum.	140 "Now, go there to the riverbank.
Kächäxla jiñ la jukub'.	Tie up your canoe.
Lok'eñla' tyi mal ja'.	Get out of the water.
Ya mi la maj tyi pañlum.	Go over there to the land.
Ya mi la wotzañ la jol	There put your heads in
b'a' tyokoltyak jiñ lum."	145 where the earth is all cracked."
'A mañik,	Ah, no,
tzäch 'i jak'äyob' añ cha' tyikili.	just two of the men obeyed.
Jiñ 'añ juñ tyikil,	One of the men
woli k'el chu' mi ki' meltyak	was watching what Our Grandfather
jiñ lak mam.	150 was doing.
Mak wol 'i ña'tyañ,	He didn't know
mi mi ki' xä'tyaj ja'el	that Chajk's lightning bolt
'i xu'il chajki.	could hit him, too.
Che jale 'ora,	And then it happened,
k'iñlaw 'ab'i,	155 flashing, they say,
ñup'law 'ab'i,	crashing, they say,

tza' tyojmi jiñ chajki,		lightning exploded,
b'a' tzi' ñijka 'i b'ä jiñ lak mami.		when Our Grandfather shook himself.
Tza jach 'i ñijka 'i b'ä,		He just shook himself,
tza' tyojmi jiñ chajki.	160	and lightning exploded.
Tza' tyiki jiñ ja'.		The water dried up.
Tza säjp'i jiñ ja',		The water went down,
ma che' ku 'añix ja'.		there wasn't any water anymore.
K'iñlaw,		Flashing,
ñup'law 'ab'i 'añ.	165	crashing, they say, it was.
'Añ 'i chäñil ja',		The water animal
tza' chämi.		died.
'Añ che jiñ,		So it was,
tza ki' sub'eñob' 'añ 'ub'i lak mam.		Our Grandfather told them.
"La'ix kulaj," che 'ab'i tzi' sub'eñob'	170	"You all come over here," they say he said
yamb'ä cha'tyikil wiñik.		to the other two men.
'Añ koñ juñtyikil		Since one of them
tzäch 'ab'i xä'tyaj ja'el 'ili chajki,		had been hit by lightning, they say,
tza' 'ab'i jum pajk chämi.		he was half dead, they say.
Che jiñ,	175	So it was,
tza ki' sub'eñ,		he told them,
"Lotyoxla jiñ la' chäy.		"Gather up your fish.
B'uty'ux la' jukub',		Fill your canoe,
chañ max tyo metza 'añik ja'.		because there isn't any water yet.
Ch'ämä,	180	Grab them,
mero tyikiñ tyo me ja'.		the river is still dry.
Machiki,		If you don't,
jal tyo mi ki' tyilel jiñ ja'.		the water is coming back.
Lotyolaj!		Gather them up!
Tyi 'ora jach mi la loty,	185	Gather them up right now,
chañ 'ame 'i päyetyla majlel b'uty' ja'."		so that the flood doesn't carry you off."
"Yoñku," che ja'el wiñiki.		"Okay," the men agreed.
Tza' ki' b'uty'ob' 'i chäy.		They started to fill their canoe with fish.
Tza' ki' yotzañob' tyi jukub'.		They started to put them into the canoe.
Che tza'ix 'ujtyi 'i lotyob' jiñ chäyi,	190	When they had finished gathering up the fish,
tza' ki' k'elob' mak tzikil juñtyikil pi'äl.		they saw that their companion wasn't in sight.
Tza' ki' k'ajtyib'e 'añ lak mami:		They asked Our Grandfather:
"Ixku juñtyikil jpi'äl?		"What about our companion?
B'aki tza' käle," che'eñ.		Where did he end up?" they said.
"Bä 'i b'ä.	195	"It's his own fault.

Majki mi jsub'eñ ke mi' k'eloñ,		Who did I tell to watch me,
chu' ka kmel.		what I was going to do.
Tza ksub'e,		I told him,
b'ajche tza ksub'etyla ja'el.		like I told you all as well.
'I kom mak tzi' jak'ä,	200	And since he didn't obey,
yomäch 'i k'el chu' mi kaj kmel,		he just wanted to see what I was doing,
tzi' yila.		he watched.
Pero mak woli 'i ña'tyañ		But he didn't know
mi mi kaj kxä'tyaj.		that I was going to throw lightning.
Tzäch ktyaja ktz'ij ja'el.	205	It hit him as well.
Machikix; la'tyo 'ajñik,		Never mind; you all go on,
mu tyo ki' k'uñ tyejchel.		he will recover after a while.
Señoñla,		Hurry,
lotyo la' chäy.		gather your fish.
Tyalix me tzal ja.'"	210	The water is coming back already."
"Yoñku," che'eñ.		"Okay," they said.
'Ujtyi 'i lotyob' añ chäyi.		They finished gathering the fish.
Tza' ki' k'elob'		They saw
wolix 'i tyejchel yambä wiñik,		that the other man was getting up,
k'uñ tyejchi majlel.	215	he was slowly getting up.
'Añ che jiñ,		So it was,
tza'ix k'otyi b'uty' ja'.		the flood came already.
Tza'ix meku majliyob' tyi jub'el;		They all went downstream;
k'otyiyob' tyi yotyoty.		they arrived at their house.
Tza' ki' sub'eñob' pejtyel xpampañ chumtyil,	220	They told everybody in the village
b'ajche' tza' 'ujtyityak.		how everything happened.
'Añ mach mi ñopob',		Ah, but they didn't believe them,
ma tza' 'añ b'a mi laj k'el ja'el		since at no time had we ever seen
mi jub'eltyak tyi mäk' b'itz' jiñ chajk.		Chajk coming down to eat bitz'.
'I jiñ cha'añ,	225	And for this reason,
woläch 'i yixña mero ñopob' tz'itya',		they really had to believe some of it,
porke komo tzäch 'i ñopoyob' ja'el,		since they had to believe it, too,
koñ kab'älob' 'i chäy		because it was a lot of fish
tza' k'otyiyob'.		they came home with.
'Añ che jiñi,	230	So it was,
che jach tza' 'ujtyi b'ajche jiñi.		thus it ended like that.

9

The Cave of Don Juan

Ausencio Cruz Guzmán

This is the first Chol story we recorded. In 1978 we (Hopkins and Josserand) were in Palenque to attend the Third Palenque Round Table and to begin our fieldwork on the Chol language. After Merle Greene Robertson introduced us to Ausencio Cruz Guzmán (Chencho), we elicited some of the standard word lists and then asked if he knew any stories. Over the next few days he told us a number of stories, including this one about Earth Owner in his guise as an old man who visits Palenque to drink with a poor but honest man. He is referred to as Lak Tyaty, "Our Father," but this is just a polite way to refer to or address a respected male.

The Earth Lord is known all over Mesoamerica. He is known to the Chols as yum witz, "Owner/Lord of the Mountain(s)," and he also appears in these stories under the names Don Juan (Mr. John) and Lak Mam (Our Grandfather). To the Tzotzil he is yahval balamil "Earth Owner" (Vogt 1969). He is Witz-'ak'lik "mountain plain" and Cu:l Taq'a "mountain valley" to the Chuj and Kekchi (both terms metonyms for "the Earth"; Hopkins, field notes; Carlson and Eachus 1977). Outside the Maya area he is known as Labijna Guijuala and Taba Yucu "Owner of the Mountain" to the Tequistlatecs and the Mixtecs (Turner and Turner 1971; Romney and Romney 1966), and he is the Central Mexican "rain god" Tlaloc (a name derived from *tlalli* "earth").

The morals expressed by this story are central to Chol religious practice and, for that matter, everyday life. Do what you are told (by elders and other authorities, including supernaturals), a principle also expressed in Our Grandfather, where the

DOI: 10.5876/9781607324881.c009

violator was struck by a lightning bolt. And don't take anything that doesn't belong to you, more forcefully expressed in The Messengers, where the guilty party loses his life because he ate forbidden food.

We published an early version of this story in *Third Palenque Round Table, 1978; Part 2* (Robertson 1980:116–23) and dedicated it to Dennis Puleston, whom we had just met. Dennis was an archaeologist with an interest in caves who was struck down by lightning at Chichén Itzá, just after the Palenque meetings.

THE CAVE OF DON JUAN

Ty'añ Jiñi Yotyoty Don Juan
Ausencio Cruz Guzmán (Josserand, Hopkins, and Cruz Guzmán 1978a)

Wajali tyi wajali,	1	A long time ago,
'añ 'ab'i wiñik b'ä		they say there was a man who was
laj tyaty don Juan.		Our Father Don Juan.
Don Juan, wajali kuxuläch 'ab'i,		Don Juan, a long time ago, was really alive,
mi yälob'.	5	they say.
'Ili Palenke, wajali 'alä tyejlum,		Palenque, a long time ago, was a little town,
mach kolem tyejklumik b'ajche wäle.		not a big town like it is now.
'I komo wajali,		And since long ago,
jiñi lak tyaty don Juan yujil 'ab'i lemb'al,		Our Father Don Juan drank liquor, they say,
mu 'ab'i yajñeltyak 'ilayi.	10	he used to come down here all the time.
Che 'ab'i,		They say that
ya' ñojab'ä laj tyaty.		then he was short, Our Father.
Ya' tyamtyak 'i tzuktyi';		Then his beard was long;
mero ya' säkix 'ab'i tzuktyi',		then his beard was already white,
säkix 'i jol tz'itya'.	15	his hair was already a little white.
'Entonses,		So,
mu 'ab'i yajñeltyak,		he used to come down all the time,
mi yajñel.		he would come down.
Komo 'añ 'ab'i lak tyaty		Since they say he was Our Father,
mero ñoxix b'ä lak tyaty wajali.	20	he was old, Our Father, a long time ago.
Buen pobre.		[And he saw a man who was] really poor.
'I tzi k'elb'eñ 'i wokolel,		And he saw his trouble,
'i tzi k'ele 'i puñtyiñtyel.		and he saw his suffering.
Tzi k'ele ke weñ wiñik,		He saw that he was a good man,
'i mi k'otyel tyi yotyoty,	25	and he would arrive at his house,
mi yotzañ tyi we'el,		he would go in and eat,
mi yotzañ tyo jab' lemb'al,		he would go in and drink, too,
mi yäk'eñ 'i majtyañ lemb'al.		he would give him a gift of liquor.
'I jiñ cha'añ,		And for that reason,

tzi k'uxb'iñ jiñ don Juan.	30	Don Juan took pity on him.
Tzi sub'eñ, "B'ajche' mi kaje,		He said, "How does he do it?
mi kaj tyi we'el."		How does he manage to eat?"
Porke mi k'el ke weñ pobre,		Because he saw that he was really poor,
mañik chu''i k'äñib'al.		there was nothing he could do.
Lo 'añich ka tza' chu''añ,	35	In vain he had very little,
pero mi b'ajb'eñ 'e'tyel,		but he worked alone,
cha'añ jach mi jap lemb'al,		because he just drank it up,
cha'añ mi jap tyi lemb'al,		because he drank liquor,
mi komo japob' tyi lemb'al.		they just drank liquor.
'I komo mi k'elb'eñ 'i k'uxlel jiñi wiñik,	40	And since he saw the poverty of that man;
cha'añ,		for that reason
'añ 'ab'i 'i majtyañ mi yäk'eñ 'ab'i wiñike.		they say there were gifts he would give him.
Jiñ cha'añ tzi kuxb'eñ jiñi don Juan.		For that reason Don Juan took pity on him.
'I tzi yäk'etyak 'i majtyañ chityam,		And he would give him lots of gifts of pigs,
'i majtyañ muty,	45	his gifts of chickens,
'i majtyañ tyak'iñ,		his gifts of money,
chu'tyak,		everything,
me', chu'tyak 'ab'i, tzi yäk'e.		deer, anything, they say, he gave to him.
'I wajali,		And long ago,
mu jach 'ab'i 'i majlel	50	they say he would just go
'ila tyi pañlum.		there to the graveyard.
'A ko 'añ 'alä tz'ityak jamil		And there was a little clearing
ya' weñ 'utz'atyax,		it was very pretty there,
ya' 'alä jamil, b'a jamäl.		there was a little grass there, in good weather.
Ya jach mi k'otyelob',	55	They would just go there,
mi k'oty jiñi lak tyaty don Juan.		Our Father Don Juan would go there.
Mi mutz' 'i wuty.		He [the man] would close his eyes.
Mi ki 'i kañ 'i wuty,		When he opened his eyes,
yax 'añ tyi mal yotyoty		there he was inside the house of
lak tyaty Juan.	60	Our Father Juan.
'Entonse,		Then,
tza kaji 'i sub'eñ don Juan,		Don Juan would say,
"Chuki 'a wom, 'alä?		"What do you want, child?
Chuka 'a wom, kal?		What do you want, my son?
'A wom chityam?	65	Do you want a pig?
'A wom muty?		Do you want a chicken?
'A wom chu' b'u 'a wom,		Want whatever you want,
jatyety ma k'el.		whatever you see.
Chu' b'u 'a wom,		Whatever it is you want,

<table>
<tr><td>

'a ch'äm majlel."
'Entonse,
mañik chu' tzi mula,
jiñi jach tzi mula
'i käch jiñi chijmay,
tzi wa' tyujk'a juñ p'e laso,
tzi loñ k'ele,
pero mach lasojik;
lukum.
'A che jiñi,
tzi wa' kächb'e ya' tyi b'ik',
tza ki tyujk'añ majlel.
"Weno, mutz'ux 'a wuty.
Wäle, mux ka cha' majlel.
Kukux, 'añix 'a majtyañ.
Pero 'ili 'a we'el,
wo b'ä käk'eñety,
mach mejlik 'a choñ.
Mach mejlik 'a b'a' 'a majtyañ 'ak'.
Mi majki yom we'el,
majki yom 'i k'ux,
la tyo 'i k'uxob' ya' tya wotyoty,
lat yo 'i b'uk'ob', ya' tya wotyoty,
pero mach 'añ mak 'aja majtyañ 'ak'
tyi yambä 'otyoty,
porke mach mañik
maj mi sub'eñoñlaj.
Mañik mach 'añ 'i wenta
yambä 'otyoty.
Si mach tzi k'uxu waj
mach 'i wenta joñlaj.
'Entonse, jiñ cha'añ mik sub'eñety."
'A komo mañik,
pejtye 'ora mi ch'äm majlel me',
mi ch'äm majlel 'i chityam,
'i mi k'ux ya' tyi 'otyoty.
'A mañik,
jiñi yijñam
tza kaj tyi k'otyel 'i tyaty, 'i ña',
tza ki 'i sub'eñ 'i k'ux 'i waj, chu'b'u.

</td><td>

70   you take it."
So,
there wasn't anything he wanted,
he just wanted
to tie up a deer,
75   he tied it up with a rope
that he thought he saw,
but it wasn't a rope at all,
it was a snake.
So it was,
80   he tied it around its neck,
he started to take it away.
"Okay, close your eyes already.
Now, you're going to go again.
Go on, you have your gift.
85   But this is your food
that I am giving you,
you can't sell it.
You can't give it away.
If someone wants food,
90   someone wants to eat it,
let them eat it there in your house,
let them drink, there in your house,
but it is not meant to be a gift
to some other house,
95   because there is not
anyone who tells us to.
There is nobody with the responsibility
for another household.
If they didn't eat a meal
100   it's not our responsibility.
So, for that reason, I'm telling you this."
Ah, but no,
all the time he took deer,
he took his pigs,
105   and he would eat there at home.
Ah, no,
his wife,
when her father, her mother, would arrive,
she would tell them to eat the food,
     whatever.

</td></tr>
</table>

Pero, "B'aki mi la puñtyuñtyaj,"	110	But "Where did you get it?"
che'eñ 'i ña', 'i tyaty.		said her mother, her father.
Pero, "Mach kujilaj b'aki mi tyaj."		But "I don't know where he finds it."
'A che jiñi,		So it was,
wowoli 'i chäñ k'ux,		they would just eat it,
woli k'ux;	115	they ate it,
mañik mi k'ajtyib'eñ tyi 'i tyojol.		they didn't ask about its price.
Pero, "Majtyañ jach, 'ab'i,		But "It's a present, they say,
chañ jach mach mi majtyañ 'ak.'"		so I can't give it away."
'A mañik,		Ah, no,
jiñi yijñam,	120	his wife,
koñ tzax lujb'i 'i k'ajtyib'eñ 'i ñoxi'al.		she got tired of asking her husband.
"Mach mejk sub'eñety,		"I can't tell you,
mach mejk sub'eñety,		I can't tell you,
porke mañik 'orden mik sub'eñety.		because I don't have permission to tell you.
K'uxu 'a waj;	125	Eat your food;
la laj k'ux," loñ che'eñ.		let's eat," he would just say.
'A mañik,		Ah, no,
tzi tyajb'e 'i yora,		the time came,
tza kaji yäl 'i yijñam,		his wife began to say,
"Repente, mach lekojik	130	"After all, it can't be bad
mik tz'itya' 'ak'eñ 'i majtyañ kña',		if I give a little gift to my mother,
mik tz'ijtya' majtyañ 'ak'eñ		if I give a little gift
majch mi tyilel."		to someone who comes to visit."
Tzi wa' k'o' 'ak'eñ 'i majtyañ yamb'ä wiñik,		She gave a gift to another man,
yamb'ä x'ixik, jula',	135	another woman, a visitor,
tzi yäk'e.		she gave it to them.
'A che jiñ,		So it was,
tza kaj tyi cha' lemb'al,		He came to drink liquor again,
'ub'i lak tyaty don Juan,		Our Father Don Juan,
tza majli.	140	they left.
"Weno,		"Okay,
wäle kom ty'añ 'awik'oty;		now I want to talk with you;
koñlaj.		let's go.
Laj majlel tyi ty'añ tyi kotyoty,"		We're all going to talk at my house,"
che'eñ lak tyaty don Juan.	145	said Our Father Don Juan.
"Koy," che ja' wiñiki.		"Okay," said the man.
Tza kajiyob' tyi majlel,		They started off,
mero yäkix ja'el lak tyaty don Juan.		and Don Juan was already very drunk.
Tza majliyob' b'a 'alä jamil,		There went to where the little clearing was,
'ila tyi pañlum, tyi pañlumi.	150	there in the graveyard, in the graveyard.

Tza k'otyiyob' ya' tyi pañlumi,
"Mutz'u 'a wuty,"
che'eñ 'i sub'eñ lak tyaty don Juan.
Tzi wa' mutz'u 'i wutyi;
tza ki kañ 'i wuty.
Tza tyejchi ya' tyi kañ 'i wutyi,
pero yax 'añ tyi mal 'otyoty;
mach tzi k'ele b'ajche' tza k'otyi.
Jiñ jach, tza ki k'el,
yax 'añ tyi yotyoty laj Juan.
'A che jiñi,
tza ki 'i sub'eñ,
"Tzak sub'ety,
mach mejk 'a majtyañ 'ak';
mach mejk 'a choñ jiñi 'a we'el,
porke 'a majtyañ.
Joñoñlaj,
mañik mach la wentajik
yambä 'otyoty,
porke laj wentajiki.
Mach yoñk lak laj käk'eñ
mach 'i k'ux 'ili kälak,"
loñ che' tzi sub'e.
"Pero mak tza käk'e."
"Mañik,
pero jiñ tzi yäk'ä 'a wijñam.
Wäle,
koñ tzaj k'ele 'a päñtyiñtyel,
mañix 'a b'ujk,
mañix chu 'añ 'a cha'añ,
pejtye tzax jili,
lo 'añich ka 'a we'el,
pero mañix 'a b'ujk,
mañix chu' ma k'äñ 'a mäñ 'a b'ujk,
loñ kitz'i jok'oletyix.
Weno, mi käk'eñety,
wäle mi käk'eñety tyak'iñ.
Pero 'ili tyak'iñ,
chañ jach me ma k'äñ tyo mäñoñel;
chañ jach ma k'äñ chu' ma mäñ.
'A mäñ 'a b'ujk,

They arrived there at the graveyard,
"Close your eyes,"
so Our Father Don Juan told him.
He quickly closed his eyes;
155 he opened his eyes.
He woke up there when he opened his eyes,
but there he was already inside the house;
he didn't see how he got there.
Just so, he saw
160 there he was in the house of our Juan.
So it was,
he started to tell him,
"I told you,
you couldn't give it away;
165 you couldn't sell your food,
because it was your gift.
Of all of us,
none of us has responsibility
for another household,
170 because we have our own responsibilities.
It's not right for us to give away
my animals for someone to eat,"
so he said.
"But I didn't give any away."
175 "No,
but your wife gave it away.
Now,
since I saw your poverty,
you don't have a shirt,
180 you don't have anything of your own,
everything is worn out;
you might have food,
but you have no shirt,
you have nothing you can buy a shirt with,
185 everything you have is patched and mended.
Okay, I'm going to give you something,
now I'm going to give you money.
But that money,
it's just for you to use for purchases;
190 it's just for you to use to buy things.
Buy yourself a shirt,

'a mäñ 'a pislel.		buy yourself some clothes.
Pero mach mi kaj 'a majtyañ 'ak',		But don't start giving it away,
porke 'ili tyak'iñ		because that money
woli käk'eñety cha'añ ma k'äñ.	195	I am giving it to you for you to use.
Porke wolij k'el 'a puñtyiñtyel.		Because I see your poverty.
K'ux mi kub'iñety,		I care for you,
porke jatyety,		because you,
weñ k'ux tza wub'iyoñ ja'el;		you cared for me as well;
b'ajche' jay p'e 'ora tzajñoñ,	200	whenever I came,
pejtye 'ora ma wäk'eñoñ kmajtyañ lemb'al,		you always gave me my gift of liquor,
kmajtyañ waj.		my gift of food.
'Entonse,		So,
juñ lajal mik tyob'eñety ja'el.		in the same way I am paying you also.
Mi käk'eñety 'a majtyañ tyak'iñ,	205	I'm giving you your gift of money,
chu' b'ä," che'eñ.		whatever," he said.
Tza ki sub'eñ don Juan,		Don Juan told him,
"Wäle, ma päy majlel 'ili xña' me';		"Now, call out that doe;
mi jkächb'eñety ma ch'äm majlel.		I'll catch her so you can take her away.
Jiñi, che' b'a 'ora mi tyijkañ 'i chikiñ	210	She, any time she shakes her ears
che' tyi yojlil 'ak'älel,		in the middle of the night,
kaña meko 'a wuty,		open your eyes, wake up,
mu me tyi 'i tyijkañ jub'el jiñi tyak'iñ.		because she shakes out money.
Tziñla mi ki jub'el.		It will tinkle as it falls.
'Entonse, che jiñi,	215	So, it's like this,
'antes ke mi säk'ajel,		before it gets light,
mux meku 'a tyejchañ 'a loty jiñi tyak'iñ,		you must get up and gather the money,
cha mach mi k'elob' b'a ma ka loty jiñi tyak'iñ."		so that nobody will see where you got it."
'A che jiñi,		Ah, so it was,
tza kaj tyi tyejchel ja' wiñik;	220	the man would wake up,
ñich'ñayix,		the night would be calm,
'i woch' 'i ñich'tyañ ja' pañimil,		he would be listening to the world,
che mi ki 'i tyijkañ 'i chikiñ jiñi me.		when the doe would begin to shake her ears.
Mañik,		No,
tza kaji 'i yub'iñ	225	he would be listening
wox 'i tyijkañ 'i chikiñ ja'e me'.		for the deer to shake her ears.
Tziñla jub'e ja' tyak'iñ;		Tinkling the money would fall;
tza majli b'äk' loty ja' wiñiki.		the man would quickly go gather it.
'I wa' b'uty' tyi moral,		He quickly filled his bag,
chu'tyak tzi wum b'uty'u.	230	whatever he found he would fill it.
'A mañik,		Ah, no,

ko 'añix cha'p'e,		there would soon be some two
'ux p'e 'alä koxtyal.		or three little sacks.
Ko 'añix 'i tyak'iñ,		Since he now had money,
tzi k'ele ja' yijñami,	235	his wife saw it,
tzi wersa k'ajtyib'eñ,		and she had to ask him,
"B'aki tza tyaja tyak'iñ?		"Where did you find money?
Kasä 'añ laj tyak'iñ 'ili,		You don't mean that money is ours,
b'aj tza ka' tyaj."		where did you find it?"
"Mañik, tza ktyaja kmajtyañ,"	240	"No, I found my gift,"
loñ che'eñ wiñik.		the man just said.
Pero mach tzi ñopo 'añ x'ixiki.		But the woman didn't believe him.
Tza ki wersa k'ajtyiñ.		She had to keep on asking.
'A mañik,		Ah, no,
tza k'oty 'i ña'.	245	her mother arrived.
Tza ki sub'eñ, "Wäle, kab'älix ktyak'iñlojoñ.		She told her, "Now, we have a lot of money.
Mach pobrejoñix lojoñ.		We aren't poor anymore.
Wäle, ma wom tyak'iñ,		Now, if you want money,
ch'ämä jiñ,		take it,
ya' 'añ tyak'iñ,	250	there is money there,
ya' 'añ cha' p'e koxtyal jiñi tyak'iñ.		there are two bags of money there.
B'uty'u 'a moral;		Fill your shoulder bag;
b'uty'u 'a chim.		fill up a bag.
Ch'ämä majlel," che' tzi sub'e 'i ña'.		Take it," she told her mother.
"Koy," che ja' 'i ña'.	255	"Okay," said her mother.
Tza kaj 'i wa' b'uty' 'i moral,		She would fill up her shoulder bag,
tza kaji b'uty' 'i chim;		she would fill up her bag,
tzi b'uty'u tyak'iñ;		she filled them with money;
tza'ix meko 'i ch'äm majlel.		she took it away.
'A che jiñ,	260	So it was,
tza 'i ch'ämä majlel 'i tyak'iñi.		she took that money away.
Komo kab'äl tyak'iñ tzi k'ele ja'el jiñi x'ixiki,		Since that woman saw so much money,
tza ki yäk'eñ 'i ña'.		she started giving it to her mother.
'A, tza majli 'i ña'.		Ah, the mother left.
Tzi b'äk' b'uty'u;	265	She quickly filled her bags,
tza majli.		and left.
'A che jiñi,		So it was,
tza k'otyi 'ub'i lak tyaty don Juan.		Our Father Don Juan arrived.
Tza ki sub'eñ,		He told him,
"Koñ laj;	270	"Let's go;
wäle, ma ka majlel ya' tyi kotyoty;		now, you're going there to my house;
kom ty'añ 'a wik'oty.		I want to talk with you.

Ma majlel; wäle, ma majlel,"
che'eñ don Juan.
Che jeñ,
tza tyejchi 'ub'i wiñiki.
Tza ki 'i sub'eñ 'i ña',
"Mi kaj 'i lok'el."
'A, mañik chuk tzi sub'e;
che jach ñich'ña tza majli.
"Tza majliyoñ ya' tyi pañlumi,"
tza kaji sub'eñ.
"Wäle, mutz'u 'a wuty,"
che'eñ don Juan.
"Koy," che'ja' wiñiki.
Tzi wa' mutz'u 'i wuty.
Tza kajñi 'i wutyi,
pero yax 'añ
tyi yotyoty don Juan.
Che jiñi,
tza kaji 'i sub'eñ 'ub'i lak tyaty don Juan,
"Tzak sub'ety, wajali tzak sub'ety.
Mik käk'eñety chu' mi käk'eñety;
'a majtyañ tza käk'ety.
Tza kcha' 'ak'ety jiñi me'
chañ ma tyaj 'a tyak'iñ,
chañ ma mäñ 'a wom.
Pero mak tza ksub'ety
chañ ma majtyañ 'ak',
chañ ma majtyañ 'ak'eñ
majch ma majtyañ 'ak'eñ.
Pero jiñ 'a wijñam, mak tzi jak'ä.
Tzi wa' 'ak'e 'i majtyañ 'i tyak'iñ 'i ña';
tzi wa' b'uty'b'e 'i moral;
tzi b'uty'b'e 'i chim.
Wäle, ma k'otyel,
mañix 'a tyak'iñ.
Pero koñ tzax tyiliyety 'ila tyi kotyoty,
wäle, ch'ämä majlel 'a majtyañ.
Päyä majlel 'a chityam,
chu' b'u 'a wom.
Chuki 'a wom;
jay kojty 'a wom,"

275

280

285

290

295

300

305

310

You're going; now, you're going,"
said Don Juan.
So it was,
the man got up.
He told his mother,
"I'm going out."
Ah, no, he didn't say anything;
he just quietly left.
"I went there to the graveyard,"
he told him.
"Now, close your eyes,"
said Don Juan.
"Okay," said the man.
He quickly closed his eyes.
When he opened his eyes,
he was already there
in the house of Don Juan.
So it was,
Don Juan started to tell him,
"I told you, a long time ago I told you.
I give you what I give you;
your gifts I gave to you.
Again I gave you that deer
so you would find some money,
so you could buy what you wanted.
But I didn't tell you
that you could give it away.
that you could give it away
to whoever you gave it to.
But your wife, she didn't understand.
Right away she gave a gift to her mother;
right away she filled her shoulder bag;
she filled up her bag.
Now, when you arrive
there won't be any money anymore.
But since you came here to my house,
now, take away your gift.
Call out a pig,
whatever you want.
What do you want?
How many animals do you want?"

loñ che'eñ.		he told him.
Tzi loñ 'ak'e juñ kojty chityam.	315	He just gave him one pig.
Tzi wa' kächb'e;		He tied it up for him;
tzi päyä tyilel.		he led it to him.
"Mutz'u 'a wuty,"		"Close your eyes,"
loñ che'eñ.		he said.
Chä'ixtyo 'añ che jiñi.	320	So it was like that.
Pero tzi wa' mutz'u 'i wuty,		But right away he closed his eyes,
'i tza juli tyilel.		and he came back.
Jiñi jax,		So it was,
tza ki k'el 'ab'i 'añ wiñikob'i.		some men saw him, they say.
Loñ kotyañob' 'i päy majlel,	325	They just helped him lead it,
päy k'otyel 'i yälak' tyi yotyoty,		they led the animal to his house,
pero mach mi ña'tyañob' b'ajche mi tyaj.		but they didn't know where he got it.
'I jiñ 'i cha'añ,		And for that reason,
mero tz'a mi k'elob' ja' wiñikob',		those men looked at him with anger,
kom mach mi mejle 'i chukob' 'ajñel.	330	since they couldn't grasp it.
"B'ajche mi tyaj?"		"Where does he find them?"
loñ che'ob'.		they asked in vain.
'I che jiñi.		And so it was.
Tza ki 'i chijtyañob'.		They started to follow him.
Tza ki 'i chijtyañob';	335	they started to follow him;
joyokña 'i chijtyañob',		they followed him around,
yub'iñob'.		they eavesdropped.
"Jala mi lok'el,		"Whenever he goes out,
b'ajche mi majlel,		wherever he goes,
b'ajche mi majlel,	340	wherever he goes,
la laj ty'um majlel."		we will all follow him."
'A kom wajali,		Ah, but before,
mutyo 'i mutz' 'i wuty,		he would just close his eyes,
mi loñ majlel.		and just go there.
Pero che jiñi,	345	But then,
tzi sub'e lak tyaty Juan,		Our Father Juan told him,
"Kojix meko ma tyilel, porke wäle.		"This is the last time you come, now.
K'elex b'ajche ma tyilel,		We'll see how you come,
b'ajche ma xäñ tyilel,		how you come walking,
porke mak tza jak'ä	350	because you wouldn't listen to
chu' tza ksub'ety.		what I told you.
Wäle, la'ix b'ajche' 'a wom tyilel."		Now, come as best you can."
'Añ che jiñi,		So it was,
tza ki 'i ña'tyañ ja' wiñik,		the man thought about it,

"Pero chex b'ä wä' 'añ 'i tyojel,
b'a tza tyiliyoñtyak wajali;
wu 'añ 'i tyojel mi kub'iñtyak."
'A che jiñi,
tza ki 'i ña'tyañ 'ub'i wiñik.
Tza ki 'i sub'eñ 'i yijñam,
"Wäle, ma wäk'eñoñ sa',
ma wäk'eñoñ chu' mik ch'äm majlel.
Chañ cha' samoñ tyo paxi'al."
'A che jiñ.
"Koy," che' ja' yijñam.
Tzi yäk'e 'i sa', 'i waj, chu' b'u.
Tza lok'i majlel;
weñ 'ik' tyo tza majli.
Tzi ch'ämä majlel 'i yalä machity
'añ b'a tza k'otyi tyi wa'tyil
tyi yañtyakb'ä 'ora
che mi mutz' 'i wutyi.
Ya' tza ki k'el 'i yäk'eñ 'i tyojel.
Che jiñ,
tza ki tzep majlel 'i yalä b'ijlel;
'i tzep 'i yalä b'ijlel.
Tza k'otyi.
Jiñ jax tza ki k'el
lak tyaty don Juan.
Yax k'otyeli,
tza ki sub'eñ,
"Wäle, chuki tza tyili 'a mel?
Tzak sub'ety,
max ma ch'äm tyilel,
pero kom mak tza jak'ä,
wäle, chuki 'a wom?" che'eñ.
"Mañik,
tzak tyili jk'ajtyiñ perdon,
chañ ma puñtyañoñ,
repente mi mux tyo 'a puñtyañoñ,
porke komo mañix chu' 'añ
cha'añ tza k'otyiyoñ,
mañix tyak'iñ,
koñ chich b'ajche tza wälä,
che mij k'otyili

355　"But it seems like this is the right direction,
where I used to come all the time;
This is the way I was told so many times."
So it was,
the man started to think about it.
360　He told his wife,
"Now, give me some pozol,
give me something to take with me.
Because I'm about to go out again."
So it was.
365　"Okay," said his wife.
She gave him his pozol, whatever.
He went out;
it was still dark when he left.
He took his little machete
370　to the place he had gone to stand
so many times
when he would close his eyes.
There he began to see the path he had taken.
So it was,
375　he started to cut out a little path;
he cut out a little path.
He got there.
Our Father Don Juan
just looked at him.
380　As soon as he arrived,
he told him,
"Now, what did you come to do?
I told you,
you aren't going to take anything,
385　but since you didn't understand,
now, what do you want?" he said.
"Nothing,
I came to ask your pardon,
so you will take pity on me,
390　to see if you won't still take pity on me,
because since there wasn't anything left
when I got home,
there was no money,
just like you said,
395　when I got there,

mañix tyak'iñ.
Loñ chich kuyi;
mañix chu' añ.
Tyo' joch koxtyalix tza k'otyi jk'el.
'Wäle, mañix tyak'iñ,' loñ cho'oñ;
tzak sub'e kijñam.
Tza majli k'el ja'el;
joch koxtyalix."
"Weno.
Wäle, kojix meko ma tyilel che jiñi;
päyix majlel 'a chityam;
jay kojty 'a wom, 'a päy majlel."
"K'eb'oñix tyi juñ kojty,
tyik'i mi k'eb'oñix,
kom mañix mik mejle jch'äm majlel.
K'eb'oñix tyi juñ kojty,"
loñ che'eñ.
Tzi wa' käche juñ kojty 'i chityam
lak tyaty don Juan.
Tzi wa' päyä tyilel;
tza k'otyi tyi yotyoty.
Tza ki 'i mel, 'i mel.
Lujb'i 'i chijtyañob' ja' wiñikob',
koñ tzi k'ele ke b'ajche mi tyaj.
Tza'ix meku kaji chijtyañob';
tza ki yub'iñob',
'i yorajlel che mi kaj tyi majlel,
lok'el majlel.
Tzax meku kaji 'i ty'umob'.
Tza ki k'elb'eñob' 'i yalä b'ijlel.
"Wä' tza majli," loñ che'ob' wäle.
Tza ki ty'umob' majlel.
Che' yomix k'otyel jiñi 'ub'i wiñiki,
tza ki k'el 'i patyi.
Yax tyilelob'.
Kab'älel wiñik.
Tza ki ña'tyañ wiñik,
"Wäle, mux ki yub'iñob' 'ili,
mach ka la' cho'oñ," tzak sub'e.
"B'ä job'ix 'i b'ä;
tza tyiliyob' 'i tzaj kañoñob'

there was no money anymore.
That's the way it was;
there was nothing left.
Just empty bags was what I arrived to see.

400   'Now, there isn't money anymore,' I said;
I told my wife.
She went to see as well;
empty bags was all."
"Okay.

405   Now, this is the last time you come here, so
call out your pig;
however many you want, call them out."
"One is more than enough,
maybe one is enough,

410   since I can't carry more.
One is more than enough,"
he said.
Our Father Don Juan
quickly tied up a pig.

415   He led it off;
he arrived at his house.
He started to prepare it; he prepared it.
The men had tired of tracking him,
but they saw where he found it.

420   They had started tracking him;
they eavesdropped;
and whenever he went out,
they went out.
They were following him.

425   They saw his little trail.
"He went here," they said now.
They went following him.
Just when he was about to get there,
he looked over his shoulder.

430   There they came.
A lot of men.
He started to understand,
"Now, they know already,
but I didn't tell them," he said.

435   "They did it all by themselves;
they came and spotted me

'a tza k'otyiyoñ tyi 'otyotyi.
Loñ tyojächka tza 'ochiyoñ 'aja',
pero tza kaj jk'eli ya' seletyak lukum.
'Añtyak k'äñchoj.   440
Jiñi jax tza kaj k'eli,
tza ki ch'ojob'.
K'äñchoj,
jiñi jax tzi k'eleyob' añ wiñikob',
'ub'i k'äñchoj,   445
tyejchiyob' majlel 'i laj k'uxuyob' 'ub'i wiñik.
Che jiñi.
Kojix meku tza k'otyiyoñ.
Jiñix meku yorajlel,
che tza laj tyiliyob'.   450
Ma che ku 'añix tza chäñ k'otyiyoñ ja'el.
Jiñix meku b'u 'ora.
Wajali,
jamä tyo jiñ 'i tyi' 'i yotyoty
'ila tyi 'eñtyil.   455
Che tza tzax 'ujtyi lojoñ tyi ty'añ yik'oty,
koñ kojixb'ä tza k'otyiyoñ ja'el,
koñ ñoxoñix ja'el,
tzax meku kaj tyi mäkel tyi' yotyotyi wäle.
'Añtyo ku tyi' 'otyotyi,   460
pero 'añix tyo chañ.
Mux lak xoy lak b'ijlel;
lak letzel ya' tyi pam tyek'oñib'.
Tyek'oñib'ix lak letzeltyak;
letzeltyak ya' tyi tyi' 'otyotyi.   465
Lak letzeli;
mi laj cha' jub'el;
che jach meku b'ajche jiñi.
K'älä wäle,
'añix tyo majch mi k'otyel   470
pero tyo tz'uk' ñichim,
'ak' lemb'al, chu'tyak,
chañ jach mi k'ajtyiñob',
chu' b'u, chuki mi kole 'i cha'añ,
mi k'ajtyiñ chañ mi kole 'i yich,   475
chañ mi kole yixim,
'o chu' mi kolel 'i cha'añ.

when I got to the house.
I just came straight in, uh-huh,
but I saw a bunch of coiled snakes there."
There were many moccasins.
As soon as they saw them,
they began to strike.
Moccasins,
just as soon as they saw those men,
those moccasins,
they rose up and bit them all.
So it was.
That was the last time I went there.
That really was the time,
when they all came.
I never went there again.
That was the time.
A long time ago,
the door to the house was still open
down below.
When we last went to talk to him,
the last time I went as well,
he was old already, too,
he began to close the door of his house then.
There is still a door to the house,
but now it's high up.
We have to go a long way around;
we climb up on ladders.
We climb various times on ladders;
we climb up to the door of the house.
We climb up;
we come down again;
that's just the way it is.
Even now,
there are still people who arrive
but just to burn candles,
offer liquor, whatever,
so that they can ask for
whatever, what they grow for themselves;
they ask for their chiles to grow,
so that their corn will grow,
or whatever is theirs will grow.

Che jax jiñi.		That's the way it is.
Pero k'älä wäle,		But still today,
'añix tyo chu' 'añ.	480	there is still something there.
Pero komo jiñi wajali,		Because since long ago
kab'äl tyo majch mi yochel		a lot of people used to enter
mi lok'sañ jiñi xajlel,		to take out stones,
chu' b'ux ka sañtyu.		things like idols.
Sañtyu,	485	Idols,
yik'oty laj ch'uj tyaty.		and Our Holy Father.
Wajali,		A long time ago,
'añ tyo xchajpayaj;		there were looters;
tzi laj chajpañob' majlel pejtyelel,		they looted everything,
tzi laj xujchiñob' majlel.	490	they stole it and took it away.
'Añ tyo ku ya' 'añ,		There are still a few things,
pero xejty' p'ejty,		but pieces of pots,
'i kolob'al 'i xujty' ñichim jax.		and just the stubs of candles.
Yax 'añ.		Just over there.
Ya' tza jili ty'añ b'ajche jini.	495	There the story ends, like that.

10

A Visit to Don Juan

Mariano Mayo Jiménez and Ausencio Cruz Guzmán

This personal history was recorded by Ausencio Cruz Guzmán (ACG) in the Chol ejido of La Providencia, in the municipio of Salto de Agua, Chiapas. The narrator was Mariano Mayo Jiménez (MMJ), a twenty-five-year-old native of Salto de Agua. The story was told on May 17, 1981, and the events described must have taken place around 1966. Also present at the interview was a woman named María Cruz (MC), who makes only one brief intervention. The text was first transcribed by Cruz Guzmán, who prepared a rough translation to Spanish. An English translation was made from the Spanish and used as a source by Joanne M. Spero in the 1980s, when she was writing her master's thesis on lightning gods under the direction of the late Linda Schele at the University of Texas at Austin. Her translation (Spero 1987:135–39) was consulted in preparing this version in the summer of 2007.

This is the story of a visit to the cave of Don Juan to ask for rain. Don Juan is one of the guises of the Earth Lord, who also appears as the rain god Chajk and the lightning god Lak Mam. This multifaceted deity is best approached in the limestone caves that are ubiquitous in the Chol region. Each of the caves has its attendants and its particular place in the ceremonial life of the Chols and other local people. A small shelter cave on a mountain facing Tila has become associated with the Black Christ of Tila and plays a central role in Chiapas and Tabasco Catholicism, drawing pilgrims from distant locales (Josserand and Hopkins 2007). The legitimization of the cave as a site of Christian worship has in effect legitimized all cave worship in the Chol area, including offerings directed to Don Juan. No

DOI: 10.5876/9781607324881.c010

one sees any contradiction in going to Catholic mass and then to a cave to pray for rain or other desires. As Oliver LaFarge's informants in Santa Eulalia told him, they practice the whole religion, not just partial religion—not just the offical church activities, not just the traditional cave-centered practices, but both (La Farge 1947).

The Tila cave and several other nearby caves are visited by shamans-in-training in a ritual sequence that ends at the Joljá or Joloniel caves near Tumbalá (Bassie 2001). Major caves related to rain petitions are found throughout the mountain range known as the Sierra de Don Juan, between Palenque and Tumbalá. Since many of these caves are known locally as "the cave of Don Juan," we once asked a Chol informant how they could all be "Don Juan's cave." He thought for a minute and then replied, "Es que tiene muchos despachos" (The fact is, he has a lot of branch offices).

In this long narrative, after Mariano has finished his tale, Chencho takes the lead and begins to tell a short version of The Cave of Don Juan, but now he relates it as a story told to him personally by the man Don Juan befriended. This inspires Mariano to recall more details.

A Visit to Don Juan

Una Visita a Don Juan
Mariano Mayo Jiménez [MMJ]
with Ausencio Cruz Guzmán [ACG] (Mayo Jiménez 1980)

ACG: *'Ili ty'añ mu b'u kaj käl,*	1	ACG: This story we're going to tell you,
'iliyi, tza 'ujtyi 'añix wäle		this, it took place now
komo jo'lum p'e jab'.		about fifteen years ago.
'Alä tyo 'ili Mariano.		Mariano was a young boy still.
MMJ: *Wajali che' ya tyo 'añoñ . . .*	5	MMJ: A long time ago, when I was still . . .
ya tyo 'añoñ b'añ kerañob'		when I was still where my brothers are
tyi Paso Naranjoji,		in Paso Naranjo,
'i koñ . . . en el Paso Naranjo . . .		and so . . . in Paso Naranjo . . .
koñ mi yälob' ke 'añ 'ab'i		since they say that there was [a certain]
San Juañ 'ab'i,	10	San Juan, they say,
b'añ laj k'ajtyiñ chu' pejtye laj k'ajtyiñ.		where we asked for everything we asked for.
'Añ wajali che' b'ajche' laj mel laj chol.		A long time ago that's how we made milpa.
Che' b'ajche' mak mi seb' tye' [tyilel] ja'al,		Since the rain didn't come soon enough,
mi chämel laj chol.		our milpa was dying.
'I tza kub'i lojoñ	15	And we heard—
ñaxañ tzajñi juñ tyikil		first one man came,
jiñi jyumijel lojoñ,		an uncle of ours,
'i tza juli 'i sub'eñoñ lojoñ		and he came and told us
ke "Weñäch," che'eñ,		that "okay," he said,

"Koñ laj,"
tza k'otyi 'i yäle.
'I che jiñi,
tza' i tyempañob' 'i bä
jyumijelob' yik'oty kerañob'i,
"Koñ laj k'ajtyiñ ja'al chañ laj chol.
Mañik ka laj k'ux 'ixim.
Woli 'i laj chämel laj kixim,
chañ weñ kab'äl jajmel,
koñ weñ kab'äl jajmel ja'el.
Cha' p'e 'uj,
pejtyelel abril yik'oty mayo,"
che'eñ.
Tza majliyoñ lojoñ,
tza majyoñ [majliyoñ] ja'el,
koñ 'alob'oñ tyo,
chañ k'ajalix jcha'añ.
Che jiñi,
"Jmajle ja'el," che'oñ.
"Chuk 'a majl 'a mel, 'aha?
Weñ ñajty. Weñ 'añ witz,"
che' tzi sub'eñoñ.
"Che muk a k'otye, ma wub'iñ,"
che tzi sub'eñoñ.
"Muku mi jk'otyel."
"Koñ laj," che'eñ,
che 'añ kerañob'.
Majliyoñ lojoñ,
tzi mäñob' majlel
jum p'e litro lemb'al
yik'o jum p'e pakete ñichim,
yik'o juñ kojty 'i mutyob',
tza majyoñ lojoñ.
'I sujmäch,
ñajtyäch,
'i puru witzäch,
ñajtyäch, tza kub'i.
Tzäch k'otyiyoñ lojoñ,
k'otyiyoñ komo las kwatro la tarde.
Che jiñi,
k'otyiyoñ lojoñ b'añ yotyoty

20 "Let's go,"
he came and told us.
And so it was,
they got themselves together,
my uncles and my brothers,
25 "Let's go ask for rain for our milpas.
We're not going to have corn to eat.
Our corn is all dying,
because there is a really big drought,
since there is a really big drought, too.
30 Two months,
all of April and May,"
they said.
We all went.
I went, too,
35 although I was small,
I still remember.
So it was,
"I'm going, too," I said.
"What are you going to do, huh?
40 It's a long way. It's very mountainous,"
so they told me.
"So you think you'll get there?"
so they said to me.
"I certainly will get there."
45 "Let's go," they said,
said my brothers.
We all went;
they went to buy
a liter of aguardiente
50 and a package of candles,
and a chicken,
and we all left.
And it was really true,
it was a long way,
55 and all mountains;
a long way, it seemed.
We all arrived there,
we arrived about four in the afternoon.
So it was,
60 we arrived at the house of

jiñi sañ kristañ, mi yälob'i.
K'otyi jpejkañ lojoñ.
ACG: *¿B'aki 'añ 'añ sakristañ?*
MMJ: *Ya'añ tyi 'Aktyepa' Yochib',*
mi yälob'. Jum p'e Yochib'.
"¿Chuki la wom?" che' 'ab'i laj tyaty ñox.
"Mañik. Tza tyili jpejkañety
mi k'el chañ ma majle 'a ñusäb'eñoñ lojoñ
'ix . . . 'ixi b'añ laj ch'uju tyaty

Sañ Roñ Juañ."
"A, bweno. ¿Tyi la pusik'al woli la tyilel?
Ma ma wub'iñ."
"Jiñäch kuyi mi kub'iñ lojoñ."
"A, bweno. 'Utz'aty che jiñi," che'eñ.
"¿Chuk me woli la k'ajtyiñ, ma wub'iñ?"
"Este . . . kom tyej kaj k'ajtyiñ lojoñ ja'al
chañ jchol lojoñ,
koñ woxi laj, weñ chämel jchol lojoñ.
Mach yomix kolel,
loñ tzax cha' päk'ä lojoñ,
woli 'i cha' chämel,
weñ tzax wäle jajmel.
Jiñ cha'añ tza jpeñsariñ,
yub'ili tza tyi jk'ajtyiñ lojoñ
tz'itya' ja'al.
Koñ mu 'ab'i yäk' . . .
la käk'eñtyel ja'al
che' mi laj k'ajtyiñ 'ab'iyi,
'ila tyi San Ron Juañi,"
che tzi yälä jkerañ yik'o jyumijelob'.
"A weno, yomäch che jiñi.
Weñ chapal tza tyiliyety laj."
"Chapaloñ ku."
"Weno, weno, koñ laj che jiñi.
Pero tyi laj kuleli, laj kulel,
laj mel koleñ k'iñ 'ila tyi kotyotyi,"
che' 'ab'i 'ub'i sañ kristañ.
"Chañ ku yomäch tzax ch'ämä loñ tyilel . . ."
ACG: *Jiñi . . . 'a . . . ¿b'ajche 'i k'ab'a*
'añ jiñi sakristañ che tyi ty'añ?

the sacristan, they call him.
We arrived to make our petition.
ACG: Where was this sacristan?
MMJ: There at Actiepá Yochib,
65 they say. A place called Yochib.
"What do you all want?" said the elder.
"Nothing. We came to ask you
to see if you can go take us
to that . . . that place where Our Holy Father
is,
70 San Don Juan."
"Ah, good. Do you come with your hearts?
Do you feel it?"
"We really do feel it."
"Ah, good. That's good," he said.
75 "What are you asking for?"
"Well . . . since we came to ask for rain
for our milpas,
since it's dying, our milpas are really dead.
They don't want to grow,
80 in vain we planted a second time,
and it is dying again,
it's really a drought now.
So we thought about it,
we felt that we should come ask
85 for a little rain.
Since they say it hasn't . . .
we haven't been given rain,
so we petition, as they say,
here to that San Don Juan,"
90 so said my brothers and my uncles.
"Ah, good, that's what you want.
You all came well prepared."
"We're really prepared."
"Okay, okay, let's go then.
95 But when we return, on our return,
we'll make a big fiesta here in my house,"
said the sacristan.
"It's a good thing we already brought . . ."
ACG: Uh . . . What do you call
100 the sacristan in Chol?

MMJ: *Este, 'i k'ab'a' jiñi b'ajche katekista*
  yub'il,
koñ jiñtza' mi pejkañ cheñ.
ACG: *¿Jiñ kuyi ñusa jty'añ?*

MMJ: *Nusa jty'añ,*
che b'ajche misionero, yub'il.
Che' majleloñ,
"Koñ laj che jiñi," cho'oñ
"Mero ñajtyäch ku," che'eñ,
chañ ku mach chäkäch.
"¿Tza laj ch'eñlel [ch'äm¨tyilel] la poko?"
"Tza ku."
"Weno, koñ laj," chejeñ.
Majyoñ lojoñ chejax k'iñ,
majyoñ loñ ja'el, majyoñ tyak ja'el.
"Wix ma käleli," che'eñ kerañob',
"'ila tyi 'otyotyi, yotyo laj tyatyi,"
che'eñ añ kerañob'i.
"Mañik much jkälä, jmaj ja'e," cho'oñ.
Majyoñ tyak ja'el.
'Ochiyoñ majleli.
Wox tyi b'äjlem 'aj k'iñ
tza k'otyiyoñ lojoñ.
Läpä ch'ikijach ku b'ih,
pero puro b'äjlel tzäch majyoñ lojoñ.
Che b'a tza 'ochiyoñ lojoñ
koleñ b'ujtyil, koleñ 'otyoty yilal.

Pero selekña jach, wolokña jach,
tye'el, ñuke xajlelol.
"Wex 'ilali," che'eñ 'ub'i,
"tza b'u jpejka lojoñ laj tyatyi,
mi yälob."
"'A weno," che'eñ . . . cho'oñ lojoñ.
'Ochiyoñ loñ majlel che ya tyoktyil 'i tyi',
tza 'ochi maj ya che li,
'aya tyi mali, koleñ mal.
ACG: *¿B'ajche ñojal, 'am b'ä jum p'e metro?*
MMJ: *Ñajty mi laj xän majlel, che' ñajtye . . .*
ACG: *¿Jiñ ku 'añ 'i tyi' ch'eñ?*

MMJ: Uh, he was called like a catechist,

it seems, since he's the one who prays.

ACG: He's the one who passes on the
  requests?

MMJ: He passes on the requests, — 105
like a missionary, it seems.
Thus we went,
"Let's go then," we said.
"It's really a long way," he said,
but it really wasn't so much. — 110
"Did you bring your flashlights?"
"We did."
"Okay, let's go," he said.
We all went when the sun was like this,
we all went, too, I went along, too. — 115
"You're going to stay here," said my brothers,
"here in the house, the house of the elder,"
said my brothers.
"No, I'm not staying, I'm going, too," I said.
I went along, too. — 120
We started to go.
The sun was going down
when we got there.
The trail was full of potholes,
and it was a steep drop when we got there. — 125
There where we entered
there was a big hill, it looked like a big
  house.
But it was round, circular,
with trees, and big piles of rocks.
"This is it," that guy said, — 130
"where we petition Our Father,
they say."
"Ah, good," he said . . . we said.
We entered where the mouth was open,
we went in like that, — 135
there inside, it was big inside.
ACG: How big was it? Would it be a meter?
MMJ: We walked a long way, so far . . .
ACG: And the mouth of the cave?

MMJ: *Chäch ku, tyoktyil che li,*　　　　　140　　MMJ: Yes, it was open like this,
tyoktyil che li.　　　　　　　　　　　　　　　　　open like this.
ACG: *Jum p'e metro.*　　　　　　　　　　　　　　ACG: A meter.
MMJ: *Jäjä. Mi cha' ñume 'i ñup'ob' tyi jum*　　　MMJ: Uh-huh. When we came out again
　p'e . . .
yik'o che wechtyil koleñ xajlel.　　　　　145　　they closed it with a . . . with about this size
　　　　　　　　　　　　　　　　　　　　　　　　　of a big rock.
ACG: *'Aja.*　　　　　　　　　　　　　　　　　　ACG: Aha.
MMJ: *Mi ñup'ob' che tza 'ochiyoñ lojoñ*　　　　MMJ: They closed it when we all entered.
　majlel.
"Weno, tzuk'ux la b'ela," che'eñ.　　　　　　　"Okay, light your candles." he said.
Che kälä lojoñ, tzuk'u lojoñ jb'ela.　　　　　　So they told us, to light our candles.
Tzuk'uloñ b'ela, tzaj xäñäloñ majlel,　　　150　　With our candles lit, we walked along,
che b'ajche 'ixi yotyo 'Umberto,　　　　　　　it was about like to Humberto's house,
weñ k'otyiyoñ lojoñ.　　　　　　　　　　　　and we arrived.
'Añ ja'i ya tyi mali,　　　　　　　　　　　　There was water there inside,
'añ 'alä pa',　　　　　　　　　　　　　　　　there was a little stream,
ya mi jub'e tye ja',　　　　　　　　　155　　there water was falling,
pero tzuwañ 'a ja'i,　　　　　　　　　　　　but that water was cold,
pero 'ik'yoch'añ tza majli.　　　　　　　　　but it was dark where it went.
Koñ 'añtza jb'ela,　　　　　　　　　　　　Since I had a candle,
tza majyoñ, chañetyak xajlel.　　　　　　　　I went on; there were a lot of big rocks.
Weñ b'ojy tyak mi yajle ja'　　　　　160　　It was slippery all over where the water fell
ya tyi mal.　　　　　　　　　　　　　　　　there inside.
Che'i majliyoñ lojoñ.　　　　　　　　　　　So we went on.
K'otyiyoñ lojoñ b'añ mi mero pejkañob'　　　We arrived at the place to do petitions
laj tyaty San Roñ Juañ.　　　　　　　　　　to Our Father San Don Juan.
'Ub'i sankristañ, "Wex 'ilali," che'eñ.　　　165　　The sacristan, "It's here," he said.
"Wäxka b'uchi' ya'i," che' kälälojoñ.　　　　　"Sit down over there," so we sat down.
B'uchle lojoñ che jiñi. Che 'añ,　　　　　　　We sat down, so. So it was,
che li, ya wa'al 'añ krusi.　　　　　　　　　like that, there was a cross there.
Koleñ krus 'ixi ch'ujtye'.　　　　　　　　　A big cross, of cedar.
Mi melob' ya b'añ koleñ krus.　　　　　170　　They do it there where the big cross is.
'I che jiñi,　　　　　　　　　　　　　　　　And so it was,
tzaj tzololoñ b'ela lojoñ, tzololojoñ.　　　　　we lined up our candles, we lined them up.
Koñ tzi ch'ämäyob' majlel　　　　　　　　　Since my brothers had brought
'i lemb'alob' kerañob'i,　　　　　　　　　　their liquor,
tza ki yäk'eñob' 'ixi sakristañ.　　　　175　　they began giving it to the sacristan.
ACG: *¿Chuki ya' 'añ ya tyi jol 'añ rus?*　　　　ACG: What is there at the head of the cross?
MMJ: *Mañik chu' añ.*　　　　　　　　　　　　MMJ: There isn't anything.
Jiñjach ñichim mi k'otye 'i tzuk'ob'.　　　　　Just the candles we came to light.

ACG: *¿'Añ ku tza 'uj, ma wäl?*		ACG: Isn't there a moon, didn't you say?
MMJ: *'A, 'añ ku jum p'e 'uj ya'i che li.*	180	MMJ: Ah, there is a moon there, like this.
ACG: *¿'Uj?*		ACG: A moon?
MMJ: *Yejtyal 'uj, ya' selel che*		MMJ: The image of a moon, it's round,
tyi ñäk' otyoty, yilal.		on the wall of the house, it seems.
Tzi sub'oñ lojoñ,		He told us,
much b'u 'i pejkañ sañ kristañ,	185	the one who asked the sacristan,
"Jiñi laj ch'uju ña' woch la käñ.		"That is Our Holy Mother you are meeting.
Woli ku 'aweno,		[If] you are all right,
wä tyo laj b'ej majlel 'ilali."		we are going further on."
Che' kälä lojoñ majloñ lojoñ,		Thus they told us, and we went on,
tza k'otyiyoñ lojoñ.	190	we arrived.
"Wex 'ila. B'uchi laj 'ilali.		"This is it. Sit down here.
Wä tza 'añ 'i tyi' 'i yotyoty		Here is the door to the house of
la yum San Juañi."		your lord San Juan."
"'A weno," cho'oñ lojoñ.		"Ah, good," we said.
B'uchleyoñ lojoñ.	195	We all sat down.
"'I tza tyo la ch'äñtyile 'añ laj tyäkäjib'",		"And did you still bring our 'warmer'
che'eñ.		[our liquor]?" he said.
"Tza ku ya witz'tyil," che'añ yumijel,		"Yes, there is a little there," said an uncle,
ki yäk'eñob'.		he began to give it to him.
Che jiñ,	200	So it was,
"Weno, ñich'tyañ, me ku la," che'eñ,		"Okay, listen up, all of you," he said,
"'i much kaj pejkañ," che'eñ.		"and I'm going to start praying," he said.
'Añ yalä Biblia, che ya wistyil,		There was a little Bible, small like this,
ki k'ele, chejiñ laj k'ele.		he started to read, he read it all.
B'ajche, jay p'e ty'añ mi yäk',	205	How many words he said,
ki ch'uyb'añ, ki päye',		he started to whistle, he started to summon,
'i jatz' 'i mesa che li ki ch'uyb'añ.		he hit the table like this when he whistled.
Jiñjax tza kaj kub'iñ tyejchi 'a Sañ Juañi,		So just like that San Juan started to wake up,
jiñi wäyäl, wele b'ajchex che jiñi,		he was asleep, perhaps, who knows,
tyejchi, ki . . . ki pejkañ,	210	he got up, he . . . he started to pray,
ki k'äy majlel 'orasiyoñ,		he started to sing out prayers,
jin jach tza kub'ilojoñ.		that's what we heard.
"¿Chuki la wom ma wäl," jiñi . . .		"What do you say you want?" the . . .
che tyilel weñ koleñ ty'añ		thus came a big voice
tyi mal tyi mali.	215	from inside that interior.
ACG: *¿Ch'ojla tye 'i sapato?*		ACG: Did his shoes make noise?
MMJ: *'Inki, ch'ojch'oña tyile che jiñi,*		MMJ: Yes, indeed, loud footsteps came
wä'le tyi tyi' 'otyoty wäleyi,		from there at the door of the house in there,
che jiñi weñ jumuk' 'i ñäch'äloñ lojoñ.		so for a good time we were quiet.

"Wenas noche, 'ijo," che tyaki.   220   "Good evening, son," he said.
"Wenas noches, papá," tza laj jak'älojoñ.   "Good evening, papa," we answered.
ACG: *¿Tyi ty'añ ma wäl 'aja papa?*   ACG: In Chol, do you say "papa"?
MC: *Laj tyaty.*   MC: Our father.
MMJ: *"Laj tyaty," chojoñ lojoñ.*   MMJ: "Our father," we said.
"Weno, ¿chuki la wom, 'ijo?" che'eñ.   225   "Okay, what do you want, son?" he said.
"Jiñi . . . tza' ab'i tyili jpejkañety lojoñ,   "The . . . We came here to ask you,
tyaty lojoñ, este . . .   Our Father, uh . . .
cha'añ chañ jchol lojoñ,   just on behalf of our milpas,
woxi laj chämel,   they are all dying,
koñ mach yoñx kolel 'ixim, kixim.   230   since the corn doesn't want to grow, our
                                                               corn.

Mi käl cha'añ tzax wa'le jajmel, yilal.   I say that it's because of the drought, it
                                                               seems.

Chuxka jmul loñ b'ajche jiñi,"   Whatever our sin was, it's like that,"
tzi cha'le ty'añ kerañob'.   said my brothers.
"'A, weno. ¿Chuki la wom?"   "Ah, good. What do you want?"
"Mañik. Chañ kom ma wäk'eñoñloñ ja',   235   "Nothing. We just want you to give us rain,
yilal, chañ mi koleloñ jchol.   it seems, so our milpas will grow.
Eske maxi koleloñ jchol loñ.   It's that our milpas don't grow.
Yub'il tzax cha' päk'ä lojoñ,   It seems we already planted a second time,
mak mi kolel,   it doesn't grow,
woli 'i cha' chämel,"   240   it's dying again,"
che cho'oñ lojoñ   so we said
tza kajiyoñ lojoñ tyi ty'añ.   when we started to speak.
'A weno, este . . .   Ah, okay, well . . .
tzi ki pejkañob' 'i b'ä   They started to ask for themselves
yik'o much b'u 'i pejkañ sañkristañ.   245   along with the sacristan that petitioned.
"¿B'ajche 'a wälä?   "What do you say?
De 'akwerdojety laj,"   Are you all agreed?"
che'eñ, che kuyi 'ixi.   he said, really like that.
ACG: *¿ "Tyeme la ty'añ," che'eñ?*   ACG: He said, "Speak all together"?
MMJ: *"Tyeme la ty'añ," che'eñ.*   250   MMJ: "Speak all together," he said.
Tzi cha' sub'eñoñ lojoñ sakristañ,   The sacristan asked us again,
"La wom chañ ja'ali."   "You all just want rain?"
"Komäch ku lojoñ."   "Indeed we all do."
Weno, tzi cha' sub'eñ ja'el,   Well, he spoke again,
"'A weno, weno,   255   "Ah, good, good,
'orita samoñ tyi Soyaló," che jiñi.   right away I'm going to Soyaló," he said.
"Sami jpejkañ Sañ Miwel   "I'm going to ask San Miguel
b'ajche 'i yälä,   what he says,

mi much ki chok jub'el 'añ ja'ali."		if he will start throwing down some rain."
"Yoñku," cho'oñ lojoñ.	260	"All right," we said.
Cha' ch'ojch'oña tza letzi majlel.		Once again, his footsteps sounded as he left.
Che jiñi,		So it was,
"Ma pityañoñ jumuk,"		"Wait for me a bit,"
che' 'ab'i tzi sub'e,		they say he said,
b'uchuloñ lojoñ.	265	and we all sat down.
Che jiñi,		So it was,
weñ ñajtye 'ora,		a good while later,
weno, cha' k'otyi,		well, he arrived again,
cha' jujukña tyilel,		he came making noise again,
cha' ch'ojch'oña tyile.	270	his footsteps rang out again as he came.
"Weno, tzax cha' juliyoñ," che'eñ.		"Okay, I'm back again," he said.
"Tza'ix ku papa," cho'oñ lojoñ.		"It's true, papa," we said.
"Weno, tyaläch 'añ ja'ali.		"Okay, the rain is going to come.
Chäch yälä 'añ San Mikel		So said San Miguel
ke tyaläch 'añ ja'ali,	275	that the rain is going to come,
pero ma me ku la b'äk'ñañ.		but don't you all be afraid.
Che jiñi,		So it is,
tyal me ku pejtye 'ik'		a really big wind is coming
yik'o tyuñi ja'		with hailstones
yik'o weñ ja'lel.	280	and heavy rain.
Ya jax tyo la majle tyi 'ojli b'ij,		You all go out to the middle of the road,
maxtyo mej k'otyemety laj		and before you have arrived
tyi 'otyoty 'ixi . . . 'ili sañ kristañi,		at the house of that . . . the sacristan,
b'äk' tyile ja'al,		suddenly a rain will come,
mi tyajety laj tyi b'ij,"	285	it will catch you on the road,"
che kälä lojoñ.		so he told us.
"Weno, kukux laj tyi lok'el,		"Okay, get out of here,
por ke yax tye ja'al,"		because a big rain is coming,"
che'eñ.		he said.
Che jiñi,	290	So it was,
yorajlel tza b'äk' lok'iyoñ majlel,		right then we left quickly,
lok'iyoñ loñ majlel.		we all left.
Che jiñi,		So it was,
ya' jpoj majle lojoñ tyi yojli b'ij,		there just as we were halfway down the road,
majlel b'äk' tyili ja'al.	295	there came a sudden rain.
Lekoj ja'al yik'o 'ik'.		A terrible rain with wind.
K'otyiyoñ loñ tyi yotyoty 'ub'i sañkristañ,		When we got to the house of that sacristan,
weñ ja'lel, ik', 'asta tza yajli tyuñi ja', jiñi.		a good rainstorm, wind, even hail was falling.

Pero che tyo woli 'i pejkañ jiñi sakristañ,		But when that sacristan was praying,
koñ tanto tza … tzi leme ja'el jyumijelob',	300	since so … he drank as well as my uncles,
koñ max tz'äkäl,		maybe it wasn't complete,
wo tyi resar.		what he was praying.
Wäle wo tyi 'orasyoñ 'añ sakristañ,		There he was praying,
tzi b'ajb'e,		and it struck him down,
jiñ jach tzaj k'ele tyo lepelej yajlel.	305	I just saw him fall down.
"Chuk tza mele, kermañu,"		"What are you doing, brother,"
cho'oñ lojoñ.		we said.
"Mañik. Mañik. Ma jña'tyañ		"Nothing. Nothing. I don't know
b'ajche mi kujtye, 'aja," che'eñ.		how this happened to me," he said.
"Tzi jatz'äyoñ chañ weñ yikoñix 'ab'i,	310	"It hit me because I'm really drunk, they say,
koñ 'oñatyax tza wäk'eñoñ lemb'al," che'eñ.		since you all gave me a lot of liquor," he said.
"Che ja'el San Juañi, yikix ja'el.		"Also that San Juan, he was drunk, too.
Ki jatz' 'i witara.		He started to play his guitar.
Tzäntzäña kaj tyi k'aytyak.		He started to sing songs beautifully.
Che jiñi, tza mich'a chañ yikix.	315	So, he got mad because he was drunk.
'I jatz'äyoñ koñ che b'ajche woj kap ja'eli.		He hit me since I was drinking like that, too.
Woch' 'ab'i jap ja'el jiñi la lemb'al		They say he was drinking your liquor, too,
ya b'u b'uty'u tyi la limetyeji.		that you had filled your bottle with.
Max 'ab'i … mach' 'ab'i tz'a'añix,		He wasn't … he wasn't, they say, strong,
tzax 'ab'i 'i laj ch'ämb'e 'i ch'ujlel,"	320	they say it took away his soul,"
che'eñ 'añ 'ub'i sankristañ.		said the sacristan.
"Mi laj k'otye laj kap ya tyi kotyotyi,		"When we arrive to drink at my house
mañix ka laj yik'añ tyo,		we aren't going to drink anymore,
che jax la kañ la wuty,"		so you will keep your eyes open,"
'ab'iyi ch'eñ.	325	they say he said.
"Chañ ku. Chäch yom.		"So be it. That's what it needs.
Wäle, kox la,"' 'ab'i,		Now, let's go," it was said,
"koñ yax 'ab'i tye ja'ali		"since a heavy rain is coming, they say,
'ojli b'ij," che kälä lojoñ.		halfway down the road," he told us.
B'äk' lok'iyoñ loñ majlel,	330	Quickly we left,
che jax tyo ñajtye,		and about so far,
che tyo ñajtye,		just so far,
mach kom loñ k'otyel tyi yotyoty sañkristañ,		we weren't quite at the house of the sacristan,
b'ajche 'ixi b'ujtyil		about where that hill is,
ya tye ñuke 'ik', ñuki ja'lel.	335	there came a big wind, heavy rain.
K'otyiyoñ loñ tyi 'otyoty,		We arrived at the house,
pero weñ koleñ ja'lel,		but it was really a big rain,
pero ja'lel chalchaña jach ka yub'ili ja'le,		but rain beating down, it seemed,

tyuñi ja'.
and hail.

Juñ yajlel ch'ejla jach ka tyuñi ja' 340
All of a sudden the hail started

tyi 'otyotyi.
at the house.

Pero 'ik',
But wind!

juñ yaj tzi laj k'äsätyak tye', pimeltyak.
Suddenly it shattered trees, bushes.

Che jiñi,
So it was,

tzi ki melob' k'iñ 345
they started to make a fiesta

ya tyi yotyoty 'ub'i sañkristañ.
there at the house of the sacristan.

Ki melob' we'eläl,
They prepared food,

tzäñsayob' chityam.
they killed a pig.

Che tyi 'ak'älel ki japob' lemb'al,
At night they started to drink aguardiente,

kaläyob' soñ, ñijkañob' b'iolin, witara, 350
they made music, played the violin, guitar,

che tza k'älä säk'ayoñ loñ b'ajche jiñi.
until dawn came it was just like that.

Yiktyakob' tza k'älä säk'ayob' b'ajche jiñi.
They drank until dawn like that.

Yäktyakob' tza k'älä säk'ayob'.
They were all drunk when the sun came up.

'I tzi laj 'alä 'añ San Miwel
And all that San Miguel said

chañ jiñi Sañ Juañ, ke 355
through that San Juan was

"Mach la womik
"If you don't want

chañ mi laj kom la b'äj tyi la' chol,
to have your milpas fail,

much majle la sewuro
be very sure

ke mi ka la b'ajb'eñ me',
that when you shoot a deer,

tyoj mi la b'ajb'eñ, 360
hit it straight on,

machank mi ka la säl jul,
don't just wound it,

tyoj mi la jule,"
shoot it right,"

che kä lojoñ.
he told us.

'I che jiñi,
And so it is,

'i sujmäch. 365
it's really true.

Tza laj k'aj lojoñ,
We asked for everything,

b'ajche mi weñ mi laj chumtyil,
how we could live well,

mi tyajoñ laj k'amijel
if we encountered sickness,

pejtye laj muty,
all our chickens,

pejtye laj chityam, 370
all our pigs,

'i chäch 'i laj 'ak'eñoñ lojoñ b'endisyoñ.
and so he gave us all a blessing.

'I tzi yäk'eñtyakob' 'i ch'ujlel 'ixim
And he gave each one the Soul of the Maize,

'a kerañob', jyumijelob',
to my brothers, my uncles,

che much'tyil, che li, che tyo,
like a handfull, like this,

welweltyil 'i wuty 'ixim 375
big grains of maize

b'ajche 'ixim 'ib'ido, mi yälob' säk,
like hybrid maize, they say it was white,

weñ säsäk 'ixim k'otye laj päk'
really white corn we were going to plant

ya tyi laj chol,
there in our milpas,

jiñ 'i ch'ujlel me 'ixim 'ilili,
that was the Soul of the Maize,

che kälä lojoñ.	380	he told us.
"Jiñ la sujty'um la ñichim,		"Those ends of your candles,
woli la ch'äm lok'el 'ilali,		you are going to take them there,
majle la pul tyi la chol.		go burn them in your milpas.
Yojli la chol mi la pule.		In the middle of the milpa, burn them.
Che mi la xujty'um la ñichimi,	385	When you are burning your candle stubs,
mi la ñoktyil		kneel down
ya tyi yojli la choli.		there in the middle of your milpa.
Cha'leñ la resal chañ weñ 'utz'aty mi lok'el,		Pray that it will turn out well,
b'ajche jiñi,"		like that,"
che kälä loñ jäjä', che jiñ.	390	he told us, uh-huh, like that.
Chäch meleyob' añ kerañob'.		Just so my brothers did it.
Chäch tzaj mele lojoñ tyi chol lojoñ.		Just so we did it in our milpas.
'I che jiñi,		And so it was,
poj chäb'iji tza' tzajñoñ		after about two days we went
ya'i 'añ yumijel,	395	there where my uncles are,
'ixi 'añ jyumijel ya'i.		I have an uncle there.
B'äk' maj tyi chol,		He went right to his milpa,
maj tyi puleñ lumi.		he went to burn the land.
Tz'äch 'i b'äk' ak'eñtyi 'añ me',		Right away he was given a deer,
b'äk' b'ajb'e juñ kojty koleñ tyaty me',	400	right away he shot a big male deer,
che k'iñ, majli che li . . .		the sun was like this, he went like this . . .
woli k'otyel yik'o 'i me'.		he arrived with the deer.
"'Umb'a'añ laj we'el," che'.		"Here's our food," he said.
K'otyel koleñ tyaty me'.		He comes in with a big buck.
Che jiñ,	405	So it was,
kaj tz'u lojoñ tyi 'ak'älel,		we started to skin it at night,
kaj k'ux lojoñ,		we started to eat it,
chäch jomokñayoñ lojoñ.		just all of us together.
Che tyi 'ak'älel jk'ux lojoñ,		So at night we ate it,
che tyo 'añ me'i.	410	since there was still venison.
Che b'ajche chab'i		About two days later
tza majli 'ak'älelix.		he went out at night.
Tza majliyob' yik'o yamb'u jyumijelob',		He went with another of my uncles,
cha' kojty b'ajb'e me', koleñ me'tyak.		they shot two deer, big does.
Cha' kojty tzi b'ajb'eyob' yorajlel.	415	Two deer they shot at the same time.
Tzi b'ajb'e tyi cha' p'e 'ak'älel.		They shot on two nights.
Tyi jum p'e 'ak'älel		In one night
che tza k'uxu loñ me' b'ajche jiñi.		we ate venison like that.
'I cheäch 'añ jmuty lojoñi, chityam.		And thus we had chickens, pigs.
Tzäch kaj tyi poj p'ojlel ja'el jcholoñ lojoñ.	420	Thus our milpas began to produce as well.

Tzäch kaj tyi kolel
koñ tzäch ki yulmul tyi ja'a,
tyi ja'al, che jiñ.
ACG: *Si, pues.*
MMJ: *Lekoj tza tyili 'i kuch 'añ 'iximi,*
pak'akña chixka.
Chächixka b'omb'ontyil 'ixim.
Tza jpoj k'ajatyak lojoñ,
lok'otyak syento b'eynte sonte
juju p'e cholel
tza jmele lojoñ.
ACG: *'Aja'a.*
MMJ: *Weñ kolen 'otyoty b'ajche 'ilili,*
tza b'ujty'i,
cha' p'ej lajtz 'ixim,
pero puro ty'uñul 'ixim.
Jiñ me ku cha'añ mi jña'tyañ wäle
ke 'i sujmäch b'ajche jiñi mi yälob',
ke 'añäch b'a mi laj k'ajtyiñ ja'al,
koñ tzäch jmero yäxña k'ele ja'el.
Wajali jiñi.
Mi chäñ wox tyo,
chäñ melob' 'añ wäleyi,
b'ajchex.
Koñ wajalix b'a tza mele lojoñ,
wajali.
ACG: *Che kuyi.*
MMJ: *'I sujmlel.*
ACG: *'I wäleyi,*
mañix b'a'añ
b'a ma maj la k'ajtyiñ ja'al,
mi la wäl 'iliyi.
MMJ: *B'ajchexka. 'Añtza' wäle,*
pero ñajtyix, wäle, 'ilali.
Koñ maj ña'tyañ b'a' kälem,
koñ wajalix tzajñoñ lojoñ,
ma chäñ k'ajalix jcha'añ.
ACG: *Mach ku.*
MMJ: *Mi yälob' ke läk'äl 'ab'i,*
'i tyoje ya tyi läk'ä Wenab'ista.
'Añ mi yälob', b'ajchexka.

Thus it started to grow
since it started to get wet from the rain,
from the rain, like that.
ACG: Yes, indeed.
MMJ: Fiercely came the load of corn,   425
it was huge, like that.
Just like this, the ears were thick.
When we went to harvest,
we took out 120 tzontes [120 × 400 ears]
from each milpa   430
that we made.
ACG: Aha.
MMJ: A really big house like this one,
we filled it,
two stacks of maize,   435
but all big ears.
So that's why I think now
that it's true what they say,
that there is a place where we ask for rain,
since I really did see it before, myself.   440
It was a long time ago.
If it's still like that,
if they still do it now,
who knows.
Since it was a long time ago we did it,   445
long ago.
ACG: It really was.
MMJ: It's true.
ACG: And now,
isn't there a place   450
where you go to ask for rain;
do you say so, here?
MMJ: Who knows? There might be, now,
but it's a long way, now.
Since I don't know where it was,   455
since it was a long time ago that we went,
I just don't remember.
ACG: Not really.
MMJ: They tell me that it's close, they say,
right there close to Buenavista.   460
So they say, who knows.

Yab'i 'i tyoje 'ila tyi Palenke, ja'el.
They say it's right by Palenque, too.

'Ila tyi che tyi 'añtza' säkjak'añ b'ä xajlel,
It's there where there are loose white rocks,

che li.
like that.

Jiñ 'ab'i 'i witzlel jiñi. 465
They say that is his mountain.

Jiñ 'ab'i 'i witzlel Sañ Juañ.
They say that is Don Juan's mountain.

ACG: *Jiñ 'ab'i kuyi.*
ACG: That's it alright, they say.

MMJ: *Jiñ 'ab'i ku.*
MMJ: That's really it, they say.

Pero mi yälob' ke mach 'ab'i chäñ ya
But they say that it isn't still there

xchumul 'ab'i doñ Juañ. 470
that Don Juan lives, they say.

Tza'b'i lok'i ya'i.
They say he left there.

Koñ jiñtza' tzi pulb'eyob'
Since they burned that place

jiñi xk'ayob', x'eb'anjeliko.
those Singers, the Evangelicals.

ACG: *Chuxka 'i k'aba'ob'.*
ACG: Whatever they're called.

MMJ: *Prespiteriano.* 475
MMJ: Presbyterians.

ACG: *Jiñ 'ab'i.*
ACG: That's them, they say.

MMJ: *Tzax 'ab'i pulb'e 'i yotyoty.*
MMJ: They say they burned his house.

ACG: *Tza ku 'i pulb'eyob' 'i yotyoty*
ACG: They really did burn his house,

wajali.
a long time ago

Che tziji kajel 'añ tyo jiñi k'ay. 480
When the Singers were just starting out.

MMJ: *'Aja.*
MMJ: Aha.

ACG: *Jiñ 'ab'i tzi puluyob'.*
ACG: They say they burned it.

Che jiñi, jiñ 'ab'i 'i lok'el, 'añ che jiñi.
So, they say he left, and so it is.

MMJ: *'Ixku mi sujmäch.*
MMJ: That's right, it's true.

Wäle, koñ mach mij chäñ 'ub'iñ 'i tyilel 485
Now, since I don't hear anyone go,

ke mi chäñ k'otyelob'.
that anyone just goes there.

ACG: *Mach ku wäle.*
ACG: Not anymore.

MMJ: *Che wajali,*
MMJ: So it was a long time ago,

che ya tyo 'añoñ tyi Pasoji,
when I was still in Paso [Naranjo],

weñ kab'ä maj ki mi k'otyelob'. 490
a lot of people went there.

K'älä ch'oyolob' tyi Tumb'ala,
Even those who lived in Tumbalá,

k'älä ch'oyol tyi Trinida
even those who lived in Trinidad

mi k'otyelob',
went there,

mi ñumelob' wiñikob' ya'i.
people passed by going there.

Pejtye ya mi majlelob' ab'i, 495
Everybody went there, they say,

mi k'otyelob' wajali.
they went long ago.

ACG: *Che jiñi.*
ACG: So it was.

MMJ: *Pejtye 'ab'i mi k'otyelob',*
MMJ: Everybody went, they say,

b'ajche Nuebo Mundo,
like Nuevo Mundo,

b'ajche' läk'ä ch'oyolob' tyi Palenke. 500
like even people who lived in Palenque.

Pejtye ya mi k'otyelob', mi yälob' wajali.
Everybody went there, they say, long ago.

Che kuyi.
It was like that.

ACG: *Tzi sub'eñoñ juñ tyikil laj tyaty ñox,*
wajali 'añ,
ya tyo 'añoñ tyi San Peru',
tzi sub'eñoñ ke yax 'ab'i
tza k'axi maj tyi Jolja', jiñi Ichtye'ja'.
MMJ: *'Aja.*
ACG: *Ya tza maj tyi 'Ichtye'ja'i,*
wäle, che mi yom tye ja'al,
ya ñaxañ mi tyoj meltyak jiñi chajk,
mi yälob'.
MMJ: *Jäjä.*
ACG: *'I 'añ 'ab'i tzi tyajayob'*
jiñi xlukb'älob'
che wo tyo 'i poj k'exe tyo majlel.
MMJ: *Che'i.*
ACG: *Tzab'i 'i k'eleyob'.*
MMJ: *'Aja.*
ACG: *Weñ kab'ä wu 'i k'axetyak majlel*
jiñ kox chäk muty.
MMJ: *'A weno.*
ACG: *Yik'oty 'ab'i b'ätye'el,*
che tyi 'ak'älel 'ab'i.
MMJ: *'A ja'a.*
ACG: *Tzolokña k'axe ya tyi kolen ja' 'ab'i,*
mi yälob'.
MMJ: *'A weno.*
ACG: *Kox chäk muty 'ab'i,*
ya tza k'axi tyi Troncha Pie, 'a mi yälob'.
MMJ: *'Aja'a.*
ACG: *'Ub'i li bätye'eli,*
mu b'u 'i xäñ tyi yok.
MMJ: *Jäjä'.*
ACG: *Wä 'ab' tyi tyi'*
kayejoñob' Tyemopa',
ya ... ya 'ab'i tza laj k'axi majlel,
mi loñ 'alob'.
Bajchexka mi 'i sujm ka.
MMJ: *'A weno. 'Ixku mi sujmäch wäle.*
ACG: *Bajche'äch.*
MMJ: *Jiñi ... pero puro wiñikax*
mi yochel 'ab'i.

ACG: An old man told me,
it was a long time ago,
I was still in San Pedro,
he told me that from there, they say,
he crossed over to Joljá, that Ixtiejá.
MMJ: Aha.
ACG: There he went to that Ixtiejá,
now, when he wants rain to come,
there he first makes a lot of lightning,
they say.
MMJ: Aha.
ACG: And there was a time when
fishermen saw him, they say,
when he was crossing over.
MMJ: So.
ACG: They saw him.
MMJ: Aha.
ACG: A lot of crested guans
were crossing over.
MMJ: Ah, okay.
ACG: With animals, they say,
just at nightfall, they say.
MMJ: Aha.
ACG: In a line they crossed over the river,
they say.
MMJ: Ah, okay.
ACG: Crested guans, they say,
they crossed over at Troncha Pie, so they say.
MMJ: Aha.
ACG: Those animals, they say,
walked on their feet.
MMJ: Uh-huh.
ACG: They say they were at the edge of
the little streets of Tiemopá,
there ... there, they say, they crossed over,
so they say.
Who knows if it's true.
MMJ: Ah, okay. It's probably true.
ACG: It could be like that.
MMJ: It ... but only men
entered there, they say.

505
510
515
520
525
530
535
540

Ya' i mach 'ab'i mi yochel x'ixik.
ACG: *¿Mach mi yochel x'ixik?*
MMJ: *Mi tza 'ochi x'ixik*
ya jach tyi pwerta yotyoty,
mi yajlel, mi chämel.
ACG: *'Aha'a.*
MMJ: *Juñ yaj mi chämel, 'ab'i.*
ACG: *¿Chuki mi cha'leñ?*
MMJ: *Koñ b'äk' ora mi ch'oj lukum, 'ab'i.*

ACG: *¿Lukum mi ch'oj?*
MMJ: *Machki, b'ajlum mi k'ux, 'ab'i.*
ACG: *'Aja'a.*
MMJ: *Jiñ cha'añ puro wiñikach*
mi yochelob' ab'i ya'i.
ACG: *'Aja'a.*
MMJ: *Jäjä'. Che mach laj pusik'al*
mi laj majlel 'ab'iyi,
much' 'ab'i laj päs'eñtyel,
mi cha' p'e laj pusik'al laj majlel 'ab'iyi,
mu 'ab'i laj päs'eñtyel lukum,
b'ajlum, 'ab'i.
ACG: *'Aja'a.*
MMJ: *Ya hach 'a mi ch'ojoñ laj jiñi,*
mi tza laj cha' 'alä,
machikax tza loñ tyiliyoñ.
B'äb'äk'echix cho'oñ laj, 'ab'i,
ya jach 'a, mi laj kälel 'ab'i.
ACG: *'Aja'a.*
MMJ: *Che mi yälob' wajali.*
ACG: *B'ajche'äch mi sujmäch,*
koñ 'añ che mi laj kub'iñ,
mi mach mi laj ñop,
pero jiñ tyo, mi laj ñop che wox laj k'el.
MMJ: *Jiñtyo kuyi.*
ACG: *Wox la kub'iñ.*
MMJ: *'I sujmäch wäle,*
koñ b'ajche wajali,
che mi kajñeloñ tyi Tila wajaliyi,
koñ tyi kok mi jkälä majleloñ,
k'älä tyi Korosal.

There, they say, no women entered.
ACG: Women didn't enter?
MMJ: If a woman entered
there at the door of the house,
she would fall down, she would die.
ACG: Aha.
MMJ: All at once she would die, they say.
ACG: What do they do?
MMJ: Since right away a snake strikes them,
      they say.
ACG: A snake strikes?
MMJ: If not, a jaguar eats them, they say.
ACG: Aha.
MMJ: For that reason, only men
enter there, they say.
ACG: Aha.
MMJ: If not with our hearts
we go, they say,
we will be taught a lesson,
if with a divided heart we go, they say,
the snake will teach us a lesson,
or a jaguar, they say,
ACG: Aha.
MMJ: Right there they will bite us,
if we spoke with two tongues,
we shouldn't have come in vain.
If we speak in fear, they say,
right there, we will remain, they say.
ACG: Aha.
MMJ: That's what they said, long ago.
ACG: It's probably true,
since that's what we feel,
we might not believe it,
but still, we believe because we are seeing it.
MMJ: That's right.
ACG: We feel it.
MMJ: It's really true,
as it was a long time ago,
when we went to Tila a long time ago,
since on foot we went the whole way,
all the way from Corozal.

(Line numbers: 545, 550, 555, 560, 565, 570, 575, 580)

'Añ juñ tyikil x'ixik,	585	There was a woman,
ch'oyol tyi Palenke,		a resident of Palenque—
'ixi mach a käñäyik.		don't you know her?—
Chepa, mi yälob'.		Chepa, they call her.
ACG: *'Aja'a. Jäjä'.*		ACG: Aha. Uh-huh.
MMJ: *Tza majliyoñ loñ tyi b'ih,*	590	MMJ: We went along the road,
tyi kok tza majliyoñ lojoñ,		on foot we all went,
'i primera b'esax tza majli jiñ x'ixiki.		and it was the first time that woman went.
'I tzi ki yäl majlel		And she started to talk as she went
'ixtyi chañelal Perlaji,		there up above Perla,
chañ, koñ puro witz 'añ,	595	high up, it's all mountains,
che jiñi, xäñ loñ majlel.		so it was, we were walking along.
ACG: *Jiñch kuyi.*		ACG: Just like that.
MMJ: *Ya tza lujb'a.*		MMJ: She fell down there.
'I koñ jujp'eñjax ja'el 'añ x'ixiki.		And she was really fat, too.
ACG: *'Aja.*	600	ACG: Aha.
MMJ: *"'Añ jlujb'oñix.*		MMJ: "I'm falling down already.
Mach k'otyoñix.		I won't get there.
Matzax tza tyiliyoñ,"		I shouldn't have come,"
che tzi cha'le ty'añ,		so she said,
b'ajche jiñi.	605	like that.
ACG: *'Aja.*		ACG: Aha.
MMJ: *'I jum p'e jach 'ora,*		MMJ: And just then,
tza laj k'uña yoki, 'i k'äb'.		her legs got all weak, her arms.
Tz'itya' ma tza yälä chämel		She almost died
tyi b'ij.	610	on the road.
ACG: *'Aja'a.*		ACG: Aha.
MMJ: *Chañ mach jum p'e 'i pusik'al*		MMJ: Because her heart wasn't one
tza majli Tila.		when she went to Tila.
Tza loñ tyi tyi Tila.		She went in vain to Tila.
"Mach 'a wäl b'ajche jiñi.	615	"Don't talk like that.
'Entonse ma ka wilañ		Don't you see
ke mi cha'leñ tyi kastigar Señor," cho'oñ.		that the Lord will punish you," I said.
ACG: *'Aja'a.*		ACG: Aha.
MMJ: *"Mak wäle.*		MMJ: "Not here.
Mi käl mach ñajty,	620	It's not far,
läk'äl tza,"		it's really close,"
mi loñ 'alob',		they told her,
che tzi cha'le ty'añ.		thus they spoke to her.
'I tyik'i woj chäñ loñ majlel lemb'al.		And since we brought aguardiente,
woj chäm maj lemb'al, 'aja,	625	we brought liquor, uh-huh,

yik'o 'ixi 'Umbertoji.
ACG: *Yik'o Polo.*
MMJ: *Yik'o Polo, 'ixi Polo.*
Polo, yalob'il laj tyaty Bentura.
'I tza jkaj käk'eñ lojoñ 'añ lemb'al.   630
Tza ki p'ätyañ 'i yok,
b'ajche jiñi.
Machiki, ya tza käle,
ya tza chämi, wäle.
Tza laj k'uña 'i pejtye 'i yok,   635
max tza mej tyi xämb'al.
Puro jach [b'uchul] tza majli,
'i sujmäch b'ajche mi yälob' wajali.
ACG: *'I sujm ku wäle.*
MMJ: *Jiñ me ku cha'añ ya tza jñopo ja'el,*   640
'i sujmäch mi yälob' wajali.
ACG: *Che kuyi.*
Pero 'añ 'ab'i jiñ laj tyaty, wajali,
mu 'ab'i 'i yajñel tyi Palenke 'ab'i,
mi yälob' jiñ laj tyaty Don Juañ.   645
MMJ: *'A me muk'äch wäle.*
ACG: *'Añ 'ab'i . . . 'añ 'ab'i juñ tyikil kaxlañ*

jkäñä b'ä ya tyi Palenke,
weñ 'ab'i yujil 'ab'i lemb'al
laj tyaty bäyi.   650
MMJ: *Jäjä'.*
ACG: *Max 'ab'i 'i b'ujk.*
Max 'ab'i chu' añ 'i cha'añ,
wajali.
MMJ: *Jäjä'.*   655
ACG: *Che maxtyo koleñ tyejklumik*
jiñi Palenke.
MMJ: *Jäjä'.*
ACG: *Mu 'ab'i k'otyetyak*
jiñ laj tyaty Juañ.   660
MMJ: *Jäjä'.*
ACG: *Mu' 'ab'i 'i ñochtyañtyak*
tyi lemb'al 'ab'i.
MMJ: *'A weno.*
ACG: *Che 'ab'i, mi yälob',*   665

with that Humberto.
ACG: With Polo.
MMJ: With Polo, that Polo.
Polo, the son of Señor Ventura.
And we started to give her liquor.
Her foot began to get its strength,
like this.
If it hadn't, she would have stayed there,
she would have died there, then.
All of her legs got soft,
she couldn't walk.
Just so [seated] she went,
and it's true what they say, long ago.
ACG: It's really true, now.
MMJ: For that reason I believe it, too,
it's true what they used to say, long ago.
ACG: That's the way it is.
But there was a gentleman, they say,
they say he used to come down to Palenque,
they called him Our Father Don Juan.
MMJ: He really did, then.
ACG: They say . . . they say there was a
Ladino
—I knew him there in Palenque—
he really liked to drink aguardiente,
that old man.
MMJ: Aha.
ACG: He didn't have a shirt.
They say he didn't have anything,
a long time ago.
MMJ: Aha.
ACG: Then Palenque wasn't yet
a big town.
MMJ: Uh-huh.
ACG: They say Our Father Don Juan
used to go there all the time.
MMJ: Aha.
ACG: He used to hang around
the firewater, they say.
MMJ: Ah, okay.
ACG: So, they say,

jiñ tzi sub'eñoñ juñ tyikil laj tyaty ñox,
laj tyaty ya' añ tyi Palenke.
MMJ: *'Aja'.*
ACG: *Mach weñ tza k'otyi wäle,*
porke 'i yalob'ilob' mero jontyolob'.　　670
MMJ: *'Aja.*
ACG: *Tzi tyajayob' 'i mul.*
MMJ: *'A, jiñ wokol 'añ, che jiñi.*
ACG: *'I jiñ tzi sub'eñoñ*
ke mu 'ab'i k'otyetyak,　　675
mu 'ab'i yajñetyak ja'eli
ya tyi yotyoty doñ Juañ.
Mu 'ab'i yäk'eñtyak 'i majtyañ,
chu mi yäk'eñtyak.
MMJ: *'Aja.*　　680
ACG: *'Ab'i . . . tzab'i yäk'e 'i tyak'iñ,*
chu'tyak.
MMJ: *'A weno.*
ACG: *Tzi yäk'e ja'el.*
MMJ: *Jäjä'.*　　685
ACG: *Jiñ cha'añ,*
much jñop 'i ty'añ ja'el,
koñ 'arapente . . .
MMJ: *'I sujmäch b'ajche mi yälob'.*
ACG: *'I sujm ku.*　　690
MMJ: *Che 'ab'i jiñi.*
Ya tyi San Roñ Juañ
'añ mi lok'el burro 'ab'i.
ACG: *¿'Añ?*
MMJ: *Kuchu 'ab'i 'i cha'añ tyak'iñ.*　　695
ACG: *'Aja'a.*
MMJ: *Cha' p'e' kajoñ tyak'iñ kuchul,*
pero 'i ch'ajañal puro jiñ 'ab'i nabuyaka,
puro lukum.
ACG: *'Aja.*　　700
MMJ: *'A las dose mi lok'el tyi jum paty 'ab'i.*

ACG: *'Aja.*
MMJ: *"Jijiji," che 'ab'i b'uro 'ab'i*
mi lok'el tyi 'oñel.　　705
Che 'ab'i majch mi k'el b'ajche wiñikoñlayi,

an old man told me this,
Our Father was there in Palenque.
MMJ: Aha.
ACG: It's not good that he came now,
because his children are really mean.
MMJ: Aha.
ACG: They found their sin.
MMJ: Ah, there is that problem, like that.
ACG: And he told me
that he would arrive frequently; they say,
he often would come down also they say,
there to the house of Don Juan.
They say he would often give him gifts,
whatever he would give him.
MMJ: Aha.
ACG: They say . . . he gave him money,
whatever.
MMJ: Ah, good.
ACG: He gave it to him, too.
MMJ: Uh-huh.
ACG: For that reason,
I believe his story, too,
since from time to time . . .
MMJ: It's true what they say.
ACG: It's really true.
ACG: They say it's like that.
There where San Don Juan is,
a burro comes out, they say.
ACG: It does?
MMJ: Loaded with money, they say.
ACG: Aha.
ACG: Two boxes of money are loaded,
but the ropes are all bushmasters, they say,
all snakes.
ACG: Aha.
MMJ: At midnight it comes out at one side,
they say.
ACG: Aha.
MMJ: "Heeheehee," they say the burro says
when he comes out to bray.
When, they say, he sees a person like us,

mi muy chiñwoñ 'ab'i layi,
mak laj b'äk'ñañ jiñi laso
chuk kächäl 'i cha'añ.
Mu 'ab'i maj laj kitye',   710
mi tzäch laj kityiyi laj cha'añ 'ab'i tyak'iñ.
ACG: *'Aja.*
MMJ: *Che tzi laj sub'eñoñ lojoñ*
che tzajñoñ lojoñ,
majchixiki mi jity,   715
che koleñ lukumächix tz'oty kächäl 'i cha'añ.

ACG: *Mach mi mejle laj kitye'.*
MMJ: *Mach mi mejle laj kitye',*
che tza sub'etyiyoñ lojoñ.   720
ACG: *¿Majki 'añ tzi sub'ety laj?*
MMJ: *Jiñch'a 'ub'i sañkristañ.*
ACG: *'Aja.*
MMJ: *Mu b'u 'i pejkañ laj tyaty Wa'añ.*   725

ACG: *Jiñ tzi sub'ety laj.*
MMJ: *Jiñ tzi sub'oñ loñ.*
ACG: *'Ixku jiñi laj tyatyi,*
¿mak chu' mi k'ajtyi,
mak chu' mi yäk'eñtyel,   730
'aja?
MMJ: *Mañik.*
ACG: *B'ajche yilal 'añ tyi yotyoty.*
¿Weñäch 'añ?
MMJ: *Weñ ku. Koleñ 'otyoty yotyoty,*   735
'añ 'ab'i 'i kajpelel.
Lekoj mi choñ 'ixim,
lekoj wo 'i kolel 'i chityam,
p'ulukña 'i chityam pam 'otyoty, tzajñoñ.   740

ACG: *'Aja.*
MMJ: *Che 'a kuyi.*
ACG: *Jiñch mi yäk'en laj tyaty.*
MMJ: *Jiñ kuyi. Jiñ jach mi 'añ laj tyak'iñi,*
mi laj käye' cha' p'e peso,   745
jo' p'e peso, b'ajche'
chañ mi cha' mäñ ñichim

if we are really chingón [tough], they say,
we aren't afraid of the ropes
that are tied on it.
We can go untie them, they say,   710
if we untie them, the money is ours.
ACG: Aha.
MMJ: Thus they told us
when we went,
if anyone should untie it,   715
when such big snakes were wrapped up in
   knots to tie it.

ACG: It wouldn't be possible to untie it.
MMJ: It wouldn't be possible for us to untie
it, like we told you.   720
ACG: Who was it that told you all that?
MMJ: It was that sacristan.
ACG: Aha.
MMJ: The one who petitioned Our Father   725
   Juan.

ACG: He told you all.
MMJ: He told us.
ACG: As for that gentleman,
was there anything he asked for,
was anything given to him,   730
huh?
MMJ: Nothing.
ACG: What did it look like in his house?
Was it good?
MMJ: Really so. His house was a big   735
house, they say there was a coffee grove.
Abundantly he sold maize,
abundantly did his pigs grow,
they were crowded into the patio of his   740
   house when we went there.

ACG: Aha.
MMJ: That's the way it was.
ACG: That's why he gave to Our Father.
MMJ: Just so. Just so, if we had money,
if two pesos were left to us,   745
five pesos, like that,
we would just buy candles again,

chañ mi tzuk' ya tyi yotyoty 'ab'i.

ACG: ¿Majki jiñ?

MMJ: Jiñ 'ixi sañkristañ.

ACG: 'A, ¿jiñ mi la käk'eñ tyak'iñ?

MMJ: Jiñ 'ab'i kuyi.

ACG: 'Añ sakristañ.

MMJ: Jiñ 'ab'i kuyi,
jäjä',
che kuyi.

we would just burn them there at his house,
  they say.

750   ACG: Who is that?

MMJ: That sacristan.

ACG: Ah, to him you give money?

MMJ: Him exactly, they say.

ACG: The sacristan.

755   MMJ: Him exactly,
uh-huh,
just like that.

PART 3

Things That Come Out of the Woods

11

The Messengers

Ausencio Cruz Guzmán

This is another of the stories Ausencio (Chencho) Cruz Guzmán first heard while making a canoe at Arroyo Palenque (see also The Celestial Bird). It was narrated by Cruz and recorded by Josserand and Hopkins in Mexico City in 1979. Cruz Guzmán's father, also named Ausencio and universally addressed as "Don Chencho," was a master canoe maker who in his youth ferried goods up and down the Río Tulijá, carrying supplies upriver from the Salto de Agua railhead to the plantations and settlements and bringing products downriver for shipment to other areas. His sons became skilled canoe masters themselves and often went with him to make new canoes (see Hopkins, Josserand, and Cruz Guzmán 1985).

In the old days, there was no postal service, and messages had to be sent by courier. The messengers traveled on foot or on mule-back. The work of a messenger could be dangerous, and there are many stories of encounters between messengers and demons. We have heard at least four versions of this story in the Chol area, with small variations. Another version, very brief and somewhat garbled, is published in the collection *Chol Texts on the Supernatural* (Whittaker and Warkentin 1965:98–101). A more complete version is found in *Walalix bä t'an* (Alejos García 1988:75–80).

In these witch stories, the animals that accompany the Lord of the Underworld, the principal demon, are owls, foxes, and a wooly dog. The owls, which can change into demons or just disappear, come along first as scouts, to warn of any dangers to be encountered. The foxes are like the dogs of the chief demon. The wooly dog, or sheep dog, can also change into a demon. The people who accompany the head demon are those who have made pacts with the devil or the children of those who made such pacts (if the devil demanded the child in place of the adult, to pay a debt). At the end of this story, one of the messengers meets this fate.

Music and noise always accompany the band of demons. The demons play flutes, violins, guitars, marimbas, drums, and many other instruments. The head demon may come mounted on a deer, which he rides like a horse. He treats the belly of the deer like a drum, pounding out the rhythm of the music.

In this story we learn some of the techniques for repelling—or at least momentarily distracting—the demons. Tobacco powder, tobacco smoke, urine, garlic, peppers, and salt all offend the demons. They block up their noses, and they can't continue to follow a scent on the trail. The *mam k'ujtz* or *pi'iläl* mentioned in the story is a native tobacco, called *pisiete* in the Spanish of the Chiapas Highlands. The leaves from near the tips of the branches are picked and dried, then ground into a rough powder, like snuff. The tobacco is then mixed with ashes and kept in small gourds with waists (Chol *bux*, local Spanish *buxito*). These are hung over the fire to dry the mixture before it is used. Women use the gourds of tobacco to protect their children from demons. They are left at the sides of newborns to keep demons away. Men put the mixture between their lower teeth and their cheeks; this tobacco preparation is said to be dangerous, as overuse results in the body swelling up and the skin turning pallid.

The varieties of maize can be divided into good ones and bad ones. White, yellow, and red corn are good; black corn is bad. In this tale the black corn, *'i'ik'bä 'ixim*, 'black corn' or *xchäkchab' 'ixim* 'red-wax corn,' is also referred to despicatively as *tya'chab' 'ixim* 'shit-wax corn' or *'ik' tyäk'añ 'ity* 'black sticky butthole,' likening it to the dark sticky excrement of infants. The maizes demand to be treated with respect. If the corn is not stacked neatly, it will complain, even cry, in protest to its owner. Thus when the messengers refuse to help pick up the scattered ears of black corn, it is a direct insult intended as revenge for the black corn's betrayal.

Among the demons, the head demon is called Xib'aj, and the demons are often referred to collectively as *xib'ajob'*. Xib'aj is the personage with whom evil people make pacts to work witchcraft on others, to seek riches, and for other reasons. Another prominent demon is *Tzimajol*, Gourd Head, so called because he is bald, that is, his head (and probably the rest of him) is skeletal. At times his head comes bouncing along by itself, making a noise like pumpkins being rolled across a floor. This bouncing head is *Puk'puk' Jol*, Bouncing Head, a name that preserves the ancient term for the Maya ballgame (cf. Yucatec Maya *pok'ol pok'*). There are other demons who leave their heads or their bodies and travel about without them, the head or the body or the bones moving about all alone. There is a woman with no head and a man with two heads. (For a survey of the cast of threatening characters, see Josserand et al. 2003; Further Reading, below).

Apart from the demons, there are other woods spirits, including elves who delight in leading people astray. When they are nearby, a person loses track of where he is and can't find the road home. One must master a number of techniques to escape; one such is to make a small musical instrument and leave it on a stump. The elves are fascinated by music, and when they come to try out the instrument, they get involved with it and forget about the person, whose head then clears up and he can get away. With all these creatures lurking in the woods, it is no surprise that messengers lead a dangerous life!

THE MESSENGERS

Ty'añ Jiñi X'ak'juñ
Ausencio Cruz Guzmán (Josserand, Hopkins, and Cruz Guzmán 1978c)

'Ili ty'añ	1	This story
mu bu kaj jsub'eñety laj,		that I'm going to tell you all,
tzi sub'eñoñ lojoñ juñ tyikil wiñik,		a man told it to us
che' tzajñi jpajlib'eñ lojoñ 'i jukub'		when we went to carve out his canoe
'ila tyi Arroyo Palenque.	5	there at Arroyo Palenque.
Jiñi jukub' tza pajli lojoñ		That canoe, we carved it
tyi Arroyo Palenque,		in Arroyo Palenque,
wajalix;		a long time ago;
'añix wälej		it must have been
komo chäñ p'ejl—jäñ'äñ—	10	some four—
hu'uh—lujum p'ejl, o b'ulux p'ejl jab'.		ten or eleven years ago.
'I ya' b'a woliyoñ lojoñ tyi 'e'tyel,		And there where we were working,
tzi sub'eñoñ lojoñ juñ p'ejl kwento,		he told us a story,
'o jun p'ejl ty'añ,		or a tale,
ty'añ b'ä wajali, ke:	15	a tale from long ago, that:
'Añ 'ab'i juñ tyikil korreyo'		There was, they say, a messenger,
mu 'ab'i 'i majlel tyi 'ak'juñ.		who was, they say, going to deliver a letter.
Pero komo wajali		Because since long ago
maxtyo 'ab'i 'añik xchumtyil;		there still were no settlements, they say,
maxtyo 'añik xchumtyil.	20	there still were no settlements.
'I tza majli;		And he left;
tzi tyaja jochob' b'ä 'otyoty.		he came upon an abandoned house.
Jocholix b'u 'otyoty;		A house that had been abandoned;
mañik 'i yum.		it had no owner.
Chex b'u b'ajche' jochol 'otyoty,	25	It looked like an abandoned house,

ba tzi käyä 'i yum,	where its owner had left it,
'i tza majli,	and he left,
'o tza chämi,	or he died,
'o chuka tzi cha'le.	or whatever he did.
'Entonse,	30 So,
tza 'ab'i ñumi.	they say he came by.
Pero komo 'ik'ajelix,	But since it was getting dark,
max tzi chäñ jak'ä xämb'al,	he didn't want to go on walking,
porke max b'a mi ki tyaj 'i wäyib',	because there was no place to find a bed,
'o b'a mi majlel tyi wäyel.	35 or where he could go to sleep.
'I che jiñi,	And so it was,
tza wäyi ya'i.	he slept there.
Cha' tyikilob' wiñik.	There were two men.
'Entonses,	So,
tza letzi tyi jol 'otyoty,	40 they climbed up to the rafters,
tyi tapanko,	to the tapanco,
tyi jol 'otyoty;	to the head of the house;
'i tza letziyob' tyi wäyel.	and they climbed up to sleep.
'Entonses,	So,
che tzi tyajayob' yojlil 'ak'älel,	45 when it was close to midnight,
tza 'ab'i ki yub'iñ	they say they began to hear
ju'ukña, tyilelob' xty'añ,	noisily, voices were coming;
ju'ukña, tyilel xkuj;	noisily, owls were coming;
ju'ukña, tyilel stzuk b'ajlum;	noisily, jaguarundis were coming;
chu'tyak bä 'animal.	50 all kinds of animals.
Tza 'ab'i kaj tyi k'otyel 'i yum pañimil—	They say it was the Earth Lord coming—
'i yum xib'aj.	the Lord of the Demons.
Xib'aj, xib'ajixtyi,	Demons, devils,
chuxka.	whatever.
Pero Xib'ajäch,	55 But the real Xib'aj,
'añ mi yälob'.	as they call him.
'Entonses,	So,
ya 'ab'i 'añob' 'ub'i wiñikob';	there were the men, they say;
mi kuchob' 'i mam k'ujtz,	they carried a bundle of tobacco,
mam k'ujtz.	60 native tobacco.
'Entonse,	So,
wäyälob' tyi jol 'otyoty.	they were asleep in the rafters.
Pero mach wäyälob'ik,	But they were not really asleep,
che jach kañalob' 'i wuty;	they just had their eyes closed.
'i ñich'tyañtyak	65 They heard everything,
chu mi ki melob',	whatever they did,

chu mi ki yälob'.
'Entonse,
tza k'otyi 'ub'i Tzimajol,
mi sub'eñob',
Tzima Jol.
'Entonse,
tza ki yäl jiñi:
"Weno,
melex laj k'ajk;
xik'ix laj k'ajk;
melex lak we'el,
porke joñoñ, 'añix jwi'ñal.
Se'ñuñ laj,"
che mi sub'eñob'
pejtye x'ixikob', wiñikob',
wo bu 'i ty'umob' tyi xämb'al.
Tza kajiyob' tyi xik' k'ajk;
tza' ki sik'ob' 'i käk'al;
tza' kaji 'i melob' 'i we'el.
'Entonse,
tza ki po'ob';
tza' ki ch'äxob'.
'Entonse,
komo lak ña' 'añ tza bä chämi,
'i max tyo 'i k'ele pañumil 'i yalob'il,
'entonse tzi yälä 'ub'i Xib'aj:
"Joñoñ, mi la lotyb'eñoñ 'i ch'ok tyuñ;
joñoñ, mi kaj jk'uxb'eñ 'i ch'ok tyuñ,
porke jcha'añ me jiñi."
Che tza ki yäl 'añ Xib'aj bäyi,
ñoj xib'aj b'äyi,
mero 'i tyatyob' bä xib'aj.
'Entonse,
tza ki melob' 'i we'el,
woyob'ix tyi we'el.
Tza ki yub'iñ 'i yujtz'il 'ub'i wiñik,
wäyälob' b'u tyi jol 'otyoty.
"Pero chex bä 'añ majch 'añ wä' tyi 'otyoty,"

che' tza ki yäl Xib'aj;
tza ki letzel.

whatever they said.
So,
that Gourd Head arrived,
70 as they call him,
Gourd Head.
So,
he began to say:
"Okay,
75 get our fire going;
fan our fire;
make our food,
because I am hungry.
Hurry up,"
80 he told them,
all of the women, all of the men,
who accompanied him on the trip.
They started to light a fire;
the flames began to rise;
85 they started to make their meal.
Then,
they started to cut her up;
they started to cook her.
So,
90 since it was a woman who had died,
and her child still hadn't been born,
then Xib'aj said:
"For me, set aside that tender egg.
Me, I'm going to eat that tender egg,
95 because it belongs to me."
That's what the one who was Xib'aj said,
the one who was the big demon,
the very father of the demons.
So,
100 they started to make their meal,
they were already eating.
He began to smell the scent of the men,
who were sleeping in the rafters.
"It seems there is someone here in the
 house,"
105 said Xib'aj.
He got up.

"Weno, letzen laj k'ele,"
che tzi sub'e 'i mosojtyak,
'i mosojtyak,
wo b'u 'i k'elob' majlel,
'i pi'leñ tyi xämb'al.
"Weno, kukulaj k'ele,"
che' 'i sub'e.
'Entonse tza letziyob':
"Cha' tyikil,
'um b'a 'añob' cha' tyikil.
¿Chuk mi lak sub'eñ?"
"La' jub'ikob',
'i k'uxob' 'i waj."
Che jiñ,
mak chu' tzi yäläyob' 'añ wiñik.
Tza jub'iyob' cha' tyikilob';
tza jub'i tyi lum.
Loñ much ki paxoñ k'ux 'i waj,
tzi yälä.
Pero che jiñi,
che jax tza ki k'el,
koñ woli 'i ña'tyañ'
tza ki yub'iñ
ke mach weñ we'elik.
"Ch'ok muty",
mi yäl.
Pero machiñ;
lak pi'äl jach.
Chañ jach koñ x'ixik
'i tza' chämi,
'añ tyo ke ma tza k'ele tyi pañumil
jiñi 'i yalob'il.
Pero kom ma tza mejli tyi 'aläñijel,
ma tza mejli tyi k'ok'añ,
'i tza' chämi,
yik'oty yalob'il ya' tyi mal.
Tza' chämi.
Jiñ meku "ch'ok muty",
mi yäl.
'Añ jiñi.
Na' muty, mi yäl.

"Okay, go up and look,"
he said to his servants,
his peons,
110 who were going up to look,
his companions on the trip.
"Okay, y'all go up and look,"
he told them.
Then they went up:
115 "Two men,
there are two men here.
What do you tell us to do?"
"Let them come down,
and eat some food."
120 So it was,
the men didn't say anything.
The two men came down;
they came down to the ground.
They were just going to pretend to eat,
125 they said.
But so it was,
they just started to see,
and they were thinking
it seemed
130 that it wasn't good food.
"Tender hen,"
they called it.
But it wasn't.
It was really a person.
135 It was just that the woman
died,
and still had not been born
her child.
But since she wasn't able to give birth,
140 she wasn't able to deliver,
and she died,
with her child inside her.
She died.
That was the "tender hen,"
145 as they called her,
It was her.
A hen, they say.

Pero ya 'añ 'i "ch'ok tyuñ",
ya' tyi yojlil 'i ñäk,
mi yäl.
Jiñ ch'ok tyuñ
'añ 'aläli,
che mi yäl.
'Entonse,
tza ki k'elob' 'añ wiñiki;
much ki k'ux 'añ jun tyikil,
tzi yälä.
Pero tza ki cha' sub'eñ 'i pi'äl,
"Mach yomik 'a k'ux jiñi,
porke mach weñ we'elälik."
'Entonse,
tza ki 'i lok'sañ
'i yaläl mam k'ujtz.
Koñ 'añix ku tza 'i yaläl b'uxi,
tza ki lok'sañ.
Tza' kaji tyity 'i wejtyb'eñ
ya' tyi pam 'i we'el.
Tzi tyity wejtyb'eñob'
pejtye wiñikob' xwe'elälob'.
Tzi wejtyb'eñob'.
'A che jiñi,
tza laj chämiyob'.
Paxoñ chämiyob';
pero che jach tza jum pajk chämiyob'.
'I che' tza 'ujtyiyob' tyi yajlel,
tzi k'ele.
Chukuyob' 'i yajñel 'ub'i wiñik.
'I welekñayob' majlel tyi b'ij.
Loñ 'ak'älel,
pero chäch wo 'i yajñesañob' majlel.
'A mañik,
che yomix 'i tyajob' majlel tyi b'ij,
tza yub'i 'añ wiñikob'.
Che yox k'otyel tyi yotlel 'ixim,

tza kaji yub'iñ yax tyileli.
'A komo yujil 'i ñuk' k'ujtz 'añ juñ tyikili,
tzi wa' ñuk'u 'i k'ujtzi.

But there was her "tender egg,"
there in the inside of her belly,
150   they say.
That tender egg
was her child,
That's what they called it.
So,
155   the men began to see;
one did want to eat,
he said.
But his companion told him again,
"It's not right to eat that,
160   because it's not good food."
So,
he started to take out
his little bundle of tobacco.
Since he had a little gourd full of tobacco,
165   he began to take it out.
He started to sprinkle it
there on top of the food.
He sprinkled it
on all the people they were eating.
170   He sprinkled it on them.
So it was,
they all died.
Well, they half died,
but only for a little while did they die.
175   And when they finished falling down,
the men saw it.
The men took off.
They hit the road flying.
It was dark,
180   but they were being pursued.
Ah, no,
they were almost going to catch them,
the men felt.
When they were just getting to a corn
   granary
185   they felt they were coming near.
Ah, since one of the men smoked,
he lit up a smoke.

Chol		English
'A che jiñi,		So,
tza' ki 'i käy 'i k'ujtz		he started to leave tobacco
ya' tyi b'ij;	190	there on the road;
tzi käyä 'i k'ujtz.		he left his tobacco.
'A koñ mach weñik mi yub'iñ		Since they don't like
'i yujtz'il 'i b'utz' k'ujtz xib'aj,		the smell of tobacco, those demons,
tzi sätyb'e 'i yujtz'il;		they lost the scent of them;
tza sajtyi 'i yujtz'il 'ub'i wiñiki.	195	the scent of the men was lost.
'A mañik,		Ah, no,
b'ajche kaj tzi xoyob' 'i b'ijlel;		whatever twists and turns they took,
tza 'i xoyo 'i b'ijlel 'añ Xib'aj.		Xib'aj took those twists and turns.
Tza ki cha' tyumb'eñ 'i yok.		He began to follow their trail again.
'A yomix 'i cha' tyaj,	200	Ah, they almost caught them again,
tza yub'i 'ub'i mero laj tyaty bä;		so felt the man who was in charge;
mero yujiläch 'i käñol wälej.		he really knew his craft.
Tza ki 'i pichiñ jiñ b'ij;		He started to urinate on the road;
tzi pichi 'i b'ij.		he urinated on the road.
'A che jiñi,	205	So it was,
tzi cha' pichi.		he urinated again.
'I 'añ Xib'aj		And Xib'aj
max tzi k'ele		couldn't see
b'a tza' cha' majli.		where they had gone.
Ya tzi sätyb'e 'i yujtz'il ja' wiñiki;	210	He lost the scent of the men;
tza majli.		he went on.
'Añ winiki		The men
tza k'otyi 'i tyaj		arrived to find
'i yotlel 'ixim.		a corn granary.
Weñ b'uty'ul tyi 'ixim jiñi 'otyoty.	215	It was really full of corn.
'Entonse,		So,
tza ki sub'eñ 'ub'i säk waj bä 'ixim:		the white corn began to tell them:
"'Ocheñ 'ilali,		"Come in here,
mak chu' mi tyumb'eñety.		nothing will happen to you.
'Ocheñ," che'eñ.	220	Come in," it said.
'A koñ ya 'añ xchäkchab' 'ixim,		Ah, but since there was red-wax corn,
'i'ik' bä 'ixim,		black corn,
tzi sub'e:		it said:
"Ma'añik,		"No,
joñoñ mi kaj jsub'."	225	I will tell!"
Che tzi sub'e 'i'ik' 'ixim,		That's what the black corn said,
tya'chäb' 'ixim.		the shit-wax corn.
Che jiñi:		So it was,

"Mach ma jak'b'eñ,"		"Don't pay any attention to him,"
che' añ säk waj.	230	said the white corn.
"'Ocheñ."		"Come in."
'A che ja'el,		So, also,
koñ ya p'uchul ja' ch'ujmi		since there were pumpkins piled up there, too,
tyi papaty 'otyoty,		at the entrance to the granary,
tza ki sub'eñ:	235	it started to say:
"Mach ma la' bäk'ñañ;		"Don't be afraid;
joñoñ, mi jtyejchel ja'el.		as for me, I will rise up, too.
Wi'ilix mi la' wochel ja'el,"		You all will get into it later, too,"
che'eñ tzi jak'ä ja'el ch'ujmi.		so said the pumpkins as well.
'A tza 'ochi 'añ wiñik	240	So the men went in
tyi jajp jiñ 'ixim.		to the middle of the corn.
Ya 'añ xk'añal:		There there was yellow corn:
"'Ocheñ ku laj;		"Do come in, you all;
mach mi la' bäk'ñañ.		don't be afraid.
Joñoñ laj, kab'äloñ laj;	245	All of us, there are a lot of us,
'a b'ajñel xchäkchab'.		and the red-wax corn is all alone.
¿Chuk ye'tyel?		What good is it?
¿Chuki 'i k'äjñib'al		What use does it have,
jiñ x'ik' tyäk'añ 'ity?"		that black sticky butthole?"
Che mi sub'eñ 'an xchäkchab'.	250	That's what it was telling the red-wax corn.
Tza 'ochi tyi jajpi.		They went into the middle of the corn.
"Machikix,		"Never mind,
mu tyo jtyejchel ja'		I'm still going to rise up, too,
tyi la' kontra."		as your enemy."
Che tzi sub'e x'ik' tyäk'añ 'ityi.	255	That's what the black sticky butthole said.
'A che jiñ,		So it was,
tza 'ochi 'añ wiñikob'i;		the men went inside;
tza 'ochi tyi jajp 'añ 'iximi.		they went in to the middle of the corn.
Tza ki yub'iñ		They started to sense
che' yax k'otyelob' añ xib'aj;	260	that the demons were coming close;
tza ki b'ajb'eñob' letyu yik'oty ch'ujm.		they started to fight with the pumpkins.
Ñaxañ tza' tyejchi ch'ujm		First the pumpkins rose up
'i b'ajb'eñtyak.		and struck them over and over.
Ch'umlaw jach,		Smash!
kaj tza' k'otyi	265	They started to reach
ya' tyi jol 'añ Xib'aj.		the head of Xib'aj.
P'uslaw jach,		Splat!
kaj tyejchel ja'el ch'ujmi.		The pumpkins began to rise up.

'A che jiñ,	So it was,
tza' ki yub'iñ 'añ 'ili 'ixim	the corn began to sense
ke max wo 'i mejlel 'i cha'añ ch'ujm;	that pumpkins couldn't do it by themselves;
tza tyejchi jiñi xk'añal.	the yellow corn rose up.
K'añal bä 'ixim	The yellow corn
tza' kaj tyi tyejchel;	began to rise up;
tza' ki b'ajb'eñ ja'el.	it began to hit them also.
'A ko max wox 'i mäjlel 'i cha'añ,	Ah, since it couldn't do it by itself,
tza yub'i,	it seemed,
tza' kaji ja'el säk waj 'iximi.	the white corn started in, too.
"Joñoñ lojoñ,	"As for us,
mero 'añoñ lojoñ tyi yeb'al,	we are down in the bottom,
yojlil jiñ säk waji,"	in the middle of the white corn,"
che' mi yälob' 'añ wiñikob'.	the men told them.
Ya jax tza' kaj tyi tyejchel ja' säk waji;	There now the white corn started to rise up;
tza' ki b'ajb'eñ.	it started to strike them.
Tza ki b'ajb'eñ 'an Xib'aji.	It started to strike that Xib'aj.
'A koñ yax tyilel ja'el 'i säk'ajeli,	Ah, but since dawn was coming soon,
k'iñlawix pañumil.	the earth was getting brighter.
Tzax kaj tyi putz'el ja'el Xib'aj;	Xib'aj started to take flight;
komo mach 'a wilañ	since don't you see
koñ ma tza mäjli 'i cha'añ 'añ Xib'aj.	that he couldn't stand it himself.
'I tzäx 'i chuku 'i yajñel,	And he just took off,
chañ säkix pañumil.	because the earth was getting brighter.
Majli.	He left.
Che jiñ,	So it was,
tza k'otyi 'i yum 'añ cholel,	the owner of the milpa arrived,
'i yum 'añ 'ixim.	the owner of the corn.
Tza' ki k'ajtyib'eñ:	He started to ask them:
"¿Chuk tza mele 'añ b'ajche 'iliyi?	"What did y'all do to make it like this?
¿B'ajche tza la' yäsa pejtyel kixim?	How did y'all get all my corn down?
¿B'ajche tza la' mele 'ili jch'ujmi?	What did y'all do with the pumpkins?
Tzax la' laj tyop'o.	Y'all have busted them all!
Wäle, kaj la' koltyañoñ jlitz,"	Now you're going to help me stack them,"
che'eñ 'i yum 'añ 'ixim.	said the owner of the corn.
"Pero mañik, yaj,	"But no, sir,
much lätzb'eñety lojoñ,"	of course we'll stack them for you,"
che tzi jak'äyob' 'añ wiñik.	answered the men.
"Tzi koltyañoñ 'ili 'a wiximi;	"Your corn helped us out;
mero weñ p'uñp'uñ jax 'ili 'a wixim.	your corn is really tough.
'Aktyañ 'ili xchäkchab',	Except that red-wax corn,

Line numbers (center column): 270, 275, 280, 285, 290, 295, 300, 305

mach k'uxik ma wub'iñ,
porke jiñ, tzi kontrajiyoñ lojoñ."
tzi yälä.
"Tyeme mi ki k'uxoñ lojoñ
yik'oty jiñ Xib'aj,"
tzi yälä.
"Wäle, mach mi laj k'uxb'iñ
jiñ 'ik' tyäk'añ 'ity."
Che tza' kaj 'i sub'eñ 'añ 'iximi,
'i ya tzi pul käyäyob'.
'Añ che jiñ,
tza' 'ujtyi 'i lätzob' 'añ 'iximi.
"¿A b'ak samety laj?"
che tzi sub'e 'añ 'ub'i 'i yum 'añ 'ixim,
'i yum yotlel 'ixim.
"Sami käk' loñ juñ.
'Ak'juñoñ lojoñ.
Pero tzax tza 'ochi 'ak'älel jcha'añ lojoñ
ya tyi b'ij.
'I ko mañix b'a mi tyaj lojoñ läk'äl bä 'otyoty,
yax tza wäyäyoñ loñ tyi joch 'otyoty.

Pero ma' wo jña'tyañ lojoñ,
mi yotyoty xib'aj,
b'a mi k'otyelob' 'i melob' chu' mi melob'.
'A che jiñ,
jiñ jax tza' kaj kub'iñ lojoñ
che tyi yojlil 'ak'älel,
tza k'otyiyob' xib'aj,
tza k'otyiyob' tyi we'el.
Yax meku tza kaj jp'ujp'ujb'eñ lojoñ
xmam k'ujtzi.
Tzax meku jchuku loñ kajñel.
Tza' tyiliyoñ tyi koltyäñtyel
'ila tyi yotlel 'a wixim.
Weñ, mik sub'eñety,
mach yomik 'a cha'leñ letyu,
mach yomik 'a tz'aleñoñ,
porke mach 'a wilañ
ke tzi koltyañoñ laj 'a wixim.
Machki,

310 don't look on it with favor,
because it went against us,"
they said.
"It was going to eat us together
with that Xib'aj,"
315 they said.
"Now, we don't like
that black sticky butthole."
Thus they spoke to that [black] corn,
and they left it scattered about.
320 So it was,
they finished stacking up the corn.
"Where are y'all going?"
asked the owner of the corn,
the owner of the corn granary.
325 "We're going to deliver a letter.
We are messengers.
But the nightfall caught us
there on the road.
And since we couldn't find a nearby house,
330 we just went to sleep in an abandoned
   house.
But we didn't know
it was a house of the demons,
where they go to do whatever they do.
So it was,
335 we started to sense
around about midnight,
the demons arrived,
they came to eat.
First we began to sprinkle on them
340 native tobacco.
We took off running.
We came to be helped
here at the corn granary.
Okay, I tell you,
345 it's not right for you to fight us,
it's not right you should dislike us,
because don't you see
that your corn helped us.
If not,

wajalix tza kub'i,	350	a long time ago, I feel,
sajmäx kub'i,		early on, I feel,
wolikix 'i k'uxoñ,		they would have eaten us,
wolikix 'i buk'oñ,"		they would have swallowed us,"
che' tza ki yälob' 'añ wiñik.		so said the men.
Che jiñ,	355	So it was,
"Yonku che jiñ,"		"Okay then,"
che 'añ wiñik,		said the man,
'i yum bä cholel.		the owner of the milpa.
"Tzax 'ujtyi lak lätz;		"The stacking is finished;
kox laj chejeñ."	360	let's go, then."
Che jiñ,		So it was,
tza' tyem majliyob'.		they left together.
Tza' k'otyiyob' 'a tyi xchumtyil,		They arrived at the settlement
b'a sami 'i yäk'eñ juñi.		where they were going to deliver the letter.
Tzi yäkä 'añ juñi.	365	They delivered the letter.
Che jiñ,		So it was,
tzi yälä		[the recipient] said
tza bä 'ak'eñtyi 'añ juñ:		when the letter was delivered:
"Wäle, ¿mu tyo kaj la' sujtyel 'ili?"		"Now, are you still going back there?"
che jiñ.	370	he said.
"Mu tyo ku,"		"Still, indeed,"
che 'ab'i 'añx 'ak'juñ.		they say the messengers said.
"Weno, kuku laj che jiñi,		"Okay, then get going,
pero tzajalety meku laj, che jiñ.		but be very careful, then.
Jun yajl 'ak'älelixtyo,	375	When it is still dark
mi la' lok'el majl 'ilayi,"		y'all leave for there,"
che tzi sub'e		he said to
'añ tza bä 'i ch'äm 'añ juñ.		the one who took the letter.
"Chañ p'is mi la' ñumel jiñ		"So that in good time you'll go by
b'a tza la' tyaja jiñ Xib'aj;	380	where you encountered Xib'aj;
chañ mach mi la' chän cha'leñ wäyel		so y'all don't just sleep again
ya' tyi jochol b'u 'otyoty."		there in the abandoned house."
"Weno,"		"Okay,"
che ja' wiñik.		said the men.
Tza sujtyiyob' majlel.	385	They turned and went back.
'A pero koñ 'añ tyo juñ tyikil jiñ wiñik		Ah, but there was still one of those men
tza bä 'i mero mitz'añ 'ub'i we'eli;		who had really tasted that food;
mach 'ab'i 'utz, tza yub'i.		that wasn't good, it seemed.
Jiñäch 'a mi ki k'extyañ,		He himself would have to replace it,
'o jiñ mi ki majlel tyi wentajil	390	or go in place of it,

'añ tza b'ä 'i k'uxu 'i waji.	the one who ate that food.
'I k'exol 'ab'i,	Its replacement, they say,
'añ waj tzi k'uxu.	for the food he ate.
Machiki,	If not him,
jiñ 'ab'i 'i kuktyal,	his own flesh, they say,
'o 'i pi'äl,	or his wife,
'o 'i ña',	or his mother,
mi cha' k'extyiyel 'i cha'añ.	would be exchanged for it.
'A che jiñi,	So it was,
tza ki sujtyiyob' majlel.	they turned and went back.
Pero mak b'ajche yub'il tza' yub'i,	But he didn't feel anything;
tza k'otyiyob' tyi yotyoty.	they arrived at their houses.
Tza' ki sub'en 'i yijñam,	He started to tell his wife,
tza ki sub'eñ 'i tyaty, 'i ña'.	he started to tell his father, his mother.
'A che jiñ.	So it was,
Tzax b'äk'ñi wälej.	He was frightened now.
Tzax kaj tyi tzäñal.	He began to have chills.
Tzax kaj tyi k'ajk.	He began to have fever.
Max tzi ñusa jum p'ejl semanaj	Not even a week went by
tza' chämi.	and he died.
Chämi.	He died.
Che jax b'ajche jiñi	Just like that
tza' 'ujtyi jsub'eñety laj.	ended what I am telling you all.

Line numbers in margin: 395, 400, 405, 410.

12

The Jaguar-Man

Nicolás Arcos Alvarez, Mateo Alvaro López,
and Ausencio Cruz Guzmán

This story was recorded in Palenque in 1985 by Josserand and Hopkins. The principal narrators are Nicolás Arcos Alvarez and Mateo Alvaro López, both from the ejido León Brindis. Ausencio (Chencho) Cruz Guzmán was also present and occasionally intervenes. Mateo is Nicolás's uncle, and Chencho owned an ejido property that Nicolás worked, so Nicolás was definitely the junior partner in the telling of the story, as can be seen in the interaction of the three. The occasion was the re-thatching of the house of Merle Greene Robertson, in the neighborhood of Palenque known as La Cañada. Josserand and Hopkins were sharing the house with Carolyn Tate, who was working on her dissertation on Yaxchilán (Tate 1992). The old thatch had disintegrated after the fall of the acidic ashes of the Chichonal volcano eruption and badly needed to be replaced. We recruited a team of thatchers from León Brindis, acquired thatching palm from La Cascada, and began to work. In the evenings, after a hard day's work, we would sit on the back porch and have the first beers of the day, a natural setting for storytelling. We livened up the group by offering a prize for the best story, but somehow nobody ever lost—all the stories were prize-worthy.

This tale represents a major genre of Chol folktales, stories that symbolize the dangers of Nature and feature a wide range of threatening characters. People living in isolated areas or camped out in their fields are subject to encounters with Blackman, Spiny Man, the Savage, the cannibal Maternal Uncles, Feet on Backward, Bouncing Head, Big Hat, and the demons of the underworld (Josserand et al.

DOI: 10.5876/9781607324881.c012

2003). The key to coping with all these creatures is Culture. They are all dangerous but unacquainted with human things or repelled by them. They can be outsmarted by a clever human. In fact, in none of our stories do the humans actually get eaten, except offstage (as in this tale).

One set of menaces are the transformers, supernaturals who can take human shapes in order to deceive people, usually with the goal of eating them. Some of these are human witches who can take on animal forms (normally those of their animal counterparts, their *wäy*); others are animals who take on human shape. The transformed supernatural may live undetected among humans for a long time, even be married and have a family. Flesh Dropper, for instance, lived as father to his human children, but at night he would drop his flesh and go out to party with other skeletons. He was ultimately discovered by his children, who against his instructions spied on him in the kitchen and saw him drop his flesh. They rid themselves of him by sprinkling the fallen flesh with salt and chile. He could not call his flesh to rise, and he fled with the coming of the dawn (Pérez Chacón 1988:169–72).

In this story and in The Comadre story in this collection, the transformers are jaguars who have taken the shapes of the humans they have killed and eaten. They cannot maintain the human shapes, however, and are soon found out. It is notable that they also speak broken Chol.

The Jaguar-Man

Ty'an Jini Bajlum Winik
    Nicolás Arcos Alvarez
    Mateo Alvaro López
    Ausencio (Chencho) Cruz Guzmán

[Nicolás:]		[Nicolás:]
Jiñäch 'i tyejchb'ali:	1	This is its beginning:
Tza majli 'añ wiñiki		A man went out
tza säk'a;		at dawn;
pero mañik tza k'otyi;		but he didn't return
k'äläl tyi ak'lel.	5	until nightfall.
Woli 'i pijtyañob'		They were waiting for him
che b'u tza k'ele		when they saw
mak tzikil tyilel.		that he didn't show up.
Wo 'i k'el		She looked
pero wo tyi 'e'tyel jiñ x'ixik	10	but the woman was still working
ya tyi mal.		there inside.
'I yalob'il		Her daughter
tza bäk' kaj tyi seb'e wäyel.		soon started to go to sleep.

Che jiñi,		So it was,
tza kaji 'i k'el	15	she started to see
yax tyilel 'ub'i wiñiki.		the man was coming near.
Tzi ña'tya chañ 'i ñoxi'aläch;		She thought it was really her husband;
pero mach 'i ñoxi'alik.		but it wasn't her husband at all.
Che jiñi,		So it was,
tzi k'ele chañ tza k'otyiyi.	20	she saw that he had arrived.
Tzi ki sub'eñ chañ		She started to ask him
mi mu tyo 'i jape' sa'		if he still wanted to drink atole
'o mu tyo 'i k'uxe waj.		or still eat some tortillas.
[CHENCHO:]		[CHENCHO:]
¿'Añ tza juñ p'ejl tyejklum?		Was there a town there?
[NICOLÁS:]		[NICOLÁS:]
Ya tzi tyejche lemb'al.	25	That's where he started drinking.
[CHENCHO:]		[CHENCHO:]
Chäch ma tyech.		Start there.
[MATEO:]		[MATEO:]
Weno, chäch ma tyech weñ, yub'il:		Okay, start it better there, it seems:
'a me jinch wiñik		that there was a man
mi jap tyi pejtyelel 'ora.		who drank all the time.
Mi ki k'otyel tyi yotyoty,	30	He would arrive at his house,
mi maj tyi tyejklum mi jap;		he would go to town to drink;
mi k'otyel tyi yotyoty.		he would arrive at his house.
Pero juñ p'ejl k'iñ		But one day
tzi tyaja b'ajlum tyi b'ij.		he encountered a jaguar on the road.
[NICOLÁS:]		[NICOLÁS:]
Pero lajal	35	But it's the same
chañ mi laj cha'leñ ty'añ cha' tyikil,		if two of us are talking,
koñ jiñ tza che'		since it seems like
ma'añik mi lak laj ña'tyañ.		we don't know it all.
[CHENCHO:]		[CHENCHO:]
Laja wejläch yom mi la cha'leñ ty'añ.		You both need to talk.
[NICOLÁS:]		[NICOLÁS:]
Jäjä'.	40	Okay.
Mu b'u 'i ñajäyel jcha'añi,		That which I forget
jatyety ma jak'e.		you can tell.
[MATEO:]		[MATEO:]
Eso.		That's it.
[NICOLÁS:]		[NICOLÁS:]
Che jach.		Just like that.
'Añ 'ab'i jun tyikil wiñik wajali;	45	They say there was a man, long ago;

weñ yujil 'ab'i lemb'al.
Mu 'ab'i 'i majlel tyi tyejklum;
mu 'ab'i cha'leñ lemb'al ya'i.
Che mi k'otyel tyi yotyoty,
weñ yäk, 'ab'i.
Pero pejtye 'ora
che mi majle tyi tyejklum,
mi jape' lemb'al.
Pero 'añix 'ora
tzi tyejche 'i lemb'al.
Mi majlel tyi tyejklum,
mi jape' lemb'al;
mu tyo 'i k'otyel tyi yotyoty.
Pero 'añ tzi tyajb'e 'i yorajlel
che tza k'otyi 'i tyaje'
juñ kojty b'ajlum.
Tzi tyaja ya tyi b'ij
che bä ya tyo woli 'i majlel.
Tzi chuku jiñi b'ajlum;
tzi tzäñsa.
Pero tza kaj tyi 'ik'añ.
Woli 'i pijtyañ jiñi 'i pi'äl
ya tyi yotyoty.
Woli 'i ña'tyañ jiñi x'ixiik
mu tyo 'i kaj tyi k'otyel,
pero mañik tzikil.
Tza k'otyi che' mero tz'itya 'ak'älel.
Tza k'otyi jiñi wiñik.
Pero mach jiñix 'i ñoxi'alix x'ixik;
jiñix jiñi b'ajlum.
Ko me tza 'ujtyi 'i tzäñsañ jiñi wiñik,
tzi muku kälel jiñi b'ajlum.
Tza majli ya tyi yotyoty jiñi wiñik.
[CHENCHO:]
¿Tzi päñtyesa 'i b'ä tyi wiñik?
[NICOLÁS:]
Tzi päñtyesa 'i b'ä tyi wiñik.
Che jiñi, tza majli.
Che jiñi, tza k'otyi.
Tza 'ochi.
Tzi ña'tya jiñi x'ixik

he really knew how to drink liquor.
They say he would go to town;
they say he would drink liquor there.
When he returned to his house,
50   he would be really drunk, they say.
But all the time
when he would go to town
he would drink liquor.
But it had been a while
55   since he started drinking.
He would go to town.
he would drink liquor;
he would still get back home.
But there came a time
60   when he arrived to find
a jaguar.
He met it there on the road
when he was still coming home.
The jaguar caught him;
65   it killed him.
But it was starting to get dark.
His wife was waiting for him
there at his house.
The woman was thinking
70   that he should be coming,
but he didn't show up.
He arrived just as it was getting dark.
The man arrived.
But it wasn't really the woman's husband;
75   it was the jaguar.
Since when he finished killing the man,
the jaguar left him buried there.
He went there to the man's house.
[CHENCHO:]
Did he turn himself into the man?
[NICOLÁS:]
80   He turned himself into the man.
So it was, he left.
So it was, he arrived.
He went in.
The woman thought

ke 'i ñoxi'aläch.
Che jiñi,
tza ki sub'eñ,
tza b'uchle ya tyi mal,
b'ajche mi k'otyel 'i ñoxi'al
mi b'uchtyäl.
Che jiñi,
tza ki yäle' ub'i x'ixik;
tzi sub'e mi mu tyo 'i jape' sa'
'o mi mu tyo 'i k'uxe' waj.
Tzi yälä jiñ wiñik:
"Mañix chu b'u kom,"
tzi yälä.
"Chañ mux jkaj tyi wäyel."
Tza kaj tyi wäyel.
Ko me jiñ x'ixik,
woli tyo tyi b'äjñe' e'tyel.
'Añ yalob'il,
tza wäyi.
Jiñ yalob'il,
seb' tyo mi wäyel.
Jiñ 'alob',
tza wäyi.
Che jeñ,
ya tza maj tyi wäyel jiñi wiñik.
Ko me wo 'i ña'tyañ jiñi x'ixik
'i ñoxi'aläch,
ya b'ä tza maj tyi wäyel.
Che jiñi,
tza kaji tyi wäyel jiñi b'ajlum.
Pero ma wo 'i ña'tyañ jiñi x'ixik
mi b'ajlum.
Che jeñ,
tza ki yäl jiñ 'alob':
"Mamá," che'eñ.
"¿Chuki?"
che tzi ki yäl.
"Jiñi weñ sak' 'i tzutzel jpapá,"
che 'ab'i.
"¿Weñ sak' 'i tzutzel? ¿Chukoch?"
che 'ab'i.

85	that it was her husband.
	So it was,
	she started to speak to him.
	He sat down there inside.
	Like it was her husband arriving,
90	he was sitting down.
	So it was,
	the woman began to speak to him;
	she asked if he still wanted to drink atole
	or if he still wanted to eat tortillas.
95	The man said:
	"There isn't anything I want,"
	he said.
	"I'm just going to go to sleep."
	He started to go to sleep.
100	So that woman
	went on working by herself.
	The daughter
	had gone to sleep.
	The daughter
105	was fast asleep already.
	The daughter
	went to sleep.
	So it was,
	there the man went off to sleep.
110	So the woman was thinking
	it was her husband,
	there where he went to sleep.
	So it was,
	the jaguar started to go to sleep.
115	But the woman wasn't thinking
	that it was a jaguar.
	So it was,
	the child began to say:
	"Mamá," she said.
120	"What?"
	she answered.
	"My papa's hair is really scratchy,"
	they say she said.
	"His hair is scratchy? Why?"
125	they say she said.

"Weñ sak' 'i tzutzel,"
che ab'i.
Che jiñi,
tza majli jiñi x'ixik.
Tza majli 'i k'el.
Tzi k'ele chañ jiñx b'ajlum ya 'añ.
Pero tzi pensariñ
chañ b'ajche mi lok' jiñ yalob'il.
Che jiñi,
'añ 'ab'i jun p'ejl tyem.
Tzi ch'ämä majlel.
Che ya 'añ jiñ tyem
ya tyi ty'ejl jiñi b'ajlum,
tzi k'uñtye lok'o jiñ yalob'il.
Che' tzi lok'o 'i yalob'il,
tza 'i yotzab'e jiñ tyem,
koñ mek'el 'i cha'añ jiñ 'alob',
mek'el 'i cha'añ.
Che jiñi,
tza lok'iyi.
Tza 'ujtyi 'i lok' 'i yalob'il jiñ x'ixik.

Che tza lok'i ja'el jiñ x'ixik yik'oty 'i yalob'il.
Tza lok'i yik'oty.
Che jiñi,
majli yik'oty,
b'añ juñ p'ejl tye',
juñ p'ejl way ja'as;
ya tza majli.
Tzi ña'tya jiñ x'ixik
b'ajche mi ki yäk' 'i yalob'il
ya tyi ñi' tye'.
Tzi ch'ämä majlel jiñi 'ab';
ya tzi kächä,
ya tyi ñi' tye'.
Che tza kaji 'i käch,
ya tzi jäm choko 'i yalob'il;
ya tza kaji 'i cha' wäysañ.
Pero ko me 'añ wajali che jiñi,
mu 'ab'i 'i k'äñob' jiñ ña'tyuñ.
Tzi ch'ämä majlel;

"His hair is really scratchy,"
they say she said.
So it was,
the woman went in.
130 She went to see.
She saw that it was a jaguar that was there.
But she put herself to thinking
how she could get her daughter out.
So it was,
135 there was a little bench there.
She took it in.
When the bench was there,
there at the side of the jaguar,
she slowly pulled out her daughter.
140 When she pulled out her daughter,
she put in the bench,
since the child was embraced by him,
she was embraced by him.
So it was,
145 she came out.
The child of the woman finished coming
  out.

The woman got out as well, with her child.
She got out with her.
So it was,
150 she went with her,
to where there was a tree,
a zapote tree.
They went there.
The woman thought about
155 how she could place her daughter
there in the tip of the tree.
She brought with her a hammock;
she tied it up there,
there in the tip of the tree.
160 When she tied it,
there she laid down her daughter;
there she started to put her to sleep again.
But since this was long ago,
they say they still used metates.
165 She brought it with her;

tzi ch'uyu letzel;
tza k'äjki yik'oty 'i k'äb' 'añ ña'tyuñ.
Che tza k'äjki yik'oty jiñi,
che jale' k'otyeli,
tza kaj tyi k'otyel jiñ b'ajlum.
Tza kaji 'i sik'b'eñ majlel 'i yujtz'il
b'aki tza majli jiñ x'ixik;
tza tyejchi majlel.
Che mach yax 'añ jiñi x'ixik,
tza majli;
tza k'äjki ya tyi ñi' tye'.
[Chencho:]
¿Tyoj k'äjkel?
[Nicolás:]
Yom k'äjkel ja'el b'ajlum.
Wolix 'i k'äjkel
chañ sami 'i chuk jub'el.
Pero ko me woläch 'i pensariñ
b'ajche mi ki kotyañ 'i b'ä,
'añ x'ixiki.
Tzi ch'ämä jiñi 'i k'äb' jiñi ña'tyuñ.
Che bä ya' wo 'i k'äjkel jiñi b'ajlumi,
tzi kujb'e jub'el 'ila tyi jol.
[Chencho:]
Pero ¿b'ajche? ¿Kächb'il 'i cha'añ?
[Mateo:]
Kächb'il 'i cha'añ.
[Nicolás:]
Kächb'il tyi laso.
Kächb'il
che bä tzi b'ajb'e.
Tzi b'ajb'e jub'el,
che jeñ tza yajli.
Pero mañik tza seb'e chämi.
Che tza k'äjki,
tzi cha' b'ajb'e,
jiñtyo tzi tzäñsa jiñi x'ixik.
[Chencho:]
'Aja'a.
[Nicolás:]
Che tzi' mele 'añ b'ajche jiñ.

	she carried it up;
	she climbed up with the grinding stone.
	When she climbed up with it,
	just then he was arriving,
170	the jaguar was just arriving.
	He was following her scent
	where the woman had gone;
	he started to come.
	When the woman wasn't there,
175	he left;
	he climbed up toward the tip of that tree.

[Chencho:]
He came directly up?
[Nicolás:]
The jaguar wanted to climb up, too.
He was climbing up
180   to drag her down below.
But she was really thinking
how she could save herself,
the woman was.
She grabbed the grinding stone.
185   When the jaguar was just about to climb up,
she struck down on his head.
[Chencho:]
But how? Was it tied to something?
[Mateo:]
It was tied to something.
[Nicolás:]
It was tied by a rope.
190   It was tied
when she hit him.
She struck down at him,
so he fell.
But he didn't die right away.
195   When he climbed up,
she hit him again,
until she killed him.
[Chencho:]
Aha.
[Nicolás:]
That's the way she did that.

[CHENCHO:]		[CHENCHO:]
Tza chämi 'añ b'ajlum.	200	The jaguar died.
[NICOLÁS:]		[NICOLÁS:]
Tza chämi 'añ b'ajlum.		The jaguar died.
[CHENCHO:]		[CHENCHO:]
¿A b'ajche tza 'ujtyi che tza chämi?		How did it end when he died?
[MATEO:]		[MATEO:]
Jiñtyo tza säk'a;		Until it was dawn;
k'äläl jum p'ejl 'ak'älel,		all during the night,
woli 'i jatz'e',	205	she was hitting him.
koñ mak tza seb' chämi 'ab'i,		Since he didn't die right away, they say,
'añ b'ajlum.		that jaguar.
Che jiñi,		So it was,
mi yajlel jub'el.		he fell down.
Che jax ñajtyel	210	Even from far away
yom 'i tyaj b'a 'añ.		he wanted to get to where she was.
Jiñ 'ab'i mi cha' b'ajb'eñ jub'el		So they say she struck down at him again
jiñ ña'tyuñ;		with the grinding stone;
k'äläl tyi lum		all the way to the ground
mi yajlel.	215	he would fall.
Pero jiñ b'ajlum,		But that jaguar
koñ kolem b'ajlum,		was a big jaguar,
ma laj kujil b'ajche pitytyäl.		we don't know what he measured.
'A che jeñ,		So it was,
k'äläl säk'ajel,	220	until dawn,
k'äläl 'ak'älel,		all night,
k'äläl tza säk'a.		until dawn came.
Jiñtyo tza k'uñ chämi,		Until little by little he died,
kome tza laj tyojp'i		since she beat in all
'i jol 'añ b'ajlum.	225	the head of the jaguar.
[CHENCHO:]		[CHENCHO:]
'Aja.		Aha.
[MATEO:]		[MATEO:]
Jiñtyo tza säk'a jiñ x'ixik.		Until dawn came to that woman.
Che jiñi,		So it was,
wolix tyi 'oñel, mi yälob';		she was crying out, they say;
wolix tyi 'oñel.	230	she was crying out.
Kome läk'äl tyi tyi' xchumtyil,		Since it was close to the edge of a village,
jiñ cha'añ tza kaj tyi 'oñel.		for that reason she started to cry out.
'Añix majki tza kaji 'i yub'iñ,		Someone started to hear
chuk wu 'i mel.		what she was doing.

Jiñ cha'añ,
tza majli 'i k'elob'
ya tyi ma tye'el.
Che tza 'ujtyi b'ajche jini.
'I k'äläl jun p'ejl 'ak'älel
tzi jatz'ä jub'el;
'i b'ajb'eñ jub'el.
[NICOLÁS:]
Jiñtyo tza jun yajlel säk'a.
[MATEO:]
Che' tza 'ujtyi b'ajche jiñi.
[CHENCHO:]
¿Tza tyili tyi koltyäñtyel?
[MATEO:]
Tza tyili tyi koltyäñtyel,
'i tza k'otyi kab'äl wiñikob'.
Tzi k'ele jiñi b'ajlum.
'I koñ jiñ tzi tzäkleñ tyilel
'i ñoxi'al jiñi x'ixik,
jiñ tzi tzäñsa jiñi.
Che tza tyajle b'ajche jiñi,
tza ku ki ña'tyañ 'añ x'ixik,
"Tza jña'tya ke ñoxi'aläch,
koñ tza kaj tyi wäyel
yik'oty kalob'il,"
che'eñ.
"Pero jiñ tzi tzäñsa jñoxi'al 'ilili,"
che'eñ.
"Ko me ñumäl jk'el jiñi jñoxi'al
b'a 'ora mi jap lemb'al,
'añix mi julel tyi 'ak'älel.
'I chäch, mi julel 'i mel,
'o 'añ mu tyo 'i julel 'i k'ux waj,

'i 'añ max mi julel 'i k'ux waj,
'I tza jña'tya
ko me lajaläch 'i b'äk'tyal
b'ajche jñoxi'al,"
che'eñ.
"Pero che wäyäli.
tza kaj tyi lok'el."

235   For that reason,
he came to look
there in the woods.
That's the way that ended.
And all night long
240   she struck down at him;
she beat down on him.
[NICOLÁS:]
Until it finally dawned.
[MATEO:]
That's the way that ended.
[CHENCHO:]
Did they come to help her?
[MATEO:]
245   They came to help her,
and a lot of people came.
They saw the jaguar.
And since he stalked
the husband of that woman,
250   he killed him.
When that was discovered,
the woman began to understand,
"I thought it was really my husband,
since he started to sleep
255   with my daughter,"
she said.
"But he killed my husband there,"
she said.
"Since I am used to seeing my husband
260   whenever he drinks liquor,
there are times when he comes back at night.
And just so, he would come back and do it,
or at times he would come back to eat
    tortillas,
and at times he wouldn't come eat tortillas,
265   and I thought
that his body was the same
as my husband,"
she said.
"But when he was asleep,
270   it started to come out."

[CHENCHO:]
Lok'el 'i tzutzel.
[NICOLÁS:]
Tza kaj tyi lok'el 'i ñej.
[CHENCHO:]
Tza kaj tyi lok'el 'i ñej ja'el.
[NICOLÁS:]
Jun yajlel b'ajlumäch, tza majli.
[MATEO:]
Mach 'añ laj pi'älix;
jun yajlel b'ajlum.
'Añ 'i k'äb',
'i tzutzel pejtyelel.
Jiñ cha'añ tzi b'äk'ña x'ixik.
[CHENCHO:]
Machiki
jiñ 'alob' tza' yub'i . . .
[MATEO:]
Machiki,
mach laj kujil
b'ajche tzi' mele,
'o mi tzi tzäñsa ja'el.
Mach la kujilik,
koñ jiñ tza ki yub'iñ 'añ 'alob',
chañ sak' 'añ 'i tzutzlel.
Che tza 'ujtyi b'ajche jiñi.

[CHENCHO:]
His hair came out.
[NICOLÁS:]
His tail came out.
[CHENCHO:]
His tail started to come out as well.
[NICOLÁS:]
All at once, he went really jaguar.
[MATEO:]
275   He wasn't a person;
all at once he was a jaguar.
He had paws,
he was hairy all over.
That's why the woman was afraid.
[CHENCHO:]
280   If it hadn't been
that the girl felt it . . .
 [MATEO:]
If it hadn't been,
we wouldn't know
how it happened,
285   or if he killed him, as well.
We wouldn't know,
except the girl began to feel it,
that his hair was scratchy.
That's the way that ended.

13

The Blackman

BERNARDO PÉREZ MARTÍNEZ

This story was narrated to us in June 1995 by Bernardo Pérez Martínez, a school-teacher from Tila, Chiapas, and the brother-in-law of Ausencio Cruz Guzmán. After he had recorded the story, the text was transcribed and then checked among the four of us. This is one of two texts in the Tila variety of Chol in this collection (see also The Comadre, below); the other texts are in the Tumbalá variety. At the time we recorded this story, a Chol friend, Marcos Arcos Mendoza, was collecting material for the Ministry of Education to put together a reader for Chol children (see his Older Brother Sun and Younger Brother Sun, above). He asked to have a copy of this story, and it was published with the title *Iyesomal ijk'al xñek* (The Tradition of the Blackman-Negro, Arcos Mendoza 1999:66–68) in *Juñ ch'älbilbä tyi lak ty'añ ch'ol* (A Treasure Book in Our Ch'ol Language), although it appears there without attribution and has been translated into the Tumbalá Chol of Marcos Arcos Mendoza.

The featured creature in this story, the Blackman, is known all over southern Mesoamerica (Blaffer 1972). He is another of the creatures that seeks to eat people, one of the menaces that lurks in the deep woods and comes to threaten people who are out alone. He is known by two names in Chol, *'ijk'al*, based on the native color term *'ik'* 'black', and *xñek*, based on a loanword from Spanish *negro* 'Black [person]'.

While surely precolumbian in origin, the Blackman has in historic times acquired some of the mythic, stereotypic aspects of Black Africans, and some authors postulate that the Blackman is based solely on African Americans. But there are many images of fierce black-painted warriors on precolumbian ceramics. Black body paint

DOI: 10.5876/9781607324881.c013

was an ethnic marker for Colonial period Chols (as reported by missionaries who tried in vain to stop the custom; Josserand and Hopkins 2007:110–11). And the creature fits too smoothly into the paradigm of other jungle menaces to have been introduced. Nonetheless, modern publications often illustrate the Blackman as a Negro, and an innovative weaver in Highland Chiapas has introduced his image in textile designs, looking like Little Black Sambo (with round white eyes, thick red lips, and nappy hair). We recently acquired a sample weaving of this character in Sna Jolobil, San Cristóbal de Las Casas, Chiapas, a weavers' co-op, and Chip Morris, an expert on Chiapas weaving (Morris 2010), said he had never before seen that motif.

Note that Bernardo, a schoolteacher, deviates somewhat from the traditional format of storytelling. He begins abruptly with the Background ("They say long ago there was a man . . ."). But the evidentiality statement is present, it's just at the end of the story, not at the beginning (see lines 241–65: "Thus said our ancestors, long ago . . .").

The Blackman

Ty'añ Jiñi Xñek
Bernardo Pérez Martínez (1995)

'Añ b'i wajali juñ tyikil lak pi'äl.	1	They say long ago there was a man.
'Añ b'i 'i yotyotylel 'ixim.		They say he had a maize granary.
'I yotyotylel 'ixim ya' tyi chol,		The maize granary was there in the milpa,
ya' b'a' añ 'i cholel.		there where his milpa was.
Komo lak pi'älob',	5	Since people
cheñ mi melob' jiñi yotyotylel 'ixim		just make their maize granaries
b'a' mi lätzob' 'ixim.		where they stack corn.
Jiñi 'i k'ab'a' 'i yotyotylel 'ixim,		That is called their maize granary,
cha'añ mi lätzob' jiñi 'ixim,		for them to stack maize,
cha'añ mi tyempañob'.	10	for them to gather it.
Pero 'añ k'iñil mi pasel 'i yumil,		But there's a season when the owner comes,
b'ajche' 'ili 'animal,		because those animals,
jiñi yujil b'ä 'i k'ux 'ixim.		they know how to eat corn.
Mi jok'e', mi jeme'.		They dig it up, they destroy it.
Wajali weñ kab'äl tyo jiñi,	15	A long time ago there were a lot of them,
b'ajche' 'ili b'ätye'el,		like the forest animals,
kab'äl tyo ma'tye'el,		many more in the forest,
chityam, tz'utz'ub', kojtyom,		peccary, coatí, andasolo,
'i yantyak b'ä b'ätye'el.		and other kinds of forest animals.
Jiñi lak pi'äli,	20	That man,
chonkol 'i weñ jilel 'i yixim,		they were finishing off his corn,
weñ k'uxtyäl jiñi 'i yixim.		his corn was being eaten up.

Ta b'i majli käntyañ 'ili yixim.		He came to take care of his corn, they say.
'I che' jiñi.		So it was.
Komo cheñak jiñi 'i yorajlel b'ajche' Xñek,	25	Like a monster, the time came for Blackman,
'añ b'ä mi la käl.		that's what we call him.
Cheñ mi yälob' lak tyat, lak ña'ob' X'ijk'al,		Thus said our fathers, our mothers, Blackman,
		the Blackman we talk about.
jiñi Xñek b'ä mi lak sub'eñ.		They say he takes out our tongues,
Mu b'i 'i lok' la kak',		they say he eats our tongues,
mu b'i 'i k'ux la kak',	30	they say he pulls our tongues,
mu b'i 'i lok'sb'eñoñ la kak',		they say he cuts off our tongues.
mu b'i 'i tzepb'eñoñ la kak'.		And like our dogs,
Yik'oty b'ajche' lak tz'i',		they say if they start to bark,
ta b'i ki 'i cha'le wojwoj,	35	he pulls out their tongues.
mi lok'sb'eñ 'i yak'.		He eats them, now.
Mi k'ux wale'.		They say that's how it happened, long ago.
Che' b'i ta 'ujtyi wajali.		That man,
Jiñi lak pi'äl,		they say he went to care for his corn.
ta b'i majli tyi käntañ 'i yixim.	40	So it was,
Che' jiñi,		he arrived there at his corn,
ta k'oti ya' tyi yiximi,		it was ugly the way it was ending, like that.
lekojix chonkol 'i jilel, b'ajche'.		There are many people
'Añ kab'äl lak pi'älob',		who harvest, like squash,
mu b'ä 'i much'kiñob' b'ajche' li ch'ujm,	45	lots of different crops,
li päkäb'tyak,		or ones that ripen there in the milpa.
'o wo b'ä 'i kolel ya' tyi cholel.		They harvest it,
'I much'kiñob',		they collect it,
'i tyempañob',		just like we gather corn.
che' b'ajche' mi lak much'kiñ 'ixim.	50	Just like they gather squash
Che' b'ajche' 'i much'kiñob' ch'ujm		there in their maize granaries.
ya' tyi yotyotylel 'ixim.		They harvest it,
'I much'kiñob',		they collect it.
'i tyempañ.		So it was,
Che' jiñi,	55	the man,
lak pi'äl,		they say he went to his maize granary.
ta b'i majli tyi yotyotylel 'ixim.		His corn harvest was finished,
Ta 'ix 'ujtyi 'i k'aj,		it was getting dark.
'ik'ix kajel.		It was twilight already.
'Ik' säpäkña 'ix.	60	So it was,
Che' jiñi,		sad,
ch'äjyem,		the earth was looking sad.
ch'äjyem pañämil.		

Ta b'i kaji 'i yub'iñ tyi ñajty,
tyi ñajty tyo 'ab'i,
ñoj ñajty 'ili Xñek, che' b'i,
chonkol 'i tyilel
yub'i jiñäch wale 'iliyi.
Mi jiñäch, che' b'i,
wo b'i ñäch'ty'añ tyilel jiñi xñek.
Chonkol tyi ch'uyub' tyilel jiñi,
mi yälob' lak tyaty, lak ña'ob', wajali.
"Whhhhi, 'hhhhi, 'hhhhi, 'hhi, 'hhi, 'hhi,
* 'hhiiiii-o'',*
che' chonkol tyi ch'uyub' tyilel li Xñeki.
'Añ b'i mi yäl yambä b'ajche' mi cha'leñ ty'añ.
Wark'iñ: "Chor, chor, chor, chor, choooor'',
che' b'i mu tyi ty'añ 'ub'i Xñeki.
Ta b'i yub'i jiñi lak pi'äl,
ñaaajty tyo b'i 'i tyilel
ti 'ub'ix tel yub'il, che' b'i.
"B'ix te b'ä?" che' jiñi.
Ta b'i kaji tyi b'äk'eñ.
Ti kaji yub'iñ, läkälix b'i tel.
Ya' b'i chonkolix tyi ch'uyub' tel:
"Whi', whi', whi', whi', whi', whi', whhiiiii-o".
Che' jiñi,
läkälix 'i tel.
'I che' jiñi,
'ub'ix 'i tel wä'i, che' b'i.
Ya' tyo tzikil wale, che' b'i.
Lak pi'äli,
ta 'ix b'i kaji 'i ña'tyañ
b'ajche' mi kajel 'i mel,
b'ajche' mi kejel 'i tel,
ti ña'tya.
"B'ajchki yom mik mel wale?" che' b'i.
"B'ajchki mi kaj 'i yujtyel wale?" che' b'i.
"Chuki mi kejel 'i tyumb'eñoñ wale?" che' b'i.
"B'ajchki yilal wale, mi kajel 'i julel?
B'ajchki yälä wale?" che' b'i.
Che' jiñi.
Yäñila, yäñila, yäñila, yäñila,
läkälix 'i tel.

They say he started to hear from far off,
from very far off, they say,
65 very far off was the Blackman, they say,
he was coming
he heard him, here and now.
But that one, they say,
they say he knew the Blackman was coming.
70 He was coming whistling,
said our ancestors, long ago.
"Whee, whee, whee, hii, hii, hii, hiiiii-o,"

thus the Blackman was whistling as he came.
They say there was another way he spoke.
75 Like: "Chor, chor, chor, chor, choooor,"
they say that's the way the Blackman spoke.
They say the man heard him,
still way off they say he was coming,
he sensed it coming, they say.
80 "What is that coming?" he said.
They say he started to be afraid.
He sensed it was coming close, they say.
There, they say, he was coming whistling:
"Whe, whe, whe, whe, whe, whe, wheee-oh."
85 So it was,
he was coming nearer.
And so it was,
he felt it coming here, they say.
He was already visible there, they say.
90 That man,
they say he started to think
how he was going to do it,
how he was going to come,
he thought about it.
95 "What should I do now?" he said.
"What is going to happen now?" he said.
"What is he going to do to me now?" he said.
"What will it be like when he comes?
What will he say?" they say he said.
100 So it was.
Closer, closer, closer, closer,
nearer he came.

'I yäx ñoj tel yub'ili.
'Ixku mi yäl lak tyaty, lak ña'ob',
che' läkäkix tel,
ta 'ix meku 'i yub'iyoñla,
mux lak señ'añ, mi yäl.
Mu b'i lak päk señ'añ.
Mach mi mejloñla tyi xämb'al,
mach mi mejloñla tyi 'ajñel,
mach mi mejlonla tyi ty'an.
Che' b'ajche' mik señ'añ laj kok,
lak pächilel, tyi pejtyelel.
'I che' jiñi.
Ta kaji yub'iñ,
weñ läkälix 'i tel,
ya' 'ix 'i tel, ta yub'i.
Yäñila, yäñila, yäñila, yäñila,
ya' 'ix b'i k'otyel tyi yotyotylel 'ixim.
Mu b'i ti ch'uyub' tel.
Mu b'i ti ty'an tel.
Che' jiñi,
wa', che' b'i, ya' tyi yotyotylel 'ixim.
Wa', che' b'i.
'I ta b'i kaji tyi ty'an jiñi Xñeki:
"¿Chuki muk'ety?" che' 'ab'i.
"Ma'añ, choñkoloñ käñtyañ kixim,
kab'äl mi yajnel 'i yumil."
"Weno", che'eñ.
'A che' jiñi,
ta b'i 'ochi majlel ya' tyi mal.
Ta b'i kaji 'i pejkañ:
"Noki! p'isi 'a wuty!" che' b'i.
Ta 'ix b'i kaji 'i p'is 'i wuty jiñi lak pi'äli,
'i ta b'i ñokle.
Ta b'i kajiyob' tyi ty'an.
Ña'tyib'ilix 'i cha'añ jiñi lak pi'äli,
b'ajche' mi kaj 'i mel je'el.
Che' jiñi.
Ta 'ix b'i ki weñ ña'tyañ
b'ajche' mi kajel 'i mel.
"Ya' tzikil wale' majch mi kajel joty,
majch mi kajel cha'leñ kañar,

And coming really close, he could hear him.
As for what our ancestors say,
105   if he comes close,
if he has sensed us,
we get numb, they say.
They say we get really numb.
We can't walk,
110   we can't run,
we can't speak.
It's like our legs get numb,
our skin, everything.
So it was.
115   He heard him
coming really close,
there he came, he heard.
Closer, closer, closer, closer,
they say he was already at the granary.
120   They say he was coming whistling.
They say he was coming talking.
So it was,
there, they say, there he was at the granary.
Right there, they say.
125   And they say the Blackman started to speak:
"Whatcha doin'?" he said.
"Nothing, I'm taking care of my corn,
a lot of owners are coming."
"Okay," he said.
130   So it was,
they say he went there inside.
They say he started to say:
"Kneel! Cross yourself!" he said.
They say the man began to cross himself,
135   and they say he knelt down.
They say he started to speak.
The man had already thought about
how he could do it, too.
So it was.
140   They say he had already thought it out,
how he would do it.
"Now let's see who is going to win,
who is going to win,

b'ajche' mi kajel yujtyel wale",	how this is going to end,"
che' yälä jiñi lak pi'äl,	145 said the man,
ti ña'tya.	as he thought.
"Ya' ti ki wale", che' b'i.	"There it has started, now," he said.
Che' jiñi.	So it was.
"'Ochen", che' b'i.	"Come in," he said.
"'Ochen", che' b'i ti sub'eñtyi li Xñek.	150 "Come in," the Blackman was told.
Ta b'i 'ochi ya' tyi malil yotyotylel 'ixim.	He came in to the inside of the granary.
Komo jiñi lak pi'äli,	Since that man
chonkol b'i 'i ñutz 'i k'ajk,	was building a fire, they say,
lemlemña.	the flames were leaping.
Ñoj k'elk'elña tyi pulel 'i si',	155 The firewood was burning wildly,
b'ajche' chäk k'elañix 'i ñich.	like a red blaze were the flames.
'I lak pi'äli,	And the man
chonkol 'i pojpoñ 'i ch'ujm,	was roasting pumpkins,
'i kolem ch'ujm,	and the pumpkins were big,
ya' tyi tyi'k'ajki,	160 there at the edge of the fire,
che' b'ajche' lak tyaty, lak ña'ob', wajali.	just like our ancestors, long ago.
Yujilob' tyo 'i pojpoñtyel 'i ch'ujm.	They still knew how pumpkins were roasted.
(Much 'i k'uxob' wale.	(Now, they eat them.
Sumukäch mi k'uxob'.	They taste good when they eat them.
'Añix tyo tyi jpojpolojoñ je'el;	165 We still roast them as well;
sumukäch tyi k'uxol.)	they are tasty to eat.)
Chonkol 'i pojpoñ ch'ujm jiñi lak pi'äl.	The man went on roasting his pumpkins.
Mi cha'leñ lojk ya' tyi mal;	Steam was building up inside them.
chijikña mi kaj tyi lojk.	The steam was beginning to hiss.
Che' b'ajche' mi cha'leñ,	170 The way he was doing it,
b'ulich ya' tyi malil,	they swelled up there inside,
b'ajche' chonkol tyi tyäk'esañ tyi pejtyelel.	as if they were all going to burst.
K'otyajax ku,	It was really beautiful,
mi luk'uñañ ya' tyi mal.	when they began to sway there inside.
Komo jiñi lak pi'älob',	175 Since the man
che' mi pojpoñob' 'i ch'ujm,	when he roasted his pumpkins,
mach chajach mi loloñ pojpoñob'.	it wasn't like they really roast them.
Mi jowob',	They poke holes in them,
cha'an mi lok'el jiñi yik',	so that the air can come out,
jini b'ulich,	180 the pressure,
'i yowixi.	the steam.
Mi ch'ub'ob',	They pierce them,
b'ajche' mi lak käl tyi yamb'ä lak ty'añ.	as we say in another dialect.
Mi lak ch'ub',	We pierce them,

<table>
<tr><td>

'o mi lak jowe'
cha'añ mi lok'el 'i b'ulich,
cha'añ mi lok'el 'i yowix.
Ta b'i käñä,
tyijikña b'i lak pi'äli.
"B'uchi 'ila tyi tyi k'ajki",
che' b'i sub'eñtyi Xñeki,
tyi X'ijk'al.
"B'uchi", che'eñ.
Jiñi xñekob'
mach b'i b'a' 'añob' jiñi 'i pislelob',
pitz'chakalob'.
Mach b'i b'a' 'añob' jiñi 'i b'ujk,
'i wexob',
pitz'chakalob'.
Chakchakñayob' tyi xämb'al.
Che' jiñi.
"Pojpoñ 'a ch'ujm",
che' b'i ti sub'eñ tyi Xñeki:
"Pojpoñ 'a ch'ujm,
'umb'a'añ 'a ch'ujm", che' b'i.
"Yomäch", che' b'i Xñeki.
Ta 'ix b'i 'i chämä li ch'ujmi;
ti kaji 'i pojpoñ 'ila tyi tyi k'ajki, che' b'i.
Che' jiñi.
Weñ tyijikña b'i lak pi'äl.
Mach b'i ma'añ tyi läkäl li tyi' k'ajki.
Ñoj tyijikña je'el li Xñek;
ti pojpo jiñi 'i ch'ujmi tyi k'ajki.
Ch'uj tzoyol yälas.
Che' b'ajche' 'i mirin, mi lak käl.
Ch'ujle'el.
Che' jiñi.
Lak pi'äl,
yujilix ma'añ ti jowb'e,
ma'añ ti tyokb'e li ch'ujmi
b'a' mi lok'el yowixi.
Ma'añ jowol jiñi ch'ujm.
Ta b'i keji tyi lok' ya' tyi malil.
Ti kaji tyi b'ulich jiñi ch'ujm.
Che' jiñi,

</td><td>

185

190

195

200

205

210

215

220

225

</td><td>

or we poke holes in them
so the pressure can come out,
so the steam can come out.
They say he knew that,
they say the man was really happy.
"Sit here by the edge of the fire,"
they say the Blackman was told,
the Blackman.
"Sit down," he said.
Those Blackmen
don't have any clothing, they say,
they are naked.
They say they have no shirts,
no pants,
they are naked.
They walk around buck naked.
So it was.
"Roast your pumpkin,"
they say he said to the Blackman:
"Roast your pumpkin,
here's your pumpkin," he said.
"All right," said the Blackman.
They say he took his pumpkin;
he started to roast it at the edge of the fire.
So it was.
The man was really happy.
They say he wasn't far from the fire.
The Blackman was very happy, too;
he roasted his pumpkin there in the fire.
His "toys" [testicles] were hanging down.
Just like trinkets, as we say.
Dangling.
So it was.
The man
knew he hadn't poked holes,
he hadn't pierced the pumpkin
where the steam could escape.
The pumpkin wasn't punctured.
They say it began to boil inside.
The pumpkin began to sweat.
So it was,

</td></tr>
</table>

che' ta 'ix k'uk'uxtyikwä	so it got hotter and hotter
jiñi ch'ujm tyi malil.	inside, that pumpkin.
Ta 'ix kej tyi k'uk'ux lojk'.	It got really really hot.
Ñoj tyikäw 'ix.	It was very hot already.
Che' jiñi.	So it was.
Ta b'i jem tyojmi jiñi ch'ujmi.	They say that the pumpkin exploded!
Ta b'i luj puli PEEEJTYELEL.	It burned him all over!
Ya-a-a-a' käñak 'añ b'i tyi ch'ujm tyi malil,	Yaah! The hot yellow flesh in the pumpkin
'i pejtyelel 'i pächilel, pejtyelel 'i ya',	burned all of his skin, all of his legs,
ta b'i lu' puli.	they say he was burned all over.
Che' jiñi,	So it was,
b'ajche' ma'añ ti yub'i panämil li Xñeki,	like he didn't even touch the ground,
ti puts'i.	the Blackman fled.
Chajach b'i ti koli lak pi'äl	Thus, they say, the man was saved
b'ajche' jiñi.	like that.
Che' jiñi,	So it was.
che' mi yäl lak tyaty, lak ña'ob', wajali.	Thus said our ancestors, long ago.
Che' tyo ti sub'oñ jiñi,	Thus still I was told
b'ajche' jiñi welito,	by my grandfather,
b'ajche' kyum, wajali.	by my father, a long time ago.
Ma'ix kuxul.	They are not alive now.
Ta 'ix sajtyi,	They have already been lost,
ta 'ix jili, wajali.	they have come to an end, a long time ago.
Jiñtyo ti sub'oñ b'ajche' jiñi.	They told me stories like this.
Ti 'ujtyi wajali,	It happened long ago,
b'ajche' 'i ty'añ	like this story,
b'ajche' 'i cha'añ Xñek,	like the story of the Black Man,
b'ajche' 'i cha'añ X'ijk'al.	like the story of the Blackman.
Jiñ ti sub'oñ,	This they told to me,
'i che' b'i ti 'ujtyi wajali.	and they said this happened long ago.
'Añ b'i lak pi'äl,	They say there was a man,
che' bä ti 'ujtyi wajali,	that this happened to, long ago,
b'ajche' jiñi.	like this.
Jiñ cha'añ,	For that reason,
mu tyo jcha' ale wa'liyi,	I still tell it here and now;
tz'itya k'ajal 'ix tyo cha'añ.	I still remember a little bit of it.
'Añ tyo juñ p'e, cha' p'e	There are one or two more stories
mach bä ma'añix ñoj k'ajal cha'an,	that I don't remember well,
pero kasi tyi pejtyelel	but almost all of them
k'ajlix tyo jcha'añ.	are still remembered by me.
Che' ti 'ujtyi wajali b'ajche' jiñi.	That's the way it happened, long ago.

14

The Comadre

RAFAEL LÓPEZ VÁZQUEZ

This story was recorded (and videotaped) in the ejido La Cascada (municipio of Palenque) in June 2002 by Josserand, Hopkins, and Cruz Guzmán during a project focused on collecting folklore and stories about the formation of the Chol ejidos (Josserand et al. 2003). Using earlier contacts in the community (we had bought thatch palm in La Cascada to re-roof Merle Greene Robertson's house in 1985), we were guided to Rafael López Vázquez, one of the original settlers, a man about seventy years of age. Don Rafael was raised in Jochintyol, municipio of Salto de Agua, Chiapas, and speaks the Tila variety of Chol. Our first interview was dedicated to his personal history and the history of the ejido, and at the end of the session he asked if we could bring him a copy of the cassette recording to use in the local school. We agreed, and a few days later we returned to give him a copy of the interview tape.

He had been thinking about the first interview, in which we had all communicated in a mixture of Spanish and Chol, and he had decided that he wanted to record again, leaving out the Spanish, to provide the schoolchildren with a better sample of Chol speech. He then gave us a rapid series of folktales, including the Comadre story as well as stories about various forest creatures (Blackman, Savage, Big Hat), a transformer story (in which a man turns into a woman), a version of the race story (in which the toads defeat the deer), a messenger story, and a version of the dog informer (see the synopses in ibid.), as well as comments on Chajk and on curers and curing. The speed of his delivery presented challenges for transcription;

DOI: 10.5876/9781607324881.c014

working on a cassette recorder with variable playback speed, his speech sounded normal only when the speed was slowed down as far as the recorder would permit.

Despite Don Rafael's expressed intent to dictate texts free of Spanish words, this presentation is salted throughout with Spanish words in various stages of assimilation. Some of this use of Spanish may be for the benefit of the interviewers, who clearly are not fluent speakers of Chol. On the other hand, like many other informants, he often clarifies the meaning of a word or phrase in Chol by citing its Spanish translation, a behavior we have also observed in interactions between native speakers.

The Comadre story is an example of a prominent motif in Chol folklore, the encounter of isolated humans with strange and dangerous creatures from the deep woods. In this case the menace is a jaguar that has killed the comadre of the woman protagonist (i.e., a ritual co-parent, the godmother of the woman's children). The jaguar then shows up at the woman's house, having taken the dead woman's form. A similar transformer is featured in the story of the Jaguar-Man. Other stories feature the Witches, Blackman, Spiny Man, Feet-on-Backward, Big Hat, and the Maternal Uncles (mother's brothers, Lacandóns). Their stories are similar. Isolated humans are approached by the creature (sometimes in the guise of another human), which ultimately would like to eat the humans. The humans escape by outwitting the dull-witted and clueless savage or by fleeing, and often relief comes only at dawn, when the woods creatures, like the demons of The Messengers, lose their powers and return to the jungle.

THE COMADRE

Ty'añ Jini Komare
Rafael López Vázquez (Josserand, Hopkins, and López Vázquez 2002)
Present: Kathryn Josserand (KJ), Nicholas Hopkins (NH), Ausencio Cruz Guzmán (ACG), Rafael López Vázquez (RLV), and occasional others.

KJ: *¿Qué tipo de cuento quiere contarnos hoy?*	1	KJ: What kind of story do you want to tell us today?
RLV: *¿Este, cha'... mismo jiñ jach b'ajche tzaj sub'ety?*		RLV: Uh, like ... the same as the one like I told you?
ACG: *Mañik, yamb'ä*	5	ACG: No, a different one.
RLV: *Yamb'ä. Yamb'ä. Äjä.*		RLV: Different one. Different one. Aha.
ACG: *Kuente che b'ajche chañ b'aki tza 'ujti walali,*		ACG: Tell like ... how it was back in the old days,
chañ mi 'añ ... Mi 'añ ... Este ... Xiba,		about if it was ... was ... uh ... demons,
KJ: *Ty'añ tyi wajali este tyi xib'aj...*	10	KJ: Story from long ago, uh, about Xib'aj ...

Tyi mañik . . .	about no . . .
ACG: *Chub'ä tyi . . .*	ACG: Something from . . .
RLV: *'Aj*	RLV: Ah.
KJ: *Tyi wiñik . . . Tzi sujtyi tyi b'ajlum . . .*	KJ: About a man . . . he turned into a jaguar . . .
RLV: *'Äjä. 'Äjä, 'äjä . . .*	RLV: Aha. Aha, aha.
NH: *Lak ch'ujlel . . .*	NH: Our souls . . .
RLV: *Pejtye 'añ jiñi. 'Añäch. 'Äjä.*	RLV: All of them are. There are. Aha.
ACG: *Che kuji.*	ACG: That's right.
RLV: *'Este . . .*	RLV: Uh . . .
Wajali, 'añ jiñi mi yälob'	A long time ago, there is one they tell
che' b'ajche jiñi,	like this one,
'ili lak sub'eñety.	this one we'll tell you.
'Añ mi yälob' b'ajche wajali,	It was, they say, like a long time ago,
por ejemplo . . .	for example . . .
Che b'ajche tyi 'antiwo	Like in ancient days,
'anterior mi yäl,	before, they say,
mi yälob' jiñi kpapá, kmamá,	my father, my mother, used to say,
por ejemplo	for example,
che b'ajche jiñi:	like this:
Choñkolob' tyi juch'b'al	They were grinding corn
jiñi x'ixikob'	these women
b'ajche jiñi yum 'otyoty.	like the owner of a house.
'Este,	Uh,
mi' ñume jiñi de . . .	there came by a . . .
juñ tyikil, che b'ajche 'i komáre.	a person, like her comadre.
Komáre che' 'ab'i.	Comadre, they say.
KJ/NH: *Komáre . . . che'ku.*	KJ/NH: Comadre, okay.
RLV: *Komáre che'. Este,*	RLV: Comadre, right. Uh,
"Buenos días, komare," che'eñ.	"Good morning, comadre," she said.
"Buenos días, komare."	"Good morning, comadre."
"'Ocheñ, komare, buchi'," che'abi.	"Come in, comadre, sit down," she said.
'A, "Yoñku," che'ab'i, b'uchtyäl.	Ah, "okay," she said; she sat down.
Yom jiñäch 'i komare yilali,	It should have been her comadre, it seemed,
che' jumuk'äch 'i lolesb'eñ 'i wuty.	thus for an instant she was fooled by her face.
Muk'äch 'i ña'tyañ	She believed it was
pero mach jiñik 'i komare je jiñ.	but that wasn't her comadre at all.
B'ajlum,	It was a jaguar,
chañ mi yom	that wanted
'i päy mal jiñi kumare	to lure out that comadre

Line markers in the gutter: 15, 20, 25, 30, 35, 40, 45.

<table>
<tr><td>

k'ux tyi matye'el.
KJ: *Mmm.*
NH: *B'ajlum.*
RLV: *'Äjä, b'ajlum, 'äjä.*
NH: *'Äjäjä.*
RLV: *Chañ mi yom majlel*
'i k'ux tyi matye'el.
Weñ, 'a ves 'i mi tyaj b'ajche
choñkol tyi juch'e 'i waj,
'i juch' 'i sa'.
Choñkol tyi juch'b'al tyi 'i ña'tyuñ,
este chañ mu b'u k'äñob' tyi juch'b'al . . .
Puru . . .
Puru piegra,
wajali.
Puru tyuñ,
ña'tyuñ.
Ña'tyuñ.
KJ/NH: *Ña'tyuñ.*
RLV: *Ña'tyuñ.*
NH: *'Äjä.*
RLV: *'I juch'ob'.*
'Añ 'i k'äb', che'
che' lak . . . tyi k'äb' ab'i.
Che' b'ajche jiñi
ke lak juch'b'al,
che jiñi.
Juch'b'al,
juch'b'al.
Weno,
"Pijtyañoñ komare,
maxtyo 'ujtyemoñ tyi k'äñol,
chañkol tyo kmele jiñ," che'.
"Jiñi ksa'," che'ab'i.
"A sa' jiñi, kumare," che'.
"Jiñ kuyi," che'ab'i.
"Weno."
"Laj wä' kotyañety, komare," che' 'ab'i.
"Kotyañ," 'i komare je.
Ke tyi juch'b'al je li b'ajlumi.
Pero mak mi ña'tyañ

</td><td>

50 and eat her out in the woods.
KJ: Mmhm.
NH: A jaguar.
RLV: Aha, jaguar, aha.
NH: Ahaaa.
55 RLV: Because he wanted to go
eat her in the woods.
Well, see, and he found her like
she was grinding her corn,
she was grinding atole.
60 She was grinding corn on a metate,
uh, because they used it to grind corn . . .
Only . . .
Only piedra,
a long time ago.
65 Just stone,
"mother stone" (metate).
Metate.
KJ/NH: Metate.
RLV: Metate.
70 NH: Aha.
RLV: They were grinding corn.
There was a mano (grinding stone),
like we . . . with a mano, they say.
It's just like that
75 that we grind corn,
so it was.
Grinding corn,
grinding corn.
Well,
80 "Wait for me, comadre,
I'm not finished with my task,
I'm still doing it," she said.
"My atole," she said.
"That atole of yours, comadre," she said.
85 "That's it," she said.
"Okay."
"Let me help you, comadre," she said.
"Help," said her comadre, too.
The jaguar started to grind corn, too.
90 But she didn't know

</td></tr>
</table>

mi b'ajlum malo,
jiñ ma mi ña'tyañ, 'äjä.
Yeye'a, 'este
"Kom laj chuk lak puy," che'ab'i.
Ma 'i chukob' puy.
Tyi ja'.
"Koñla che jeñi, komare," che'ab'i.
Majliyob' tyi chuk puyi.
'I 'entonses
ya' tyi ja' waleyi,
b'a choñkol lotyob' puyi,
'este, komo
jiñi malob'äyi b'ajlumi,
ma'ak mi ña'tyañ b'a b'ä puy,
mukach'i 'i lot'i jiñi xajwulel,
una.
Uñ tyuñ che pipi tyi tyuñ ehe',
mi chokb'e 'oxel,
mi chokb'e 'oxel ya'
tyi 'i traste komare je.
"A, ma, komare,
ma che' b'ajche jiñi.
Jiñi mi lale chuk 'ili puyi,"
che'ab'i.
"Puy che'me laj k'ux.
Puy, puy,
karakolito, karakolito."
NH: *'o . . .*
RLV: *Karakolito, 'äjä.*
B'ajlumi,
mañik mi loty,
puru xajlel,
tyuñ mi yotzañ ya' tyi traste.
NH: *Mjmhm.*
RLV: *"A, ma che' ki, komare,*
ma cheki jiñ mi laj chuke', komare.
Mach 'awuji chuko puy,"
che'ab'i.
"Ma'añ," che'ab'i.

RLV: *'i . . . 'entonses,*

---

that it was an evil jaguar,
she didn't know that, aha.
Then, uh,
"I want us to catch snails," she said.
95　They were going to catch snails.
In the river.
"Let's go, then, comadre," she said.
They went to catch snails.
And then
100　there at the river now,
where they were gathering snails,
uh, since
that evil jaguar,
he didn't know where or what snails were,
105　he picked up a rock,
una.
One rock, like a round rock, uh-huh,
he threw in three,
he threw in three there
110　in the comadre's bowl, too.
"Ah, no, comadre,
it's not like that.
That's not how to catch snails,"
she said.
115　"Snails, like those we eat.
Snails, snails.
Caracolito, caracolito."
NH: Oh . . .
RLV: Caracolito, aha.
120　That jaguar,
he wasn't picking up anything,
just rocks,
stones he was putting there in the bowl.
NH: Mmhmm.
125　RLV: "Ah, not like that, comadre,
not like that do we catch them, comadre.
You don't know how to catch snails,"
she said.
"No," he said.
[Noise, side comments, parrot squeaks]
130　And . . . then,

mux ki ña'tyañ jiñi komare,
mu b'i 'ib'äk'ñañ yub'il.
Mi b'äk'ñañ.
Mu b'i k'eb'eñ jiñi
'i paty che' b'ajche jiñi,
che' b'ajche kotyol tyi lot' puy
b'ajche 'ili
che' b'i locho 'i ñej
che'e 'añ b'i ñej,
wä tyi . . .
wä tyi b'äj.
NH: *Ñej.*
RLV: *Ñej, 'i ñej.*
Mi lochol che'ab'i
mi ch'uyb'ety 'i b'estido ya'
che'je.
'Ajä.
NH: *Mjm.*
RLV: *'Añ mi ch'uyb'e tye*
'i b'estido che'e.
Mi mi k'eb'e 'i kola,
'i kola,
'añ jiñi kola, 'i ñej.
'Ajä.
"'Aj," che'ab'i.
"Mach me jkomare," che'ab'i.
Pensar ke b'äk'iñañ,
tex ke ti b'äk'e.
"Weno, komare," che'ab'i.
"Pijtyañoñ la'i,
mik majle tyi tya'," che'ab'i.
Tya'.
[Se rien].
Tya', äjä.
"'Ä, weno," che'ab'i.
"Weno, komare," che'ab'i.
"¿B'ak 'añ 'a machity, komare?
Kom maj tya', kom maj tya',
maj tyi tya' 'ixi, komare,"
che'ab'i.
Chukox 'i b'äkñañ 'i komare,

the comadre started to understand,
she started to feel afraid, they say.
She was getting frightened.
They say she started to see
135   his back was like this,
when he bent over to pick up snails
like this
they say his tail curled out.
So he had, it is said, a tail,
140   here on . . .
here on himself.
NH: A tail.
RLV: Tail, his tail.
It came curling out, they say,
145   when his dress rose up there
like that.
Aha.
NH: Mhm.
RLV: When rose up
150   his dress like that.
His cola was seen,
his cola,
He had a cola, his tail.
Aha.
155   "Ah," she said.
"It's not my comadre," she said.
Imagine that she got frightened,
she started to be afraid.
"Okay, comadre," she said.
160   "Wait for me there,
I'm going to go shit," she said.
Shit.
[Everyone laughs.]
Shit, aha.
"Oh, okay," he said.
165   "Okay, comadre," he said.
"Where is your machete, comadre?
I want to go shit, I want to go shit,
go to shit over there, comadre,"
she said.
170   How frightened she was, the comadre,

chañ mi ki jile,
mi ki k'ux b'ajlum.
'Entonses ta majli li komare,
'iii, jiñjach lok'el ma, ti putz'i majlel.
Ta b'i k'oti tyaj jiñi che che,
ñojo kolem tye'.
NH: *Mjm.*
RLV: *'Añ 'i ... 'añ 'i jo'ñal,*
jiñi tye' añ, 'i ...
wéko, che b'ajche día.
Ya ti 'ochi majlel ja li komare je
ke b'äk'ñañ li b'ajlumi.
'I b'äk'ñañ.
Kuato ti k'otyi ty'añ li komare je,
yax muku jiñi ... de iñ ... li komare ya'i.

Choñkol tyi putz'el.
"'Ii," che'ab'i,
"Komare," che'ab'i.
Max 'i jak', che jach b'ajche 'ile.
"Komare, lok'eñix ya'.
Chuk muk'ety ya'i," che'ab'i.
"Ay, komare," che'ab'i.
Chukoch o b'ajche cheb' i ke yom b'i k'ux
yom b'i chaleñ mi läk xiñ tye',
yom b'ä 'oxe b'ajlum
mak mi yochel,
komo b'ajlumi,
kolem b'i.
'I komo lese b'i ti 'ochi
te b'i ke je ji,
'i ña'tyañ,
'añ ya'i tye' ta ki ki b'äj ya'ya',

'i 'äjä tyi mäke'.
Ya'li b'ajlumi, wérsa ... wersa.

[Visitante: "Buenas tardes," entra a la casa.]
RLV: *Buenas [al visitante] ...*
Ti ki lajchiñ, ki lajchiñ,
ti ki lajchiñ li ... li b'ajlumi.

because he could finish her off,
the jaguar could eat her.
So the comadre left,
eee, she just took off, she fled.
175 They say she went and found a big tree,
a really big tree.
NH: Mhm.
RLV: There was a ... there was a hole
in the tree, there was a ...
180 hueco, like [you could see] daylight.
There she got inside, the comadre
who was afraid of the jaguar.
She was frightened.
When she heard the voice of that "comadre"
185 she was already hidden ... that comadre
there.
She was fleeing.
"Ee," he said,
"Comadre," he said.
She didn't answer, she just stayed like that.
190 "Comadre, come out of there.
What are you doing in there," he said.
"Ay, comadre," he said.
Why or how it was he wanted to eat her
he needed to get inside the tree,
195 the jaguar needed to get in,
but he didn't get in,
since that jaguar
was big, they say.
And since he was hitting, trying to get in
200 they say that ...
her grinding stone,
there was a branch there he started to hit
with,
and so as to eat her.
There's the jaguar, fuerza, fuerza
(working ...)
205 [A visitor arrives: "Good afternoon" ...]
RLV: Good ... [to the visitor]
He started clawing, clawing,
he started clawing, that ... jaguar.

Chañ mi yom 'i k'ux 'i komare je.		Because he wanted to eat his comadre, eh.
Yom mi k'uxe.	210	He wanted to eat her.
Yom mi k'uxe.		He wanted to eat her.
Lajchiñ, lajchiñ,		Clawing, clawing,
"Ma! Ma 'i ki maj".		"No! She's not leaving!"
[Visitante: "Buenas tardes . . . " saluda a		[The visitor greets everyone.]
todos]		
RLV: *'Ay che jiñi,*	215	Ay, so it was,
ta'ix . . . mañik ti k'uxu . . . tyik tyike,		so . . . he couldn't eat her . . .
Ti 'uk'e li b'ajlumi.		The jaguar cried.
"Jii, komare," che'ab'i.		"Ee, comadre," he said.
"[Kom] mij k'uxb'e 'a chikiñ.		"[I wanted] to eat your ears.
Mij k'uxb'e 'a jol	220	To eat your head,
tyi käläl komare,"		all of you, comadre,"
che'ab'i.		he said.
"Ma te 'awäk'ä 'a b'äj		"You wouldn't give yourself up.
ti putz'iyety, komare."		You ran away, comadre."
Pero mach yälä,	225	But she didn't speak,
che' "Tyaloñ tyo, komare,"		so "Here I am still, comadre,"
che'ab'i.		he said.
Lajchiñ tyi temprano		Clawing until early morning,
ti maj lajchiñ k'älä		he went on clawing until
b'ajche 'ili tyi 'a las seis,	230	it was about six o'clock,
tex ku majli li b'ajlumi.		and the jaguar left.
Tex ke tyi lok'e te jiñi komare,		The comadre came out
je b'a putz'e jeme.		from where she had fled.
Ya' b'a tyi jowle tye'.		There in the hollow tree.
Tix majli tyi yotyoty.	235	She went to her house.
Tix majli tyi yotyoty,		She went to her house,
tix majli.		she left.
Chex ki tyi b'äk'eñ che jiñi,		She had been so afraid,
chex ki ña'tyañ.		she had believed him.
Pero mach b'i ti käña, mach,	240	But she didn't recognize him, no,
pero komaräch yilal.		but he looked like the real comadre.
Ta b'i 'i k'ajtyib'eñ 'i komare,		They say she asked her [real] comadre,
"Komare," che'ab'i.		"Comadre," she said.
"Chuki."		"What?"
"Este, jatyety ti ñum 'a k'eloñ sajmäl	245	"Uh, you . . . came by to see me
tyi loty laj puy, laj puy,"		to collect snails, our snails,"
che'ab'i.		she said.
"Ma'añ, pero mañik,		"No, but no,

ma'añik jañoñ,		it wasn't me.
mañik wä b'ä jlok'el,	250	It wasn't me that went out,
wäch 'añoñ tyi kotyoty		I was here in my house,
'a no, 'i melel ku.		ah, no, that's the truth.
Meleläch", che'ab'i.		That's right," she said.
"'A, weno," che'eñ.		"Ah, okay," she said.
"'Ay, 'Chuki yes,	255	"Ay, 'What's going on,'
che' li b'ajlum		said that jaguar
che mi tyili kolik k'uxoñ,"		when he came and almost ate me,"
che'ab'i.		she said.
"Mij k'el che jiñi		"I saw that when he
choñkol 'i loty jiñi puyi,	260	was picking up snails,
ya'ix 'i locho 'i ñej,		there his tail came out,
wä tyi patyi ya' tyejchel 'i jäpä 'i ñej," che' li.		out of his back, his tail came out," she said.
"Yom kole' 'i k'uxoñety komare," che'ab'i.		"He almost ate you, comadre," she said.
"Aj yos, komare.		"Ay, dios, comadre,
Chukoch che'ob' b'ajche jiñi," che'ab'i,	265	Why is it all like that?" she said,
"Chukoch ma majle koñ kolem b'ajlum,		"Why do you go off with a big jaguar,
chokoch maj komo me'añ trato laj cha'añ		why go when it's not our business
chañ mi laj majl tyi lot' puy,"		to go out and gather snails?"
che'ab'i.		she said.
"Fíjate, komare,	270	"Fíjate [imagine], comadre,
ma mik ña'tyañ je'el," che'ab'i.		I don't know, either," she said.
"Ti ñumi 'i päyoñ," che'ab'i.		"He came to call me out," she said.
"Fíjate,		"Fíjate,
choñkoloñ tyi juch'b'al,		I was grinding corn,
choñkol juch'e jsa',	275	I was grinding my atole
ti wa' kotyayoñ,"		it [the grinding stone] protected me later,"
che'ab'i.		she said.
"'Ora ti k'otyayoñ bavo tyi saj," che'ab'i.		"Now it protected me bravely later," she said.
"'A, weno" che'ab'i.		"Ah. Okay," she said.
"Chechi, komare," che'ab'i.	280	"So it is, comadre," she said.
"'Añ chäch wäläyi," che'ab'i.		"That's the way it is here," she said.
"Max chu laj laj tyumbeñ, komare," che'ab'i.		"Nothing we can do about it all, comadre," she said.
"Ma'ix," che'ab'i.		"No indeed," she said.
"Yamb'ä 'ora komare mach 'a jak' majlel.		"Another time, comadre, don't get called out,
Ame 'i k'uxety," che'ab'i'.	285	so he doesn't eat you," she said.
"Chi'chi komare," che'ab'i.		"All right, comadre," she said.
Weno. Ya'ix ya'.		Okay. There it was.

PART 4

Discourse Analysis of Narrative Texts

15

Discourse Analysis of Chol Narrative Texts

Nicholas A. Hopkins

In this section, each of the narratives presented above is discussed in terms of its discourse patterns, specifically in terms of the narrative structure presented by Kathryn Josserand, above ("The Narrative Structure of Chol Folktales"):

The Opening (usually an Evidentiality Statement)
Scene-Setting Background
The Event Line
The Peak Event
The Denouement
The Closing

Some deviation from this set of topics occurs in the texts, where, for example, there may be more than one Peak Event or no distinction between the Opening (Evidentiality Statement) and the start of Background information. However, the ease with which the elements of this structure can be discerned in the narrative texts argues for its validity as an instrument in the analysis of Chol narratives. Indeed, Classic period hieroglyphic texts have a notably similar structure (Hopkins and Josserand 2012:31–38).

Our Holy Mother

Lak Ch'ujul Ña'
The story of the Moon and her sons is a common narrative from the traditional repertory and has been reported several times in the published literature (Whittaker

DOI: 10.5876/9781607324881.c015

and Warkentin 1965:13–49; Arcos Mendoza 1994, 1999:75–76, 151). This narration by Ausencio Cruz Guzmán has all the elements of formal storytelling, from its elaborated opening to its unique closing. It has a very long scene-setting Background interrupted by two punctual events that anticipate the Event Line. The first Peak Event, the fatal conflict between the brothers, is followed by a Denouement that includes a second Peak Event, the transition from the old world—the pre-agricultural days before the appearance of the Sun —to the new world order.

THE OPENING: This opening (lines 1–5) is highly elaborated, beginning with the time-setting term *wajali*, placing the event —even the telling of the story by the ancestors—in the mythological past, and marking the story as traditional knowledge with the reportative *'ab'i*.

Wajali 'ab'i,	A long time ago, they say,
mi yälob' laj tyatyña'ilob' . . .	our ancestors used to say—
mi yälob', mi kub'iñ,	they say, I listen—
jtyaty, jña', tzi sub'eñoñ,	my father, my mother, told me,
wajali.	long ago.

SCENE-SETTING BACKGROUND: In sentences marked as non-completive, Our Holy Mother is introduced (6–9), and the scene is set in a time before the world as we know it existed (10–17). The long setup is interrupted by one brief statement in the completive aspect that anticipates the event line (19):

Tza 'ajñi cha' tyikil 'i yalob'il.	*She had two children.*

Having introduced these two protagonists, the background continues with details about their characters and their habitual activities (20–51).

THE EVENT LINE: The event line proper only begins when God sees what is happening and sends down to earth the "exotic bird" (52–64). The text continues to alternate between events and background information. Prior to the peak event, the only events marked as being on the event line (with completive aspect) are the following:

God's observation of, and response to, the older brother's activities:

tzi k'ele jiñ Lak Ch'ujul Tyaty	God saw it . . . (53–54)
tzi choko tyilel jiñ lekoj b'ä muty	He sent down that exotic bird. (59)

The mother's fateful failure to hide all the younger brother's toys, and the older brother's response:

max tzi laj lotyo,	She didn't gather them all up,
i tzi käyä tyi juñ paty	and they stayed out at one side. (106)

tza seb' sujtyi,	He suddenly turned around
'i tza k'otyi tyaj 'añ 'alob'	and came to find the boy. (118–19)
'i ña' . . . max tzi tyaja chuki mi yäl.	His mother . . . couldn't find anything . . . say. (122–23)
Ix ku yerañ, weñ 'utz tzi päsä 'i b'äj.	As for the brother, he made himself be good. (124–25)

THE PEAK EVENT: The long peak event begins with the younger brother's discovery of the beehive and the resulting events (146–48). These events are marked with the Focus Marker *'i*, once thought to be a borrowing from Spanish but now known to occur in Classic period hieroglyphic texts (Josserand and Hopkins 2011:12; Montgomery 2002:114):

'I 'añ tzi tyaja juñ tyejk tye' b'a 'añ chab'.	And he found a tree that had honey.
'I tza k'otyi 'i sub'eñ 'añ yäskuñ.	And he went to tell his older brother.

Now, for an extended stretch of narration, practically every sentence is marked with completive aspect, with occasional background information related in noncompletive aspects. The peak is further emphasized by the use of extended dialogue between the two brothers, a dialogue that ends when the honey tree is cut down, bringing down the older brother with it (225–33).

Che jiñi, tzi yäla: "Ma ma sek'oñ!"	So it was, he said: "Don't cut me down!"
Jiñ jax tza yub'i ke	He just felt that
wolix 'i jub'el ya' tyi tye'i,	he was falling out of the tree.
k'iñlaw, ñup'law jub'el,	Crashing! Smashing! Falling,
ya' tyi ñi' tye'	there from the tip of the tree
ya' b'a woli tyi mäk' chab',	there where he was eating honey,
tza yajli.	he fell.

The event line continues after this incident as the younger brother goes home and confronts his mother (234–63) and then brings her back to the scene and introduces her to her new animals, sprung from the body of her oldest son (289–316).

THE DENOUEMENT: The report of events to his mother (316–28) leads to a retelling of the story by the younger brother and a lengthy discussion of the results from the older brother's death, the creation of all the animals (329–42). There is also a moral to the story (329–39):

B'ä 'i b'äji; mak tzi yäk'oñ jmäk' chab'.	It's his own fault, he didn't give me honey to eat.
Jiñ cha'añ tza yajli, 'i che' tza chämi.	For that reason he fell, and so he died.

A SECOND PEAK EVENT: A second episode is introduced with the reintroduction of *wajali* and the reportative marker *'ab'i*, along with background information that sets the new scene, the world as we know it (343–46).

'Añ che'jiñi, wajali 'añ tyo 'ab'i	So it was, it was still a long time ago, they say,
mi melob' 'i chol.	they made their milpa.
'Añ tyo 'ab'i,	Still it was, they say,
mi pulob' 'ab'i 'i pulem lum.	they burned their fields for planting.

The transition from the old world to the new is expressed by the frequent use of the verb *kajel* 'to begin' as an auxiliary verb, indicating the beginning of actions that would continue:

'Añ che'jiñi,	And so it was,
tzax me ku kaji tyi 'e'tyel	he really started to work,
'ub'i 'alob'i . . .	the boy . . .
Tza kaji tyi lok'eltyak 'ab'i	He started repeatedly to go out, they say,
tyi juñ p'ejl tyi' 'otyoty . . .	through one door of the house . . . (370–73)
Tza kaji tyi kolel majlel . . .	He started to grow big . . . (382–83)
tza kaj tyi kolel.	he started to grow. (393)

As the younger brother takes on his nature as the sun, growing bigger and bigger and starting to take his walks through the sky, his old mother tries to follow him but is unable to keep up his pace, and the story closes with the final peak event, explaining why the moon falls further and further behind the sun every night (399–402):

'I che'jiñi,	And so it was,
wowoli 'i ñajtyañ,	she was falling further and further behind,
tza b'ejb'e käle majlel Laj Ña',	Our Mother was left behind,
'uj b'ä.	the one who is the Moon.

THE CLOSING: The text closes with a simple restatement of the results of the final peak event, an alternative to the usual *Che' tza 'ujtyi b'ajche jiñi*, 'That's the way that ended':

'I che' jach tzi käyäyob' 'i b'äj	And that's they way they remained
tyi xämb'al.	on their walks. (403–4)

OLDER BROTHER SUN AND YOUNGER BROTHER SUN

K'iñ 'Askuñälbä y K'iñ 'Ijtz'iñälbä

This brief telling of the story of the Moon and her sons goes right to the peak event, with other elements reduced to a minimum. In contrast, the peak events are related at some length, and the lengthy denouement, the transition from the old world to the new, is likewise detailed.

THE OPENING: The abbreviated opening (lines 1–4) nonetheless has all the elements required for a traditional story, beginning with the time-setting *wajali* 'a long time ago' and including the invocation of the ancestors as the authority on which the tale is based. The use of the reportative *'ab'i* continues through the first of the background, the existence of the two suns and their identification as brothers (lines 5–7).

'Añ wajali	It was a long time ago,
mi yäl lak tyaty, lak ña'ob',	our ancestors say,
tza' b'ä 'i k'eleyob' wajali	those who saw it long ago,
b'ajche' tza' 'ujtyi tyilel.	how it came to pass.
Jiñi mu bä 'i yälob':	This is what they say:
'añ 'ab'i jiñi k'iñ;	they say there was a sun;
pero cha' tyikil, 'ab'i.	but there were two, they say.

SCENE-SETTING BACKGROUND: The background (5–13) is as abbreviated as the opening, and in fact the two overlap. The information provided is limited to the existence of the two brothers and their identification as the white sun and the green sun. From there the text moves immediately into the event line.

THE EVENT LINE: The event line begins with the first use of the completive aspect (except as in subordinate clauses, above): *tza' majliyob' tyi matye'el 'i säklañob' chab'*, "they went into the forest looking for honey" (15–16). The ensuing events are related in great detail, with extensive dialogue between the protagonists. Anticipating the peak event, the reportative *'ab'i* returns for the first time since the opening and background when the younger brother starts to make the gophers that will bring down the tree (58–59), and *'ab'i* continues to occur periodically through the peak event.

THE PEAK EVENT: The peak event is marked by coupleting and repetition, beginning with the felling of the tree (109–12).

Che' jiñi,	So it was,
käläl tyi lum 'ab'i tza' jub'i.	all the way to the ground, they say, he fell.
Tyeme 'ab'i tza' jub'i	Together, they say, they fell,
yik'oty jiñi kolem tye'.	he and the big tree.

The following sentences repeat references to the spilling of the blood and the breaking of the body, and then relate a long litany of the animals into which the blood and body of the older brother are transformed (120–26):

. . . tza' laj sujtyi tyi b'ätye'el.	. . . it all turned into animals.
Yamb'ä tza' sujtyi tyi chityam,	One part turned into pigs,

yamb'ä tyi wakax,	another to cattle,
yamb'ä tyi chijmay…	another to deer…
Yamb'ä tza' sujtyi tyi tye'lal,	Another part turned to agoutis,
yamb'ä tyi wech,	another to armadillos,
yamb'ä tyi muty.	another to birds.

THE DENOUEMENT: The text now turns to the aftermath of the death and transformation of the older brother. As in the denouement of the preceding version, verbs in this section stress the beginning of a new era with the use of the auxiliary verb *kajel* 'to begin', with *kaji* 'he began' reduced to to *ki* (128–31):

tza' b'i ki 'i päy jiñi chityam	…he began to call the pigs…
tza' b'i ki tyuxb'añ jiñi chityam…	he began to whistle up the pigs…
Tza' ki 'i wetz' majlel jiñi 'aläk'äl.	He began to herd along the animals.

Again, as in the preceding version, the denouement contains a second peak event, as the mother creates a division between domestic and wild animals, with some animals, frightened by her crying, fleeing to the forest: *Lamtya tza putz'i, lamtya tza käle,* "half of them fled, half of them stayed behind" (167–68).

THE CLOSING: Like the opening, the closing of the narration is brief:

Che' mi yälob' wajali.	Thus they tell of long ago.
Ya' tza' 'ujtyi.	There it ended. (181–82)

The Celestial Bird

Ty'añ Jiñi Tyaty Muty

This brief story refers to celestial creatures and the establishment of elements of the world order, but it is not one of the most traditional stories that derives from the authority of the ancestors. It is, however, stated not to be from the narrator's personal experience but is something he was told.

THE OPENING: The opening is brief and to the point: *Che' jach, tzi sub'eñoñ ke che'i,* "Just like this, they told me that it's like this" (lines 1–2).

THE BACKGROUND: The background follows immediately and is correspondingly short: *Che mu tyi 'uk'el muty… ñaxañ 'añ mi yub'iñ 'ub'i tyaty muty,* "When the roosters crow… first they hear that father rooster" (3–7).

THE EVENT LINE: Since this is not so much a narrative text but a procedural, telling how something is done or why something happens, the equivalent of the event line is narrated in non-completive verb forms. Nothing punctual happens (8–14).

THE PEAK EVENT: Likewise, the peak event is narrated in non-completive verb forms (15–19):

Ñaxañ mi cha'leñ 'uk'el	First crows
'ub'i tyaty muty tyi pañchañ.	that father rooster in heaven.
'Entonses mux 'ab'i jak'ob'	Then, they say, answer
wu b'u 'añ tyi lum ja'el;	those that are on earth as well;
mux 'i laj pam jak'ob'.	from all over they answer.

THE DENOUEMENT: The denouement follows immediately after the peak event and gives the "moral" of the story: without the crowing of the "father rooster," the earthly roosters would not crow (20–27).

THE CLOSING: The closing extends the explanatory denouement: "That's why they call him 'father rooster'" (28–29).

THE TURTLE AND THE DEER

Ty'añ 'Ajk yik'oty Me'

This text is a narrative, but it is clearly not from the traditional repertory but a borrowing from the European tradition. Consequently, it has some of the elements of a traditional tale, but they are not elaborated.

THE OPENING: The opening of the narration has only the barest nod to tradition: the use of the reportative *'ab'i* to indicate that this is not a report based on the narrator's experience but something that "is said," a story passed down in the oral tradition: *'añ 'ab'i 'ajk,* "they say there was a turtle . . ." (line 1).

SCENE-SETTING BACKGROUND: Unlike most texts, the narration moves directly into the completive aspect, giving us to understand that this is a report of a singular event, not a situation that pertained over some extended time: *'añ 'ab'i 'ajk, tza kajiyob' tyi juñ p'e preba yik'oty me'.* "They say there was a turtle; he and a deer began a race" (1–3). What amounts to background is the anticipation of the upcoming events—the turtle had short legs, he knew there were two branches of a road of equal length, and he met the deer at the fork in the road (4–15).

THE EVENT LINE AND THE PEAK EVENT: The event line begins with the next use of the completive aspect (16–18):

Che jeñ,	So it was,
tza kaj tyi ty'añ jiñi me'.	the deer started to speak.
Tzi yälä che b'ajche jiñi: . . .	He spoke like this: . . .

The story continues in the completive aspect, a series of punctual events. The peak event is signaled by a couplet, followed shortly by a series of couplets (57–59):

Jiñ cha'añ,	For that reason [because the deer moved by jumping]

<table>
<tr><td>tza lujb'a;</td><td>he got tired;</td></tr>
<tr><td>tza lujb'a.</td><td>he got tired.</td></tr>
</table>

The narrator continues (76–85):

<table>
<tr><td>Tza päkle 'añ me'.</td><td>The deer laid down.</td></tr>
<tr><td>Pero jiñ 'ajk</td><td>But the turtle</td></tr>
<tr><td>ya wo tyi k'uñtye' tyilel</td><td>he was slowly coming</td></tr>
<tr><td>ya wo tyi tyilel [pero che'].</td><td>there he was coming [like this].</td></tr>
<tr><td>Tza' ochi 'i wäyel jiñi me'</td><td>The deer went to sleep</td></tr>
<tr><td>b'a tzi k'aja 'i yoj.</td><td>where he was resting.</td></tr>
<tr><td>Tza wäyi 'añ me'.</td><td>The deer went to sleep.</td></tr>
<tr><td>Tza bäläk' wäyi tyi 'ora.</td><td>He went right to sleep.</td></tr>
</table>

And finally (95–100):

<table>
<tr><td>Tza k'uñtye' ñumi 'añ 'ajki.</td><td>The turtle slowly passed him.</td></tr>
<tr><td>Tza ñumi, tza ñumi;</td><td>he passed him, he passed him;</td></tr>
<tr><td>tza majli. Tza majili</td><td>he went on by. He went on by</td></tr>
<tr><td>käläl tyi tyi' ja'.</td><td>all the way to the riverbank.</td></tr>
</table>

THE DENOUEMENT: The aftermath of the turtle's surprising win relates the "moral": the shame of the deer for having lost despite his inherent advantage (110–30), the happiness of the winning turtle (142–43). The underdog can succeed by steady effort, overcoming the advantages of the superior (but lazy) party. This part of the narration also gives the two listeners the opportunity to break in and repeat critical parts of the story and clarify some points.

THE CLOSING: The listeners having replaced the original narrator, the closing is actually voiced by one of the listeners, Nicolás (150–51):

<table>
<tr><td>Che tzi yälä b'ajche jiñi.</td><td>That's what he said.</td></tr>
<tr><td>Che tza 'ujtyi b'ajche jiñi.</td><td>That's the way that ended.</td></tr>
</table>

OUR GRANDFATHER

Ty'añ Lak Mam

This story is drawn from the repertory of traditional tales, and it has as its major protagonist one of the most important native deities, the Lightning God, who is also the master of rain known as Chajk. Both are aspects of the Earth Lord, the principal deity of the Mesoamerican pantheon (see also the next story, The Cave of Don Juan, featuring another avatar of the Earth Lord that takes the form of an elderly human).

THE OPENING: The brief opening phrase (lines 1–3) nonetheless has the critical elements: the time reference *wajali* "a long time ago" placing the action in the mythological past, and the attribution of the story to the oral tradition, *mi yälob'* and *'ab'i*, "they say." However, the opening phrase goes immediately to background.

SCENE-SETTING BACKGROUND: The background begins in the first sentence: *[mi yälob'] ke jiñ lak mam mu 'ab'i 'i jub'eltyak 'ila tyi lum*, "[they say] that Our Grandfather used to come [repeatedly] down here to earth." Continuing in non-completive verb forms, the narrator sets the scene and introduces the other protagonists, the fishermen (13–20).

THE EVENT LINE: The first use of the completive aspect signals the beginning of the event line: *tza ki k'elob k'achäkña 'ab'i tyi ñi' b'itz' jiñ lak mam*. "they saw, straddled on a limb of *b'itz'*, they say, our grandfather" (22–24). The text continues in completive aspect, with a considerable amount of reported dialogue.

Just before the peak event (119–24) there is a chronological step back in time, which we learned from this text is a device that signals the beginning of a new episode, in this case the peak. One of the fishermen has gone to get Lak Mam's hat, and he gives it to him. "But before he went" (*Pero ñaxañ che' tza majli*), the text continues, Lak Mam had warned him not to shake his shirt. In editing this text, we first suggested to the narrator that this event ought to be placed earlier, in chronological order. He agreed, and we moved the event back to an earlier point, assuming it was something he had simply forgotten to say at the right time.

None of us was satisfied with the results. The move seemed to take something away from the narration. We relented and moved the text segment back where it belonged. Only later did Kathryn Josserand discover that the step back in time was an important device used in Classic period hieroglyphic texts to mark the transition from one episode to another (Josserand 1991b).

THE PEAK EVENT: The peak event of this narration (154–67) is one of the most highly structured statements we have encountered, featuring couplets (AA), nested couplets (BCCB), and a triplet (DDD) along with a framing device (AA . . . AA) and a resolution (E) that plays against the peak action, perhaps framing the peak event with the initial phrase, *Che jale 'ora*:

	Che jale 'ora,	And then it happened:
A	*k'iñlaw 'ab'i,*	flashing, they say,
A	*ñuplaw 'ab'i,*	crashing, they say.
B	*tza tyojmi jiñ chajki,*	Lightning exploded
C	*b'a tza ñijka 'i b'ä lak mami.*	when Our Grandfather shook himself.
C	*Tza jach 'i ñijka 'i b'ä,*	He just shook himself,
B	*tza tyojmi jiñ chajki.*	and lightning exploded.
D	*Tza tyiki jiñ ja'.*	The water dried up.

D	*Tza säjp'i jiñ ja',*	The water went down,
D	*ma che' ku 'añix ja'.*	there wasn't any water anymore.
A	*K'iñlaw,*	Flashing.
A	*ñuplaw 'ab'i 'añ.*	crashing, they say it was.
E	*'Añ 'i chäñil ja', tza chämi.*	The water animal, it died.

THE DENOUEMENT: Following the peak event the moral is expressed: when Our Grandfather tells you to do something, do it! Because he didn't cover his eyes as he was told, one of the fishermen is struck unconscious—but not fatally; Our Grandfather is not a malicious deity. On the contrary, he rewards good behavior and encourages the fishermen to harvest the stunned fish before the water returns (190–210).

THE CLOSING: The fishermen having returned home with an extraordinary amount of fish (216–29), the text closes in traditional fashion (230–31):

'Añ che' jiñi,	So it was,
che' jach tza' 'ujtyi b'ajche jiñi.	thus it ended like that.

THE CAVE OF DON JUAN

Ty'añ jiñi Yotyoty Don Juan

Like the preceding story, this narration is drawn from the traditional repertory and features the Earth Lord in one of his guises. In this case, the lord of the material world appears as an old man and interacts with humans as a fellow human. While the distant Lightning God, Chajk, was referred to in the last story as Lak Mam, Our Grandfather, here the Earth Lord, one degree closer to humans, is called Lak Tyaty, Our Father. The latter is a common form of address and corresponds to local Spanish *don*, a title of respect.

THE OPENING: As in the preceding tale from the same genre, the opening contains the critical elements but moves directly into background (lines 1–3):

Wajali tyi wajali,	A long, long time ago,
'añ 'ab'i wiñik bä	there was, they say, a man who was
laj tyaty don Juan.	Our Father Don Juan.

SCENE-SETTING BACKGROUND: Expressed in non-completive verb forms, the text introduces the living Don Juan, details his appearance, and comments on his habit of coming down to earth to drink (4–20).

THE EVENT LINE: The event line begins with the first use of a completive verb form, when Don Juan becomes acquainted with a poor man (in the first of a series of couplets, 22–23):

I tzi k'elb'eñ 'i wokolel	And he saw his trouble,
'i tzi k'ele 'i puñtyiñtyel.	and he saw his suffering.

The text continues, alternating additional background information with punctual events.

THE PEAK EVENT: This text is so replete with couplets and repeated lines that it is difficult to isolate a single peak event. Rather, there is a series of minor peaks leading to the last incident on the event line (440–46):

Añtyak k'äñchoj.	There were many pit vipers (snakes).
Jiñi jax tza kaj k'eli,	As soon as they saw them,
tza ki ch'ojob'.	they began to strike.
K'äñchoj,	The pit vipers,
jin jax tzi k'elelob' 'añ wiñikob',	just as soon as they saw the men,
'ub'i k'äñchoj,	those pit vipers,
tyejchiyob' majlel	they rose up
i laj k'uxuyob' 'ub'i wiñiki.	and bit them all.

THE DENOUEMENT: After this last event, the text changes in character to the reminiscences of the narrator, who now seemingly takes on the character of the poor man protagonist (447–94). In this section of the text there are no punctual events other than retrospective ones (447–52):

Che jiñi.	So it was.
Kojix meku tza k'otyiyoñ.	That was the last time I went.
Jiñix meku yorajlel,	That really was the time,
che tza laj tyiliyob'.	when they all came.
Ma che ku 'añix tza chäñ k'otyiyoñ ja'el.	I never went there again.
Jiñix meku b'u 'ora.	That was the time.

And again (456–59):

Che tza tzax 'ujtyi lojoñ tyi ty'añ yik'oty,	When we last went to talk to him,
koñ kojixbä tza k'otyiyoñ ja'el,	the last time I went as well,
koñ ñoxoñix ja'el,	he was already old, too,
tzax meku kaj tyi mäkel tyi' yotyotyi wäle.	he began to close the door of his house then.

And finally (487–90):

Wajali,	A long time ago,
'añ tyo xchajpayaj;	there were looters;
tzi laj chajpañob' majlel pejtyelel.	they looted everything,
tzi laj xujchiñob' majlel.	they stole it and took it away.

Otherwise this last section of the text employs non-completive verb forms, and topics are introduced with the time-setting term *wajali* 'a long time ago' (453, 487). The theme has clearly shifted from the interactions of the poor man and Don Juan to personal recollections and the current situation of Don Juan's cave.

THE CLOSING: The closing is a simple one-line statement:

Ya' tza jili ty'añ b'ajche jiñi.   There the story ends, like that.

A Visit to Don Juan

Una Visita a don Juan

This text is a personal narrative, not a story drawn from the traditional repertory. As a consequence, it lacks the markers that identify a text as something passed down from the ancestors. On the other hand, it does illustrate the normal interaction between a narrator and his audience. The story told by Mariano Mayo Jiménez (MMJ) is introduced by Ausencio Cruz Guzmán (ACG), who takes his own turn as narrator from time to time.

THE OPENING: The narration is actually introduced by the listener, who gives the evidentiality statement (lines 1–4): *'Ili ty'añ mu bu kaj käl, iliyi, tza 'ujtyi 'añix wäle komo jo'lum p'e jab'. 'Alä tyo 'ili Mariano.* "This story we are going to tell you, this, it took place now about fifteen years ago. Mariano was a young boy still."

SCENE-SETTING BACKGROUND: Mariano begins his narration by placing the events in the distant past (5–7): *Wajali che' ya tyo 'añon . . . b'añ kerañob' tyi Paso Naranjoji . . .* "A long time ago, when I was still . . . where my brothers are in Paso Naranjo . . ." The use of *wajali* in a personal narrative is not uncommon. While it does not relegate the events to a mythological past, it does place them in a past that is remote as far as the speaker is concerned.

In this passage *wajali* appears twice, and some facts are attributed to the common tradition (9–10): *mi yälob' ke 'añ 'ab'i San Juañ 'ab'i . . .* "they say there is a San Juan, they say . . ." The background ends with the situation that brought about the visit to Don Juan (13–14):

Che' b'ajche' mak mi seb' tye' ja'al,   Since the rain didn't come soon enough,
mi chämel laj chol.   our milpa was dying.

THE EVENT LINE: The event line begins with the first instance of the completive aspect, the report of the arrival of an uncle, who has come to organize a trip to the cave (15–17): *'I tza kub'i lojoñ ñaxañ tzajñi juñ tyikil jiñi jyumijel lojoñ . . .* "And we heard first one man come, an uncle of ours . . ." The text continues relating events in completive aspect, with considerable dialogue to carry the action along (18–424).

THE PEAK EVENT: As in the preceding story, more a personal narrative than a traditional folktale, the peak event in this narration is difficult to identify. The end of the string of punctual events (425–36) could be considered the peak; more reflexive text follows that amounts to the denouement, and the huge maize harvest is the culminating event of the story:

Lekoj tza tyili 'i kuch 'añ 'iximi,	Fiercely came the load of corn,
pak'akña chixka.	it was huge, like that.
Chächixka b'omb'ontyil 'ixim.	Just like this, the ears were thick.
Tza jpoj k'ajatyak lojoñ,	When we went to harvest,
lok'otyak syento b'eynte sonte	we took out 120 tzontes [48,000 ears]
juju p'e cholel tzaj mele lojoñ . . .	from each milpa that we made . . .
Weñ kolen 'otyoty b'ajche 'ilili,	A really big house like this one,
tza b'ujty'i,	it filled,
cha' p'ej lajtz 'ixim,	two stacks of maize,
pero puro ty'uñul 'ixim.	but all big ears.

THE DENOUEMENT: Immediately after the last quoted sentences, the text reverts to non-completive aspects (437–46):

Jiñ me ku cha'añ mij ña'tyañ wäle	So that's why I think now
ke 'i sujmäch b'ajche jiñi mi yälob',	that it's true what they say,
ke 'añäch b'a mi laj k'ajtyiñ ja'al,	that there is where we ask for rain,
koñ tzäch jmero yäxña k'ele ja'el.	since I really did see it before, myself.
Wajali jiñi.	It was a long time ago.
Mi chäñ wox tyo,	If it's still like that,
chäñ melob' 'añ wäleyi,	if they still do it now,
b'ajchex.	who knows.
Koñ wajalix b'a tza mele lojoñ,	Since it was a long time ago we did it,
wajali.	long ago.

The narrator has effectively ended his story, and the remaining conversation goes back and forth between the two participants, bringing in other observations and speculations.

THE CLOSING: The text ends without any formal closing. In response to a question about whether money was paid to the *sacristán* (the human guardian of the cave), the narrator says (755–57) *Jiñ 'ab'i kuyi, jäjä', che kuyi.* "Him exactly, they say, uh-huh, just like that."

The Messengers

Ty'añ jiñi X'ak'juñ

The Chol folktale repertory is filled with stories about the savage creatures that come out of the woods to threaten humans. These stories are not attributed to the ancestors but are told as if they came from a much more recent time and represent situations that could occur in contemporary times.

THE OPENING: This story is attributed to a known person, although the events reported are not said to be events he actually witnessed. The evidentiality statement (lines 1–15) simply states where and when the narrator, Ausencio Cruz Guzmán, learned the story. In that statement, however, he makes use of the time-setting term *wajali*, suggesting that the tale is an old one (13–15):

. . . tzi sub'eñoñ lojoñ juñ p'ejl kwento,	. . . he told us a story,
'o jun p'ejl ty'añ,	or a tale,
ty'añ bä wajali, ke:	a tale from long ago, that:

SCENE-SETTING BACKGROUND: The next sentences introduce the protagonists and set them on their journey to deliver a letter (16–20). Here the text is marked as reported knowledge with the reportative *'ab'i*:

'Añ ab'i juñ tyikil korreyo'	There was, they say, a messenger,
mu 'ab'i 'i majlel tyi 'ak' juñ.	who was . . . going to deliver a letter.
Pero komo wajali	Because since long ago
maxtyo 'ab'i 'añik xchumtyil;	there still were no settlements;
maxtyo 'añik xchumtyil.	there still were no settlements.

THE EVENT LINE: The event line begins immediately after this brief setup with the first use of the completive aspect (21–22). While there are clearly two messengers, not one (as we learn in line 38), Chol cares little about marking the number with precision.

'I tza majli;	And he left;
tzi tyaja jochob' b'ä 'otyoty.	he came upon an abandoned house.

The event line continues, alternating punctual events in completive aspect with background information in non-completive verb forms.

THE PEAK EVENT: The peak event, following a number of minor peaks, is the fight with the demons at the granary, where the maize and the pumpkins defend the messengers (256–93). This episode culminates when, as the white corn is making its move, the sun comes up and the demons flee (283–93):

Ya jax tza' kaj tyi tyejchel ja' säk waji;	There now the white corn started to rise up;
tza' ki b'ajb'eñ.	it started to strike them.

Tza ki b'ajb'eñ 'an Xib'aji.	It started to strike that Xib'aj.
'A koñ yax tyilel ja'el 'i säk'ajeli,	Ah, but since dawn was coming soon,
k'iñlawix pañumil.	the earth was getting brighter.
Tzax kaj tyi putz'el ja'el Xib'aj;	Xib'aj started to take flight;
komo mach 'a wilañ	since don't you see
koñ ma tza mäjli 'i cha'añ 'añ Xib'aj.	that he couldn't stand it himself.
'I tzäx 'i chuku 'i yajñel,	And he just took off,
chañ säkix pañumil.	because the earth was getting brighter.
Majli.	He left.

THE DENOUEMENT: Immediately after the last-quoted passage, the text moves into a new episode; the milpa owner arrives and asks how the devil they had made such a mess (294–324). This opening allows the messengers to retell the whole story (325–54) and suggest the first moral: they shouldn't be punished for making the mess, because otherwise they would have been eaten by the demons. Besides, the owner's maize took their side in the fight.

The messengers proceed with the milpa owner to the village and deliver their letter. The recipient gives them the second moral: don't leave on a trip too late; start before dawn so you will arrive before darkness (366–82).

The third and most important moral is still coming (anticipated by lines 385–98): if you take something that doesn't belong to you, you will suffer from it. Something will have to be paid in its stead. Arriving home, the messenger who ate forbidden flesh pays the price (405–11).

THE CLOSING: The text closes with a standard couplet (417–18):

Che jax b'ajche jiñi	Just like that
tza' 'ujtyi jsub'eñety laj.	ended what I am telling you all.

The Jaguar Man

Ty'añ jiñi B'ajlum Wiñik

This story is one of what we have called "transformer stories," in which some character, usually a jaguar, devours a human and takes his or her shape. In this story the victim is a drunken husband; in the Comadre story the victim is a female, the comadre (ritual co-mother, godmother of one's children) of the protagonist. These stories revolve around the ways the human escapes the clutches of the transformer, and the moral of these stories is that the savages are less intelligent than people, and a clever and resourceful person can overcome the menace. In that aspect they are similar to stories of the Blackman, the difference being that the latter exists independent of humans and is not a transformer.

This particular narration, by Nicolás Arcos Alvarez, illustrates the expectations of the listeners that stories will be told a certain way. The two listeners, one the narrator's uncle (Mateo Alvaro López) and the other his mentor (Ausencio "Chencho" Cruz Guzmán), are both senior to Nicolás and do not hesitate to call him down when they think he isn't telling the story well (24–44). When Nicolás declares the story to be over (199), Mateo retells it (203–94), with back-channeling from the other two, and finally ends it himself (294).

THE OPENING: Nicolas's first opening is a brief statement (1) that has none of the markers of traditional storytelling: *Jiñäch 'i tyejchb'ali*, "This is its beginning." Likewise, he launches immediately into the event line, with no background information (2–23): *Tza majli 'añ wiñiki . . .* "A man went out . . ." He manages to get through the first epoisode, the arrival of the (supposed) man to his house and his wife's greeting, before he is called down by his listeners. Chencho breaks in to ask for some background: *¿Añ tza juñ p'ejl tyejlum?* "Was there a town there?" (24) and tells Nicolás to start there. Mateo agrees and offers an alternative beginning, using non-completive verb forms for background and culminating in the first event, expressed in the completive: *Pero juñ p'ejl k'iñ tzi tyaja b'ajlum tyi b'ij.* "But one day a jaguar found him on the road" (27–34).

After further discussion (35–44), Nicolás starts again and shows he has grasped the point as he lays it on thick, using non-completive background statements as well as the reportative *'ab'i* and placing the action in the distant past with *wajali* (45–50). He then continues with less marking (51–55) but ends the background with a triplet (56–58):

Mi majlel tyi tyejklum,	He would go to town,
mi jape' lemb'al;	he would drink liquor;
mu tyo 'i k'otyel tyi yotyoty.	he would still get back home.

THE EVENT LINE: The new event line begins with the first use (other than in subordinate sentences) of the completive aspect: *Pero 'añ tzi tyajb'e 'i yorajlel che tza k'otyi 'i tyaje' juñ kojty b'ajlum* "But there came a time when he arrived to find a jaguar" (59–61). The text continues, relating minor peaks and adding background information.

THE PEAK EVENT: Just as Nicolás is getting to the peak event (163–76), the triumph of the woman over the jaguar, Chencho and Mateo interrupt with questions (177, 187–88):

Pero ko me 'añ wajali che jiñi,	But since this was long ago,
mu 'ab'i 'i käñob' jiñ ña'tyuñ,	they say they still used metates.
tzi ch'ämä majlel;	She brought it with her;

tzi ch'uyu letzel;	she carried it up;
tza k'äjki yik'oty 'i k'äb' 'añ ña'tyuñ.	she climbed up with the metate.
Che tza k'äjki yik'oty jiñi,	When she climbed up with it,
che jale' k'otyeli,	just then he was arriving,
tza kaj tyi k'otyel jiñ b'ajlum.	the jaguar was just arriving.
Tza kaji 'i sik'b'eñ majlel 'i yujtzil	He was following her scent
b'aki tza majli jiñ x'ixik;	where the woman had gone;
tza tyejchi majlel.	he started to come.
Che mach yax 'añ jiñi x'ixik,	When the woman wasn't there,
tza majli;	he left;
tza k'äjki ya tyi ñi' tye'.	he climbed toward the tip of the tree.
[CHENCHO:]	[CHENCHO:]
¿Tyoj k'äjkel?	He came directly up?
[NICOLÁS:]	[NICOLÁS:]
Yom k'äjkel ja'el b'ajlum.	The jaguar wanted to climb up, too.
Wolix 'i k'äjkel	He was climbing up
chañ sami 'i chuk jub'el.	to drag her down below.
Pero ko me woläch 'i pensariñ	But she was really thinking
b'ajche mi ki kotyañ 'i b'ä	how she could save herself,
'añ x'ixiki.	the woman was.
Tzi ch'ämä jiñi 'i k'äb' jiñi ña'tyuñ.	She grabbed the grinding stone.
Che bä ya' wo 'i k'äjkel jiñi b'ajlumi,	When the jaguar was just about to climb up,
tzi kujb'e jub'el 'ila tyi jol.	she struck down on his head.
[CHENCHO:]	[CHENCHO:]
Pero ¿b'ajche'? ¿Kächb'il 'i cha'añ?	But how? Was it tied to something?
[MATEO:]	[MATEO:]
Kächb'il 'i cha'añ.	It was tied to something.

DENOUEMENT AND CLOSING: Nicolás makes one last attempt to control the story (178–97) and then tries to end the narration (199): *Che tzi' mele 'añ b'ajche jiñ,* "That's the way she did that." Chencho intevenes (200). Nicolás couplets him, again to end the story (201), but Chencho asks another question (202), and then Mateo picks up the narration, with occasional back-channeling from Chencho and even Nicolás (203–41), and attempts to bring the narration to an end: *Che' tza 'ujtyi b'ajche jiñi,* "That's the way that ended" (243). But Chencho intervenes again (244), and Mateo returns to the story (245), retelling most of the early incidents. After some back-channeling from both Chencho and Nicolás, Mateo finally manages to close with one final *Che tza 'ujtyi b'ajche jiñi* (289).

The Blackman

Ty'añ jiñi Xñek

In this narration, one of two Tila Chol texts in this collection, some words take shapes distinct from those in the Tumbalá variety (the rest of the collection except for The Comadre). Tila Chol has undergone (or is undergoing even as we speak) a number of innovations. For one thing, the verbal preclitics are changing. The completive aspect preclitic in Tumbalá Chol, *tza' ~ tzi*, is matched by Tila Chol *ta' ~ ti*. This seemingly minor change has considerable implications for the technical description of Tila Chol, because it puts unpalatalized *ta'* in direct contrast with palatalized *tya'* 'excrement'. Unlike Tumbalá Chol, where essentially all alveolar stops are palatalized *ty*, in Tila Chol we have to distinguish between *ty* and the *t* that comes from old *tz* and occurs only in this morpheme. (The earlier form is attested for Tila Chol in a 1789 wordlist; Hopkins, Cruz Guzmán, and Josserand 2008.) Because of a desire to unify and normalize the script, Chol writers frequently ignore these phonetic details and transcribe this morpheme, albeit unpalatalized, as *tya ~ tyi*. In Tila Chol there is also reduction in the forms of many other verbal morphemes. As an auxiliary (before the main verb) or as a directional verb (afterward), the verbs *kajel* 'to begin to', *majlel* 'to go to', and *tyilel* 'to come to' frequently occur in such reduced shapes as *ke* or *ki*, *ma* or *maj*, and *te* or *ti*. The reportative *'ab'i* 'it is said' is often reduced to *b'i*. The progressive *woli* of Tumbalá Chol is matched by *chonkol* in Tila (see line 21).

THE OPENING: There is no formal opening to this story; the narrator moves directly to background (1), although the background information is marked with the reportative *'ab'i* (here *b'i*) and the time-setting *wajali*. However, a long evidentiality statement is given at the end of the narration (241–65), replacing the usual denouement.

SCENE-SETTING BACKGROUND: The background introduces the protagonist, a farmer who has a maize granary; places the granary in his milpa, and discusses the custom of keeping a maize supply in the fields and the necessity to guard it against marauding animals, especially in earlier times (1–19). It ends with the farmer's current situation (20–22):

Jiñi lak pi'äl,	That man,
chonkol 'i weñ jilel 'i yixim,	they were finishing off his corn,
weñ k'uxtyäl jiñi 'i yixim.	his corn was being eaten up.

THE EVENT LINE: The event line begins with the first use of the completive aspect, in smooth transition from the background (23): *Ta b'i majli käntañ 'ili yixim*, "He went to take care of his corn, they say." The event line continues, alternating as usual between non-completive background information and event-line events. The Blackman is introduced as background (24–36), and the story returns to the event line (37). Repetition of words and phrases (70–73, 101), phonological lengthening (78), and unusually strong stress (116) all help to build tension as the Blackman approaches the milpa:

(70, 73) *Chonkol tyi ch'uyub' tyilel jiñi . . .*	He was coming whistling . . .
che' chonkol tyi ch'uyub' tyilel li Xñeki.	thus the Blackman was whistling as he came.
(101) *Yañila, yañila, yañila, yañila . . .*	Closer, closer, closer, closer . . .
(78) *ñaaajty*	looong
(116) *Weñ läkälix 'i tel,*	coming *really* close . . .

THE PEAK EVENT: Tension builds up through a series of couplets as we approach the peak event, but the actual peak is expressed here with vocal alterations more than syntactic structures, although there are parallelisms in the text (217–35):

Che' jiñi.	So it was.
Lak pi'äl,	The man
yujilix ma'añ ti jowb'e,	knew he hadn't poked holes,
ma'añ ti tyokb'e li ch'ujmi	he hadn't pierced the pumpkin
b'a' mi lok'el yowixi.	where the steam could escape.
Ma'añ jowol jiñi ch'ujm.	The pumpkin wasn't punctured.
Ta b'i keji tyi lok' ya' tyi malil.	They say it began to boil inside.
Ti kaji tyi b'ulich jiñi ch'ujm.	The pumpkin began to sweat.
Che' jiñi,	So it was,
che' ta 'ix k'uk'uxtyikwä	so it got hotter and hotter
jiñi ch'ujm tyi malil.	inside that pumpkin.
Ta 'ix kej tyi k'uk'ux lojk'.	It got really really hot.
Ñoj tyikäw 'ix.	It was very hot already.
Che' jiñi.	So it was.
Ta b'i jem tyojmi jiñi ch'ujmi.	They say that the pumpkin exploded.
Ta b'i luj puli peeejtyelel.	It burned him *all over*!
Ya-a-a-a'	Yaaah!
k'äñak 'añ b'i tyi ch'ujm tyi malil,	The hot yellow flesh in the pumpkin
'i pejtyelel 'i pächilel, pejtyelel 'i ya',	burned all of his skin, all of his legs,
ta b'i lu' puli.	they say he was burned all over.

THE DENOUEMENT: The denouement now takes the role of the opening evidentiality statement, the attribution of the story to the ancestors of the narrator (241–65).

THE CLOSING: The closing is the traditional *Che' ti 'ujtyi wajali b'ajche' jiñi,* "That's the way it happened, long ago" (266).

The Comadre

La Comadre

Like the Jaguar-Man story, this is another tale of jaguar transformers. Here, the jaguar has apparently devoured the protagonist's neighbor and comadre and comes over for a visit. Typically, the jaguar says little and sometimes speaks broken Chol. Likewise, the jaguar does not understand human culture and makes mistakes that reveal his true identity. Also speaking broken Chol are two of the principal investigators, who prompt the speaker to tell some story in the traditional mold.

The conversation begins (1–19) with a discussion of what kind of stories Don Rafael would like to tell today (to complement the stories he had given us on an earlier occasion). Once he settles on a topic, he launches immediately into the opening.

THE OPENING: The opening (lines 20–29) is more or less standard, with the use of *wajali* (and *tyi 'antiwo, anterior*), the reportative in the form of *mi yälob'* "they say," and attribution to the ancestors, here called *kpapá, kmamá*, "my poppa, my momma."

SCENE-SETTING BACKGROUND: The narration goes directly into what appears to be the event line, but the verb forms are non-completive: *mi ñume(l) . . . juñ tyikil . . . 'i komáre*, "A person . . . her comadre comes by" (34–36). The text continues in incompletive aspect, implying ongoing or habitual actions rather than punctual ones. In fact, the completive aspect does not occur until much later in the narration, at line 89, and then in an auxiliary verb: *Ke tyi juch'b'al je li b'ajlumi (= [ta] kaji tyi juch'b'al ja'el li b'ajlumi)*, "The jaguar started to grind corn, too." The completive occurs in a main verb at line 98: *Majliyob' tyi chuk puyi*, "They went to catch snails." This is either an extemely lengthy background episode or a deviation from the traditional norm.

THE EVENT LINE: If we hold to the principle that the event line does not begin until the first use of the completive aspect, then it begins at line 89 or 98 (above), but the intervening text is all non-completive. Much later in the text (173–76), the completive again occurs, and after that instance it is fairly frequent:

Entonses ta majli li komare,	So the comadre left,
'iii, jiñjach lok'el ma,	eee, she just took off,
ti putz'i majlel.	she fled.
Ta b'i k'otyi tyaj jiñi che che'	They say she went and found a big tree,
ñojo kolem tye'.	a really big tree.

At this point in the story we seem to be approaching the peak event. That is, in this narration there seems to be a shift in the use of completive and incompletive forms in that the early event line is narrated in non-completive verb forms and the peak episode is marked by the use of completive verb forms.

THE PEAK EVENT: Coupleting increases as the peak event nears (207):

Ti ki lajchiñ, ki lajchiñ,	He started clawing, clawing,
ti ki lajchiñ li . . . li b'ajlumi.	he started clawing, that . . . jaguar.
Chañ mi yom 'i k'ux 'i komare je.	Because he wanted to eat his comadre, eh.
Yom mi k'uxe'.	He wanted to eat her.
Yom mi k'uxe.	He wanted to eat her.
Lajchiñ, lajchiñ,	Clawing, clawing,

The jaguar makes one last attempt to reach the woman and then sits down and cries (217–21).

Ti 'uk'e li b'ajlumi.	The jaguar cried.
"Jii, komare," che'ab'i.	"Ee, comadre," he said.
"[Kom] mij k'uxb'e 'a chikiñ.	"[I wanted] to eat your ears.
Mij k'uxb'e 'a jol	To eat your head,
ti käläl komare,"	all of you, comadre,"
che'ab'i.	he said.

The jaguar departs, and the woman comes down and goes home (227–36).

THE DENOUEMENT: The story is now retold to the actual neighbor, the comadre that somehow was not in fact devoured by the jaguar (242–83), and the moral comes out (284–85):

"Yamb'ä 'ora komare	"Another time, comadre,
mach 'a jak' majlel.	don't get called out,
Ame 'i k'uxety," che'ab'i'.	so he doesn't eat you," she said.

THE CLOSING: The closing is a simple *Weno. Ya'ix ya'.* "Okay. There it was" (285–86).

References

Alejos García, José. 1988. *Wajalix bä t'an*. Centro de Estudios Mayas, Cuadernos 20. México, DF: Universidad Nacional Autónoma de México.

Alejos García, José. 1994. *Mosojäntel: Etnografía del discurso agrarista entre los ch'oles de Chiapas*. México, DF: Universidad Nacional Autónoma de México.

Alejos García, José, and Elsa Ortega Peña. 1991. *El Archivo Municipal de Tumbalá, Chiapas, 1920–1946*. México, DF: Universidad Nacional Autónoma de México.

Altman, Heidi M. 1996. "Evidentiality and Genre in Chol Mayan Traditional Narrative." MA thesis, Florida State University, Tallahassee.

Arcos Mendoza, Marcos. 1986. "'Askuñil bä K'iñ yik'oty Yijtz'iñ bä K'iñ" (The Major Sun and the Minor Sun). Story #3 in "Stories," by Kathryn Josserand (researcher), Nicholas Hopkins (researcher), Nicolás Arcos Alvaro (speaker), Mateo Alvaro López (speaker), Marcos Arcos Mendoza (speaker), and Ausencio Cruz Guzmán (speaker). *Mayan Languages Collection of Nicholas Hopkins*. The Archive of the Indigenous Languages of Latin America: www.ailla.utexas.org. Media: audio. Access: public. Resource: CTU006R012.

Arcos Mendoza, Marcos. 1994. "K'in askunälbä y k'in x'ijtz'inälbä [Older Brother Sun and Younger Brother Sun]: El cuento del sol mayor y sol menor." In *Chol Texts, Vocabulary and Grammar*, by Nicholas A. Hopkins and J. Kathryn Josserand, 187–204. Final Technical Report to the National Science Foundation, Grant BNS-8308506, 1983–86. Tampa, FL: Institute for Cultural Ecology of the Tropics.

DOI: 10.5876/9781607324881.c016

Arcos Mendoza, Marcos, ed. 1999. *Juñ ch'älbilbä tyi lak ty'añ ch'ol: libro de literatura en len-gua Chol de Chiapas.* México, DF: Dirección General de Educación Indígena, Secretaría de Educación Pública.

Aulie, Wilbur, and Evelyn Aulie. 1978. *Diccionario Ch'ol-Español: Español-Ch'ol.* Serie de Vocabularios y Diccionarios Indígenas Mariano Silva y Aveces 21. México, DF: Instituto Lingüístico de Verano.

Bassie, Karen. 2001. *The Jolja' Cave Project.* Crystal River, FL: Foundation for the Advancement of Mesoamerican Studies, Inc.; http://www.famsi.org/reports/00017/index.html.

Bassie-Sweet, Karen, Nicholas A. Hopkins, and J. Kathryn Josserand. 2012. "Narrative Structure and the Drum Major Headdress." In *Parallel Worlds: Genre, Discourse, and Poetics in Contemporary, Colonial, and Classic Maya Literature,* ed. Kerry Hull and Michael Carrasco, 195–219. Boulder: University Press of Colorado.

Blaffer, Sarah C. 1972. *The Black-Man of Zinacantan: A Central American Legend.* Austin: University of Texas Press.

Breton, Alain. 1988. "En los confines del norte Chiapaneco, una región llamada 'Bulujib.'" *Estudios de Cultura Maya* 17: 295–354.

Brody, Jill. 1986. "Repetition as a Rhetorical and Conversational Device in Tojolabal (Mayan)." *International Journal of American Linguistics* 52 (3): 255–74. http://dx.doi.org /10.1086/466022.

Cahn von Seelen, Kristin. 2004. "'This Place Was Paradise': Consumption as Metaphor and Material Concern on Mexico's Southern Frontier." PhD diss., University of Pennsylvania, Philadelphia.

Carlson, Ruth, and Francis Eachus. 1977. "The Kekchi Spirit World." In *Cognitive Studies of Southern Mesoamerica,* ed. Helen L. Neuenswander and Dean E. Arnold, 38–65. Museum of Anthropology Publication 3. Dallas: Summer Institute of Linguistics.

Cruz Guzmán, Ausencio (consultant). 1978a. "The Tale of Lak Mam (Lightning)." *Mayan Languages Collection of Nicholas Hopkins.* The Archive of the Indigenous Languages of Latin America: www.ailla.utexas.org. Media: audio. Access: public. Resource: CTU002R017.

Cruz Guzmán, Ausencio (consultant). 1978b. "The Tale of the Lightning." *Mayan Languages Collection of Nicholas Hopkins.* The Archive of the Indigenous Languages of Latin America: www.ailla.utexas.org. Media: audio. Access: public. Resource: CTU002R003.

Cruz Guzmán, Ausencio (consultant). 1978c. "The Tale of the Moon." *Mayan Languages Collection of Nicholas Hopkins.* The Archive of the Indigenous Languages of Latin America: www.ailla.utexas.org. Media: audio. Access: public. Resource: CTU002R002.

Cruz Guzmán, Ausencio, J. Kathryn Josserand, and Nicholas A. Hopkins. 1980. "The Cave of Don Juan." In *Third Palenque Round Table, 1978, Part 2,* ed. Merle Greene Robertson, 116–23. Austin: University of Texas Press.

de la Torre Yarza, Rodrigo. 1994. *Chiapas: Entre la Torre de Babel y la lengua nacional.* México, DF: Centro de Investigaciones y Estudios Superiores en Antropología Social.

de Vos, Jan. 1980. *Fray Pedro Lorenzo de la Nada: Misionero de Chiapas y Tabasco; en el cuarto centenario de su muerte.* [No publisher or place of publication listed].

de Vos, Jan. 1988. *La Paz de Dios y del Rey: La conquista de la Selva Lacandona, 1525–1821.* 2nd ed. México, DF: Fondo de Cultura Económica.

de Vos, Jan. 1990. *No queremos ser cristianos: Historia de la resistencia de los lacandones, 1530–1695, a través de testimonios españoles e indígenas.* México, DF: Dirección General de Publicaciones del Consejo Nacional para la Cultura y las Artes, Instituto Nacional Indigenista.

Diarassouba, Sidiky. 2007. "Establishment of Literary Standards for an Oral Language: The Case of Nafara Discourse Patterns, Côte d'Ivoire, West Africa." PhD diss., Florida State University, Tallahassee.

Folan, William J., J. Kathryn Josserand, and Nicholas A. Hopkins. 1983. "Una nota sobre paleoclimatología, prehistoria y diversificación lingüística de los mayas a través de los tiempos." *Información* 7: 3–18.

Folmar, T. Lee. 1996 "Chol Bird Taxonomy." Honors thesis, Florida State University, Tallahassee.

Gossen, Gary. 1974. *Chamulas in the World of the Sun: Time and Space in a Maya Oral Tradition.* Cambridge, MA: Harvard University Press.

Hopkins, Nicholas A. 1964. "A Phonology of Zinacantán Tzotzil." MA thesis, University of Chicago.

Hopkins, Nicholas A. 1967a. "The Chuj Language." PhD diss., University of Chicago.

Hopkins, Nicholas A. 1967b. "Summary of the First Seminar for the Study of Maya Writing." *Latin American Research Review* 2 (2): 91–94.

Hopkins, Nicholas A. 1968a. "Estado de la lingüística mayance." *Escritura Maya* 2 (3): 33–35.

Hopkins, Nicholas A. 1968b. "A Method for the Investigation of Glyph Syntax." *Estudios de Cultura Maya* 7: 79–83.

Hopkins, Nicholas A. 1970. "Estudio preliminar de los dialectos del tzeltal y del tzotzil." In *Ensayos de antropología en la Zona Central de Chiapas*, ed. Norman A. McQuown and Julian Pitt-Rivers, 185–214. Colección de Antropología Social 8. México, DF: Instituto Nacional Indigenista.

Hopkins, Nicholas A. 1974. "Historical and Sociocultural Aspects of the Distribution of Linguistic Variants in Highland Chiapas, Mexico." In *Sociocultural Dimensions of Language Change*, ed. Ben Blount and Mary Sanches, 185–225. New York: Academic.

Hopkins, Nicholas A. 1980. "Chuj Animal Names and Their Classification." *Journal of Mayan Linguistics* 2 (1): 13–39.

Hopkins, Nicholas A. 1983. "Knowledge and Use of Dialect Variants in Lowland Chol." Paper presented to the Annual Meeting of the American Anthropological Association, Chicago, IL, November.

Hopkins, Nicholas A. 1984. "La influencia del yucatecano sobre el cholano y su contexto histórico." In *Investigaciones recientes en el área maya: XVII Mesa Redonda; 21–27 junio 1981*, 191–207. San Cristóbal de Las Casas, Chiapas: Sociedad Mexicana de Antropología.

Hopkins, Nicholas A. 1985. "On the History of the Chol Language." In *Fifth Palenque Round Table, 1983*, ed. Merle Greene Robertson and Virginia M. Fields, 1–5. San Francisco: Pre-Columbian Art Research Institute.

Hopkins, Nicholas A. 1988. "Classic Mayan Kinship Systems: Epigraphic and Ethnographic Evidence for Patrilineality." *Estudios de Cultura Maya* 17: 87–121.

Hopkins, Nicholas A. 1991. "Classic and Modern Relationship Terms and the 'Child of Mother' Glyph (T I:606.23)." In *Sixth Palenque Round Table, 1986*, ed. Merle Greene Robertson, 255–65. Norman: University of Oklahoma Press.

Hopkins, Nicholas A. 1995. "Ch'ol." In *Encyclopedia of World Cultures*, vol. 8: *Middle America and the Caribbean*, ed. James W. Dow and Robert V. Kemper, 63–66. Boston: G. K. Hall.

Hopkins, Nicholas A. 1997. "Decipherment and the Relation between Mayan Languages and Maya Writing." In *The Language of Maya Hieroglyphs*, ed. Martha J. Macri and Anabel Ford, 77–88. San Francisco: Pre-Columbian Art Research Institute.

Hopkins, Nicholas A., Ausencio Cruz Guzmán, and J. Kathryn Josserand. 2008. "A Chol (Mayan) Vocabulary from 1789." *International Journal of American Linguistics* 74 (1): 83–114. http://dx.doi.org/10.1086/529464.

Hopkins, Nicholas A., and J. Kathryn Josserand. 1986a. "The Characteristics of Chol (Mayan) Traditional Narrative." Paper presented to the Symposium on Mayan Discourse, 25th Conference on American Indian Languages, American Anthropological Association, Philadelphia, PA, December.

Hopkins, Nicholas A., and J. Kathryn Josserand. 1986b. "Proposal to the National Science Foundation (1983): Chol Texts, Vocabulary and Grammar." In *Handbook for Grant Proposal Preparation*, ed. Ann M. Peters, Lise Menn, Paul G. Chapin, and Helen C. Aguera, 2.1–2.16, 2.35–2.39. Washington, DC: Linguistic Society of America.

Hopkins, Nicholas A., and J. Kathryn Josserand. 1990. "The Characteristics of Chol (Mayan) Traditional Narrative." In *Homenaje a Jorge A. Suarez: Lingüística indoamericana e hispánica*, ed. Beatriz Garza Cuarón and Paulette Levy, 297–314. Mexico, DF: El Colegio de Mexico.

Hopkins, Nicholas A., and J. Kathryn Josserand. 1994. *Chol Texts, Vocabulary and Grammar*. Final Technical Report to the National Science Foundation. Grant BNS-8308506: 1983–86. Tampa, FL: Institute for Cultural Ecology of the Tropics.

Hopkins, Nicholas A., and J. Kathryn Josserand. 1995. "El desciframiento y la lingüística." Paper presented to the plenary session on Maya epigraphy, Tercer Congreso Internacional de Mayistas, Chetumal, Quintana Roo, Mexico, July.

Hopkins, Nicholas A., and J. Kathryn Josserand. 1998. "La lingüística y el desciframiento de las inscripciones mayas." In *Tercer Congreso Internacional de Mayistas: Memoria*, ed. Ana Luisa Izquierdo, 447–78. México, DF: Universidad Nacional Autónoma de México. (Reprinted 2002, Chetumal: Universidad de Quintana Roo.)

Hopkins, Nicholas A., and J. Kathryn Josserand. 2012. "The Narrative Structure of Chol Folktales: One Thousand Years of Literary Tradition." In *Parallel Worlds: Genre, Discourse, and Poetics in Contemporary, Colonial, and Classic Maya Literature*, ed. Kerry Hull and Michael Carrasco, 21–42. Boulder: University Press of Colorado.

Hopkins, Nicholas A., J. Kathryn Josserand, and Ausencio Cruz Guzmán. 1985. "Notes on the Chol Dugout Canoe." In *Fourth Palenque Round Table, 1980*, ed. Merle Greene Robertson, 325–29. San Francisco: Pre-Columbian Art Research Institute.

Hopkins, Nicholas A., J. Kathryn Josserand, and Ausencio Cruz Guzmán. 2011. *A Historical Dictionary of Chol (Mayan)*. http://www.famsi.org/mayawriting/dictionary/hopkins/dictionaryChol.html.

Houston, Stephen D. 1997. "The Shifting Now: Aspect, Deixis, and Narrative in Classic Texts." *American Anthropologist* 99 (2): 291–305. http://dx.doi.org/10.1525/aa.1997.99.2.291.

Instituto Nacional de las Lenguas Indígenas. 2000. "Variantes lingüísticas: Cuadro 1, Población de 5 años y más hablante de alguna lengua indígenas y número de localidades por variante lingüística según sexo: localidades con asentamientos históricos, 2000." XII Censo General de Población y Vivienda. www.inali.gob.mx/component/content/article/63.

Instituto Nacional de las Lenguas Indígenas. 2008. "Catálogo de las lenguas indígenas nacionales: variantes lingüísticas de México con sus autodeterminaciones y referencias geoestadísticas." Diario Oficial de la Federación, 14 de enero de 2008. http://www.inali.gob.mx/component/content/article/49-404.

Jones, Linda K., ed. 1979. *Discourse Studies in Mesoamerican Languages*. Arlington: Summer Institute of Linguistics and University of Texas at Arlington.

Josserand, J. Kathryn. 1968. "Complex Sentence Formation in Yucatec." Paper presented to the American Anthropological Association, Seattle, WA, November.

Josserand, J. Kathryn. 1975. "Archaeological and Linguistic Correlations for Mayan Prehistory." In *Actas del XLI Congreso Internacional de Americanistas, México, 2 al 7 de septiembre de 1974*, ed. José Carlos Chiaramonte, vol. 1:501–10. México, DF: Instituto Nacional de Antropología e Historia.

Josserand, J. Kathryn. 1986. "The Narrative Structure of Hieroglyphic Texts at Palenque." Paper presented to the Sixth Mesa Redonda de Palenque, Palenque, Chiapas, June.

Josserand, J. Kathryn. 1987a. "The Discourse Structure of Maya Hieroglyphic Texts." Paper presented to the symposium The Linguistic Structure of Maya Hieroglyphic Writing, XXVth Conference on American Indian Languages, American Anthropological Association, Chicago, IL, November.

Josserand, J. Kathryn. 1987b. "La estructura y contenido de las inscripciones clásicas." Paper presented to the Taller Maya IX, Antigua, Guatemala, June.

Josserand, J. Kathryn. 1987c. "Tipos de material literario y modos de presentación." Paper presented to the Taller Maya IX, Antigua, Guatemala, June.

Josserand, J. Kathryn. 1989. "A New Reading for the Palenque Sarcophagus Lid Inscriptions." Paper presented to the Seventh Palenque Round Table, Palenque, Chiapas, June.

Josserand, J. Kathryn. 1991a. "Linguistic and Literary Models of Text Analysis: Scene Changers and Temporal Adverbs in Hieroglyphic Texts." Paper presented to the 47th International Congress of Americanists, New Orleans, LA, July.

Josserand, J. Kathryn. 1991b. "The Narrative Structure of Hieroglyphic Texts at Palenque." In *Sixth Palenque Round Table, 1986*, ed. Merle Greene Robertson, 12–31. Norman: University of Oklahoma Press. [Spanish translation published as Josserand 1997, "La estructura narrativa en los textos jeroglíficos de Palenque." In *Mesas Redondas de Palenque*, ed. Silvia Trejo, 445–81. México, DF: Instituto Nacional de Antropología e Historia.]

Josserand, J. Kathryn. 1992. "Deciphering Verbal Morphology in Maya Hieroglyphic Writing." Paper presented to the symposium Attestation and Preservation, XXXIst Conference on American Indian Languages, American Anthropological Association, San Francisco, CA, December.

Josserand, J. Kathryn. 1994. "Royal Names and Titles in Classic Maya Hieroglyphic Inscriptions." Paper presented to the American Anthropological Association, Annual Meeting, Atlanta, GA, November.

Josserand, J. Kathryn. 1995a. "Historia y literatura en los textos jeroglíficos clásicos." Paper presented to the V Encuentro: Los Investigadores de la Cultura Maya, Universidad Autónoma de Campeche, Campeche, Mexico, November.

Josserand, J. Kathryn. 1995b. "The Literary Structure of the Tablet of the 96 Glyphs, Palenque." Paper presented to the Latin American Indigenous Literatures Association, XIIth Symposium, Mexico City, June.

Josserand, J. Kathryn. 1995c. "Participant Tracking in Hieroglyphic Texts: Who Was That Masked Man?" *Journal of Linguistic Anthropology* 5 (1): 65–89. http://dx.doi.org/10.1525/jlin.1995.5.1.65.

Josserand, J. Kathryn. 1996. "The Emergence of Modern Chol Dialects." Paper presented to the 35th Conference on American Indian Languages, Symposium on Mayan and Other Mesoamerican Languages, American Anthropological Association, Annual Meeting, San Francisco, CA, November.

Josserand, J. Kathryn. 1997a. "La estructura narrativa en los textos jeroglíficos de Palenque." In *Mesas Redondas de Palenque*, ed. Silvia Trejo, 445–81. México, DF: Instituto Nacional de Antropología e Historia. [Spanish translation of Josserand 1991b.]

Josserand, J. Kathryn. 1997b. "Participant Tracking in Hieroglyphic Texts: Who Was That Masked Man?" In *The Language of Maya Hieroglyphs*, ed. Anabel Ford and Martha Macri, 111–27. San Francisco: Pre-Columbian Art Research Institute.

Josserand, J. Kathryn. 1998. "The Art of Political Discourse in Classic Maya Hieroglyphic Inscriptions." Paper presented to the symposium The Poetics of Ideological Discourse in Mesoamerica, American Anthropological Association, Annual Meeting, Philadelphia, PA, December.

Josserand, J. Kathryn. 1999. "Social Interaction and Linguistic Practice." Keynote Address: Linguistics, Third Palenque Round Table [new series], Palenque, Mexico, June.

Josserand, J. Kathryn. 2002. "Women in Classic Maya Texts." In *Ancient Maya Women*, ed. Traci Ardren, 114–51. Walnut Creek, CA: Altamira.

Josserand, J. Kathryn. 2004. "Language and Dialect in the Classic Maya Lowlands." Paper presented to the Maya Meetings at Texas, Symposium, Austin, TX, March.

Josserand, J. Kathryn. 2007a. "Literatura e historia en los textos jeroglíficos clásicos." *Gaceta de la Universidad Autónoma de Campeche* 17 (93): 39–46.

Josserand, J. Kathryn. 2007b. "The Missing Heir at Yaxchilán: Literary Analysis of a Maya Historical Puzzle." *Latin American Antiquity* 18 (3): 295–313. http://dx.doi.org/10.2307/25478182.

Josserand, J. Kathryn. 2011. "Languages of the Preclassic along the Pacific Coastal Plains of Southeastern Mesoamerica." In *The Southern Maya in the Late Preclassic: The Rise and Fall of an Early Mesoamerican Civilization*, ed. Jonathan Kaplan and Michael Love, 141–74. Boulder: University Press of Colorado.

Josserand, J. Kathryn, and Nicholas A. Hopkins. 1984. "Materials for the Advanced Seminar on Mayan Hieroglyphic Writing, Austin, Texas, March 12–17, 1984." Unpublished manuscript in possession of the author.

Josserand, J. Kathryn, and Nicholas A. Hopkins. 1988. *Chol (Mayan) Dictionary Database*. 3 vols. Final Performance Report, National Endowment for the Humanities Grant RT-20643-86.

Josserand, J. Kathryn, and Nicholas A. Hopkins. 1991. *A Handbook of Classic Maya Inscriptions: The Western Lowlands*. Final Performance Report, National Endowment for the Humanities Grant RT-21090-89.

Josserand, J. Kathryn, and Nicholas A. Hopkins. 1994. "Recent Investigations in Maya Hieroglyphic Writing." In *Proceedings of the 47th International Congress of Americanists, New Orleans, Louisiana, July 1991*, ed. E. Wyllis Andrews, 221–24. Publication 63. New Orleans: Middle American Research Institute.

Josserand, J. Kathryn, and Nicholas A. Hopkins. 1996. "Chol Ritual Language." With Terrence Lee Folmar, Heidi Altman, Ausencio Cruz Guzmán, and Bernardo Pérez Martínez. Crystal River, FL: Foundation for the Advancement of Mesoamerican Studies, Inc. http://www.famsi.org/reports/94017/index.html.

Josserand, J. Kathryn, and Nicholas A. Hopkins. 2000. "Classic Maya Grammar and Discourse Structure." Paper presented to the symposium Linguistic Bases of the Ancient Maya Script, Annual Meeting of the American Anthropological Association, San Francisco, CA, November 16.

Josserand, J. Kathryn, and Nicholas A. Hopkins. 2002a. "Classic Maya Social Interaction and Linguistic Practice: Evidence from Hieroglyphic Inscriptions and Mayan Languages." In *La organización social entre los mayas: Memoria de la Tercera Mesa Redonda de Palenque*, vol. 2, ed. Vera Tiesler Blos, Rafael Cobos, and Merle Greene Robertson, 355–72. México, DF: Instituto Nacional de Antropología e Historia.

Josserand, J. Kathryn, and Nicholas A. Hopkins. 2002b. "La lingüística y el desciframiento de las inscripciones mayas." In *Tercer Congreso Internacional de Mayistas* [Chetumal, 1998], ed. Ana Luisa Izquierdo, 447–78. México, DF: Universidad Nacional Autónoma de México.

Josserand, J. Kathryn, and Nicholas A. Hopkins. 2005. "Lexical Retention and Cultural Significance in Chol (Mayan) Ritual Vocabulary." *Anthropological Linguistics* 47 (4): 401–23.

Josserand, J. Kathryn, and Nicholas A. Hopkins. 2007. "Tila y su Cristo Negro: Historia, peregrinación y devoción en Chiapas, México." *Mesoamerica* 49: 82–113.

Josserand, J. Kathryn, and Nicholas A. Hopkins. 2011. *Maya Hieroglyphic Writing: Workbook for a Short Course on Maya Hieroglyphic Writing*. 2nd ed. http://www.famsi/org/mayawriting/hopkins/index.html.

Josserand, Kathryn (researcher), Nicholas Hopkins (researcher), and Ausencio Cruz Guzmán (speaker). 1978a. "Story of the Cave of Don Juan." Story #3 in "Stories," by Kathryn Josserand (researcher), Nicholas Hopkins (researcher), and Ausencio Cruz Guzmán (speaker). *Mayan Languages Collection of Nicholas Hopkins*. The Archive of the Indigenous Languages of Latin America: www.ailla.utexas.org. Media: audio. Access: public. Resource: CTU006R006.

Josserand, Kathryn (researcher), Nicholas Hopkins (researcher), and Ausencio Cruz Guzmán (speaker). 1978b. "Story of the Rooster." Story #2 in "Stories," by Kathryn Josserand (researcher), Nicholas Hopkins (researcher), and Ausencio Cruz Guzmán (speaker). *Mayan Languages Collection of Nicholas Hopkins*. The Archive of the Indigenous Languages of Latin America: www.ailla.utexas.org. Media: audio. Access: public. Resource: CTU006R006.

Josserand, Kathryn (researcher), Nicholas Hopkins (researcher), and Ausencio Cruz Guzmán (speaker). 1978c. "Story of the Witches." Story #1 in "Stories," by Kathryn Josserand (researcher), Nicholas Hopkins (researcher), and Ausencio Cruz Guzmán (speaker). *Mayan Languages Collection of Nicholas Hopkins*. The Archive of the Indigenous Languages of Latin America: www.ailla.utexas.org. Media: audio. Access: public. Resource: CTU006R006.

Josserand, J. Kathryn, Nicholas A. Hopkins, Ausencio Cruz Guzmán, Ashley Kistler, and Kayla Price. 2003. "Story Cycles in Chol (Mayan) Mythology: Contextualizing Classic Iconography." Research Report to the Foundation for the Advancement of Mesoamerican Studies, Inc. www.famsi.org/reports/01085/index.html.

Josserand, Kathryn (researcher), Nicholas Hopkins (researcher), and Rafael López Vázquez (speaker). 2002. "Interview 2002-2." *Mayan Languages Collection of Nicholas Hopkins.* The Archive of the Indigenous Languages of Latin America: www.ailla.utexas.org. Media: audio, video. Access: public. Resource: CTU010R002.

Josserand, J. Kathryn, and Laura Martin. 1986. "Introduction to Mayan Texts." Paper presented to the Symposium on Mayan Discourse, XXVth Conference on American Indian Languages, American Anthropological Association, Philadelphia, PA, December.

Josserand, J. Kathryn, and Linda Schele. 1984. "Discourse Analysis of Narrative Hieroglyphic Texts." Paper presented to the symposium Mayan Hieroglyphs: Papers in Memory of Marshall Durbin, American Anthropological Association, Denver, CO, November.

Josserand, J. Kathryn, and Linda Schele. 1985. "Discourse Analysis of Narrative Hieroglyphic Texts." Unpublished manuscript in possession of the author.

Josserand, J. Kathryn, Linda Schele, and Nicholas A. Hopkins. 1979. "La relación del chol a la jeroglífica maya." Paper presented to the Taller Maya IV, Palenque, Chiapas, July.

Josserand, J. Kathryn, Linda Schele, and Nicholas A. Hopkins. 1985. "Linguistic Data on Mayan Inscriptions: The *ti* Constructions." In *Fourth Palenque Round Table, 1980,* ed. Merle Greene Robertson, 87–102. San Francisco: Pre-Columbian Art Research Institute.

Kistler, Sarah Ashley. 2003. "Spanish Loan Phenomena in Chol Maya." MA thesis, Florida State University, Tallahassee.

Koob, Maria. 1979. *Fonología del chol de Salto de Agua, Chiapas: Tesis de licenciatura.* México, DF: Escuela Nacional de Antropología e Historia.

La Farge, Oliver. 1947. *Santa Eulalia: The Religion of a Cuchumatán Indian Town.* Chicago: University of Chicago Press.

Laughlin, Robert M. 1999. "We Are the Real People: Tzotzil-Tzeltal Maya Storytelling on the Stage." In *Traditional Storytelling Today: An International Sourcebook*, ed. Margaret Read MacDonald, 494–97. Chicago: Fitzroy Dearborn.

Laughlin, Robert M., and Sna Jtz'ibajom. 2008. *Monkey Business Theater.* Austin: University of Texas Press.

Litka, Stephanie. 2011. "Mayas, Markets, and Multilingualism: The Political Economy of Linguistic and Social Exchange in Cobá, Quintana Roo, Mexico." PhD diss., Florida State University, Tallahassee.

Longacre, Robert E. 1979. "Introduction." In *Discourse Studies in Mesoamerican Languages,* ed. Linda K. Jones, vii–ix. Summer Institute of Linguistics Publications in Linguistics 1, no. 58. Arlington, TX.

Longacre, Robert E. 1985. "Discourse Peak as Zone of Turbulence." In *Beyond the Sentence: Discourse and Sentential Form*, ed. Jessica R. Wirth, 81–98. Ann Arbor, MI: Karoma.

Longacre, Robert E. 1986. "The Semantics of the Storyline in East and West Africa." *Journal of Semantics* 5 (1): 51–64. http://dx.doi.org/10.1093/jos/5.1.51.

López, Montejo, Jorge Guzmán Gutiérrez Bernabé, Rubén López López, Enrique Jiménez Jiménez, and Ernesto Martínez López. 2000. *Säkläji'b ty'añ ch'ol*. Tuxtla Gutiérrez: Servicios Educativos para Chiapas.

Mayo Jiménez, Mariano (consultant). 1980. "Visit to Don Juan." *Mayan Languages Collection of Nicholas Hopkins*. The Archive of the Indigenous Languages of Latin America: www.ailla.utexas.org. Media: audio. Access: public. Resource: CTU002R005.

McQuown, Norman A., and Julian Pitt-Rivers, eds. 1970. *Ensayos de antropología en la Zona Central de Chiapas*. Colección de Antropología Social 8. México, DF: Instituto Nacional Indigenista.

Metz, Brent E., Cameron L. McNeil, and Kerry M. Hull, eds. 2009. *The Ch'orti' Maya Area: Past and Present*. Gainesville: University Press of Florida. http://dx.doi.org/10.5744/florida/9780813033310.001.0001.

Montgomery, John. 2002. *How to Read Maya Hieroglyphs*. New York: Hippocrene Books.

Mora-Marín, David, Nicholas A. Hopkins, and J. Kathryn Josserand. 2009. "The Linguistic Affiliation of Classic Lowland Mayan Writing and the Historical Sociolinguistic Geography of the Mayan Lowlands." In *The Ch'orti' Maya Area: Past and Present*, ed. Brent E. Metz, Cameron L. McNeil, and Kerry M. Hull, 15–28. Gainesville: University Press of Florida. http://dx.doi.org/10.5744/florida/9780813033310.003.0002.

Morris, Walter F. (Chip), Jr. 2010. *Guía textil de los Altos de Chiapas*. San Cristóbal de Las Casas, Chiapas: Asociación Cultural Na Bolom.

Pérez Chacón, José L. 1988. *Los choles de Tila y su mundo: Tradición oral*. San Cristóbal de Las Casas, Chiapas, Mexico: Dirección de Fortalecimiento y Fomento a las Culturas de la Sub-Secretaría de Asuntos Indígenas, Secretaría de Desarrollo Rural.

Pérez Martínez, Bernardo (consultant). 1995. "The Xnek's Tale." *Mayan Languages Collection of Nicholas Hopkins*. The Archive of the Indigenous Languages of Latin America: www.ailla.utexas.org. Media: audio. Access: public. Resource: CTU002R019.

Redfield, Robert. 1941. *The Folk Culture of Yucatán*. Chicago: University of Chicago Press.

Robertson, Merle Greene. 1983. *The Temple of the Inscriptions*, vol. 1: The Sculpture of Palenque. Princeton: Princeton University Press.

Robertson, Merle Greene. 1985a. *The Early Buildings of the Palace and the Wall: Paintings*, vol. 2: The Sculpture of Palenque. Princeton: Princeton University Press.

Robertson, Merle Greene. 1985b. *The Late Buildings of the Palace*, vol. 3: The Sculpture of Palenque. Princeton: Princeton University Press.

Robertson, Merle Greene. 1991. *The Cross Group, the North Group, the Olvidado, and Other Pieces*, vol. 4: The Sculpture of Palenque. Princeton: Princeton University Press.

Robertson, Merle Greene. 2006. *Never in Fear*. San Francisco: Pre-Columbian Art Research Institue.

Robertson, Merle Greene, ed. 1980. *Third Palenque Round Table, 1978*. Austin: University of Texas Press.

Romney, A. Kimball, and Romaine Romney. 1966. *The Mixtecans of Juxtlahuaca, Oaxaca*. Six Cultures Series 4. New York: John Wiley and Sons.

Schele, Linda, and Mary Ellen Miller. 1986. *The Blood of Kings: Dynasty and Ritual in Maya Art*. Fort Worth: Kimbell Art Museum.

Spero, Joanne M. 1987. "Lightning Men and Water Serpents: A Comparison of Mayan and Mixe-Zoquean Beliefs." MA thesis, University of Texas, Austin.

Stephens, John Lloyd. 1841. *Incidents of Travel in Central America, Chiapas, and Yucatan*. 2 vols. New York: Harper. http://dx.doi.org/10.5962/bhl.title.84376.

Tate, Carolyn E. 1992. *Yaxchilan: The Design of a Maya Ceremonial City*. Austin: University of Texas Press.

Taube, Karl A., William A. Saturno, David Stuart, and Heather Hurst. 2010. *The Murals of San Bartolo, El Petén, Guatemala*, Part 2: *The West Wall*. Ancient America 10. Barnardsville, NC: Boundary End Archaeology Research Center.

Thompson, J. Eric S. 1938. "Sixteenth and Seventeenth Century Reports on the Chol Mayas." *American Anthropologist* 40 (4): 584–604. http://dx.doi.org/10.1525/aa.1938.40.4.02a00040.

Thompson, J. Eric S. 1960. *Maya Hieroglyphic Writing: An Introduction*. 2nd ed. Norman: University of Oklahoma Press.

Turner, Paul, and Shirley Turner. 1971. *Chontal to Spanish Dictionary: Spanish to Chontal*. Tucson: University of Arizona Press.

Vázquez Álvarez, Juan Jesús. 2011. "A Grammar of Chol, a Mayan Language." PhD diss., University of Texas at Austin.

Vogt, Evon Z. 1969. *Zinacantan: A Maya Community in the Highlands of Chiapas*. Cambridge, MA: Belknap Press of Harvard University Press. http://dx.doi.org/10.4159/harvard.9780674436886.

Warkentin, Viola, and Ruby Scott. 1980. *Gramática ch'ol*. Serie de Gramáticas de Lenguas Indígenas de México, no. 3. México, DF: Instituto Lingüístico de Verano.

West, Robert C., Norbert P. Psuty, and Bruce G. Thom. 1985. *Las tierras bajas de Tabasco en el sureste de México*. Villahermosa: Gobierno del Estado de Tabasco.

Whittaker, Arabelle, and Viola . 1965. *Chol Texts on the Supernatural*. Summer Institute of Linguistics Publications in Linguistics and Related Fields 13. Norman: Summer Institute of Linguistics of the University of Oklahoma.

Further Reading

While many of the publications listed below are unlikely to appear in your local library, they do show up in bookstores in Mexico, and in any case they give an idea of the recent proliferation of published materials in Chol, as in other indigenous languages. This compilation includes only stories told in (or translated to) Chol (Chol Folktales, below) and articles and monographs devoted specifically to Chol grammar (Chol Grammar, below). For a review of Chol literature and similar stories in other Mayan languages, see our 2003 research report (Josserand et al. 2003; we have not included here the prior appearances of our texts in Hopkins and Josserand 1994). Except for *ä*, the original orthography is preserved in these bibliographic entries.

CHOL FOLKTALES

Alejos García, José. 1988. *Wajalix bä t'an* [Ancient Words]: *Narrativa tradicional ch'ol de Tumbalá, Chiapas*. Centro de Estudios Mayas, Cuaderno 20. México, DF: Universidad Nacional Autónoma de México.

Anderson, Arabelle. 1957. "Two Chol Texts." *Tlalocan* 3 (4): 313–16. [How Monkeys Came into Being, and How Snakes Came into Being, dictated by Mateo Guzmán Sánchez.]

Arcos, Francisco. 1988. "Bajlum yik'ot uch [The Jaguar and the Possum]." In *Wajalix bä t'an: narrativa tradicional ch'ol de Tumbalá, Chiapas*, by José Alejos García, 47–50. Centro de Estudios Mayas, Cuaderno 20. México, DF: Universidad Nacional Autónoma de México.

Arcos, Francisco. 1988. "Juan Sol [John Sun]." In *Wajalix bä t'an: narrativa tradicional ch'ol de Tumbalá, Chiapas*, by José Alejos García, 103–7. Centro de Estudios Mayas, Cuaderno 20. México, DF: Universidad Nacional Autónoma de México.

Arcos, Francisco. 1988. "Kolem bä xiye' [Big Eagle]." In *Wajalix bä t'an: narrativa tradicional ch'ol de Tumbalá, Chiapas*, by José Alejos García, 25–30. Centro de Estudios Mayas, Cuaderno 20. México, DF: Universidad Nacional Autónoma de México.

Arcos M., Miguel. 1986. "Ili xtiklaya ik'aba' Xpuk'puk'jol [The Witch Named Bouncing Head]." In *K'uk' Witz, Cerro de los Quetzales: tradición oral chol del Municipio de Tumbalá*, by Miguel Meneses López, 64–66. Tuxtla Gutiérrez: Dirección de Fortalecimiento y Fomento a las Culturas, Sub-Secretaría de Asuntos Indígenas, Secretaría de Desarrollo Rural, [Estado de] Chiapas.

Arcos Mendoza, Marcos, ed. 1999. *Juñ ch'älbilbä tyi lak ty'añ ch'ol* [Treasure Book in Our Ch'ol Language]: *Libro de literatura en lengua Chol de Chiapas*. México, DF: Dirección General de Educación Indígena, Secretaría de Educación Pública. [A collection of 106 stories.]

Attinasi, John. 1979. "Chol Performance: Do Not Talk to Dogs, They Might Talk Back to You." In *Mayan Texts II*, ed. Louanna Furbee-Losee, 3–17. International Journal of American Linguistics, Native American Texts Series. Chicago: University of Chicago Press.

Cristobalito. 1988. "Pu'pu'k jol [Bouncing Head]." In *Wajalix bä t'an: narrativa tradicional ch'ol de Tumbalá, Chiapas*, by José Alejos García, 71–74. Centro de Estudios Mayas, Cuaderno 20. México, DF: Universidad Nacional Autónoma de México.

Díaz, Margarita. 1988. "Ak'jun" [Messengers]. In *Wajalix bä t'an: narrativa tradicional ch'ol de Tumbalá, Chiapas*, by José Alejos García, 75–80. Centro de Estudios Mayas, Cuaderno 20. México, DF: Universidad Nacional Autónoma de México.

Díaz, Margarita. 1988. "Meba' alälob" [The Orphan Children]. In *Wajalix bä t'an: narrativa tradicional ch'ol de Tumbalá, Chiapas*, by José Alejos García, 41–43. Centro de Estudios Mayas, Cuaderno 20. México, DF: Universidad Nacional Autónoma de México.

Díaz, Margarita. 1988. "Mu'bä i lok'el ti ak'lel" [Things That Go Out in the Night]. In *Wajalix bä t'an: narrativa tradicional ch'ol de Tumbalá, Chiapas*, by José Alejos García, 81–84. Centro de Estudios Mayas, Cuaderno 20. México, DF: Universidad Nacional Autónoma de México.

Díaz, Margarita. 1988. "Tsi' ts'aka i yijnam" [He Cured His Wife]. In *Wajalix bä t'an: Narrativa tradicional ch'ol de Tumbalá, Chiapas*, by José Alejos García, 85–90. Centro de Estudios Mayas, Cuaderno 20. México, DF: Universidad Nacional Autónoma de México.

Díaz Vázquez, Crescencia. 1998. "La buena niña y los muertos: Jiñi wembu shi choc yicot jiñi chumeñobu" [The Good Girl and the Dead]. *Cuentos y Relatos Indígenas* 7: 233–36.

Centro de Investigaciones Humanísticas de Mesoamérica y el Estado de Chiapas. México, DF: Universidad Nacional Autónoma de México.

Martínez, Alfredo E. 1994. "El dueño del cerro: iyum jiñi wits" [The Lord of the Mountain]. *Cuentos y Relatos Indígenas* 4: 209–17. Centro de Investigaciones Humanísticas de Mesoamérica y el Estado de Chiapas. México, DF: Universidad Nacional Autónoma de México.

Meneses López, Miguel. 1986. *K'uk' Witz, Cerro de los Quetzales: tradición oral chol del Municipio de Tumbalá.* Tuxtla Gutiérrez: Dirección de Fortalecimiento y Fomento a las Culturas, Sub-Secretaría de Asuntos Indígenas, Secretaría de Desarrollo Rural, [Estado de] Chiapas.

Meneses Méndez, Domingo. 1994. "Cuando muere la persona que tiene su nahual: Che' mi' chamel amba way lak pi'alo'b" [When a Person Who Has a Nagual Dies]. *Cuentos y Relatos Indígenas* 4: 191–208. Centro de Investigaciones Humanísticas de Mesoamérica y el Estado de Chiapas. México, DF: Universidad Nacional Autónoma de México.

Meneses Méndez, Domingo. 1997. *Kolen ik'ajel* [Great Darkness]: *La Gran Oscuridad.* Serie Nuestras Raíces. Centro Estatal de Lenguas, Arte y Literatura Indígenas; Consejo Estatal para la Cultura y las Artes de Chiapas. San Cristóbal de Las Casas: Gobierno del Estado de Chiapas.

Meneses Méndez, Domingo. 1998. "Xu'ok; Xu 'ok" [Short Leg]. *Cuentos y Relatos Indígenas* 7: 213–31. Centro de Investigaciones Humanísticas de Mesoamérica y el Estado de Chiapas. México, DF: Universidad Nacional Autónoma de México.

Montejo Vázquez, Cristóbal. 1994. "El rayo y la formación del río Agua Azul: Jiñi chajk yik'oty bajche' tsa' ajñi Xäx K'elam Bä ja' " [Lightning and Where the Agua Azul River Came From, a Yajalón Tzeltal story translated to Chol by José Díaz Peñate]. *Cuentos y Relatos Indígenas* 5: 345–53. Centro de Investigaciones Humanísticas de Mesoamérica y el Estado de Chiapas. México, DF: Universidad Nacional Autónoma de México.

Morales Bermúdez, Jesús. 1999. *Antigua palabra: Narrativa indígena ch'ol.* México, DF: UNICACH and Plaza y Valdés Editores. (First edition, 1984, *On ot'ian; antigua palabra; narrativa indígena chol.* México, DF: Universidad Autónoma Metropolitana, Azcapotzalco.)

Moreno, Nicolás. 1988. "Lak kichan" [Our Mother's Brother]. In *Wajalix bä t'an: narrativa tradicional ch'ol de Tumbalá, Chiapas,* by José Alejos García, 37–40. Centro de Estudios Mayas, Cuaderno 20. México, DF: Universidad Nacional Autónoma de México.

Moreno, Nicolás. 1988. "Lak Ña' yik'ot i yalobil" [Our Mother and Her Children]. In *Wajalix bä t'an: narrativa tradicional ch'ol de Tumbalá, Chiapas,* by José Alejos García, 60–64. Centro de Estudios Mayas, Cuaderno 20. México, DF: Universidad Nacional Autónoma de México.

Moreno, Nicolás. 1988. "T'ul yik'ot i ko'" [Rabbit and His Grandmother]. In *Wajalix bä t'an: narrativa tradicional ch'ol de Tumbalá, Chiapas*, by José Alejos García, 51–59. Centro de Estudios Mayas, Cuaderno 20. México, DF: Universidad Nacional Autónoma de México.

Moreno, Nicolás. 1988. "Winik-bajlum" [Man-Jaguar]. In *Wajalix bä t'an: narrativa tradicional ch'ol de Tumbalá, Chiapas*, by José Alejos García, 31–36. Centro de Estudios Mayas, Cuaderno 20. México, DF: Universidad Nacional Autónoma de México.

Moreno, Nicolás. 1988. "Xmeba' winik" [The Orphans]. In *Wajalix bä t'an: narrativa tradicional ch'ol de Tumbalá, Chiapas*, by José Alejos García, 65–67. Centro de Estudios Mayas, Cuaderno 20. México, DF: Universidad Nacional Autónoma de México.

Oleta Lara, Lisandro. 1994. "La aparición del Señor de Tila: Bajche' tsa' ipäsä ïbä jiñi Ch'ujulbä Laktyaty tyi Tila" [How Our Holy Father Showed Himself to Tila]. *Cuentos y Relatos Indígenas* 4: 219–25. Centro de Investigaciones Humanísticas de Mesoamérica y el Estado de Chiapas. México, DF: Universidad Nacional Autónoma de México.

Peñate Montejo, Juana Karen. 1999. "Kabäl xtyañob [Many Poets]: tantos poetas." In *Palabra conjurada (Cinco voces, cinco cantos)*, by Josías López K'an, Juana Karen Peñate Montejo, Ruperta Bautista Vázquez, Nicolás Huet Bautista, and Enrique Pérez López, 19–28. San Cristóbal de Las Casas, Chiapas: Espacio Cultural Jaime Sabines, Fondo Nacional para la Cultura y las Artes (FONCA), CEJUV A.C., Causa Joven. (Contains her poems Ñatyibal/Pensamiento, Jiñi Witz/El cerro, Säk'an/Amanecer, and ¿Chukoch?/¿Por qué? [Thoughts, The Mountain, Dawn, and Why?].)

Peñate Montejo, Juana Karen. 2002. *Mi nombre ya no es silencio*. Tuxtla Gutiérrez: Gobierno del Estado de Chiapas. [Eighteen poems in Chol and Spanish.]

Pérez Chacón, José L. 1988. *Los choles de Tila y su tradición: Tradición oral*. Tuxtla Gutiérrez: Dirección de Fortalecimiento y Fomento a las Culturas, Sub-Secretaría de Asuntos Indígenas, Secretaría de Desarrollo Rural, [Estado de] Chiapas.

Sánchez Díaz, Juan. 1986. "Ili xiye' tzabu ik'uxu wiñikob" [The Eagle That Ate People]. In *K'uk' Witz, Cerro de los Quetzales: Tradición oral chol del Municipio de Tumbalá*, by Miguel Meneses López, 62–63. Tuxtla Gutiérrez: Dirección de Fortalecimiento y Fomento a las Culturas, Sub-Secretaría de Asuntos Indígenas, Secretaría de Desarrollo Rural, [Estado de] Chiapas.

Sánchez Díaz, Juan. 1986. "Jiñi bajlum yombu mantyar yik'ot wiñikob" [The Jaguar That Wanted to Rule over People]. In *K'uk' Witz, Cerro de los Quetzales: Tradición oral chol del Municipio de Tumbalá*, by Miguel Meneses López, 57–59. Tuxtla Gutiérrez: Dirección de Fortalecimiento y Fomento a las Culturas, Sub-Secretaría de Asuntos Indígenas, Secretaría de Desarrollo Rural, [Estado de] Chiapas.

Sánchez Meneses, Juan. 1998. "Cuento del tigre y el tlacuache: Bajlum yik'oty uch" [Jaguar and Possum]. *Cuentos y Relatos Indígenas* 7: 237–43. Centro de Investigaciones

Humanísticas de Mesoamérica y el Estado de Chiapas. México, DF: Universidad Nacional Autónoma de México.

Sántiz Gómez, Roberto. 1999. *Xäte' yik'oty pejpem* [Eagle and Butterfly]*: El águila y la mariposa*. Translated from the original Tzeltal by Nicolás López Arcos. Serie Tyuch'k'iñ. Centro Estatal de Lenguas, Arte y Literatura Indígenas (CELALI). San Cristóbal de Las Casas, Chiapas: Consejo Estatal para la Cultura y las Artes de Chiapas (CONECULTA).

Torres A., Pedro. 1986. "Ili wiñik ambä ich'ujlel bajche' tentzun" [The Man Who Had a Nagual Like a Goat]. In *K'uk' Witz, Cerro de los Quetzales: tradición oral chol del Municipio de Tumbalá*, by Miguel Meneses López, 60–61. Tuxtla Gutiérrez: Dirección de Fortalecimiento y Fomento a las Culturas, Sub-Secretaría de Asuntos Indígenas, Secretaría de Desarrollo Rural, [Estado de] Chiapas.

Vásquez, Sebastián. 1988. "I yum ch'en" [Lord of the Cave]. In *Wajalix bä t'an: narrativa tradicional ch'ol de Tumbalá, Chiapas*, by José Alejos García, 92–98. Centro de Estudios Mayas, Cuaderno 20. México, DF: Universidad Nacional Autónoma de México.

Vázquez Álvarez, Juan Jesús. 2001. *Palabras floridas: pejkaj ch'utyaty. Actividad oral de los choles dedicada a las deidades* [Flowery Words: Petitions to God. Speech by Chols Dedicated to the Deities]. Tuxtla Gutiérrez: Gobierno del Estado de Chiapas.

Whittaker, Arabelle, and Viola Warkentin. 1965. *Chol Texts on the Supernatural*. Summer Institute of Linguistics Publications in Linguistics and Related Fields 13. Norman: Summer Institute of Linguistics of the University of Oklahoma.

CHOL GRAMMAR

Altman, Heidi M. 1996. "Evidentiality and Genre in Chol Mayan Traditional Narrative." MA thesis, Florida State University, Tallahassee.

Arcos López, Nicolás. 2009. "Los clasificadores numerales y las clases nominales en chol." MA thesis, Centro de Investigaciones y Estudios Superiores en Antropología Social (CIESAS), México, DF.

Attinasi, John Joseph. 1973. "Lak t'an, a Grammar of the Chol (Mayan) Word." PhD diss., University of Chicago.

Aulie, Wilbur. 1957. "High-Layered Numerals in Chol (Mayan)." *International Journal of American Linguistics* 23: 281–83.

Coon, Jessica L. 2004. "Root, Words and Split Ergativity in Chol: Grammar and an Analysis of a Mayan Language." BA thesis, Reed College, Portland, OR.

Coon, Jessica L. 2006. "Existentials and Negation in Chol (Mayan)." In *Camling: Proceeding of the Fourth University of Cambridge Postgraduate Conference in Language Research*, ed. Charles Chang, Esuna Dagarova, Irene Theodoropoulou, Elina Vilar

Beltrán, and Ellis Wilford, 51–58. Cambridge: Cambridge Institute of Language Research.

Coon, Jessica L. 2009. "Interogative Possessors and the Problem with Pied-Piping in Chol." *Linguistic Inquiry* 40: 165–75.

Coon, Jessica L. 2010a. "Rethinking Split Ergativity." *International Journal of American Linguistics* 76: 207–53.

Coon, Jessica L. 2010b. "VOS as Predicate Fronting in Chol." *Lingua* 120: 354–78.

Coon, Jessica L. 2010c. "Complementation in Chol (Mayan): A Theory of Split Ergativity." PhD diss., Massachusetts Institute of Technology, Cambridge.

Gutiérrez Sánchez, Pedro. 2004. "Las clases de verbos intransitivos y el alineamiento agentivo en el chol de Tila, Chiapas." MA thesis, Centro de Investigaciones y Estudios Superiores en Antropología Social (CIESAS), México, DF.

Koob Schick, Hildegard Maria. 1979. "Fonología del chol de Salto de Agua, Chiapas." BA thesis, Escuela Nacional de Antropología e Historia, México, DF.

Martínez Cruz, Victoriano. 2007. "Los adjetivos y los conceptos de propiedad en chol." MA thesis, Centro de Investigaciones y Estudios Superiores en Antropología Social (CIESAS), México, DF.

Martínez Pérez, Carolino. 2005. "Análisis morfosintáctico de la frase nominal y la construcción de los nombres de acción en la lengua chol de tila, Chiapas." MA thesis, Centro de Investigaciones y Estudios Superiores en Antropología Social (CIESAS), México, DF.

Meneses Méndez, Domingo. 1987. "Morfología de los elementos del sintagma nominal en ch'ol." BA thesis, Programa de Formación Profesional de Etnolingüistas, Tlaxcala.

Ramírez Figueroa, Jesús. 1998. "Análisis comparativo de variantes de la zona chol, Chiapas y Tabasco." MA thesis, Centro de Investigaciones y Estudios Superiores en Antropología Social (CIESAS), México, DF.

Schumann Gálvez, Otto. 1973. *La lengua chol de Tila, (Chiapas)*. México, DF: Universidad Nacional Autónoma de México.

Vázquez Álvarez, Juan Jesús. 2002. "Morfología del verbo de la lengua chol de Tila, Chiapas." MA thesis, Centro de Investigaciones y Estudios Superiores en Antropología Social (CIESAS), México, DF.

Vázquez Álvarez, Juan Jesús. 2007. "Los tres tipos de estructuras de complemento en chol." *Proceedings of CILLA-III*. www.ailla.utexas.org/site/cilla3_toc.html.

Vázquez Álvarez, Juan Jesús. 2010. "Los depictivos analíticos y sintéticos en la lengua chol de Tila, Chiapas." In *La predicación secundaria en lenguas de Mesoamérica*, ed. Judith Aissen and Roberto Zavala, 61–85. México, DF: Centro de Investigaciones y Estudios Superiores en Antropología Social (CIESAS).

Vázquez Álvarez, Juan Jesús. 2011. "A Grammar of Chol, a Mayan Language." PhD diss., University of Texas at Austin.

Warkentin, Viola, and Ruth Brand. 1974. "Chol Phonology." *Linguistics* 132: 87–101.

Warkentin, Viola, and Ruby Scott. 1980. *Gramática ch'ol*. Serie de Gramáticas de Lenguas Indígenas de México 3. México, DF: Instituto Lingüístico de Verano.